THE SECRET PASSION OF ANGELA CLAYFORTH

An English Murder Mystery

The Secret Passion of Angela Clayforth

An English Murder Mystery

by

Lindsay Greatwood

John James Publications

ISBN 978-2-940509-09-6

Cover: © 2017 Lindsay Stuby Greatwood
A manor house in southern England

Design: movingis.com

www.johnjamespublications.com

PROLOGUE

She could still see the old manor house as it was on that summer's evening: abandoned, ready to be bulldozed by the developers; beautiful in an empty, haunted way. The red brick facade, its weathered beams covered in thick, twisting tendrils of wisteria, wore a soft, secretive look. The house, already minus one of its Elizabethan chimneys, seemed quaint yet forbidding under the mossy, uneven roof. And all around, neglected lawns resembled small meadows and flower beds overflowed with unpruned roses and colonies of speedwell.

In the pink evening light, the lattice windows, their leaded lights caving inwards, held rippled reflections of ancient oaks moving gently in the breeze. Some of the casements were broken and swallows darted in and out of the missing panes. Inside, field mice scuttled behind the wainscoting of echoing rooms, rats nested in fireplaces and bats hung upside down from the ancient rafters. Some of these creatures, thought Stella, must have seen Mrs Clayforth lying in one of the upstairs rooms, cold and white, eyes staring at the ornate ceiling.

They might even have seen the knife enter the woman's body, over and over, in that furious attack.

But it would be years, whole decades, before Stella would find out what really happened on that July night, back in 1965; though she'd long had her suspicions. And, even when the evidence finally stared her in the face, she had good reasons, she told herself, for not going to the police.

CHAPTER 1

"Don't gimme that old bullshit!" Gordie snorted at the estate agent as he turned his Rolls Royce into the driveway of Hadham Manor.

"But Mr Harris – "

"Haunted! Got enough bloody women haunting me for alimony and child maintenance, as it is, without taking on a bleedin' ghost. And I'll tell you somethin' else: the last cow took me to the cleaner's, so I'm boracic lint – skint, right? You tell your clients that. Tell 'em just 'cos I'm a TV personality it don't mean I'm a soft touch for an over-priced gaff. Needs knocking down and startin' again, by the looks of it."

The limousine halted in front of a studded oak entrance door, its wrought ironmongery festooned with padlocks. Gordie Harris switched off the engine and peered up at the Grade II listed building while Dudley Crompton busied himself shuffling the papers from which he'd been reciting since they'd left Crompton and Co. in the High Street. He tried again.

"There is, in fact, rather a history to the house which could be useful for – ah – publicity.

A talking point, perhaps. Apart from the ghost, someone was found here once … "

Gordie turned his perma-tanned face towards the passenger seat and scowled. "Watchya mean, someone was found? Found wandering, out of their mind? Found, trying to burn the place down? Found, chopped up in a dozen pieces?"

"Well, no; not exactly. It seems the lady – "

"Not rape. I don't need that. I'm not that bleedin' desperate for publicity."

Crompton consulted his top sheet again. "It seems the woman might have taken her own life. It was, ah, never really established how she died. A local woman. She'd wandered into the house, one summer's evening when it was empty. Couldn't find her way out again. Fell on something sharp. A knife, possibly, left lying on the floor. Simply an accident. But if you wanted to embellish the story – "

"I want to look around first, that's what I want. Come on, sunbeam, open up then."

Gordie Harris swung himself out of his Roller, stepped over the clumps of weeds pushing up through the gravel driveway and made his way to the entrance door. As he stood there, waiting for Crompton to stow his papers in his slim leather briefcase, he sniffed the sharp, autumnal air. An involuntary shiver ran through him, and he was glad he'd worn a cashmere coat and silk scarf and his suéde driving gloves. He watched the estate agent select various keys on a substantial key ring and unlock the heavy duty padlocks on the door. After that, it still took the shoulders of both men to persuade the thick wood to give way. Finally, they found themselves standing in the middle of a dark, high-ceilinged hallway, dominated by a wide staircase and lined with oak panelling.

"Blimey O'Riley!" said Gordie, taking in the partially-collapsed staircase and the fractured panelling. "No wonder she bloody topped herself, spending a night here! What'd she do – jump from the gallery and take the banisters with her?"

"Oh, the local woman? Actually, I think she tripped on a loose floorboard in one of the upper rooms. We can view the first floor if we keep to the left of the staircase. It's structurally sound – "

"Listen, mate, I'm not chancing me arm on that lot," the quiz show host held a fist to his chest in a mock gesture. "My public would never forgive me."

"Then you don't think the house would suit ... "

"I don't think nothin', mate," Gordie told him. "Let's do the ground floor. See how it goes."

Crompton led the way to the back of the house where the rooms seemed to be less gloomy. They entered a long salon with three French windows on the far wall, leading to a garden terrace. Shafts of dusty light filtered through the long panes, illuminating the walls and parquet floor, and the building seemed at once more cheerful.

"All right for a billiard table, then," Gordie glanced up and down the length of the room. "Drinkies on the terrace, what-ho," he mimicked a plummy voice as he walked over to one of the French windows. "Have to lose some of them trees; look bleedin' menacin' – "

"The garden would be magnificent if it were restored to its former glory. The late Sir Charles Trington held a fête here, every June. It's his family who are selling the property, now that Lady Trington has passed away in a nursing home. I think you'll find the extensive grounds will afford you sufficient privacy when you want to relax, away from the spotlight."

Gordie Harris sniffed and screwed up his eyes against the autumn light. "Let's see the view from upstairs, then. Don't want to see them houses down the road. Not an effin' rooftop. Not a bloody satellite dish."

They made their way back to the entrance hall and Crompton trod carefully on the staircase. Gordie followed close behind, noting where the estate agent placed his feet.

"All the housing estates in this area are high-class ones," Crompton said over his shoulder. "Although none of the properties are large. The development you're thinking of, Manor Close, was built in the late Fifties when the Trington family began to sell off some of their land. The manor had been a substantial one before the First World War. But many of the gardeners and agricultural labourers never came back from the trenches. The estate became difficult to manage. Then the housemaids went off to the munitions factories at the start of the Second World War and they didn't want to return to the old life, below stairs. It was the same with other manor houses, all over the country: no staff for the upkeep. So more and more land was sold for housing as more people wanted to live outside London and commute to the city. The suburbs mushroomed and merged into the great conurbation we know to – "

"This the Long Gallery, then? Where the ol' ghost struts his stuff?" They had paused at the top of the staircase and a long, wide corridor stretched before them. "My son'll love this for skateboarding."

Crompton gave a thin smile. "It's an historic part of the house – " he began. "I don't think – "

Gordie cuffed the other man's arm. "Only joking, mate. The old cow won't hardly let me see the kids. Dunno what they look like, these days. What's through that door at the end? That the master bedroom?" And he was off, trotting along the gallery, ahead of the estate agent.

"Now this is what I call a room!" the TV host stood in the middle of a large panelled chamber dominated by a cavernous fireplace. He raised his hands, palms upwards. "Get the old four-poster creaking in here on a Saturday night, eh?"

Dudley Crompton repeated his weak smile and cleared his throat. "I, ah, believe this was where they found the local lady. In – let me see – " he consulted the sheet of particulars in his hand. "Yes, nineteen sixty-five. A long time ago now, but it may still be of local interest. The ghost, however, has a more colourful history: a Cavalier, hiding from the Roundheads during the Civil War – "

"Clock that ceiling, will you? Look at them roses and leaves and stuff, up there. Fancy drifting off, looking at that lot – whoah -" Harris tottered backwards, having caught his heel on a loose floorboard. "Bleedin' 'eck! Nearly lost me ratings, there! Tell you what, this whole place needs redoin'. How long's it been empty, then? Twenty years?"

"They were going to demolish the property, I believe, when they found the woman in the house. But, by the time the police investigation was completed, the developer had gone bankrupt. Then a preservation order was put on the building; it was listed and taken off the market – "

"Just tell me how long, willya?"

"It was used by television and film companies," Crompton continued to ignore the question, "for costume dramas in the eighties and nineties. The advantage for production teams being that they had the run of the place."

"You mean no one's lived here for forty-odd years? Blimey, that'll cost a bomb to sort out: structure problems, galloping rot, plumbing and guttering to do – "

"The cost of the renovation is reflected in the very reasonable asking price – "

"Reasonable, my arse! Listen, mate: 'The Sky's the Limit!' that's the name of my show. But it ain't my name, see? I'm a wheeler-dealer, like them money spots with the contestants. I push 'em to the limit, right? Don't give the stuff away. And I'm not giving my own dosh away, neither." The TV personality began listing points on his fingers. "First off, there's a bloody housing estate all round this place – "

"But Hadham Manor is very convenient for London ... "

"Second, the effin' roof is caving in – "

"It's also well-situated for Gatwick Airport. And there's talk of another runway – "

"Third off, I don't like bleedin' aeroplanes swooping low over me swimmin' pool – "

Crompton sighed. The agent was fast running out of selling points and knew the time had come to do a deal. "I'm sure," he said to Gordie with a conspiratorial nod of his head, "that if you made the Trington family a reasonable offer, they'd – "

"They'd take it, mate. Half the asking price and they'd take it. I bloody would, looking at this place. Tell you what I'll do – and don't forget I'm skint, like I said. Cash. No chain, no mortgage company sticking their oar in 'bout the condition of the building. Cash, and completion within the week. I'm off to Barbados for a winter break, so we'll get it sorted before I go. Half the asking price, and that's my final offer."

"But, Mr Harris, I couldn't possibly let a building of historical interest go for less than – "

"You get back to them people, that family. Tell them what I said. Place is fallin' down. Half the price it says on that piece of paper in your mitt, and ghosts and bodies in the library or anywhere else don't count for nothing. Got a week to sort it. You get on the blower. You tell 'em that."

Stella told herself a car alarm had gone off somewhere down the street. She turned over in bed, pulled the duvet up to her ears and shut her eyes tight. But the keening sound of the siren soon penetrated the bedclothes, and she realised a squad car had drawn up outside her apartment building.

She threw back the covers and peered at the illuminated hands on her bedside clock. Two in the morning; though she hadn't really slept. She'd known, as soon as she'd seen the evening news, they'd come calling for her. That TV quiz show host with the bow tie and the quiffed hair, spouting to the cameras, arms windmilling, explaining the excavations for his swimming pool, a busty blonde in a skimpy bathing suit and high heels towering beside him.

So, they'd found another body. Well, bully for them after forty years. She wondered if Neil was lying awake, as well, somewhere on the other side of London, waiting for the rozzers to call. The wailing siren reminded Stella of those high-pitched screams, rising and falling, all those years ago. She remembered the blood on

Neil's hands. There'd been moments in the past when she'd felt guilty about the happiness she'd found with him. And it could have lasted if she hadn't been so jealous, if she'd had more self-control. But Neil had more to worry about than her, and she was sure he was worried tonight. So why hadn't he phoned? Didn't she deserve a phone call, at least, after all she'd said and done?

Heavy feet on the stairs, waking up the whole building. As if the siren hadn't got everyone up and to their windows, already. Stella knew she'd upset the neighbours a couple of weeks ago, when Francine's office bash had ended up at her place. Now, she thanked God she'd never told Francine about Angela Clayforth, though she'd often been tempted to do so. Even when her mother had died, Stella had kept quiet about the discovery she'd made, and the light it could have shed on the whole affair.

Now, something told her Francine and her husband, Michael, would soon put the jigsaw together for themselves. And she was glad. The episode had been a burden for her to carry, she'd realised that recently. Tonight would be the beginning of the end of all those years of pretence and lies.

The doorbell. They leaned on it long and hard. "Police! Open up! Mrs Martin, we know you're there – "

"Alright, alright," muttered Stella, groping for the light switch. She plucked at the dressing gown on the back of the chair and wrapped it around her as she crossed the hallway. Unlocking the door, she opened it just a fraction and slotted her nose in the crack. "Yes? Who is – ?"

The door shuddered and flew inwards, sending her flying backwards against the opposite wall. Winded and stunned, she held the side of her face where the door had scraped it. All the phrases of explanation she'd rehearsed in the bathroom mirror that evening were forgotten. This was not the way they had treated her the last time they'd questioned her, when they'd found Mrs Clayforth.

"Get dressed, Mrs Martin. This police officer will accompany you."

Stella looked from the florid features of the plain clothes detective to the weasel-faced woman constable. The woman's eyes narrowed as she stared back at Stella, unsmiling.

"Alright, officer. There's no need to – Where are those men going? This is a private home – "

"We have a warrant to search this flat," the red-nosed detective barked. Stella didn't hear the rest. Police swarmed past her and she was pushed roughly into her bedroom by WPC Weasel. The woman followed her into the room and stood there, arms folded, waiting for her to get dressed. Stella decided she wasn't going to strip for the old stoat face. She turned her back and tugged up her underwear and jeans underneath her dressing gown. She grabbed a tee-shirt and a light sweater from the chair, then thought about taking a jacket but reckoned she'd wouldn't be gone long. She had nothing to add to the police files on Mrs Clayforth, she would make that clear from the start. And, as for their new find, well, she knew nothing about that, did she? What possible motive could a sixteen year-old girl have had for killing her best friend?

"Mr Taylor?" The man in a trench coat on the doorstep was probably reporter; he had a photographer with him. "Mr John Taylor, formerly of Manor Close, Hadham?"

John Taylor stood there, not knowing what to say. The nightmare was starting all over again. Would they never leave him in peace? He remembered the reporters who'd gathered around him, outside the police station, forty years ago. Question after question about his neighbour and why he thought she'd killed herself. Then there'd been the insinuations: he was a widower and she'd been a widow. She'd been supportive when he'd lost his wife, the neighbours had seen that. But Angela Clayforth had also been a woman of strong emotions, everyone agreed, and they'd said so to the press, further muddying the waters for him. Could Mr Taylor give them a statement on his relationship with the deceased? That was all he'd heard for weeks after they'd found Angela.

"Could you spare us a moment, Mr Taylor?" The reporter gave him a friendly smile, but Taylor didn't relax his guard. "Could we step inside, Charlie and me? Bloody taters out here ... "

John Taylor thought for a moment, then let out a sigh. It was useless to send them away. And it might make matters worse if he didn't give his side of the story, yet again. When they'd found Angela in the old manor house, tongues had started to wag almost immediately. Someone, and he didn't know who, but he had his suspicions, had said that he and Mrs Clayforth had been more than just neighbours. "You'd better come in," he said, and opened the door wide.

The reporters followed Taylor into his front room. He had lived in this shabby, semi-detached house on the North Circular for the last twenty years, ever since the children had left home and he and Eileen had returned from Ireland.

"Sorry to disturb you this late at night," the reporter said, settling himself into an armchair. "It took us a while to track you down, Mr Taylor. The archives said you'd moved to Ireland after the – er, demise of Mrs Angela Clayforth. Sit yourself down Charlie; don't stand there like a lemon."

"Can I take your coats? I'm afraid this room isn't very warm. I'm a pensioner, on benefits. We have to be careful with light and heat. We were just going to bed – "

"Oh, don't let us disturb your wife, sir. And we won't keep you very long. Charlie, can you get a couple of Mr Taylor standing by the fireplace? And get those pics on the mantelpiece, the school kids in the background. Look straight at the camera, Mr Taylor. And another one. One more, then a couple of you sitting in the armchair. That's it. Nice one. OK, Charlie."

Taylor sank back in the chair. He was tired. It was gone midnight and he wished he were upstairs with his wife. They'd only stayed up to watch a film, and that had turned out to be a bad remake of the one they thought they were going to see. He'd tell these people the facts, straight, then they'd go. And, hopefully, they wouldn't take any more interest in him. "Look, you're wasting your time here, lads," he said. "I've nothing more to add. I said it all, years ago. This new body – the one they talked about on the news tonight – I don't know anything about it. And I don't want to know, see?"

Poor old boy, thought Andy Ware, regarding the sunken shape in the armchair opposite. John Taylor seemed as worn out as the furnishings in the room. His baggy jumper looked home-knitted and was coming apart at the cuffs, his trousers were shiny at the knees and threadbare like the carpet which didn't quite touch the walls of the room. Andy reckoned Taylor had been shouldering a problem or a bad memory for the last four decades and it had worn him down to the core. Give the bloke a bit of sympathy and understanding, and he, Andy Ware, would have a scoop that would make the nationals, never mind the weekly in Hendon where he worked.

"Nice place you have here, Mr Taylor ... "

Taylor blinked at him. "You think so?"

"Well, for retirement, like. Compact. Just right for you and the missus. Children all gone now? Grandchildren? You had two young 'uns, didn't you? Is that them, in the photos? We did some checking, you see. You lost your wife – "

"In a car accident. Yes. She was very young." John Taylor spoke mechanically now. "A lorry went into her car. She was driving the children to school. They reckoned she turned to say something to one of the kids. Pulled out into the traffic at the same time. She was killed instantly. The children were unhurt. That's all I can tell you. Was there anything else you wanted to ask?"

"We're sorry about your late wife, Mr Taylor. It must have been very hard. The shock. Difficult to cope. A young family. You at work all day. The neighbours, I expect they were helpful – "

John Taylor grabbed the arms of his chair and leant forward, his brow deeply furrowed. "The neighbours were shits, all of them. They said they wanted to help, but they were a load of voyeuristic busybodies. They weren't interested in how I was coping when I lost Susan. They just wanted some scandal to brighten up their small, suburban lives. They were a clutch of bored housewives, that's all, and their husbands weren't much better, as it turned out." He sat back and glared at the reporter, daring him to ask more.

Andy dared. "So, the rumours about you and Mrs Clayforth were – "

"Completely unfounded. Mrs Clayforth didn't kill herself because of an unhappy love affair with me. She lived opposite my house, and she sometimes knocked at the door with something she'd cooked for the children. She was just a neighbour, like all the other neighbours – "

"A shit, you mean?"

Taylor didn't trust the reporter. He'd made that mistake before. "I didn't know her well. She cooked a few meals for Sally and Ross, that's all. She wasn't the only one who helped with the kids at that time. There were others ... " He let his head fall forwards, as if he were too exhausted to say any more.

Charlie was checking his camera over, wanting to be gone now his job was done. Andy Ware was conscious of the photographer's restlessness but, at the same time, he smelt a story and wanted to be the one to uncover it. He decided he could get more detail on Mrs Clayforth from the Surrey papers' archives, but he'd give John Taylor one more try before calling it a night. He shot a swift glance at Charlie, to let the photographer know he was nearly through, then he cleared his throat. "The body they've just uncovered at Hadham Manor. Have you any idea – "

"I've told you, I don't know who she is – "

27

"She? It's a woman, then?"

John Taylor turned pale and held the arms of his chair again. "I don't know. I've told you I don't know anything about it." He rose and went towards the door and held it open, signalling the end of the interview. "Now, will you please go. I have nothing more to say."

Charlie stood up immediately. Andy got up, too, knowing he'd be back to see John Taylor when he'd checked with his pals in the Surrey Police force on the sex of the body they'd found. The reporters paused at the front door to shake Taylor's limp hand. "Thanks for your time, Mr Taylor. We appreciate it very much. If I need to speak to you again, I'll – "

"You won't need to speak to me again. There's nothing more to say. This all happened forty years ago and it's over and done with now. Let people rest in peace, and let the living in peace, will you?"

"Right you are, Mr Taylor," said the reporter, pulling up his coat collar. Then, looking straight at the glowering pensioner on the doorstep: "Who was the other woman who died? Who killed her and buried her there?" The front door closed with a slam. The reporter shrugged. "We'll know soon enough, anyway."

"No tea, only coffee from the machine. Take it or leave it."

Stella shifted in the plastic chair and stared at the two detectives across the table. She was tired now, ready to comply with anything that would get her out of the police station and back to her flat in World's End. It might have had something to do with her being left alone in the interview room for nearly an hour. They were giving her time to think. Getting her worried, maybe. Well, they hadn't cautioned her, so she wasn't under arrest. She was simply helping the police with their enquiries, as they called it. Then why drag her from her bed in the middle of the night? What was so urgent that it couldn't wait for the day shift?

"Coffee. Milk, no sugar." She rubbed her eyes. The detectives exchanged satisfied glances. One of them rose from his chair and headed for the door.

"Want one an' all, Graham?" he asked, holding the door open as he spoke. Cool air wafted into the small room. It felt fresh on Stella's face. Her temperature had been rising steadily since they'd left her in that box-like space. She told herself the problem was claustrophobia, not nervousness or one of those hot flushes. The room was barely big enough for a table and four chairs and it smelt of stale cigarette smoke. No windows, nothing to look at on the walls, not even a police notice to fix on. The interviewee had no choice but to make eye contact across the scratched tabletop.

The detective called Graham nodded his vote for coffee as his colleague left the room. Then he opened the dog-eared file in front of him and perused the notes inside. The two of them sat in silence, Stella trying to read the file upside down and guessing the papers were the originals on the Angela Clayforth case. After a few minutes, the other detective returned, distributed plastic cups of sludge-coloured liquid, then resumed his place opposite Stella. Detective Graham reached over and switched on the recording machine at the end of the table. This took Stella by surprise, and alarmed her.

"Commencing the interview with Mrs Stella Martin, at ... " Detective Graham glanced at his watch, " – four five a.m., Wednesday twelfth October. Present: Detective Super¬intendent Graham Binns and Detective Inspector Barry Carver."

Stella gulped at her coffee, hoping it would lessen the tension that had begun to knot her insides. She'd never been in this kind of situation before, not even when they'd found old Angela. Back then, Stella had just turned sixteen and was still at school. The police had been friendly, almost avuncular, when they'd asked their perfunctory questions. They'd wanted to know how well she knew the deceased. She'd told them Mrs Clayforth was a neighbour who had coffee with her mother sometimes. Were they good friends, your mother and Mrs Clayforth, they'd asked? Yes, she'd answered. They sometimes had a drink together in the evenings, as well. Stella hoped she'd said the right thing. It wasn't the moment to drag her mother into the situation. The woman already had her problems, some of them connected with Angela Clayforth.

What about Mr Taylor? Did Stella know the man who lived opposite Mrs Clayforth? Yes, she'd baby-sitted for him a few times after his wife had died, she lied. And did Mr Taylor know Mrs Clayforth well? Stella had to think. She said: a little, though she didn't know how well. She'd seen Mrs Clayforth take a casserole dish over to Mr Taylor's one evening, when she, Stella, was on her way to – to her friend's house.

Don't mention the friend, not ever. And don't mention Neil. And don't mention mothers, if you can help it, or fathers, for that matter. Talk about the baby-sitting, even if it wasn't true. Yes, say how much you enjoyed the baby-sitting, or some such similar rot. It doesn't matter about Mr Taylor. Who cares if they were having an affair? She tried to picture old Angela and John Taylor in bed together and nearly started to laugh. That big, bosomy woman with her loud voice and jangling bracelets and her bright red lipstick. What was it about Mrs Clayforth that men had found attractive?

The phone rang and Neil snatched it up. He listened for a moment, then his face relaxed. "Hi, Michael. Fine, and you? Yes, I heard. It was on the news. Yes, it's incredible. What? Francine thinks that? No – you're kidding! Who on earth put that idea into her head? Stella? Stella? Do me a favour ... "

He listened while his younger brother outlined the theory his wife had developed over the past couple of years. Francine had been close to Neil's first wife during their marriage and, when Neil and Stella had divorced, Francine had remained close friends with her ex-sister-in-law. Soon after Neil's divorce, Michael began working long hours to build up his architectural practice, and Francine, after two miscarriages, had taken to spending several evenings a week in the company of Stella. They would hit the wine bars in and around the King's Road and mull over various events in their lives, for two or three hours at a time. After countless discussions, fuelled by glasses of red, dissecting their respective pasts, Francine had formed her own idea as to why the Boyds' marriage had failed.

The way she saw it, the relationship had been a non-starter. Something had happened back in Hadham, when they were teenagers living in Manor Close. It was linked to that Clayforth woman, the one who'd committed suicide. But there was more, and it was connected with someone else who had gone missing around that time. Stella didn't often refer to Tanya, by name, although they'd been best friends, according to Michael. Yet, when Tanya had left home, the light seemed to have gone out of both Neil and Stella's lives. Francine reckoned Tanya's departure was the event that had united the Boyds, then torn them apart for some reason. And now, they'd found a body in the grounds of Hadham Manor. Oh, yes; Francine had an idea who it was, alright.

CHAPTER 2

Angela Clayforth sat in front of her dressing table mirror and congratulated herself. The new hairstyle took years off her, and that was a fact. Not that she was old, she told herself. She may have been forty last birthday but she didn't look a day over thirty-two. Well, thirty-five, maybe. Doreen said she looked thirty-two, and friends always told the truth, didn't they? She could rely on Doreen. Poor Doreen: the woman was looking older than ever since she'd found out about Ray.

"You have your whole life before you!" Angela told the face in the mirror. The face nodded emphatically back, and she added a touch more lipstick and primped her newly-cut hair. The hairdresser hadn't made it too short but had given it more height and volume. The style lifted her face, Angela thought. Not that she had jowls or a sagging chin. Heaven forbid. In fact, she could swear that she was looking younger each day. Each day since Frank had died.

He had been so careful with their money over the years, and what good had it done him?

Or her, for that matter? Frank had died ten months after he'd retired from the bank and, now, finally, the tiresome argument with the life insurance company had been resolved. He'd fallen down the stairs as a result of the heart attack, not had a cardiac arrest as a result of – well, what were they suggesting? Thank goodness for Doreen Reynolds. If Doreen hadn't been there at the time and corroborated her account of what had happened, Angela might not be as well off as she was today.

'Thank you, Frank, for being such a careful, miserable, penny-pinching bastard!' She fluttered the false eyelashes she'd bought in the hairdresser's, studying their effect in the mirror. They were all the rage now: Jean Shrimpton and Twiggy, they all wore them.

Frank would have had something to say about them. "What on earth have you done to your face, woman? You look as though you've got two black eyes!" He would occasionally make comments about her clothes and fashion accessories, but never appreciative ones. Angela sighed. Frank had been much older than she; not just in age, but in his staid mind. She'd hardly been out of her teens when she'd married him, and he had been over forty.

Back then, Angela had no particular ambition beyond marriage and a nice house with deep pile carpets and bone china on the table. And Frank, the assistant manager at the bank where she was a junior secretary, seemed a quiet and steady man who, she knew, lived with his widowed mother. It wasn't until about a year after Angela had started work there, that Frank's mother had died. Frank suddenly looked so lost and alone to Angela that she would bake him small cakes and scones to take home for the weekend. And the assistant manager seemed to appreciate it.

It was about two months after his mother's death when, one morning, during a lull in the number of customers in the bank foyer, the assistant manager had stood beside his junior secretary and cleared his throat quietly. "I wonder, Miss Rees – ah, could I ask you, would you like to come to the cinema with me, one evening?"

Angela had almost jumped in her chair. She made an error on the money transfer form she was typing while day-dreaming of Bobby Darin and his latest hit song. The secretary pursed her lips, telling herself she'd have to type the document and its carbon copies all over again. Then she looked up at Mr Clayforth and gave him a chaste smile, just like the ones Audrey Hepburn gave her leading men in the movies.

"There's an Ealing comedy at the Regal, this week. I'd be delighted if you would like to see it with me."

Angela lifted her pencilled eyebrows. The assistant manager, talking to her like this; you could have knocked her down with a feather. She said, in a voice as hushed as Frank Clayforth's, 'They're showing 'A Streetcar Named Desire' at the Odeon," Angela had the hots for Marlon Brando at the time, and Paul Newman, and Burt Lancaster.

"They always made my mother laugh, those Ealing films." Frank spoke gently but firmly, ignoring the information the secretary had volunteered. To Angela, it didn't seem the moment to argue the point. He'd asked her for a date, hadn't he? Leave it at that. She gave a weak smile. Yes, she said, she'd love to come. She didn't suppose it mattered what film she saw, just this once. After all, the man who'd asked her out was the assistant manager, who would, one day, be a manager. And, taking the situation to its logical conclusion, she would then be a bank manager's wife with a nice house and deep pile carpets. That was what Angela was thinking as she slotted another money transfer form and two carbon copies into her typing machine.

Angela Clayforth sighed and got up from her dressing table and went to the wardrobe that ran the length of one wall of her bedroom. She loved to open the doors wide and look at her new clothes all at once, and take her time in choosing what she would wear that day. It gave her a particular thrill to know there was another wardrobe full of her clothes in the other bedroom: Frank's old room. She had emptied his wardrobe and two chests of drawers the evening he'd been taken to hospital and pronounced dead on arrival.

It had taken rather longer to rid the house of the smell of pipe tobacco. And she still had Mitzi, although the short-haired dachshund was getting on in years. Frank had adored Mitzi. As the marriage had gone stale and their lives had become quite separate, Frank had got into the habit of taking Mitzi to the Hadham Arms for a pint of bitter, every evening. After that, he would retire to his garden shed where, pipe clamped between his teeth and transistor radio tuned into the Third Programme, he'd sit at his bench, constructing mechanical objects with the Meccano set his mother had bought him during the war, after his father had been killed in action.

Angela had been delighted to give the Meccano set to the two boys who lived at

Number 21. Neil and Michael Boyd were well-behaved brothers who always said hello to Mrs Clayforth when they met her in the street. She guessed that Neil was too old to play with Meccano, even though Frank had never stopped amusing himself with the metal plates and bars. Neil, she knew, was studying hard for his university entrance exams and enjoyed playing sport for his school at weekends. But young Michael had already built a crane and an engine with the different pieces of red-painted metal he'd found in Mr Clayforth's carefully preserved boxes.

Just after Angela had given them the Meccano set, Mrs Boyd had sent her eldest son over to ask if there were any jobs the widow needed doing in the house or the garden. Angela smiled, thinking of the tall, good-looking teenager and his eagerness to please, as she selected a Mary Farrin dress and slipped it carefully over her head, trying not to muss her new hairstyle. Neil would be coming to clean the windows at ten, this morning. Nice boy. Nice young man. If only she were ten years younger. Maybe, fifteen ...

"Sandwiches, John," said Susan Taylor, handing the lunch box to her husband and brushing the shoulder of his jacket. He nodded, kissed her on the cheek and opened the front door. She stood on the step, watching him walk down the path and unlock the car. She felt proud of her handsome husband. John had worked hard on his day release course at the local technical college, the previous year. And now, with his mechanical engineer's diploma, he'd got a new job, heading the drawing office team at Mortimer's Engineering Ltd. It had meant they'd been able to move from their damp Victorian flat in North London to this new housing development in the Surrey hills. A dream come true for Susan; perfect for bringing up their young family.

They had seen the show house advert in the London evening paper. Hadham had turned out to be a small village but it had a primary school and a general stores, a church and a pub. Not that the Taylors were regular church goers and they had no spare cash to spend in pubs. But Susan loved the little Close, with its bright, detached houses and their mock Tudor facades and lattice windows. Each plot had a small garden at the front and a medium-sized garden at the rear, and, best of all, they backed on to dense woodland that belonged to a beautiful Elizabethan manor house.

To Susan, a Londoner, born and bred, it was like living deep in the countryside. There were two large commons nearby where the twins could roam and play when they were older, and there were other families in the road with young children they could play with. The only problem was the nearest town, with its main stores, was ten miles away. It meant going to work with John on Thursdays and bringing the car home for the weekly shop, the twins yelling and fighting in the back. At four years old, they were full of energy and, generally, Susan was pleased about this. But she was a nervous driver at the best of times, and she found it difficult to concentrate with Sally and Ross squabbling noisily behind her.

When John and Susan had first looked at their house in Manor Close, the cul-de-sac had resembled a muddy field, which was exactly what it had been before Sir Charles Trington had sold some of his redundant farm land to a firm of developers. New housing estates like the one in Hadham were springing up all around London now, and small construction companies were making good money, snapping up country estates.

Susan thanked God for the opportunity to leave Willesden. There was nothing to keep them in London after her parents had died. She had stopped working as a clerk at Tyler and Jenkins, where she'd first met John, seven years earlier, and become a full-time mother. A year ago, he'd landed the job at Mortimer's, an engineering firm with contracts in Third World countries. The business was expanding and John Taylor had already proved to his bosses he was capable and energetic and committed to his work. Yes, Susan was proud of her husband, and he had given her two beautiful, if exhausting, children.

Of course, money was short. The new mortgage seemed enormous compared to the rent on their damp flat in London. And clothes and shoes and bikes for the twins were becoming more expensive as they got older. But John's recent promotion had been a cause for celebration. They'd taken the children to Brighton and stopped for a picnic on the South Downs, on the way. Susan smiled now, as she waved to John backing out of the driveway, recalling the warm sunshine that Sunday and how the children had laughed as they'd rolled down a hillside into the arms of their father. It was one of those perfect moments she would remember all her life.

As she went to close the front door, she looked up for a moment and caught a glimpse of Mrs Clayforth in the house opposite; a face at the downstairs window, half-hidden behind a net curtain, watching them. She felt sorry for the widow. Angela Clayforth had been alone in that house for nearly a year now and she didn't seem to have many friends. Susan made a mental note to call on the woman and invite her over for coffee or afternoon tea. She had nothing in common with Mrs Clayforth but she felt she ought to make the effort, for the sake of neighbourliness. She gave a small wave to the face at the window, stepped inside and closed the door.

Angela let go of the net curtain and stepped back into the room. Damn that Mrs Taylor, catching her looking at them. Watching her neighbours' comings and goings had become part of her daily routine since Frank had died. She liked to imagine the kind of relationships these people had by watching them getting in and out of their cars together, whether they looked at each other or not, spoke or laughed together. She knew which couples were happy to walk around their front gardens in the evenings, discussing their lawns and flowers. She and Frank had never stood together on the front lawn, at any time, to admire the shrubs he had planted. If one was in the garden, the other would be in the house.

Angela squinted in the sunlight streaming through the sitting room window and put her hand up to shade her eyes. The ideal couple, she thought, and pursed her lipsticked lips, thinking about the Taylors. Why hadn't she and Frank smiled and waved to each other when he'd left the house in the mornings? Where had it all gone wrong? The answer was that it had never been right. Angela knew she had married for practical reasons, for status and security, not love. Back then, twenty years earlier, it had not seemed important they had nothing in common; not interests or sense of humour, nor outlook on life.

Angela had believed they could rub along together, sharing social occasions and their neat home. She hadn't given much thought to the bedroom, to spending a night with Frank Clayforth and waking up with him, there, in the morning. Her thoughts had focussed on the two negligées she had seen in the local lingerie boutique, in her favourite colours of peach and rose. That first night – she didn't want to think about it now. She had the dog to feed. They'd bought the dachshund, she supposed, to give them a reason to continue living together. Not that they'd ever sat down and discussed how their lives had drifted apart.

"Who's a lovely girl, then?" Frank would bend over the dog, several times a day, and rub her behind the ears. He'd adored Mitzi from the start and the short-haired dachshund lived for

Frank's attention. She would sit at his slippered feet whenever he played his Gilbert and Sullivan records or read his newspaper from cover to cover, and she would accompany him to the garden shed where he spent hours at his bench with his Meccano set, the Third Programme on in the background.

Now, the dog trotted after Angela, up and down, all over the house. She'd stepped on the animal several times and it had always responded with an ear-splitting yelp. Angela had thought about having Mitzi put down. But she'd been afraid of what the neighbours would say. She promised herself the moment the animal became incontinent or rheumatic, she would take it to the vet. But the dachshund remained annoyingly healthy and continued to follow Angela around the house. It was a relief when Doreen Reynolds' awful child, Stella, had offered to take it for a walk every day, after school. Correction: Doreen had volunteered her daughter for the job. Stella was a pudgy, awkward teenager with a spotty complexion and straight, lank hair. The girl had little or no conversation, let alone any social graces. Angela couldn't abide the teenager. Well, neither could Doreen, come to that.

"For God's sake, look at the mud on your shoes! Do you think I was put on this earth to clear up after you?" Doreen, standing at the sink doing the dishes, turned her head to glare at her sixteen year old. She knew Stella expected a confrontation as soon as she came in the back door. It was almost a daily occurrence now: Doreen shouting at her, often several times a day. But girl seemed to accept it. It was as if she understood she would never be able to please her mother, and had long ago stopped trying.

"How many times do I have to tell you to change into your slippers, especially in this weather? God, what have I done to deserve a child like you!" Doreen returned her flushed face to the dishes, satisfied she'd voiced her complaint. But Stella could already smell the real reason for her mother's mood. And tonight, when her father came home late, as he did more often than not these days, the shouting would begin, all over again.

"I'm going down to the Williams's after I've taken Mitzi for a walk," said her daughter without looking at her, untying her shoe laces and putting on her slippers. "I've got to see Tanya about a class project."

"Don't you come back late, waking up the whole household, like you usually do!" responded Doreen, scouring a saucepan with vigour. But she was relieved. She preferred it when her oldest child was out of the house. Thomas didn't provoke the animosity she felt towards her daughter. Her son was a quiet, studious child. He never answered back. And he never mentioned the empty bottles that appeared in the kitchen, ready to be disposed of, after Ray had gone to work.

"You're a selfish, good-for-nothing girl and I'll be glad to see the back of you soon!" She turned her head again but found she was talking to an empty room. Stella had already exited through kitchen door and into the hallway. Doreen heard the teenager's plodding tread on the stairs and, suddenly, she had an overwhelming need for another sherry. She glanced at the bottle on the side, then at the kitchen clock. Angela was coming over this evening. She must pace herself; she must. Just a small one for now. What? The bottle nearly empty? She could have sworn – Well, never mind. There was another in the cupboard. And there was gin for tonight. Angela liked a gin and orange. As for Doreen, she would drink anything these days. Anything to blot out what was happening in her marriage.

"Here, you mutt!" shouted Stella as she picked her way along a narrow path that led deep into the woods. But Mitzi took no notice, as usual. The dachshund was on a mission that only another dog would appreciate; there were smells in the undergrowth of foxes, rabbits and other dogs, plus a human being or two. Even more pressing was that other activity all dogs got up to when out for a walk. Mitzi knew Stella would wait until she'd done her business, even if the teenager's tone of voice wouldn't be exactly welcoming when she returned.

For her part, Stella didn't care about Mitzi or what the dog got up to in Hadham Woods. About a year ago, when Mr Clayforth had died and her mother had volunteered her to walk Mrs Clayforth's dog, the girl had hardly uttered a word in protest. One reason was that it gave Stella an opportunity to meet her friends, Tanya and Neil, Michael and Francine, who'd be playing or, now they were older, walking and talking in the lanes and woods nearby.

The other reason for her not minding was that it got her out of the house after school, which meant an extra hour or so away from the war zone that her home had become in the last three or four years. It wasn't her mother's drinking that bothered Stella. In fact, she was relieved when her mother was practically comatose. But there followed that most dangerous period, when Doreen was coming out of one of her drinking sessions. The woman had a temper at the best of times but, when she was withdrawing from an alcoholic binge, she became a monster. At the slightest provocation or for no reason at all, it seemed to Stella, if her path crossed with her mother's anywhere in the house, the woman would clout her around the head or violently slap her face. These walks in the woods in the late afternoon gave the girl a brief respite from all of that.

Stella had already learnt to use food, particularly doorstop sandwiches and whatever was in the biscuit tin, as an antidote to her home life. Every time she felt low and, lately, even if she didn't, she found she could get a temporary fix from something sweet or filling, or both. The problem was, these temporary lifts out of her general misery had caused her 'puppy fat', as the doctor had called it, to inflate, turning her into something resembling the Michelin Man. Her body had ballooned and so had the tops of her arms and legs, and her face had become round and featureless. Her waistline was non-existent now, measuring almost the same as her large bust.

Stella's unattractiveness, compared to other girls in her class, and especially to her friend, Tanya Williams, had begun to make her miserable at school these days, as well as at home. In games lessons, Stella noticed, none of the girls wanted her to be on their team for netball or rounders. She was always the last one to be picked by the captains.

"Hey, Fatty!" Marcia Ackroyd had called out as they'd packed up their books after French that afternoon. Stella had automatically looked round and seen Marcia standing at the door with Jennifer Rawle, Gillian Cotterell and Tanya. "See!" whooped Marcia. "She knows her name!" The girls laughed as they left the classroom and she could still hear them in the corridor.

Tanya, laughing at her! Stella could have died. She didn't care what buck-toothed Jennifer Rawle thought of her, or dopey Gillian Cotterell with her acne and square-framed glasses. But Tanya lived in Manor Close, just a few doors down from Stella. They had played together after school and during the long holidays ever since they'd been at primary school. They'd made camps in Hadham Woods with the Boyd brothers and little Francine, and picked wild flowers and pressed them in telephone directories. Now, Stella began to notice how Tanya hung around with Marcia Ackroyd and her friends in the lesson breaks, and she realised, with dismay, that her old friend hadn't called at her house for a very long time.

"Taylor, drop whatever it is you're doing and knock out this drawing for me, pronto." John Taylor had no need to look up from his drawing board. He knew the voice; he loathed the man. "I told Durrell I'd let him have the plans by tonight." Ash, the drawing office manager, threw a sheaf papers on the desk beside John's drawing board and walked on, out of the office. Taylor looked up then, and narrowed his eyes as he watched the back of Neville Ash disappearing through the frosted glass door. John loved his job: the pay was good and his colleagues were fine and the journey to work took only twenty minutes. But there was one problem, and it was a daily irritation that was starting to get him down.

The moment John had started at Mortimer's, his immediate boss, the drawing office manager, had seemed to dislike him. At first, John thought it was a situation he could overcome. He worked hard, stayed late and tried to engage Ash in conversation whenever the man walked through the office. But, after several weeks of effort, Taylor was getting nowhere. Then a final attempt at a friendly exchange gave him a clue to the problem. "Morning, Neville. How are you – "

"I'll ask you not to call me by my Christian name, Taylor. I'm Mr Ash to you."

There was a slight curl to his boss's upper lip. "If we don't maintain the difference in our status, the office will descend into chaos."

"Oh, I don't think that would – "

"I'd prefer us to keep to a working relationship. We know where we are, then. Don't we?" Before Taylor could respond, the manager had turned on his heel and left the office. Heads bobbed up at the other drawing boards. Everyone had heard what Ash had said.

"Don't take it to heart, mate," said Ian Tyler, over his board to John. "Ash knows he's only squeaked into the manager's post. If you'd joined the firm six month's earlier, he'd never have got the promotion. It would have been you and he knows that. And now, he reckons you're chasing his tail. Everything you do, he sees as competition. Like the other day, when Mr Mortimer stopped by your board and looked at your drawing. Old Ash was wetting himself, watching you talking to the boss like that. His mouth was down for the rest of the day."

At first, Taylor was surprised to hear this. Then he recalled other exchanges with the manager during the last few weeks and Ian's words began to make sense. Ash's personal insecurity was at the heart of the matter, no mistake. Not that it helped John, knowing the reason for his boss's hostility. He had no idea how he could change the situation. He hadn't a clue where to start. And the more he thought about the problem and how he might go about solving it, the more there seemed no solution.

The dark red liquid slipped down her throat like soothing cough mixture. She felt the chemicals hit her brain and her eyes shone mistily. That was better. She would just sit down and relax for a minute. Where was that other bottle of sherry? Not in that cupboard, try the next one along. No. Try the next. Not there. But they had been there: six bottles at the beginning of the week. She'd bought them herself. Was Ray pouring them down the sink in the middle of the night? That would be the sort of stunt he'd pull: any subterfuge to undermine her when he could.

But, these days, he spent more time at the golf club than at home. "Don't try to get up, you'll fall over," was his only greeting when he put his head around the sitting room door, late at night, and saw her slumped in an armchair in front of the television. Doreen was beginning to feel frightened now. And it wasn't because of anything Ray had said. More to do with Angela Clayforth's words, last summer.

They'd been reclining on sun loungers in the Reynolds' garden with their second jug of Pimm's that afternoon. "Doreen," said Angela, her glass raised, "if a man's still at the golf club at eleven o'clock every night, take it from me, he's seeing someone other than the barman."

A mental picture of Ray in the golf clubhouse, talking and laughing with Vic and Audrey and an unknown woman was more than Doreen could bear. She'd done her best over the years, cleaning the home and bringing up the family, but she knew it hadn't been enough. She'd let her appearance go. She was overweight and she drank to help her get through the day. Last Christmas, Ray hadn't even mentioned his office party, let alone the golf club dance. Their marriage had disintegrated. If they had the occasional conversation, it was only to discuss the children's schooling. Doreen took the sherry bottle down from the kitchen cupboard. She placed it on the worktop and held on to it, then let out a sob. She felt afraid, terrified of the future. She unscrewed the cap. Best to have a drink now, she told herself, sliding a glass next to the bottle, and the world will seem a better place.

Angela Clayforth did her best to avoid conversations with Doreen Reynolds' daughter when the girl rang the doorbell to take Mitzi for a walk. Stella reminded Angela uncomfortably of herself at that age. Not that Angela had been as podgy as the unfortunate Stella. "It's your bones," her mother had told her. "You've always been a big girl, Angela, and now you've got large breasts." Angela had hung her head. "Oh, for heaven's sake!" her mother admonished her, "stop feeling sorry for yourself. You'll find it useful to have a rounded figure when you're older. I don't know who you take after, though. Must be Grandma Clough. She had an enormous bust. Could hardly get about because of them!" Angela's head sank lower.

Why hadn't she been more like her mother? wondered the gawky teenager. She longed for her mother's svelte attractiveness, and her abilities. Both of Angela's parents were achievers in life. Doctor Rees was a research scientist at one of the London institutes and Mrs Rees taught history and geography at the local grammar school. Her parents were an energetic couple who spent summer weekends playing tennis at the local club and took ski-ing holidays in the Alps every winter. Angela never accompanied them. "Oh, Angela's useless at games," she'd overheard her mother tell a neighbour, one day, when she was about eleven. "A great, gallumping girl! I've paid for her to have tennis lessons at the club but, you know, they make jokes about her all the time. I can't believe I've given birth to such an elephant!"

And the neighbour had laughed and shaken her head, then nodded in agreement.

When Angela Rees failed her eleven-plus exam, it was no surprise to anyone. Her parents decided she should go to a boarding school in Kent. "You'll love those extra classes, Angela," her mother told her as they drove up to the grey square building on her first day of term. "You can learn to play an instrument and take speech and drama lessons. Both will give you confidence and poise. And there's swimming. That'll firm you up ... "

But Angela knew her mother didn't hold out much hope for her. During her time at Oakley, she was content to be the girl her mother had pronounced her to be. Academically, she bumped along near the bottom of the class. Her reports were never glowing. She never learnt to play a musical instrument and she hated swimming almost as much as she hated tennis. But in speech and drama lessons, the girl could forget who she was and what she looked like. She became someone else completely. She was rarely chosen to be a princess or a queen, but she didn't mind being a soldier with a spear or even an old man with a beard. She was someone else, not 'Big Angela'.

There were two Angelas in the Upper Fifth at Oakley, and one of them was a slim, sporty girl with honey blonde hair called Angela Harvey. So different from 'Big' Angela Rees. Years later, Mrs Clayforth would look at Tanya Williams, another schoolgirl who lived in Manor Close, and be reminded of Angela Harvey. The attractive classmate, all those years ago, had underlined her own gawkiness. Her hostility towards the girl had grown so intense that, one games lesson, when they were both at the far end of the hockey pitch, she had been tempted to club Angela Harvey with her hockey stick until the girl's beautiful face was damaged beyond repair. Mrs Clayforth wondered if Stella Reynolds ever felt that way about her friend, Tanya Williams.

CHAPTER 3

Neil pushed the bell on Mrs Clayforth's front door, listened to the chimes in the hallway and waited, just as he'd done every Sunday morning for the last ten months.

"I've said you'll help the lady," his mother had told him, one morning at the kitchen table after Mrs Clayforth had been round for coffee. "It'll give you some extra money to buy those pop records you go on about, and that guitar. Michael's old enough to do your paper round now and you've got exams to study for. A few Sunday mornings, cleaning Mrs Clayforth's windows and mowing her lawn, will take up all your spare time."

Neil continued to stir his coffee, staring into the swirling liquid. "And," his mother said, after a pause. He knew what was coming. "It'll give you less time to moon around that girl. There'll be plenty of opportunity for that silliness once you get to university."

Neil's mouth set in two thin lines. "And don't you look like that, young man. That Tanya's no catch, I can tell you. You want to meet a girl from a good family when you get to college." His mother got up and rinsed the cups she and Angela Clayforth had used for coffee, a quarter of an hour earlier. "Not that Mrs Williams isn't a nice woman. She's done her best for Tanya, considering the girl's lacked the discipline of a father. But this isn't the time to be thinking about things like that – "

"Things, like what?" Her son looked up, challengingly.

Mrs Boyd sighed. "Your father and I want you to have a good start in life, that's all. Just do this for us, please, Neil. Work hard and you'll have everything you want, soon enough." She rinsed the last cup and placed it on the draining board. "You'll wonder what you saw in that girl, later on."

So here he was again: standing on Mrs Clayforth's doorstep. Ten in the morning and dog-tired after one of the best Saturday nights in his entire seventeen years. Some girl called Marcia, a friend of Tanya's, had thrown a party. Her parents had been away for the weekend and –

"Hello, young man. Come along in." Mrs Clayforth held her front door open wide. God, how he hated the way she smiled and put her hand on his shoulder, and left it there too long. "I thought you could clean my car for me today. It always looks so nice when you've polished it. Now, come into the kitchen and have a cup of coffee, first, and some biscuits to give you energy."

Normally, this was the worst part of Sunday mornings. Sitting opposite Angela Clayforth at her kitchen table, her knees brushing against his, far too often. But this morning he needed the coffee. How much cider had he drunk last night? And how much had Tanya drunk? There was so much he couldn't remember. A stab of pure pain flashed between his eyes, blinding him for a moment. He followed Mrs Clayforth's large behind, sashaying before him into the kitchen.

"A strong one, please, Mrs Clayforth. Two spoons."

Angela Clayforth turned as she filled the kettle and raised her pencilled eyebrows. "A night on the tiles, young man? You are a one! I expect you're a good dancer, aren't you? I don't know, all these gyrations they do now, they're – well, so suggestive, don't you think?" The false eyelashes fluttered and the red glossy lips parted.

A wave of nausea swept over Neil. He felt last night's cider rise in the back his throat. "Can I use your toilet, please, Mrs Clayforth?" He stood up and held on to the table.

"Why, of course. It's through here."

He stumbled after her, his hand clapped over his mouth. As he closed the toilet door behind him, a strong odour of geranium pot pourri assailed his nostrils, making him feel even more nauseous. He lifted the frilled lavatory seat and knelt down and grabbed the bowl. As he threw up, he noticed the blue disinfectant which had been added to the water curdled as it received the party cider.

A tap at the door. "Are you alright, young man?"

"Fine. Thanks." He would never drink cider again. But, maybe, it had been worth it. It had got him upstairs at the party, into the parents' bedroom with Tanya. And he'd never have had the nerve to undo her blouse like that; though she'd taken the rest of her clothes off, herself. And she'd taken most of his clothes off, too –

"Coffee's on the table!"

Neil went slowly back to the kitchen, wiping his mouth with the back of his hand. He sat down gingerly on the chair and clasped his coffee mug with both hands. He felt Mrs Clayforth's knees pressing against his as she leaned across to offer him a plate of biscuits.

"These are your favourite, I know. A little bird told me. Your mother, actually."

Neil took a couple of Swiss creams and looked at them in his hand, and felt sick again. He wondered how Tanya was feeling this morning. An image of her, astride him, her breasts moving rhythmically above his head, almost made him smile. He was a man now. That party had been the best ever. And Tanya was his girl.

"My, you were thirsty! More coffee? You haven't eaten your biscuits."

Neil felt more pressure on his knees. He stood up, leaving the biscuits untouched on the kitchen table. "I'm not hungry, really." The sound of his chair scraping back made his head throb. He swallowed. He needed some fresh air. He wanted to be alone with his thoughts. He needed to put some space between himself and this woman. "I'll get the bucket and cloth and the soap stuff, Mrs Clayforth. They'll be in the garage, I expect."

Outside, he gulped in the morning air. Then he cast a sideways glance at number seventeen, the house with the blue paintwork, four doors down. Tanya was in there. Was she sleeping? Was she thinking of him? Thinking of last night? He got the bucket and filled it from the outside tap and set to work on Mrs Clayforth's Triumph Herald.

He had not been surprised at the beauty of Tanya's lithe body when he'd seen it for the first time; only full of joy. He had covertly looked at the curves of her hips and breasts over the last three or four years and mentally undressed her, many times before. As children, they had played in the woods and made camps with Michael and Francine and a few others. Tanya had been a playmate then, nothing more. But for so long, he had wanted more than her friendship. He had wanted her naked, as she had been with him last night.

She had led him up the staircase, opened the door to a bedroom and switched on a side lamp. They had stood there, kissing and stroking each other and he'd moved one hand towards her breasts. Tanya had stopped kissing him then, and pulled him towards the bed. She lay there, smiling and laughing, as his hands caressed and explored her. After a while, he had fumbled with her blouse buttons and she'd laughed again and pushed him off.

She stood up and peeled off all her clothes in front of him. He went to her, kissed her breasts, her stomach, her pubic hair. And Tanya was undressing him, leading him back to the bed. She pulled him close and, suddenly, he found himself beneath her. She guided him with her hands and he felt her deliberate pelvic movements, heard her low moaning. Then she made a sound he had never heard her make before. She cried out, a kind of scream, but it wasn't in pain. She was in ecstasy; they both were. An urgent, pulsating rapture.

"Hullo, Neil. How are you?"

He looked up from washing the front bumper. The person who'd spoken was obscured by sunlight, but he knew the voice, anyway.

"'Lo, Stella. Fine."

Stella stood there, on the driveway, watching him soaping the Triumph's headlights and rubbing them with the cloth. He didn't look up again. He didn't say anything else. The girl watched him for a couple of minutes and searched for something to say. It hadn't always been like this. When they were younger and had played together, with Tanya and the others, he'd been friendly and talkative with her. She had been one of his gang, sharing his camps over in Hadham Woods. They'd climbed trees together and he'd held her hand to stop her falling and pulled her into the uppermost branches. They'd told each other jokes, exchanged confidences, shared secrets.

Once, Stella had told him that her mother drank sherry in the mornings. Neil had looked at her in surprise. He thought for a moment, then said that Michael still wet his bed sometimes.

Stella never repeated to anyone else the things that Neil had told her. Not even to Tanya. These were their special secrets and she cherished them. It meant she was his friend. And one day soon, she would be his girlfriend. And they'd get married and she'd look after his house and they'd have children who were tall and fair like Neil. She didn't want children who looked like her, not short and stocky with mouse brown hair.

"So, I'd better be going, then."

"Yeah," Neil grunted as he wiped along the front wing.

"I'm going down to Tanya's now."

He stopped rubbing the paintwork and looked up at her.

"We've got a school project to do." She jiggled the school bag she carried in her hand. "It's about ancient Greece and Athens."

"Tell Tanya ... " What should he tell Tanya? What could he say to Stella to pass on to her? Stella wasn't the kind of person you'd pick to deliver a romantic message. A joke, yes. She'd always been one for telling a joke. "Say, I'll see her soon."

A frown of incomprehension creased Stella's brow. "That's a funny message. You see her practically every day ... " Then a glimmer of understanding came into her eyes. It dawned on her that he'd been waiting for Tanya after school, these last few months. Stella had never really questioned why he was always at their bus stop. She'd simply been happy to see him on the same bus home, most days of the week. She stared at Neil. He had gone back to cleaning Mrs Clayforth's car. And there was the woman, herself, coming out of her front door with a yellow cloth and a tin of what looked like car wax.

"Now, Stella, don't you stop Neil working. He's a busy young man." She patted him lightly on the back as he rinsed the car windscreen, as if to affirm he was her exclusive property.

"Just going." Stella moved away, back on to the street, and continued her walk down to number seventeen. She kept her head down, staring hard at the pavement, as events began to fall into place. Yes, Tanya had been different lately. Yes, it probably dated from around the time Neil had started turning up at the bus stop after school. Yes, they had all got on the bus together, most days. But Neil always sat next to Tanya. In other words, he had never sat next to Stella. That meant – what did it mean? Wasn't he going to be her boyfriend now?

She was still pondering the situation as she rang the Williams's doorbell. She stood there, not noticing the length of time it took

Tanya to come to the door. When her friend finally appeared, she was still in her nightdress, her long hair dishevelled, but her face radiant. Stella thought she looked a bit like Brigitte Bardot or Marianne Faithful or one of the Beatles' girlfriends. She decided, there and then, she would grow her hair long and go on a diet, and she would colour her hair blonde and wear the same pale lipstick as Tanya. Then Neil would be her friend again, and her boyfriend, as she'd always known he would be.

"Oh, it's you. What time is it?"

"Nearly eleven."

"Oh, God!" Tanya rubbed the back of her head and shook out her hair.

"I've got the project," Stella held up her school bag.

Tanya gave a low groan.

"We said we'd look at this morning. Can I come in?"

"Did we? Oh, right ... come in." She left the door wide and started up the stairs. "Let me put some clothes on. Come on up."

Stella closed the front door and climbed the stairs behind her friend. Tanya's bedroom was the largest one in the Williams's house and situated at the front. Most of the properties in the Close had the same layout inside. In Stella's house, the biggest bedroom was her parents' room, although her father sometimes slept in the box room on his own. Stella and Thomas had equal-sized rooms at the back of the house. Mrs Williams slept in one of the back bedrooms at number seventeen.

Although the houses had the same internal design, their facades varied in colour and in the style of their windows. But it was the small gardens in front of the properties that really stamped the personalities on the houses. Stella's home had a neglected honeysuckle hanging off the wall by the front door. The door needed varnishing, the path needed weeding. Mrs Clayforth's windows were square leaded lights, instead of the diamond-shaped ones that most people had, with a luxuriant climbing rose trained, pruned and firmly fixed across the front wall. The Taylor's house, across the road from Angela Clayforth's, had very little in the front garden except a brightly-coloured plastic children's slide. The lawn was patchy and had a track around the edge where the twins rode their tricycles most days. Their gate was nearly always left open. The house at the end of the Close, where Neil and Michael lived, was half-hidden behind maturing trees that Mr Boyd had planted when the family had moved in, ten years ago. Next door to them, Mrs Hodge's garden was very like the Hodges: fussy, busy. Mrs Hodge loved to gossip.

Tanya was in her underwear when Stella pushed open the bedroom door. The girl's light-blue matching bra and panties seemed to accentuate her slim shape. As Tanya tugged a flimsy teeshirt over her head and slid into a pair of tight jeans, Stella noticed how long her friend's legs were, how flat her stomach was, and how her breasts were full but not overflowing her low-cut bra.

"Need some breakfast, first. Got to have a cup of coffee," she said, pulling a brush through her hair in quick, long strokes. "God, I feel like death! I've only had about four hours' sleep. Marcia had a party last night. Her parents are in the South of France."

"Yes, I heard her talking about it in class on Friday. Was it good? Did many people go?" Stella trailed behind Tanya, back down the stairs and into the kitchen.

Her friend gave a snort and a giggle as she held the kettle under the tap. "Everyone was there. The place was full to bursting point."

"I wasn't there."

"Yes, well ... "

"Who was there, then?"

"Half of Neil's school, for a start – "

Stella was suddenly alert. "Did Neil go? Was he at Marcia's party?"

Tanya gave her a look of amusement, then threw back her head, laughing. The kettle boiled, she turned and poured hot water into a mug, stirring the coffee, still giggling.

"Was he there? I saw him this morning, cleaning Mrs Clayforth's car. He said hello – No, he said he'd see you soon."

"Did he?" Tanya slid into a chair at the table where Stella had already seated herself. "What else did he say?"

"So, he was there, then ... "

Tanya gave a low laugh. "Oh, he was there, alright! More than all right, I'd say!" Then her face took on a dreamy expression and she sipped at her coffee.

Stella squirmed in her seat. Normally, she hung on her friend's every word but, this morning, Tanya was irritating her. Tanya had always been the sophisticated one. She knew things Stella had wanted to know about fashion and music, and how to kiss. They'd discussed the technique of kissing, in detail, about eighteen months ago. Her friend seemed to know all about it, presumably from Marcia who had an older brother who had friends he brought home for tea. Tanya said Marcia had been kissed by one of her brother's friends and

70

he'd put his tongue in her mouth and felt her teeth.

"Did you ... ?" Stella wanted to ask Tanya if Neil had kissed her at the party, if he had put his tongue in her mouth and felt her teeth.

"What?" Tanya stifled a giggle. "Did we what!"

"Nothing." Stella wasn't ready to let go of her daydreams, yet. She thought of something else to ask. "Did your Mum mind you being out late?"

Now it was Tanya's turn to get annoyed. She didn't feel like discussing what had happened when she'd got back from the party. Her mother had been waiting for her, downstairs, as she always did when Tanya was out with her friends. She'd sat in the armchair in front of a blank television screen until four in the morning, listening for her daughter's return. There'd been the usual row about the time Tanya had got home, the usual questions about who she'd been with, what she'd been doing. Tanya, as always, was defensive, which made her mother even more anxious about her daughter's growing tendency to stay out late. Finally, Mrs Williams had become exasperated. "Don't think you can stay out half the night, every weekend, and expect me to sit here, worrying about you!"

"There's nothing to worry about, Mum. Stop imagining things. Just take a pill and go to bed. For God's sake, I was only at Marcia's – "

"And there were boys there, too?"

"Of course there were boys there. We're not training to be nuns – "

"Don't you talk back to me, my girl. I know far more about the world than you do!"

Tanya pulled a face and muttered under her breath, "I doubt it."

"If your father was still alive, he'd soon put a stop to this nonsense. I pray to him nightly to give me strength – "

"Oh, for God's sake, don't be so melodramatic. Anyway, he wouldn't be much use. He wasn't bothered about us – "

"That's not true!"

"Well, he didn't stick around, did he? Took the easy way out – "

"Stop it!"

Tanya drew herself up and spoke slowly, deliberately. "He didn't want to go on. He killed himself so he wouldn't have to live with us, with you! He couldn't sort out his own life, let alone anyone else's – "

"Don't say any more!" Mrs Williams hoisted herself out of the armchair and went towards her daughter.

But Tanya was in full flood. "Don't say what? Don't say he killed himself, you mean? Don't say he cut his wrists? That he couldn't live with you? That he preferred to die – "

Mrs Williams' hand flew out and struck Tanya across the face. The girl staggered backwards, her eyes watering. She held her cheek and lowered her head for a moment. Then she turned and left the room without another word. Her mother sank back in the armchair and stared at the blank television screen again. She would've liked to have cried, but the tears wouldn't come. She sat there and thought back to the time, fourteen years ago, when she'd been widowed.

Tanya had only been a baby when Jim had lost the house to a gambling debt. It had been his last attempt to win back all the money he'd lost over the years; to provide something for his family. And he had, indeed, provided for them. He'd taken out a life insurance policy, not long before he died. The insurance company had tried to withhold the payment, but Mavis Williams's solicitor knew all about the small print, having advised Jim about the policy, several months earlier. No, money wasn't a problem for Mavis, but her daughter was beginning to worry her. Tanya reminded her so much of Jim: the same impetuosity, the same strong emotions, the same embracing of life without a thought for the future.

She had tried to pick up the pieces. She had given all her time and effort to her daughter. They had moved to the coast and they'd been happy together. Tanya loved going shopping with her mother and walking on the beach with her. And she was content to play with her dolls while Mavis sat in the bay window, sewing or knitting. Later on, the girl did her homework in the same room, overlooking the sea, while her mother read a novel or worked on a small tapestry. Their lives had been calm and uneventful. It should have remained that way.

Then Zelda, Mavis's sister, became ill with breast cancer and Mavis looked for a house where she could be near to her. They had only been in their new home in Manor Close a few months when Zelda died. Years later, Mavis wondered if, lost in her grief for her sister, she had neglected Tanya at this time. Perhaps she should have focussed on the living and not the dying. But the girl was happy, playing on the common nearby with her new friends and in the woods at Hadham Manor. The chubby Stella Reynolds became a particular friend, living just a few doors down and going to the same school as Tanya. The girls picked wild flowers together and pressed them in scrapbooks. And they seemed to have fun making camps with Neil and Michael Boyd and even with little Francine West, although the younger girl wasn't always allowed out to play.

Then, a couple of years ago, Tanya discovered makeup and pop records and boys. She stopped going to her Girl Guide meetings and stopped going to church on Sundays. Mrs Williams found herself standing in the pew near the front of the congregation all on her own. Her daughter was spending time in a coffee bar after school, not with Stella but with two girls in her class called Marcia and Jennifer. Tanya became a different person, or so it seemed to Mrs Williams, who began to worry, more and more, where her daughter was, who she was with.

"Oh, stop asking where I am all the time!" her daughter had shouted at her one day. "You're suffocating me! Do you know that?"

Mavis didn't know what Tanya was talking about. She only knew she felt uneasy about her daughter's new attitude, not only to her mother. And now there was young Neil to worry about. Mavis liked the Boyds. They were a nice family. But Tanya had a mad streak in her. She could encourage Neil in the wrong direction. She was like Jim. Mavis saw Jim's headstrong ways, so often, in Tanya. She sighed. She couldn't think of her daughter's future without a sense of foreboding. And she knew it would break her heart if she ever lost Tanya.

Angela Clayforth watched Susan Taylor place the twins in the back of her husband's car and climb into the passenger seat, next to her husband. Ah, thought Angela. Eight o'clock, Thursday morning. Shopping day. The wife has the car, takes the twins to see her friend, Marjorie, and her children. They have lunch, then Susan goes on to the supermarket and buys the groceries for the week, collects Ross and Sally from her friend's and rushes home to give the children their tea and cook John's dinner before collecting him from work. That much she knew from the few polite exchanges she'd had with Susan Taylor in the street. But that was as far as it went. Angela realised she had never had a real conversation with Mrs Taylor in all the time they'd lived opposite each other. Not even when Frank had died.

"Is there anything I can get you from the supermarket, Mrs Clayforth?" Susan Taylor had knocked at the door, one shopping day, about a week after Frank's heart attack.

"Nothing, thank you," Angela had said, standing at the door, still in her quilted dressing gown. She hadn't meant to be rude to the woman, it was just too early in the morning to make conversation and her egg had nearly had its three minutes in the pan. Susan Taylor had paused for a moment, in case Mrs Clayforth had wanted to say something else, then said, "Well, I must be going. The children are already in the car." And she'd smiled, turned and hurried back down Angela's path. Angela had closed the door and returned to her breakfast.

Their lives were so different, Angela realised that. Mrs Taylor was always rushing somewhere, usually with her children in tow. Angela, on the other hand, had all the time in the world. She had even thought about taking a job again when Frank had first retired and begun to get on her nerves, pottering around the house for most of the day. But office work had never interested Angela. It had been something she'd accepted she had to endure on the way to her goal of domestic ease. She'd stopped working as soon as she and Frank had married and devoted her energies to decorating their home. It was the only reason she'd accepted the man's proposal. It was a pity he had to be part of the deal.

This morning, Angela wondered if she should ask Susan Taylor to buy her some of that new hair conditioner they'd been advertising on the television. Just to have contact with a neighbour, she thought. Just for something to say. Angela didn't see many people these days, except Doreen Reynolds. But Doreen was so wrapped up in her own problems, and not always sober. Angela had invited other women in the Close over for coffee, and some of them had invited her back, in return. But she didn't seem to have much in common with any of them.

All they wanted to discuss was their children, and Angela found she had nothing to contribute to that particular subject. Mrs Williams had been the worst. A thin, tired-looking woman, a widow like herself. But all Mavis Williams could talk about was her daughter and how well she was doing at school and how much she helped Mavis in the house. That was a couple of years ago, and Angela hadn't bothered to call on the woman again. She had seen Mavis's daughter going about with Doreen's plump child, laughing and swinging their satchels as they walked back from school in the afternoons. But, lately, she'd seen Tanya Williams walking past her house with Valerie Boyd's son, Neil. The two always walked slowly and close together, hands almost touching, with Stella Reynolds sometimes trailing behind them.

Angela found she spent a lot of time at her sitting room window, these days, watching the residents of Manor Close going about their daily lives. But she felt detached from them all, uninvolved, a person apart. And, in the main, she preferred it that way. She wasn't interested in people's struggles to pay their mortgages or bring up their children or grow hydrangeas in their gardens. The only thing that really interested Angela were the marital relationships in the households. After all, she didn't have one of her own to think about. She observed couples, like the Taylors, who smiled as they went in and out of their houses, who conversed with each other in their gardens, who laughed together over their children. She had become quite an expert at discerning who was in a happy relationship and who was not; those who lived together and those who merely existed under the same roof, as she and Frank had done.

Remarriage held no appeal for Angela but she craved a relationship with a man. Yes, that's what's missing from my life, she thought. A man to be happy with: romance, l'amour. Angela sighed and continued buffing her nails as she watched John Taylor back the family car out of their driveway. The children were jumping up and down on the back seat and Mrs Taylor was waving her index finger at them while her husband turned the wheel. Angela moved the net curtain slightly for a clearer view of the scene. Then she noticed her houseplants needed watering.

Three hours later, as she was snipping a dead leaf off an African Violet on the windowsill, something outside in the road caught Angela Clayforth's eye. A police car was drawing up in front of the Taylors' house. She put down the scissors and held back the curtain a fraction. Two police officers, one driving and one in the back of the car with John Taylor. Mr Taylor was hunched forward. She saw him put his hands over his face. The officer in the back of the car got out and held the door open for him. Mr Taylor didn't move straight away. He sat there, staring ahead of him. Angela Clayforth lifted the curtain back a little further. It was as if she knew, already.

CHAPTER 4

Stella Reynolds turned the corner into Manor Close, a hockey stick in one hand and her school bag, a maroon beret poking from its flap, swinging low from the other. Her tie was loose and her socks were bunched around her ankles, her suede shoes were scuffed and bald at the toes and one of the laces had come undone. She was staring at the pavement as she walked, deep in thought, going over her journey home from school.

Stella was in shock, there was no other word for it. Her world had collapsed about her ears, though it had been her eyes that had witnessed the scene. Stella had believed she and Tanya were getting along fine, that they were almost close friends again. Of course, Tanya was still spending time with Marcia Ackroyd, Jennifer Rawle and goofy Gillian Cotterell. But Tanya and Stella must have spent four or five evenings together in the last fortnight, working on their school project. And Tanya had been fun to be with: laughing with Stella, instead of at her, as she did when Marcia was around. They'd exchanged confidences again, just as they had in the past when they were much younger. Best of all, one evening, they had discussed Neil Boyd. Tanya had asked her what she thought it would be like to be married to someone like Neil.

"Well," said Stella, leaning back on her elbows on Tanya's bed amongst the brochures of ancient Greece they'd been cutting and pasting into their school project book. "I think he'd make a good husband, for the right person. I mean, you'd want to look after him and do things for him ... "

"What things?" giggled Tanya. She was kneeling on the floor with a glue pot and brush, sticking cuttings into the project book.

"Sort of cook nice dinners for him and make sure his shirts were ironed. Be nice to him – "

"Be nice to him, how?" Tanya sat up on her heels and looked at Stella with a mischievous smile. "Go on, tell me what you would do."

"It's hard to say exactly," said Stella, giving it serious thought. "It would depend on the situation – "

"Bit of canoodling in the bedroom, would that do it?"

"Well, I don't know about that ... "

"No, you don't, do you?" sighed Tanya, her smile waning. "I do, though," and she looked away, dreamily.

A slight frown crossed Stella's face for a moment, then it was gone. "But I do know someone like Neil would make a good husband. He's always friendly and kind, and he helps others. Look at what he does for Mrs Clayforth, every weekend."

Tanya gave an abrupt laugh. "Not as much as the old bat would like him to do!" And she stuck another picture in the book and pressed it down with the palm of her hand.

"Oh, she's like that with everybody. She hardly says thank you when I take Mitzi for a walk. She kind of expects everyone to run around for her. I don't know how Mr Clayforth put up with it. He must have died from overwork."

"Well, he didn't die from overwork in the bedroom. My mum went round there for coffee once, and she said Mrs Clayforth had her own room and so did Mr Clayforth. They didn't like each other, my mum says. No one likes Mrs Clayforth. She looks down on people. She looks down on my mum. My mum can't stand her. I expect your mum gets fed up with her, too."

"I don't know."

"Neil gets fed up with Mrs Clayforth. He hates going round there and mowing the lawn and cleaning the car. He says Mrs Clayforth fancies him – "

"What? No!"

Tanya nodded. "She does. He reckons she'll go after anything in trousers."

"You mean, she makes up to Neil?" Stella asked, incredulously.

"You bet she does. Pushes her knees against his, under the table – "

"Don't be revolting!"

"God, Stella. You're so dumb! Don't you know what's going on out there? Hasn't your mother told you anything?" Tanya shook her head, laughing again.

"Just 'cos your mum talks to you – you're lucky."

Her friend's face clouded over. "No, I'm not. I'm tired of my mother butting in on my life. She never leaves me alone. I can't go anywhere without her wanting to know what I've been doing and who I've been with. I wish she'd get a life of her own, I really do."

"I thought you got on well with your mum."

"I used to. But it's different now. I'm going to get away from her, just as soon as I can. I'm going to leave home after the summer exams. I'll get a job – "

Stella stared at her in disbelief. "But you can't! I thought you were going to college. What will you do if you don't go to college?"

Tanya tapped the side of her nose. "I've got plans. Big ones. I can't talk about them yet. I might tell you about them soon, but not right now."

Stella felt proud that Tanya had confided in her as much as she had. She believed they would go on being close friends, as if Marcia Ackroyd and her pals had never existed. She waited for Tanya after games, as usual, on Thursday afternoon, so they could walk home together. She was happy to have Neil walking with them, too, as he often did. She adored Neil. Neil and Tanya were her two favourite people.

She waited outside the school gate for over half an hour. By then, all the girls had gone home. The teachers were leaving now and getting into their cars. Stella couldn't understand it. She'd seen Jennifer and Gillian leave with Marcia. Of course, they'd sneered at her and made noises as they'd walked past her. Stella had ignored them. Finally, when Mrs Grove, the head teacher, came out and Ben, the caretaker, locked the gate, she began to drift down the road, alone.

Stella caught the bus, got off at Hadham and looked around, half expecting to see Tanya waiting for her. She went into the sweet shop, telling herself her friend might be in there, and bought a handful of penny chews and stuffed them in her pockets. The sweets were a comfort. Her friend hadn't waited for her but the chews almost made up for it. She began to walk slowly down the lane, unwrapping a sweet, past the woods that bordered Hadham Manor, towards home.

She was putting the third fruit chew in her mouth, kicking her school bag as she traipsed along, when she heard a sound: a squeal of laughter coming from the woods. She stood still and listened. Silence. But Stella was sure she'd heard Tanya laughing. It had sounded just like her. She crossed the road to the manor side and waited again. There it was: two voices, this time, two sets of laughter. She peered over the broken fencing posts that half-leant against the ancient trees, and thought she saw movement further in the woods. She prodded the fence with her hockey stick and a couple of rotten posts gave way in front of her. Stella stepped between the crumbling staves and into the grounds of Hadham Manor. She began to thread her way through the trees, her footsteps muffled by the woodland carpet of dead leaves.

After a couple of minutes, she stopped again and listened. A breeze rustled the leaves of the old oaks and elms and birds cawed in their high branches. Stella decided to head for the old camp she and Tanya had made with Neil and

Michael and Francine, in the long summer holidays about five years ago. The camp had been built out of branches and brambles and resembled a low hut. It even had a makeshift door you could place in the mouth of the construction, so that you were snug inside and felt hidden from the rest of the world. The shelter had been solid enough to withstand the last five winters, probably because it was in the middle of the wood where strong winds never penetrated. And, although it was on the edge of a clearing, it was far enough away from the big house, with its terraced lawns and walled gardens, to be of no interest to the men who worked at the manor.

Stella plodded deeper into the wood, using her hockey stick and her school bag to bat the brambles in her path. She knew exactly where she was going. She'd followed these paths so often in the past and, more recently, in the afternoons with Mrs Clayforth's dog. In less than ten minutes she was standing on the edge of the clearing, staring at the door of small branches covering the entrance to their old camp.

"No! That tickles!" A peal of laughter came from inside the makeshift hut. "Right, I'll get you for that!" There was more laughter. Neil's laughter, too. Stella let her bag and stick drop noiselessly to ground. She advanced on the camp, her face creased with emotion.

She got as close as she dared. She knew she could be seen through the bracken walls of the hut once she reached a certain point in the clearing. She hunkered down on the soft earth and listened. But Neil and Tanya were quiet again. There was no conversation. After a couple of minutes, Stella began to be uncomfortable in her crouched position. She leaned out from the hawthorn bush where she'd been squatting and peered towards the camp. She could now make out some movement. Silent movement. Two bodies – and they had no clothes on. She drew back quickly behind the hawthorn. She blinked. She looked out again. It was true what she'd seen: Tanya and Neil were lying on the floor of the hut, pressed together, and they hadn't a stitch on!

Five minutes passed. Ten minutes. Quarter of an hour. There was no more talking, only some low moaning, but Stella couldn't tell who it was. She had moved away from the hawthorn bush now, knowing Tanya and Neil were preoccupied in the hut, and was leaning against the trunk of an elm tree, deliberating whether to go home or not, when Tanya, it could only have been Tanya, let out a strangulated sound, the likes of which Stella had never heard before. She stood rigid against the tree, pressing against the knotted bark. She wanted to run from the clearing then, but her feet wouldn't move. All of a sudden, Neil gave a loud shout, then another, and another. Then all was quiet again. Stella peeped out from behind the elm. The bodies were still. She could make out Tanya, lying full length on top of Neil. Their heads, their arms and legs were melded together.

"Tanya, I adore making love to you." Neil's voice was hoarse and barely audible.

"We'll be like this forever," said Tanya, in a stronger tone.

"We will. We'll make our own camp – "

"We'll get married," Tanya told him.

"Right."

"And I'll live with you while you're at university."

There was a pause. "I can see you in the holidays. There'll be a lot of studying to do."

There was movement in the camp, something like a disengagement of bodies. Stella saw Tanya sit upright on Neil. She was looking down at him, her long hair hiding her face, except from Neil's view.

"You've got to take me with you. Don't you dare leave me here, stuck in this place. I'll be sixteen. I can leave home. I can share your digs and get a job. We can be like this all the time." She lowered her face to his and they kissed.

"I'll come home and see you at weekends, I promise."

"What!" Tanya sat bold upright again. She flung her mane of hair back over her shoulders, exposing her perfect breasts. "Why don't you want me to go with you? Is there someone else? Is there?" Her voice was demanding, but mischievous more than angry.

"Of course not. You're the one. You're my girl, Tanya –"

"You're not seeing Mrs Clayforth, on the sly? I know how she makes eyes at you all the time – "

"Where did you say you were ticklish?" Neil's voice sounded lighter now.

Tanya squealed with laughter and collapsed over him. Stella saw them writhing and giggling together. Then Tanya's head came up for air, still laughing. "Or Stella! What about Stella Reynolds? She moons over you! Big Stella! Yes, that's it! She's your secret love, isn't she? Tell me, right now, or I'll tickle you – "

The two of them rolled further into the camp. Stella couldn't see them, partly because of the gloom in the hut and partly because of the glistening in her eyes. She turned away and wiped her nose with the back of her hand, then pushed away from the tree. She crossed the clearing, picked up her school bag and her hockey stick and quietly left the wood.

Doreen Reynolds looked up and saw her daughter trailing round the corner of the Close. The girl looked dishevelled, a disgrace. Her tie was crooked, her socks were down. Even the expression on her face was miserable. Doreen glanced away for a moment, half in distaste and half with embarrassment. She prayed that the women standing with her, outside the Taylors' house, wouldn't notice Stella's sagging shape plodding along the pavement.

She felt Angela Clayforth give her a nudge. "There's Stella. And we were only talking about her a moment ago. Perhaps her ears were burning!"

"I don't see my daughter with her. Where's Tanya?" said Mavis Williams, standing on her toes and peering around the group.

About five or six neighbours had gathered outside the Taylors' house and were standing by the police car, waiting for news of what had happened. The moment the police had drawn up outside the house, the women in the Close, alert at their windows, had opened their front doors.

Angela Clayforth had been first out of her house. She crossed the road, just as one of the officers went inside number twenty five with John Taylor. The officer behind the steering wheel was talking on the radio as Angela walked up to the car.

"Yes, Sarge. He's just gone inside. PC Lloyd is with him. Over." A crackled voice responded on the radio. Angela stood by the open driver's window, listening as well as she could. "Right. Will do. Roger. Over and out." The officer put the mouthpiece back on the car dashboard. He looked up at Angela and raised his eyebrows. "Yes, madam? Can I help you?"

Angela gave one of her best smiles. A sweet, friendly smile, she thought. The policeman continued to regard her impassively. It crossed her mind she had too much lipstick on that morning. "Oh, officer, I'm Mr Taylor's neighbour. I live just there," she pointed to her house, opposite. "I saw your car draw up. Is everything alright? Can I do anything to help?"

The police officer cleared his throat, frowned slightly and looked straight ahead, through his windscreen. "No, madam. Nothing. Just take yourself home. Mr Taylor needs to be on his own at the moment."

As he spoke, Doreen Reynolds arrived at Angela's side, then Valerie Boyd and Mavis Williams joined them, then Sheila Hodge from the far end of the Close. The officer looked up at the women and stepped out of his car. "OK, ladies," he said, nodding round them. "A quiet word. There's been an accident: Mrs Taylor. We've just taken Mr Taylor to identify her body. He's in shock. You'd expect that. I don't think you should disturb him today. The doctor's on his way. He'll probably give him something to help him sleep. See how he is – "

Like a chorus, the women's hands went to their faces. They all wore expressions of dismay and disbelief; except, noticed the police officer, the woman who had approached his car first. She stood silently, looking thoughtful, her arms folded across her ample chest. She remained silent while the other women started asking him questions, all at once. "A car accident? What happened? Where did it happen? The children, are they alright?"

Officer Jessop held up his hands to quieten their voices. "Now then, ladies. We don't want a disturbance outside Mr Taylor's house. I can't give you any details. We're investigating the accident, see? There was a lorry involved. Mrs Taylor may have been talking to her children and pulled out into the oncoming traffic. We don't know for certain – "

"Did she die instantly?" said Angela, still with her arms folded and looking matter-of-fact rather than emotional.

"Madam, I'm not at liberty to say. Please go back to your homes now. My colleague will be out, just as soon as the doctor arrives – and here he is now."

The women fell back to let Doctor Patten through. They all knew him. His surgery was in the village and he was their doctor, too. They watched the policeman escort the doctor up the path and ring the doorbell for him. The other officer opened the door, stepped back, nodded them inside and closed it behind them. The women were left on the pavement, staring at the empty front door.

"Well," said Sheila Hodge, "there's nothing more we can do here. Best thing is to come round during the week and see if there's anything he needs, poor man." She shook her head regretfully and turned away and started to walk back towards her house.

"Sheila's right," Valerie Boyd nodded to the others. "We should leave John Taylor in peace now. We could call on him later and offer to do some shopping for him. And what about the twins? We could help him out with Sally and Ross." She glanced at Mavis Williams, and was reminded that her son was late home from school, too. She had a good idea who he was with. Valerie Boyd liked Mrs Williams as a neighbour but, lately, she had begun to worry that Tanya was distracting her son from his school work. These exams were important for Neil, she knew. She suddenly thought of something. "Perhaps Tanya could baby-sit for Mr Taylor," she suggested. "It would be extra pocket money for her. I see she buys makeup now and the latest fashions. I'm sure she'd be glad of the money."

Mavis Williams also saw an opportunity: a few evenings baby-sitting for Mr Taylor would mean she knew where her daughter was. It would restrict the time Tanya was spending with Marcia Ackroyd, whom Mavis didn't particularly like, and her friends. Perhaps, if Marcia lost interest in Tanya, Mavis and her daughter would become close again, just like old times. And Mavis longed for the old times. Those years when Tanya had been a young girl and dependent on her mother. They had been the happiest years of Mavis's life, she realised now. She had even been happier with her daughter, a few years ago, than when her husband was alive. Jim's gambling, and the problems it had brought them, had given her nothing but anxiety, right up until his death. The worry of his debts had robbed her of her youth. She'd become old before her time. But he had given her Tanya, and that was a blessing. And now, here was a chance to restrict her daughter's movements and keep her here, in Manor Close.

"Valerie, that's a marvellous idea. I'm sure Tanya will be pleased to help Mr Taylor, in any way she can. She could even do a little light housework for him at weekends." She turned to Angela Clayforth, who was glancing at Doreen Reynolds for a moment. "After all, both Neil and Stella gave up their time to help you, Angela, when you lost Frank. I'm sure you couldn't have managed without them, and John Taylor will feel the same about Tanya helping him, I expect."

In truth, Mavis Williams felt that Angela Clayforth had overdone her victim-of-circumstances role when Frank had passed away. The Clayforth's marriage had not been a close one, from what she'd seen of it, and she'd never heard Mrs Clayforth say a good word about her husband, before or after his death. But the woman clearly enjoyed being a widow, and all the attention and help the status brought her. Mavis was of a different school: she had quietly devoted her life to her daughter when she'd lost her husband, without any song and dance, or the theatricals. Mrs Clayforth seemed to wear her widowhood like a badge, like a disabled sticker that would exempt her from certain rules in society. Mavis thought Angela Clayforth a very vulgar woman, as well as a first-class snob.

"You think so, Mavis? Don't you think Tanya, at her age, would object to doing domestic tasks in her spare time?" smiled Angela. She had always sensed Mavis Williams's hostility towards her. Not that it bothered her. She was comfortable in her own role in life and didn't feel the need to imitate Mavis's acts of humbleness and fortitude in the face of widowhood. Angela was glad to have been rescued from her bad marriage, there was no denying it. She didn't know what sort of marriage Mavis Williams had had but it annoyed her to see the woman going about as though she were carrying some cross to her own special Calvary. Mavis seemed to make a virtue out of suffering for others and Angela could see that Tanya was the focus of the woman's virtuoso act. Whereas she, Angela, had embraced the good life and celebrated her freedom from the oppression of marriage. Yes, Mavis Williams irritated her with her constant expressions of sadness and suffering.

While the women talked, Doreen caught sight of her daughter out of the corner of her eye. Stella was walking slowly and heavily up the other side of the road, head down and totally oblivious of the group standing outside the

Taylors' house. Doreen quickly looked away, hoping that no one else had seen her girl. Stella looked a mess, and her continuing tendency to be overweight could no longer be called puppy-fat. The girl was nearly sixteen, for heaven's sake, and she was looking as unattractive as Doreen had as a child.

Fortunately, her son, Thomas, was quite different. A happy, well-behaved child with none of Stella's moodiness. And Thomas was academically gifted. He shone in the classroom and on the sports field. When Doreen looked at Thomas, she could see her husband, Ray; his good looks, his sharp brain. Whenever she beheld Stella, she was reminded of her own shortcomings. It had a lot to do with why she hated her daughter, for Doreen hated herself: her heavy figure, her depressive moods, her love of overeating. She often wondered if her daughter would become dependent on alcohol, like herself; if there was something in the family genes that Stella would inherit. Doreen remembered an aunt who had loved the sherry bottle too much, and her mother had once told her about a great-uncle who'd owned a pub in Woolwich and drunk himself to death.

Looking at her daughter now, sloping along the pavement, she couldn't imagine a bright future for the girl. What young man would look twice at a lumpy girl like that? At least she, Doreen, had been slim when she'd first met Ray. She'd had a twenty-four inch waist. She used to starve herself, in those days. It wasn't until Thomas had started school that everything began to slide from under Doreen. Was it Ray's working late? Or had he started working late because she'd a few drinks by the time he came home in the evenings? She couldn't remember the order of things, how the marriage had disintegrated or how her drinking had increased. She only knew that alcohol had become central to her day. If only she could lay off the bottle now. She would make the effort, she really would. She looked at Stella, dragging her feet as she walked along, her shoulders drooped. She willed the girl to turn into their front garden before the other women saw her. Then she heard Mavis Williams exclaim, "There's Stella!" and Doreen resigned herself to her daughter's presence for the next ten minutes.

"Stella, we have something to tell you." Angela Clayforth assumed the role of spokesperson, as she always did when she and Doreen were together. "It's Mrs Taylor – "

"Where's Tanya?" interrupted Mavis Williams. Apart from her concern for her daughter's whereabouts, it gave her pleasure to cut Angela Clayforth's flow of words. She'd always thought Angela had too much to say for herself, that she monopolised conversations as though she were the centre of everyone's world. "Have you seen my girl, Stella? Did she come home on the bus with you?"

"She's in Hadham Woods, lying on top of Neil Boyd, and they're both completely naked," is what Stella wanted to say. She bit her lip and looked down at the pavement, imagining the consequences of those words.

"For God's sake, child, answer Mrs Williams!" said Doreen. "She asked you a question. Where are your manners?"

"I'm not a child," Stella looked at her sullenly. Normally, her mother would have slapped her face for replying like that. But Stella knew that, outside their home, her mother played the role of the sweet and happy mother, unless she was alone with Mrs Clayforth, when all pretence was dropped.

"Mrs Taylor has been in a car accident," said Angela, reasserting her authority over the group.

"She's dead," said Doreen, hissing the words at her child.

"Mrs Taylor? She's ... what?" Stella tried to grasp the meaning of what they'd said to her, but her mind was still full of images of Neil and Tanya making love in the woods.

"Stella, dear," said Mrs Boyd, looking at her kindly. "There's been a terrible accident. Mr Taylor has come home and the doctor is with him now. Can you tell us where Neil and Tanya are? Did you see them on the bus? Neil's tea is ready for him and he's got so much homework to do for his exams next month."

"Uh, no. I haven't seen them. They probably took the bus after mine. I don't know." Stella turned to go. Her emotions were in turmoil and she felt hot tears welling up. The news about Mrs Taylor; kind, friendly Mrs Taylor, was starting to penetrate her consciousness. Stella had liked Mrs Taylor a lot. The woman had always waved to her and taken the time to talk to her whenever they'd met at the shops or in the Close. Stella wanted to get away from these women. She needed to run up to her bedroom and throw herself on her bed and cry for so many reasons, mostly for herself.

As she moved away from them, she heard Angela Clayforth say, "Ah, there's the doctor now. Hello there, Doctor Patten! Can we have a word ... "

The doctor was closing his bag as he came down the Taylors' front path with the two police officers. He looked up when he heard Mrs

Clayforth, and saw her stride across the road towards him with two other women behind her. Mrs Clayforth: how well he remembered that woman. Her husband had died last year. Heart attack, wasn't it? The woman had clearly not felt the loss. Since then, she'd looked younger every time she'd been to the surgery. She'd asked him about cosmetic surgery, vitamin shots, hormone replacement therapy. He guessed she'd met someone else. Perhaps she'd already met someone before the poor fella had died. And how well she was looking now: upright, shoulders back; firm, striding steps; glowing with health, even happiness. By the time he'd managed to close the clasp on his bag, Mrs Clayforth and her band were upon him.

"Doctor Patten, how is he? We were so sorry to hear about Mrs Taylor. Is there anything we can do?"

The officers walked on ahead of him, going through the gate and getting into their car. Doctor Patten felt a moment of slight panic. They were leaving him alone with this woman. But, why should that worry him? he asked himself. What was it about it the woman's manner? Was it that self-assurance in the way she carried herself or her strong, almost imperious voice when she required information? He remembered, at the surgery, his receptionist's expression darkening as Mrs Clayforth had strode to the desk to make another appointment. She was not a woman one warmed to, he decided. For the first time, he wondered if she was lonely. "He needs to rest, Mrs Clayforth. That's all for now. His children are being cared for by a friend of his wife for a few days. I've given him a sedative. He'll be sleeping soon. Best not to disturb him today."

"We wouldn't dream of it, Doctor Patten! Not if you say so. I'll call on him tomorrow. I live just opposite, you know. I'm sure there must be something I can do to help the poor man. Don't you worry, now. He'll be in good hands. I'm a widow, remember, with time on my hands. I'm the best person to help him through this sad time."

Doctor Patten opened his mouth to say something but, just then, one of the women exclaimed, "There's Neil, with Tanya!" and the conversation came abruptly to an end.

CHAPTER 5

John Taylor let his head fall back in the armchair. His hands lay limp on the arms. He was drained of all feeling, numb. This was her chair. She always sat in this one. It was just the way it was, he didn't know why. Maybe it was because the other chair was near the standard lamp, where he could read his paper in the evenings. Susan liked the television shows. She would sit there with her sewing, laughing at the comedies. She always had sewing to do. The twins needed patches on the knees of their trousers, or she'd be tacking a dress for Sally, ready for the sewing machine. That was Susan: industrious, a good wife and a good mother. Irreplaceable. God, what was he going to do?

A sob exploded from him, travelling up from somewhere deep in his soul. "Susan, come back to me!" he cried out loud and let the tears roll down his cheeks. He would have pounded the arms of the chair in his emotion but the sedative the doctor had given him had drained all his strength. He felt he was floating, he was adrift in a sea of despair. He couldn't go on without Susan. He saw no future. His life had ended that morning with his wife's. There was nothing left, now that she had been taken from him.

What was it the doctor had said to him? "You have to think of your children, now. Your wife would have wanted you to take care of them. You must deal with this. I'm only a phone call away. Let me know if you want some pills to help you sleep." John had shaken his head. He hadn't even wanted the shot Doctor Patten had given him. But the doctor had insisted, and those two police officers were standing there with their arms folded, watching him. He knew he had behaved badly when they'd turned up at his office. But what would either of those men have done if someone had come to the police station and said the same thing to one of them?

At first, when Neville Ash had called him into his office, John had hoped Ash had given up his hostility towards him and wanted a civilised, working relationship that would benefit them both. After all, Ash had worn a sympathetic, almost friendly expression when he'd come over to John's drawing board and placed a hand on his shoulder. "Will you come through to my office, John? Just a few words, in private." Taylor had risen from his chair. Ash had called him John, for the first time. He walked behind the manager's narrow frame through the drawing office, towards the frosted glass door. He hadn't seen the two dark shapes in the office until he'd followed Ash into the room. The manager had gone round to his desk, indicating a chair to John. The two uniformed officers had remained standing, nodding at him with a serious expression.

Was he in trouble? What had he done? The tax on the car? No, that was OK. Speeding? Not that he remembered. Susan: perhaps she'd been speeding. She had the car today. Shopping. Kids to school. Maybe she'd dented the car. Maybe the kids were shaken, or she was. Maybe she'd had a more serious accident –

"Mr John Taylor?" One of the policemen stepped forward, holding a notebook in his hand but not referring to it. Taylor nodded. His heart began to race. His hands were sweating. Had he done anything wrong? "Are you the husband of Mrs Susan Taylor of twenty five, Manor Close, Hadham?"

It was an effort to reply. "Yes." His mouth was dry. Thoughts raced in his head.

"I'm afraid we have some bad news for you, sir. I'm sorry to say your wife had an accident this morning, driving a Riley 1.5 on the Brighton Road, just outside Redhill. The car was involved in an accident with a tanker. I'm sorry to inform you that we were unable to save your wife –"

"What! What are you saying?" John jumped up. "What are you trying to tell me? Susan! Where is she? Which hospital have they taken her to? Is she alright – " He stared at each of them in turn, uncomprehending.

"What I'm trying to tell you, sir, is – "

"No! She's alright!" John went towards the policeman and shook him by the shoulders. "Tell me, she's alright!"

"Now then, sir," the second officer stepped up to him and gently pulled him back. Taylor shook him off, violently.

"John, get a hold of yourself," said Neville Ash, standing up behind his desk. "Stop behaving in a such a ridiculous – "

John Taylor's fist shot out and landed on one side of Neville Ash's angular face. The force of the blow sent the manager tottering backwards, knocking his chair over as he crashed against the wall behind.

"Now then, sir," the first officer held him in a firm armhold. "We must ask you to come with us. Get your jacket, sir, and come now. We understand you're upset. There was no easy way to tell you."

John felt himself propelled out of the manager's office. "Mr Taylor's desk?" one of the policemen asked a colleague of John's. The whole of the drawing office were looking at them now, wondering what had brought the law to Mortimer's Engineering in the first place.

John didn't remember collecting his jacket and keys, or the ride to the hospital. But he remembered them showing Susan to him. God, he would never forget that. Never. There was a large drawer. A drawer, for heaven's sake! Like they'd filed her somewhere, like a statistic. That sickening rumble as the drawer was pulled out. That sheet: white, forming a shape. The cover pulled back, and Susan's darling face, the colour of alabaster.

The accident had been kind to her face. Hardly a mark. A small cut on her forehead. They didn't show him the lower part of her body. He didn't ask to see it. He heard words, something about the steering wheel crushing her chest, something about dead on arrival. But they were just words. It was Susan's face in front of him: inanimate, drained of life. He put out a hand and touched her on the cheek. It was cold, unyielding, like marble. The sheet was drawn over his wife again. He felt himself being led away. He was only an observer. It couldn't be happening to him.

And so, here he was, in Susan's armchair. What point was there in going on? The light had gone out of his life. He had a vague notion of what he had to do. He would ask Doctor Patten for those sleeping pills. Lots of them. And he would save them up. Then he'd swallow them, all together. And, then, he'd be with Susan. He was feeling heavy now, he was slipping away. Tomorrow, he'd see the doctor and get those pills ...

Angela's mind was racing. A number of possibilities began to crowd her brain. She could give comfort to John Taylor. She, who had also suffered a loss, who had known loneliness, too. She got up from the kitchen table and paced the tiled floor. She would make plans. She rubbed her manicured hands together. Where to begin?

She had never sat in the sitting room in the evenings. Not when Frank was alive. He would take the paper into the front room and settle in his chair with his pipe and the dog, and remain there all evening. Angela had never much cared for television and preferred to sit in the kitchen, poring over her cookery books. She had a fine collection, including some volumes of Cordon Bleu and Elizabeth David. In the past, after looking at these for an hour or so, she would retire to her bedroom and devour her latest romantic novel.

Angela had always been a voracious reader, mostly of popular fiction. She adored Agatha Christie novels and was half in love with James Bond. But the stories that really moved her were the tales of romance she borrowed from the local library or bought in paperback when she visited Guildford, where her parents now lived. These were the stories that lifted her. The moment where the tall, strong man carried the heroine, after many misunderstandings, into the sunset. Angela had married for practical reasons, but it didn't stop her dreaming of another kind of existence. A world where she was pretty and petite, where the hero adored her and, most of all, where they lived happily ever after. It was fiction, rather than reality, which filled Angela's mind during the daylight hours.

And the evenings – how she looked forward to the evenings! There may have been a rotund, bespectacled, balding man, puffing disgusting pipe smells into her sitting room, but once she was in her own room, her own space, tucked up in bed with a novel, she was transported to another world. The stories in the women's magazines also sustained her. She read every one of them, every week. Her interest in these magazines had begun with recipes and household tips but, soon, she was captivated by the short stories of unhappy or oppressed women who finally found the happiness they deserved.

Angela's interest in cooking coincided with her marriage to Frank. This was not because she particularly wanted to impress her husband, who never seemed to notice the food that was laid in front of him. But Angela dreamed of dinner parties. She dreamed of entertaining neighbours and receiving praise for her cuisine. When the Clayforths had first married and bought the house in Manor Close, Angela had invited their neighbours for dinner, and had gone to town on the preparation. It was a chance to use their bone china, which she had asked for as a wedding present from her parents. The elegant plates and tureens of thin white porcelain with gold edging represented the social success that Angela hoped for in her marriage.

She remembered, as if it were yesterday, the evening the Reids came to dinner. Margery and Norman were not neighbours, but friends of Frank's, or his mother's, the late Mrs Clayforth, to be precise. They had known Reginald and Edna Clayforth for nearly fifty years and had lived in the same South London street. The Reids and the Clayforths had gone through the Blitz together. Reginald had been killed by one of the last doodlebugs that fell on London.

Angela had never met her late mother-in-law, but she understood that when Frank had asked her to marry him he'd needed someone to keep house for him, as his mother had done. She had hoped for more in the marriage, companionship at the very least. But the relationship hadn't blossomed and, disappointed in their expectations, both Angela and Frank had retreated into their own interests, avoiding each other as much as they could. At the very beginning of the marriage, it had been different. Angela had been eager to show off her new home, her status as the wife of an assistant bank manager. And Margery and Norman Reid were one of the first couples to be asked to dine off the bone china tableware.

"Oh, no! Just a little for me! No, really, I'm not a big eater." twittered Margery Reid, raising her bony hands and simpering shyly at Norman and Frank. "Edna always gave me small portions. Just a taste, please. And her food was so light."

Angela looked at the Boeuf Bourgui¬gnonne, steaming in the casserole dish in front of her. She had enjoyed preparing the meal that afternoon, and had looked forward to seeing the pleasure on everyone's face as she lifted the casserole lid and they smelled the rich aroma of the herbs she'd added. She ladled a small amount onto Margery's white and gold plate and gave the woman a tight smile as she passed the plate down the table. She picked up another warmed plate and began scooping into the casserole again.

"I hope that's not for me," said Norman Reid, shaking his head with an apologetic smile. "It's my digestion, you know. And my haemorrhoids. I can't eat anything with herbs in it, or spices. Edna was a wonderful cook, you know; plain home cooking. I'm afraid I can't get on with this foreign cuisine. Well, you never know what's in it. We ate something with a strange-sounding name on holiday in Taunton, the year before last. It was my fault really. Shouldn't have been so adventurous. Turned my insides into uproar for days!"

Angela nodded, smiled again and passed a small portion of Bœuf Bourguignon to Norman Reid. She looked at Frank with a semi-smile, but her eyes were glistening and there was a lump in her throat. She felt the presence of her late mother-in-law, standing in judgement over her.

"Oh, just a small amount for me, too," said Frank from the other end of the table. "Is there any bread? If not, I'll go and cut some."

"Yes, I'd like some bread," said Margery.

"Yes, please," said her husband, as Frank rose to go into the kitchen.

Angela sat there, mortified. It was Margery who broke the silence. "Of course, during the war we had to make do with so little. Just a cube of cheese, a couple of ounces of butter, two rashers of bacon and an egg, if you could get such things. We know how to make things go a long way. We've never lost the habit of it, have we, Norman? The way people indulge themselves today ... Well, there's no such thing as self-control!"

The dinner party continued in this spirit. The Reids spent the evening reminiscing about food rationing and clothes coupons while Angela silently collected the plates. Back in the kitchen, she fished a forgotten bouquet garni out of the casserole and scraped the contents into the dog's bowl.

When she returned with the dessert, a peach and grape Pavlova she'd spent a whole hour decorating, just before the Reids had arrived, she placed it on the table and remained standing, waiting for Mrs Reid to protest at the richness of the dish.

"Oh, did you make that meringue?" said Margery, raising her bird-like claws again.

"Yes, I did," Angela replied, holding her head up, proudly.

"What a pity it's broken on one side. Now, Edna was wonderful with eggs. Her egg dishes were as light as a feather – "

"She probably watered them down," said Angela with a fixed smile and without looking at her husband. She cut into the broken side of the meringue and passed the portion to Mrs Reid.

Frank never discussed the dinner party with Angela after their guests had left. He'd sat quietly at the top of the table during the dessert, waiting to return to his armchair and fill his pipe. He didn't compliment her on the menu or the table decoration or the new dress she had squeezed into that evening. Angela realised that giving a dinner party with Frank would never amount to a pleasurable evening.

Angela didn't know why she didn't warm to any of Frank's friends. She just didn't. Not even the bank staff he had kept in touch with after his retirement, though she should have had her work experience in common with them. To her, they were conservative and small-minded people. On the one hand, she shared their values regarding houses and interior decorations but, when it came to conversation, Angela found she had nothing to say them. She would have liked to have talked to them about books, the best sellers and romantic fiction she devoured. But these people only seemed to read about cricket or macramé or the home medical encyclopaedia for their aches and pains.

She had been glad when the Reynolds family had moved into the Close. Doreen was as unhappily married as Angela and, after a few gin and oranges, would pour her heart out to her. Angela, who also enjoyed the large gins Doreen poured, though she never drank alone, found she could talk to her neighbour about her own problems. Very soon, the two were close friends, sharing confidences and sympathising with each other's domestic situation.

But their relationship seemed to change when Frank died. Angela found she didn't have any more problems to share with Doreen. At least, not of the marital kind. Angela's life was calm, domestically, if unfulfilled. Yes, thought Angela to herself, coming back from an evening at Doreen's where she had left her friend in floods of maudlin tears over Ray's constant absences, our lives have taken different paths now: Doreen is trying to keep hold of the man in her life whereas I'm looking for a new one.

And why not find a new man? thought Angela. Why not plan for the future? The past had been unpleasant, but it was gone, finished. She should simply put it down to experience. A cookery book lay open on the kitchen table. The double page photograph was a luscious picture of Porc au Cidre, garnished with apple rings and sprinkled with fresh parsley. Had Angela found someone who would appreciate her cooking, her conversation, her flamboyant dresses and her love of romance? Should she be thinking in this way? Susan Taylor hardly cold and still in the hospital morgue? Yes, she should. She was thinking of others, not just of herself. She was thinking of those poor motherless twins, Sally and Ross. And thinking how lonely John Taylor would be, by himself, in the days, months, years to come.

She could see it now: she'd be carrying a freshly-made lasagne, golden yellow and piping hot, across the road to number twenty-five. And just as she arrived at the Taylors' front door, it would open, before she even had time to press the bell. And he would be smiling. Not the shy smile he had given her on the two or three occasions where he'd been getting in his car and looked up and seen her standing at her window, watching him leave for work. John Taylor would be smiling with his eyes, as well, and he'd throw up his hands and hold the door wide and exclaim, "Angela! You're quite a woman! Come in, and let's eat your wonderful supper together. I have a bottle wine and I'll light some candles. The children are tucked up in bed, asleep. We'll have a wonderful evening together, just the two of us. I can't tell you how good it is to have someone to – to ..."

And they would look at each other, meaningfully. And he would lift the casserole from her hands and their heads would draw close. He would brush his lips against hers. Then they would remember the front door was still open, and they would laugh together and she would close it behind her. She would follow him into the kitchen and he would put her casserole down on the side. Then he'd turn to her. He'd take her in his arms and tilt her head up to his. No, that wasn't right. She was taller than John Taylor. She would have to remember not to wear high heels. Anyway, he'd take her in his arms and he'd hold her close. He would kiss her face, her neck and finally press his lips against hers, holding her tightly to him. "Darling Angela," he would murmur in her ear. "Your lasagne will have to wait. I want you, need you, more than I need food." And, with those words, he would guide her out of the kitchen, into the hallway. For a moment, she couldn't decide whether they would make love on his sofa or upstairs while the children slept. Then she thought she wouldn't want to lie in that bed, the one where Susan Taylor had slept with John. John: such a manly name. A hundred times better than the name, Frank. Yes, it would be an evening of passion in front of the fire, and she'd slip across the road to her own house at dawn.

"You should be ashamed of yourself!" Mavis heard herself shout at her daughter. She had gone up to Tanya's bedroom to find out exactly why the girl had been so late home from school. Not that Mavis was naive. She understood how hormones raged during the teenage years. After all, she had experienced the same emotions herself when she had met Jim, the young and handsome salesman with a honeyed tongue. Mavis had married young, too young. She had not had a chance to see the world or, at least, meet many people. If she had, would she have behaved any differently? Probably not. Jim Williams was irresistible. He was a smooth talker, he seemed confident in all types of company. Mavis had no idea it was the whisky bottle that gave him that relaxed and happy air. It had also addled his brains in the end, for Jim believed he only had to place one more bet and he would be lucky this time. That one last bet would change everything and then his wife would be proud of him. Tanya had the same rash approach to life as her father, Mavis could see that. Tanya would act first, following her emotions and her needs, then she would become angry and exasperated if her plans went awry.

"What is there to be ashamed of?" Tanya had shouted back. She turned her back on her mother and busied herself, unpacking her school bag.

"You looked totally dishevelled, both of you, when you came around corner, this afternoon. Do you think I'm stupid? Do you think I don't know what young people get up to?"

Tanya dropped the books she was holding in her hand on the bed and turned to face her mother, arms akimbo. "And what's that, exactly?"

Mavis bit her lip.

"Go on! Tell me! Why don't you say what you and Dad got up to in the back of his car?"

"I'm telling you not to see this boy – "

"In case – go on, say it! In case I get pregnant, like you did? In case I have to get married? Is that it?"

"Tanya, don't talk like that! Don't say such things!" Mavis put her hand to her mouth and turned her head away, but something like a small sob escaped her.

Her daughter continued to stand there, looking at her. Mavis went to leave the room. Suddenly, Tanya went over to her mother and put a hand on her shoulder. "Mum, I'm sorry. Mum ... "

Mavis looked round. Her eyes were glistening. Her normally pale face was suffused with emotion. She shook her head. "It doesn't matter. Your baby brother ... He would have been ... Well, Neil's age, I suppose."

Tanya put her arm round her mother's shoulder and kissed her cheek. She had heard the story of her stillborn brother, so many times before, and she didn't want to hear it again. She was tired of her mother, and her living in the past. She wanted a life of her own. She wanted to be free of all these ghosts: her father, her dead brother, her mother's sister who'd died of cancer. And she was tired of Manor Close and it's small-minded people and their boring ways of living. Tanya was bursting with energy. She wanted to live life to the full. She wanted to escape this dreary village and live in a big town with Neil Boyd. And, if it didn't work out with Neil – well, she would never come back. She would live her own life, free as a bird. Just a few months more. Not long now –

Her mother was talking to her again, something about a neighbour.

"And that poor man, all on his own. Losing his lovely wife, like that. I know what it's like to lose a loved one. He must be devastated, his world must be upside down." Mavis had recovered her composure and was telling her daughter about Mrs Taylor's accident and the police bringing Mr Taylor home. "So, I said you'd look after his children for him when you came home from school. You could be back by four-thirty, if you caught the early bus – "

"Mum, what are you talking about?" Tanya frowned as she caught the drift of the woman's words.

"I said you'd look after Sally and Ross for Mr Taylor until he gets back from work. Mrs Taylor's sister can have them during the day, then bring them home in the afternoon for an hour or so before Mr Taylor – "

"What are you saying? I can't baby-sit for anyone! I'm busy. I've got my own life to lead. I've got homework – "

"You can do your homework while you're over at number twenty-five. It's only for little while and it will be such a help to that poor man. You never know, you might be grateful to somebody yourself, one day; someone who helps you out when you have a problem. That's what neighbours are for, after all."

Tanya closed her eyes and prayed. She prayed that she'd be delivered from her mother and her interfering ways. She prayed that she could keep hold of her sanity, just for a few more months. Just until Neil left for university. Then, she vowed, she'd never see her mother again.

He couldn't believe it had happened over thirty-six hours ago. Had he really been without Susan for a day and a half? He'd sat in this same armchair until gone midnight the previous evening, just holding the framed photograph of the four of them, taken last Christmas, and staring at it. Would he spend every evening the same way, now, looking at the picture? Would he repeat this ritual every night for the rest of his life?

John Taylor was still in shock. He didn't really understand what had happened to him, how the world had changed. Last night, he had climbed the stairs in the early hours of the morning and fallen onto the bed. Their bed. The bedclothes smelled of Susan. And he had tried to reach out in the dark and touch her, but she wasn't there. She would never be there again. It was difficult for him to comprehend: Susan not sharing the future with him, seeing Sally and Ross as teenagers, becoming grandparents, marking off the milestones in life, growing old together. He had held on tight to Susan's pillow all night, burying his head in the centre of it, where his wife's head had always lain. The worst part was waking up in the morning and hoping it had all been a bad dream. But, the moment he had opened his eyes and seen the empty space on the other side of the bed, he knew his worst nightmare would continue, in perpetuity.

A choked sound came from the back of John's throat. He tried to blink away the tears but they were falling fast, hot rivers of grief rolling down his cheeks. He pushed a fist into each eye socket and held them there. He waited. He sniffed hard, then swallowed and opened his eyes. He was looking straight at the photograph again, where he'd put it back on the bookcase in the early hours. He stared at it for a moment, then reached over and took it down and gripped it, tight. He studied the family smiling back at him. They'd been so happy last Christmas. They'd been happy every Christmas. John had never been so content as he had been with Susan, not in his whole life.

He traced his wife's face in the photograph, her rounded features, soft and feminine. Susan had never had the figure of one of those willowy models who graced the fashion pages. She had often wished out loud that she was more like Jean Shrimpton or Patti Boyd, with legs as long and slim as racehorses. But John had laughed at her when Susan had pointed to a tiny miniskirt on a skimpy figure in a magazine and wished she could wear one like it. He had slipped his arm around her dimpled shoulders and kissed her and whispered in her ear that he liked his women well-rounded. He didn't want angular bones digging him in the ribs when he made love to her, he wanted flesh he could hold on to. And Susan had laughed and pulled his head onto her breasts, and he had buried his face in their sweet, white softness. Now, all he had left to lay his head on was her pillow. He would never be able to touch or see or inhale Susan again.

And her voice: how he would always remember that lilting, almost musical tone. Susan's voice had never been strident, like those of one or two of the women he'd heard in Manor Close. His Susan had been the perfect woman, as far as he was concerned. He could never replace her softness, her femininity, her sunny disposition. He held the photograph tightly in both hands and stared at his wife, willing her to talk to him from the picture, to say something that would comfort him. "Susan, come back to me!" he whispered. He brought the photo up close and pressed his lips against the cold glass on his wife's image. As he held his mouth to her face, a discordant sound made him jump in the chair. John realised it was the doorbell ringing, but he didn't get up. He stayed fixed in his armchair. The doorbell rang again, not once, but insistently; one long ring after another.

CHAPTER 6

"With your girlfriend again, tonight, I suppose?"

Stella could hear her mother downstairs, her slurred words loud and accusatory. A couple of minutes earlier, she'd heard her father's car door slam, then the back door open and close. She knew her mother had been watching television for most of the evening, drinking, waiting. She knew what was coming; she knew to stay upstairs in her bedroom. She went quietly across the room and opened the door a fraction, and listened.

"I said, I suppose you were with your floozie, tonight?"

Her father was in the kitchen. The fridge door opened for a moment then closed. Stella heard the kettle being filled, then switched on. A moment's silence, then: "Give it rest, Doreen."

She heard a shuffling movement. Her mother was heading for the kitchen. "So, you're not denying it, then? With her, again, were you?" Doreen must have paused by the kitchen door, probably swaying a little, glass in hand. Stella could picture her: the eyes would be bloodshot, as they so often were at this time of the day and, perhaps, she'd be resting her head on the door frame as she looked at her father, half-angrily, half-pleading.

"I said, leave it out, Doreen. It's been a long day at the office. I stopped off at the golf club for a pint or two, to relax, that's all." Stella heard the kettle boil and the chink of a coffee spoon against a mug. "Now, if you don't mind – "

But her mother was fired up. Stella knew she'd been sitting in that armchair for a couple of hours, at least. "Kind of you to come home to your family for the night. I suppose we should be grateful for that. You're lucky I'm here to come home to. Lucky I put up with you – "

The coffee mug came down on the countertop with a bang. "I'm what? I'm what?" Her father's voice no longer sounded tired, but apoplectic with anger. "Lucky? Me! For putting up with you, you lush?"

Stella slid out of her bedroom door and crept across the landing. She peered over the banisters, resting her chin on the handrail. There was a small creak behind her, and she turned. Her brother had opened his door and was standing, illuminated, in the bright shaft of light streaming from the angular lamp on his desk. Stella put a finger to her lips. "Shhh," she whispered across to him. Thomas stayed where he was, wearing the exasperated frown he often wore when his mother had been drinking.

Stella and her brother were different personalities, but they were united in their opinion of their parents' marriage and the cloud of bad feeling they had lived under for most of their childhood. Thomas was two years younger than Stella and, unlike his sister, he had never known a time when his parents had been happy together. Stella, on the other hand, could just about remember her mother and father taking the children for outings and picnics in the country. But, even for Stella, this was a hazy, distant memory. Like Thomas, all she had really known was the state of domestic war which had dragged on for years, souring the air in the house and the people who breathed it.

Thomas dealt with the situation in a completely different way to Stella. Whereas his sister was by nature a protester and had a strong tendency to answer back, and, as a result, was often involved in shouting matches with her mother, Thomas retreated into his schoolwork and stayed late after lessons to play rugby or cricket, depending on the season. During the long holidays, he would get himself invited to classmates' holiday homes on the coast and had learnt to sail with several of them. Thomas never answered his mother back; he refused to have anything to do with her, as far as he possibly could. But Doreen mistook his smouldering silence for compliance. She wanted to believe at least one member of the family was on her side. Thomas became her favourite child. The acquiescent one, the studious one, the one who understood what she was going through and acknowledged it with his own expressions of pain and fortitude. Stella's personality was too similar to Doreen's for the two of them to ever live in harmony.

"Well, what am I supposed to do, sitting here alone, night after night, while you're propping up the bar with other women?"

"Don't be ridiculous, woman. What else am I supposed to do in the evenings? Sit here, listening to your drunken ramblings? Look at you – "

"That's your fault! Look what you've done to me: staying out, night after night, for years!"

Stella saw her father appear at the kitchen doorway, stand in front of her mother and put his face close to hers. He spoke in a low, contemptuous tone. "Look what you've done to yourself, woman. My God, I don't know why I put up with it." He stood back, a look of disgust on his face, as though recoiling from a bad smell, then he placed his hands on his hips and looked at her hard, as if appraising her. "Do you know, I took a woman home from the club tonight? A lovely, bright attractive woman who, in spite of the fact she'd lost her husband ten years ago, was able to laugh and smile and socialise without whining and drinking herself into a stupor – "

"So, you're driving her home now! And does she invite you in for a drink – "

"Is that all you can think about? Bloody drink!"

"Is that all you can think about? Widows seducing you!"

"If I let a widow seduce me, Doreen, I guarantee you'd be the last to know!"

Stella heard her mother let out a whimper.

"Look, woman, you're spilling you're goddam drink. Get a cloth. I'm not clearing up after you. I'm going to bed. Goodnight!" Ray Reynolds strode past his wife. He brushed her elbow and more of the liquid in her glass spilled onto the floor. Doreen let out another sob. She closed her eyes and made a high-pitched, mewling sound. Then, clutching her glass in both hands, she slid slowly down the wall and sat on the floor in a crumpled heap, next to her puddle of spilled drink.

On the fourth long ring, John Taylor levered himself out of the armchair and went slowly into the hall. He could see a figure standing behind the pane of frosted glass in the front door but he had no idea who it could be. Nor did he care. Whoever it was, they were an unwelcome intrusion into his grief. He had sat in the same chair for the last three days, since Susan's accident, staring into space, staring at Susan's photo, staring at nothing but images in the air. He'd ignored the phone ringing and the sound of the doorbell. The twins were staying with his sister-in-law and the rest of the world could go hang itself.

He opened the front door, suddenly conscious that he hadn't shaved or changed his clothes or hardly washed since the day of the accident. He hadn't cared about himself, only the loss of his wife. But now, as he pulled back the door and blinked in the Saturday morning sunlight, he felt ashamed of his appearance, whoever it might be.

Tanya was aghast when she saw Mr Taylor standing before her on the step. He looked about ten years older than she remembered him. Not that she had seen him very often; just every now and then in the Close as she'd walked along the pavement to her own house. She'd seen more of Mrs Taylor, who'd been in and out of number twenty-five with her children, taking them shopping or to nursery school. Tanya had liked Mrs Taylor. The woman had always had a wave and a smile for her and, sometimes, a few friendly words if Tanya was passing when Mrs Taylor was in her front garden. Mr Taylor was a more remote figure, absent at work during the day and busy with his family and his home at weekends. Tanya was sure she'd never really spoken to him. And now, here she was, standing on his doorstep, looking at this wreck of a man and trying to find the right words to say to him.

"My mum sent me," she said, simply. "About baby-sitting for you."

John Taylor looked at her and frowned, as if he were having trouble comprehending her words. "It's – ah – You're the girl who lives in the blue and white house, over there, aren't you?"

Tanya nodded. She wasn't enjoying calling on Mr Taylor, one little bit. Why had she done it? Why had she given in to her mother? Why did her mother always have to break down and sob and talk about all she'd done for Tanya, every time Tanya's instincts told her to give a situation a wide berth. For a start, Tanya had exams this year. Not that she cared a great deal about that. But she'd given up the Girl Guides so she'd have time for her school work and, more importantly, for listening to her pop records, reading her magazines and going to parties. If she started child-minding for Mr Taylor, when would she have time for the essentials in her life?

And when would she see Neil Boyd? It was bad enough that Mrs Boyd kept her son on a tight rein. Tanya had the feeling that her boyfriend's mother didn't approve of her. The woman always found jobs for Neil to do whenever she called for him. And it was Mrs Boyd who'd organised the chores Neil did for Mrs Clayforth at weekends, she was sure. Neil had told her that Mrs Clayforth had come round to ask if Neil would cut the lawn and clean her car and do a few other jobs around the house. Well, Mrs Boyd hadn't objected to him spending time there, had she? And yet, she was visibly annoyed if Tanya and her son came trailing home, hand in hand, late from school, or they stayed out late at a party on a Saturday night.

Mrs Boyd was always telling her son that he must use this valuable time to study for his exams, and Neil was starting to believe it. He would repeat his mother's words to Tanya, as if they were his own. The last time they had lain in Hadham Woods, naked and satiated after making love on a Sunday afternoon, Tanya had, once again, brought up the subject of sharing a flat with him when he went to university. She had expected him to be enthusiastic, just as he had been with her, minutes earlier, as he'd caressed her body and covered her in kisses. Instead, he'd fallen silent. Then he'd started talking about his brother; how he'd seen Michael in the local record shop with Francine West, and what did Tanya think about that? Tanya had ignored his words and insisted she wanted to live with him when he left home in October. Neil sat up and started putting his clothes on, saying he didn't want to talk about it now.

Tanya needed more time to persuade Neil to take her with him to college. The last thing she wanted to do was spend time at number twenty-five, playing with a couple of four year-olds. Yes, they were nice kids, she thought. Though she'd only really seen them in the garden with their mother, or holding on to Mrs Taylor's hands in the road, on their way to kindergarten. Tanya gave a small, inward sigh as she stood facing Mr Taylor. He looked terrible. He looked shattered. She almost felt sorry for him. Except that she was feeling sorry for herself, frustrated with her life and angry with the way it was going right now.

"Baby-sitting? For me? Oh, I don't think that's necessary, really. Thank you, ah ..."

"Tanya. My name's Tanya. I'm sorry to have disturbed you. It's just that my mum said you'd need help for a while. Someone to look after Sally and Ross until you got home from work in the evenings. But – "

"Oh, I see." John Taylor scratched his head as he held on to the door. He didn't really see. He was trying to work it out, in fact. He had no idea how he would manage anything without Susan. He still had a vague idea he would swallow all the tablets the doctor had given him, so he'd never have to contemplate a life on his own. "Well, I don't know ... I suppose you'd better come in." He held the door wide for the teenage girl. He was starting to remember who she was. He'd seen her with the Reynolds girl a few times as he'd driven out of the Close. Of course, they were much younger then. This teenager was nearly a woman now. Her skinny-rib sweater outlined a distinct bust line.

"Well, if it's not a good moment ... " Tanya saw herself going home and telling her mother Mr Taylor didn't need any help.

"It's alright. You're not disturbing me. I mean, you'd better come in." John opened the door wider and stood back for the girl. "Excuse the mess. I haven't had a chance to do much ... "

Tanya stepped into the hallway. The house was similar in layout to her own. She knew the sitting room was to her right but she hesitated to go through the door without being invited to do so. And if the room was in the condition that Mr Taylor was in, she preferred to talk to him in the hall, then beat a retreat.

"Come through to the kitchen. Would you like a cup of coffee?"

She followed her neighbour into his kitchen. To her relief, the space was clean, if not tidy, with only a few cans open on the worktop.

"Sit down, Tanya."

She sat down, still wishing she could be gone.

John Taylor filled the kettle and spoke with his back to her. "I've been here on my own for a few days. The twins are with my wife's sister until Monday, when I go back to work." He put the kettle on the countertop and switched it on, and gave the teenager a weak smile. "To be honest, it'll be a good thing to be busy again, seeing and talking to people." He heard himself say these words, but he could hardly believe them. Did he really want to return to the real world? He was probably saying the first thing that came into his head, just to make conversation with the girl. She looked fresh and pretty and full of life. He realised he must appear like an old man to her: his greying hair, flat and unwashed, the stubbly beginnings of a grey beard. He reached into a cupboard for the last of the clean mugs and set them on the table. "Sugar, Tanya?"

She shook her head. "I don't want any coffee, thanks, Mr Taylor. It's just that my mum said – "

"I know. She's told you to help me out." He looked at her kindly. "The question is, do you want to help me out, Tanya? You're not obliged to, just because your mother's told you to come over here."

The girl bit her lip and looked up at him.

He let out a sigh. "You know, Sally and Ross are good children. But they're only children, and they run about and shout over their toys, just like all children do. Are you sure you want to look after them? It'll only be for an hour or so and, I have to say, I'd be grateful if you could. But I have to be sure they're with someone who wants to be with them." The kettle boiled and he slid a mug across the worktop. "Do you want to think about your offer, Tanya?" he said, spooning coffee into the mug.

Tanya was taken aback. She hadn't expected Mr Taylor to understand the situation, or be kind enough to ask if she really wanted to help him out. No adult had ever spoken to her as an equal before.

John brought his coffee over, sat down at the table and smiled across at her. He hoped the teenager would say yes and look after the twins for him. She was an attractive girl, young and attractive. It would be nice to be greeted by a pretty face when he got home after a long day at the office. He was immediately startled by his train of thought. He gulped a mouthful of coffee the wrong way and almost had a coughing fit. What was he thinking? How on earth could he have those kind of thoughts? And Susan, not yet buried, not yet cold in her grave. He was appalled. He was disgusted with himself. He turned away from Tanya and wiped coffee from the corner his mouth.

I suppose he's lonely, Tanya said to herself. He doesn't have anyone to talk to. Poor man, he's just lost his wife and here I am, refusing to say I'll look after his children for an hour or so during the week. He really does look miserable. But not in the way my mother does when she's trying to get round me for some reason.

John took another swig of coffee and put the mug down, then stood up. "So, you'll let me know on that, Tanya? You don't have to decide now – "

Tanya got up, too. She stood there for a moment, looking at him, then touched his arm lightly. "I've thought about it already, and I'd really like to look after Sally and Ross for you, Mr Taylor."

John drew a quick breath, then he grinned. "You would? Well, that's – that's good. That's great. Thank you, Tanya." He wanted to pat her on the shoulder, gratefully, but, for some reason, he didn't trust himself. Instead, he said, smiling and nodding, "Great. Great."

Tanya smiled shyly back at him. It felt good, making Mr Taylor happy. "Well, I'll come round after school, then. On Monday."

"Monday, then. Thank you, Tanya. I'll pay whatever the going rate is."

Now Tanya's heart leapt for joy: more money to buy records with, and clothes and go to the pictures. And money to save, so that she could leave home with Neil in the autumn. "OK. Thanks, Mr Taylor." She was still smiling as he opened the front door and she stepped into the sunlight. She couldn't wait to tell Neil about her plans for their future. She had it all sorted, in the bag.

John Taylor looked less happy as he closed the front door. He stood in the hall, shaking his head, telling himself the pills had addled his brains. The girl was the daughter of a neighbour, just out of childhood. He forgot to ask her age. Couldn't be more than sixteen.

Susan had been – what – eighteen when he'd met her? She was fair-haired and pretty, like Tanya; but more rounded, softer in the face, less knowing in her eyes. Tanya didn't look as innocent as Susan had at eighteen. Tanya could have passed for a woman of twenty with that makeup she was wearing, and her breasts were – John stood there and blinked, again unable to believe the way he was thinking. He needed a long shower, he needed to wash his mouth out. He needed to scrub himself clean of his thoughts.

He stood in front of the bathroom mirror and took a long look at himself. He was still a young man, but a young man who looked old and grey. His thick, dark hair had lost its lustre and was flecked with grey at the sides. Even his three day-old stubble was silver-grey, matching his once-dark eyebrows. He opened the bathroom cabinet and gazed at the array of bottles and small boxes, ranged neatly along three shelves. Most of the cartons were Susan's: her toiletries, as they called them in the chemist's, women's lotions. He had no idea what they were all for. He picked up a box and read the label. Moisture cream, deep toning, enriched with vitamins, eliminates wrinkles. Susan didn't have any wrinkles that he remembered. Susan had been perfect in his eyes, the perfect woman.

And that was what he missed right now: his lovely, perfect wife.

John shaved slowly and extra carefully and stood in the shower for a long time, eyes closed, letting the hot water cascade over his head. When he stepped out of the cubicle he felt refreshed and he rubbed himself vigorously with the bath towel. He opened the window and breathed in deeply, enjoying the late spring air that wafted in from the garden. In the bedroom, he rummaged through the chest of drawers for clean socks and underpants, then he threw open the wardrobe to find a pair of clean trousers.

Susan's skirts and dresses and blouses were neatly arrayed on hangers beside his own clothes. He fingered a dress: a summer dress with a floral print, yellow and white daises on a pale blue background. He had loved Susan in that dress, with her shoulder-length blonde hair flicked back over the cut-away neckline. She had always worn it with the gold chain and locket he'd bought her for her twenty-first birthday. John gathered up a handful of the material and held it to his face, inhaling the sweet familiar smell of his wife.

He must have stood there for five or ten minutes, he didn't really know how long. He shrugged on a shirt and, as he did up the front buttons, the thought came to him: how would he manage with the washing and ironing, the kid's clothes, changing sheets and pillowcases? Come to that, how did the washing machine work? He had never seen Susan do the ironing. His shirts just appeared on his wardrobe shelves, miraculously, ready to be worn. John looked around the room, at the floor, the furniture, the bed. Housework: he could never do it. He wouldn't know where to start. He'd never have the time. He thought, how did Susan manage all this, and the kids, as well? And she'd cooked his meals, and she'd made love to him at night, never saying she was tired.

With a sinking feeling, he thought about cooking. He would be happy to live on tins of everything, himself, but the children, he knew, would need proper meals. Could he cook for them every night? Could he, hell. He could do toast, he could boil an egg, he could open a tin of beans. And he could scramble eggs. That was it: scrambled egg and beans on toast. What else? Nothing else. That was all he could cook. Well, his sister-in-law would be happy to do them a roast on Sunday, he was sure about that. John understood in that moment he'd be relying on June a great deal now. She lived nearby and, although she had a husband, Ken, she didn't have any children and only worked part-time, in the afternoons. June was as shattered as he had been by the death of her sister. He wondered how she was today; his children, too. He would ring her in a minute and go through a few things with her.

The shower had revived him, although he was still feeling lost and distraught. But he felt he could function, albeit slowly, for the first time since he'd lost his wife. Suddenly, there was so much to think about on the practical side, especially concerning the twins. Well, the baby-sitting was taken care of. And, soon, the kids would both be at primary school, which had longer hours than kindergarten.

John sat down heavily on the bed and pulled his shoes out from underneath. He was thinking he should start by changing the bed sheets, when he noticed one of Susan's fluffy bedroom slippers under the bed. He brought it out and held it up, and looked at it hard. Only a few days ago, this object had held the bare foot of the dearest person to him in the whole world. He put the slipper to his face, the fluffy decoration slightly tickling his nose. The now-familiar, deep feeling of emptiness welled up in him and he felt his eyes pricking with tears. He pressed the slipper hard against his cheek. He heard himself sob and let the tears flow freely. He was back where he'd started. He felt his life was finished, that he couldn't go on. He didn't see the point of any of it, not even caring for his children. John fell back on the bed, still holding his wife's slipper, and howled into the pillow in loud, gasping sobs.

The doorbell sounded again. John didn't hear it. His grief was louder than any extraneous noises going on around him. But the caller was persistent and rang again. And again. Then whoever it was put a finger on the bell, and left it there. After a few minutes, John was conscious of a faraway sound. He stopped his sobbing, levered himself up and listened. The front door: Tanya had changed her mind about baby-sitting, already.

He swung his legs over the side of the bed and sat there for a moment, wiping his eyes and trying to smooth down his hair. Then he took a deep breath, exhaled and stood up, and went downstairs to answer the door. As he opened up, the caller's finger pressed on the bell once more. The hand was quickly drawn away as John stood in the doorway. At first, he thought he was looking at Tanya with her long blonde hair. But the shape of the person, fractured by the sunlight shining in his eyes, mutated into something shorter, wider, thicker in the head and neck. And the hair was teased up, the face older, the makeup far less delicate; the lips deeply lipsticked, dark red.

"Mr Taylor!" Angela Clayforth gave him a wide smile as she stood on the step holding a lidded, earthenware casserole dish in one hand, her other hand hovering near his doorbell. John blinked for a moment, then smiled at his neighbour. He was so relieved it wasn't Tanya returning to say she'd had second thoughts about their arrangement, that he returned Mrs Clayforth's beaming smile, out of relief.

"Mrs Clayforth. Sorry I didn't – ah – couldn't answer the door straightaway." He looked at the pot she was holding, now with both hands, for it had begun to feel heavy and the last thing Angela wanted to do was drop it on John Taylor's path. He stood there, awkwardly, not knowing what to say to her, though it was obvious she had brought him a gift, and he guessed it was something for his supper.

"Mr Taylor, I knew I wouldn't be disturbing you too much. I saw you talking to the Williams girl, earlier."

John's mind clicked back a few days, to when he'd noticed Mrs Clayforth's curtain drop as he'd looked up when he left for work. She must spend all day watching everyone, he thought to himself; everything going past her window.

"So, I thought I'd just pop across, and bring you this." She beamed at him, holding the casserole dish out towards him.

"You've – brought me – Well, I – You'd better come in, Mrs Clayforth." John stood back and his neighbour immediately sailed through his door. She turned and smiled at him again, and he could see her features better, now that she was out of the strong light. She appeared to be wearing a lot of makeup for so early in the day. He looked away, down at the floor, and gestured her through to the kitchen.

She strode over to the worktop and placed the earthenware dish on top of it, pushing it back carefully from the edge. "There now, Mr Taylor. I've made you a nice porc au cidre for your supper, and for the children of course. I felt I just had to do something to help you out. You'll be wanting a good meal, and I'm sure the last thing on your mind, right now, is cooking."

John looked at the dish appreciatively and nodded. "Well, it's funny. You know, I'd been wondering what to feed the children when they come home this weekend. I don't have a clue what to do in the kitchen, or where to start."

Angela Clayforth's eyebrows lifted and her eyes brightened. "Oh, now! Don't you give it another thought. You know, I'm all alone across the road. It seems so silly, cooking for one. And I do enjoy – "

"Mrs Clayforth, that's really kind. But I don't think I could burden you with that sort of thing – " But she was lifting the lid on the casserole and the smell that wafted from the pot was delicious. Suddenly, John realised he was hungry. "It smells superb," he smiled at her, gratefully.

Angela was encouraged. It had been a long time since she'd been praised. Years, in fact. And here was someone telling her she was valued, that she still had something to give. It was as though a shaft of light had pierced her lonely existence and brought with it a thousand possibilities. Angela felt, at that moment, the warm glow of being wanted. Mr Taylor was smiling at her. He looked frail, he needed someone to look after him. Suddenly, she felt an almost mystical calling, a desire to make someone happy. A purpose in life, a raison d'être.

Chapter 7

There was a small skip in Tanya's step as she walked up the path to Neil Boyd's house. She knocked at the front door, stood there in the sunshine with a smile on her face, flicked back her hair and waited. Valerie Boyd opened the door, wearing an apron and wiping flour off her hands with a cloth. She looked at the girl on the step and drew a sharp breath. Tanya was not her favourite teenager.

"Hello, Mrs Boyd," said Tanya, still smiling. Usually, Mrs Boyd asked her in straight away, knowing the girl had called to see her son. But, this time, the housewife didn't open the door wide to her. Instead, she stood in the doorway, looked slightly uncomfortable. "Is Neil there?" Tanya asked, peering round the aproned figure into the dim light of the hall.

"I'm afraid he isn't, Tanya." The woman continued wiping her hands industriously on the cloth.

Tanya frowned. "But he's always home on Saturday afternoons, doing his homework."

"Well, that's just what he's doing. He's busy. He has a lot of school work to do. You know he's – "

"Yes, I know," sighed Tanya. "He's got exams coming up. He's got to get good grades."

Valerie Boyd nodded. "It's very important. Neil had a long talk with his father last night, and he understands how crucial these next few months are. I hope you understand, too, Tanya. I hope you'll help him in this. Neil needs to concentrate on his studies. He can't go out and about with you all the time. He's got enough to do, helping Mrs Clayforth at weekends, as well as his homework."

Tanya felt a wave of frustration engulf her previously sunny mood. She had been bursting to tell Neil about her new job, baby-sitting for Mr Taylor. And now, here was Mrs Boyd, uttering stupid, irrelevant phrases and barring her way to her boyfriend's bedroom. She was starting to feel angry. The strong emotions she had inherited from her father began to pulse through her. "Look, I just want to see him, Mrs Boyd. I just want have a word, tell him something. It'll only take a minute – "

Just then, Neil appeared at the foot of the stairs. He had heard his mother go to the door. He'd guessed it was Tanya. He knew, instinctively, she would want to go for a walk with him. And he knew she would want to go to Hadham woods. Normally, he would have been delighted. But today, Tanya's calling round presented him with a problem.

There had been a seismic shift in the Boyd household the previous evening. When Mr Boyd had come home from work, his wife had told him she thought their son was spending too much time with the Williams girl. She was convinced this – she called it 'friendship' – would affect the boy's exams if he didn't spend more time studying.

Mrs Boyd had always been ambitious for both of her sons. She had wanted to go to university herself, but the war and the death of her father at Dunkirk had put paid to any ideas of staying on at school. She'd had to go out to work at sixteen to support her frail mother, who had never recovered from receiving the War Office telegram with its bare words concerning her husband's death. But Valerie Boyd had hopes and plans for both of her sons, and no pretty chit of a girl in the neighbourhood was going to stand in the way of her eldest becoming a lawyer. She had made Graham sit down with Neil that evening and impress on the boy the need to focus on his studies. And she would get her husband to do exactly the same, in a couple of years' time, with her youngest child, Michael.

"It's alright, Mum," said Neil, coming to the door and standing beside his mother. "I'll just have a quick word with Tanya, now. It'll only take a minute or two. Then I'll go back to my books. Promise."

Mrs Boyd seemed satisfied with this. She stopped wiping her hands on her cloth and turned to go back into the kitchen. Neil took her place at the door. Tanya was still left standing on the step; she couldn't believe it. This boy was supposed to be her sweetheart. They had been as intimate as it gets, he had promised to marry her. And here he was, standing, nonchalantly, with his hands in his pockets, not even inviting her into the house.

"Come on, Neil. Let's go for a walk," said Tanya, doing her best to put a smile back on her face. "It's a lovely afternoon. We could spend a couple of hours ... " she lowered her voice and threw a glance at the kitchen door behind him – "you-know-where. We could have some fun, right? Just the two of us ... "

Neil gave her a half-smile, but still looked uncomfortable.

"What?" said Tanya, a terseness in her voice now.

"It's just that, well, I had a talk with my father last night. It doesn't matter what he said. It's just that – "

"Just what?"

"So, I promised him I'd put in a bit more work for my exams, that's all. I just need to stay home this afternoon and do some book work." Neil knew how Tanya would take this. He had seen how fast her temper could flare up, several times before.

She stood for a moment, looking at him, incredulously. When she spoke, her tone of voice had altered. It was as if she were struggling to prevent it from cracking under a great strain. "Look, Neil. You can't go making love to me and then dropping me when – "

"Sshh! My mother – " he threw his head back to indicate the kitchen door.

Tanya gave a sneer and put her hands on her hips. "I won't be quiet. And I won't be used when you feel like it, and pushed aside when you don't. Let's get one thing straight, Neil, either we're in a relationship or we're not. And if we are, you have to take time out to see me."

Neil caught hold of Tanya's arm and steered her off the step and on to the path. "Look, Tanya. I'm very fond of you. You know that – "

"Do you love me?" she demanded.

"Well, yes." he shrugged his shoulders and spoke in a low voice, hoping she would do the same.

"Then listen to this: I've just got a job, looking after Mr Taylor's children for an hour after school until he comes home from work. It'll give me some extra money, so I can start saving for when you go to university and we get a flat together. And you could come and baby-sit with me and – "

He was shaking his head now, holding up his hands and backing off. "No, that's not what I want. You know that, Tanya. We've discussed this before. I told you: I'll be in a hall of residence for the first year at college, then we can see what – "

"And I told you I've got to leave home. I can't stand it – "

"You don't have to leave home, Tanya. You can do a secretarial course or something and, then, when you've got a good job – "

"Oh, stop being so practical, so unadventurous! Let's live a little now!" She reached up to put her arms on his shoulders. He backed away again and she was left with her hands in the air.

"Tanya, right now my work comes first. It's taking up most of my time, you know that. Later, we'll see. Who knows, we might be able to be together; maybe not. We have to be patient – "

"Is that what your father said?"

"Something like that ... "

"Well, all I know, Neil Boyd, is that I'm a person in a hurry. I've got lots of living to do. I don't want to spend any more time at home with my miserable mother, who does nothing but moan about everything I do. If you're too busy to be with me, I can find someone who isn't." And with those words, Tanya turned on her heels, before Neil could see the tears in her eyes, and walked stiffly down the garden path, through the gate and turned for home.

Neil stood and watched her go. He was torn between his strong urge to run after her and take her in his arms, and his father's advice the previous evening when they'd discussed his future. Neil was by nature a cautious young man. He had been a careful, practical child who'd always been prepared to go that extra mile to achieve what he wanted. He had no need for instant gratification in anything. He was prepared to hunker down and wait, and that often made the reward sweeter for him. As a boy, he would take his time, spending hours building model aeroplanes or practising the clarinet or improving his rugby kick, and before he embarked on any project, he would think it through carefully. He would always consider the end result first, and calculate the time and effort that would be involved. It was this delayed gratification that gave him a high. Looking forward to achieving a goal was as pleasurable for Neil as attaining it.

He sighed and went back to the house. He didn't know why Tanya was in such a hurry for them to be together. Surely, building their lives in a slow, orderly fashion would bring greater material rewards? This was the one aspect of Tanya that he did not particularly like: her impulsiveness, her inability to be patient, especially on the subject of his studies. She ought to be able to see the advantages of waiting for him to finish university, and allowing him to build a career that would benefit both of them in the long term.

His mother put her head around the kitchen door as he started to climb the stairs. "Everything all right, dear?"

Neil didn't answer, but kept going with his head down.

Valerie Boyd gazed after her son and gently shook her head. Then she returned to the kitchen and continued beating the mixture for a cherry cake, which she knew was her son's favourite.

Angela Clayforth was on cloud nine. She had half a dozen recipe books open on her kitchen worktop, showing pictures of steaming casseroles and elegant desserts. She had a notebook open, too, and a pen in her hand. She had written: Monday – coq au vin plus fruit compote (see what fruit available), Tuesday – moussaka (buy aubergines) plus chocolate mousse (buy decorations), Wednesday – She tapped the pen on her teeth and stared ahead of her. "No, not that," she said to herself. "It's not the weather."

She turned the page of the nearest book and squinted at the recipe on the page. She wondered for a moment if she needed glasses. How old was she? Forty-three, last birthday. Perhaps she should get her eyes tested. Not that she'd wear glasses if John – she'd called him John on Sunday evening and he hadn't objected – was having dinner with her. Glasses don't go with low cut dresses. Drop earrings and a flattering necklace were the best accessories if you were trying to attract a man. And Angela was trying hard to attract, and she had an idea she was succeeding.

She had been across to John's house three evenings in a row with a piping hot meal for him and the children. Of course, it was nuisance, the twins still being up and under his feet. He'd said something about young Tanya Williams baby-sitting for him during the week, and how grateful he was to everyone for helping him out like this. John had smiled at her as he'd said those words; a special smile, she thought. He was looking better now that his wife's funeral was over. Angela had watched him go off to work every morning with the twins dressed for nursery school and jumping up and down in the back of his car. And he'd waved to her a couple of times. She hadn't realised she could be seen so easily from her window. But, perhaps, he was looking out for her. Perhaps he was hoping she'd be there. A glimpse of her to brighten his day; his new-found soul mate, living opposite him.

Crème brûlée: that was a fine dessert for an intimate evening. A frown passed over Angela's face as she remembered the last time she'd made crème brûlée. It had been early on in her marriage. Good heavens, was it nearly twenty years since she'd made those delicious ramekins of rich custard with their crisp sugar coatings? Yes, she remembered the evening. After that, she'd never bothered to tempt Frank with haute cuisine, or anything else. But, in those early days she'd believed in marriage and thought it was her duty – yes, duty – to revive an already flagging situation. She'd wanted Frank to take her in his arms and tell her how much he loved her, how much he appreciated the way she kept house and cooked his meals. Of course, the house came first, as far as Angela was concerned. A beautiful living room and the best china and deep pile carpets were top of her list of the necessities in life. But she had wanted a loving husband to complete the set and she'd been prepared to make an effort for that.

It wasn't that Frank had repelled her, sexually, though her wedding night had been very off-putting. Angela had been a virgin that night, and remained one for nearly a week after they had wed. Only a year or so later did she realise that her husband, although he was eighteen years older than she, had also been a virgin when they'd married. It figured: he had lived at home with his mother until her death, when he'd asked Angela to marry him. Angela thought Frank had singled her out at the bank because he found her attractive, because he had fallen in love with her, the way men did in the novels she borrowed from the library. She felt proud to be Mrs Frank Clayforth, the assistant bank manager's wife. She dressed appropriately, in quality town and country clothes, matching skirts and blouses. And pearls; always the pearl earrings and the matching single strand around her neck.

It puzzled Angela, for nearly two years after the marriage, that her husband didn't seem very interested in anything she said or did. Frank had his hobbies, his Meccano set and his stamp collecting, and he read the papers avidly.

He would eat whatever Angela cooked and put in front of him; it was all the same to him. And if she became miffed when he hadn't noticed the effort she'd made her with the cooking or her appearance, he wouldn't notice that, either. As far as Frank was concerned, he wanted everything to run along the same well-oiled wheels that his life had run on when his mother had been alive. By the second year of her marriage, Angela knew that Frank Clayforth had merely been looking for a housekeeper to replace the one he'd lost when Edna Clayforth had died.

Until that point of realisation, nearly two years into her marriage, it had upset Angela that Frank had no real interest in their sex life. He would perform perfunctorily, on Tuesday evenings and Saturday evenings, then his head would fall back on his pillow and he'd begin to snore, almost immediately. He continued this routine, whether Angela wore a skimpy negligée or a flannel nightdress, whether she wore expensive perfume or not. She would lay awake for hours, listening her husband's nocturnal noise, until one evening, the last time she had made a crème brûlée, she moved herself and her clothes into the guest room, never to return to the marital bed.

"This is a special dessert for a special evening, darling," Angela had placed the pretty ramekin in front of Frank and sat down opposite him, waiting for her husband's eyes to alight on the dish with interest.

Frank picked up his teaspoon to eat the dessert. He was checked, momentarily, by the caramelised topping. Then he hammered with the back of his spoon across the delicate coating, as if cracking a hard-boiled egg, and resumed his meal while reading the share prices on the financial page of his newspaper.

"Do you like it, then?"

"What?" Her husband's eyes flickered but remained fixed on the shares page.

"The dessert. I made it specially. I thought you'd like it."

"Oh, right. I see ICI are down again. And BP. Drat." He shook the paper and turned the page.

Angela said nothing else during the meal. She cleared the table and did the dishes. She got ready for bed. She put on a black and red negligée. She put a dab of Chanel No. 5 behind each ear lobe. She got into bed and waited. Frank was looking at his stamp collection.

At eleven o'clock, the appointed hour on a Saturday evening, Frank moved at his usual measured pace from the bathroom to the bedroom. He hung his dressing gown on the back of the bedroom door and shook his slippers from his feet and got into bed beside her. After the regulation minute of silence, where they both stared at the wardrobe ahead of them, Frank's hand fell on his wife's shoulder. He gave a soft grunt.

Angela did not respond, as she normally did. She didn't give a little simper and turn to him and part her lips in an inviting smile. She continued to stare straight ahead, fixing on the wardrobe with all her concentration.

Frank's hand left her shoulder for a moment. Then it fell on her again. He gave the same low grunt and moved closer to her.

Angela sat rigid in the bed. Frank's hand slid down to her breast. He attempted to manoeuvre her backwards and lever himself onto her. She still didn't look at him but, after a few seconds, she let him mount her and do his business. He took no more, no less time than he usually did on a Saturday night. He rolled off her and she heard his head fall onto his pillow with a soft phut. A few seconds later, Angela heard Frank's first snore. As she lay there, in the dark, a large tear fell silently down her cheek. She gave a small sniff then turned over, and lay with her back to her husband.

It was when she moved into the other bedroom that Angela stopped buying flimsy underwear and started to wear nightclothes and undergarments that were practical and more comfortable. Her day clothes remained smart; she was always well turned out, as befitted a bank manager's wife, now that Frank had been promoted and was running his own branch. Frank hadn't objected to his wife having her own bedroom. In fact, he'd never commented on it. He had knocked at her bedroom door the following Tuesday evening, after he had got himself ready for bed. Angela was tucked up for the night, face moisturised, reading a romantic novel. She looked at her portly husband, standing there in his checked dressing gown, hands thrust into the pockets, his eyes almost reduced to slits without his glasses, and let her book fall onto the bedcover. "Yes?" she said in disinterested tone.

Frank cleared his throat and shifted a step to one side. "Would you like me to come into your bed for a moment?"

Angela wavered. She knew the situation was not up for discussion. Frank didn't do discussions. He avoided in-depth analysis of anything personal, in case he came out of it badly. Frank wasn't a particularly courageous man. He preferred a quiet, orderly existence.

The nearest he ever got to a personal conversation was to discuss an account with a client at the bank. But, in a situation like this, he had nothing to say. It was a plain yes or no answer he required.

"No."

"Right." Frank turned and took hold of the door knob and opened the door.

Angela watched him go. She knew it was the end of the sexual aspect of their marriage. 'No' had been a rejection, loud and clear, and Frank would always remember that. He would not lay himself open to that kind of dismissal again. Frank may not have had courage, but he certainly had pride.

The door closed behind him. Angela took a deep breath and exhaled slowly. She picked up her book and started to read the same paragraph again. Then she let the book drop. She tried to analyse her feelings: she knew she should feel a sense of loss, that something had gone from her life. But she only felt as if a great weight had been lifted from her shoulders. She actually felt happy. She started to smile.

There was not much for Angela to smile about in the years of marriage that followed, but she kept reasonably cheerful, taking a great interest and pride in her home and her cooking. Frank and Angela fell into the habit of taking their meals separately, to avoid the need for conversation at the table. Angela would cook early and leave her husband's meal on a plate for him to put in the oven. It was an arrangement that suited them both. The less they said to each other, the less they wanted to say to each other, until their cohabitation was one of almost complete silence. But Frank had his Meccano set and his stamp collection and his garden to tend. And then, one day, not long after he had retired from the bank, he brought home a short-haired dachshund and called her Mitzi.

Angela did not want a dog, not of any size or shape. It was the longest verbal exchange the couple had had in years. It was decided the dog could stay, as long as Frank took full responsibility for the animal. Mitzi trotted after Frank everywhere: to the shed at the bottom of the garden where he constructed his Meccano, to the pub where he went at lunchtimes for a pint while his wife had her midday snack. The dog lay at her master's feet while he pored over his stamp collection and when he fell asleep in his armchair in the afternoons with a newspaper over his face.

But Mitzi had outlived Frank. Angela saw the dog as a final reminder of those cold years of marital disharmony. Frank had loved Mitzi. Frank had loved his mother and had kept her memory alive by visiting her grave every Friday morning with Mitzi. Angela hated all of them: Frank, the ghost of his mother and his adoring dog. And now all that was left was the dachshund, who had, perversely, taken to adoring Angela. She supposed it was because she was now the one that fed it.

Angela had no interest in Mitzi, but she didn't feel she could get rid of the animal, so soon after Frank had died. What would the neighbours say? When Doreen had offered her daughter to walk the dog, it made the situation easier to bear. "The exercise will do Stella good," Doreen had said to her, while Angela secretly thought it would have done her friend good to take the dog out, herself. She had noticed Doreen's drinking was escalating during the day, but Angela needed a friend to talk to, even more, now that she was on her own in the world.

She found that Frank's death had left her feeling more isolated than in the loneliest moments of her loveless marriage. Before, there had been a structure to her day: cooking his meals and doing his laundry, cleaning their home, emptying the ashtray where he'd tapped out his pipe and clearing up the newspapers he'd left on the floor when he'd fallen asleep in the chair. Angela hadn't been fond of her husband, but she was even less fond of living on her own.

She started going shopping for whole afternoons. She began to look at younger people's clothes, and saucy underwear again.

And she started exercising in her bedroom in the evenings, so that she could squeeze herself into the latest mini dress. She carried the portable record player into her bedroom and bought herself a stack of pop records. She would adjust the long mirror in the corner of the room and put on her newly-purchased underwear and dance to the music. Angela would spend hours in the evenings, jigging and pirouetting around the room, her arms flying outwards as she executed small jumps in the air. By the end of an evening she was glowing from her efforts. She tingled all over, as though she'd been out dancing for a night. The beat of the music was a primeval comfort to her. She would mime the words and shake her head, her hips and her legs. Angela began to feel younger for the first time in years, jerking her arms and her body and throwing back her head and twirling about. It was the only time Mitzi left her mistress on her own in the house. The dog removed itself to the kitchen and laid down by its water bowl, shut its eyes and tried to sleep.

John finished Mrs Clayforth's delicious casserole gravy with a spoon. And why not, he said to himself. He was alone at the table; on his own in the kitchen, once again. The children were upstairs in bed, fast asleep, and he was spending another evening without company, without Susan. Was this the future, he asked himself: night after night, savouring Angela Clayforth's reheated dinners in a silent kitchen?

She had asked him to call her Angela when she'd bustled into the house one evening with another earthenware pot. John saw no reason why they shouldn't be on first name terms. It was kind of the woman to cook for them, day after day. It gave him peace of mind to know the children were eating a hot nutritious meal every night. Of course, he'd offered to pay her for the food. But she'd held up her hands, with those painted fingernails he couldn't help noticing. "No, no! Really, John, it's my pleasure!" she'd said, giving him a beaming, lip-glossed smile. That was another thing he noticed about his neighbour: the lipstick; bright orange some evenings and, sometimes, bright red. She would probably be alright, he reckoned, if she didn't put all that goo on her face, not to mention that strong perfume, whatever it was.

Still, he was grateful to the woman. He was grateful to all the neighbours for knocking on his door and asking if there was anything they could do. Mrs Boyd had baked him a cake and offered to do his ironing, but Susan's sister was taking care of that. And young Tanya had turned out to be as good as her word and was there, looking after the twins, every evening when he came home from work. She had even stayed on, one time, and helped him bath Sally and Ross before he'd given them one of Mrs Clayforth's suppers. John found he looked forward to seeing Tanya when he got home at the end of a long day. She was a bright, cheerful girl, and she laughed when he joked and horsed around with the children. Last night, he had piggy-backed the twins around the sitting room and she'd joined in, hoisting the children on his back and clapping her hands with laughter. He was sorry when she'd said she had to leave. He'd nearly asked her to stay a little longer and help him bath the twins again, but he didn't want to impose on her time, didn't want to jeopardise her helping him out in the future. He'd have been miserable if she'd stopped coming to his house. He didn't want to lose her.

"A special dessert tonight for a special person!" said Angela as John had opened the door to her, the evening before. "Crème brûlée! You'll adore this ... " and she trotted through to the kitchen and carefully slid a large ramekin dish onto the worktop. "Now, you've still got half of the lasagne I made you yesterday?"

John nodded with a smile. "Yes, thank you, Mrs – Angela. The kids loved it."

"Wasn't too herby for them, I hope?" Angela fluttered her eyelids at him and pouted a little.

What was it, thought John, about this woman's mannerisms that he found slightly irritating? He smiled and reassured her they'd loved it. They all loved her cooking, he said.

Angela looked delighted by his words. She moved a little closer and laid her hand on his shoulder. As her face came nearer to his, he could feel her warm breath on his face, "Well, you know, if you're not busy next Saturday evening, we could have a small dinner together. Here, if you like, or, perhaps, if you could get a baby-sitter, you could pop across to my place."

John was surprised, taken aback. He was wholly unprepared for her words. He moved a little, as surreptitiously as he could, to make some space between himself and his neighbour. Her bright orange lips took on a slightly menacing appearance as they widened before his eyes. He held on to the kitchen worktop for a moment, telling himself not to panic; there was no reason to be afraid of Angela Clayforth.

"I think – I believe I've got to go to my sister-in-law's that evening. I don't know ... I'll have to check. Can I let you know on that?"

The orange lips puckered slightly. "Yes, of course, John. Don't you worry about it tonight. You know, I'm always there, just across the road." Then she rallied and said brightly, "We can always have a meal together another Saturday evening. We'll make a special date for it!"

John could have kicked himself for not finding some permanent excuse for not dining with her. It was not that he disliked Mrs Clayforth. She was a good sort and she'd done him proud with all this cooking of hers. But the idea of sitting opposite the woman for an intimate supper, sharing a bottle of wine and, perhaps, a brandy with her, didn't appeal to him, at all. He would rather go to his sister-in-law with the kids, any night of the week, than listen to Mrs Clayforth cooing at him in that ingratiating tone of hers.

There was the doorbell, again. He felt his stomach churn. It had to be Angela Clayforth. John realised he was beginning to dread the woman coming round in the evenings now. He wondered how he could put a stop to it, without hurting her feelings.

CHAPTER 8

"I've stopped drinking, Ray. Honestly, I have ... " Doreen stood at the bottom of the stairs, watching her husband go wearily up to his bedroom. He had moved into the spare room a week ago, when she'd been sick on the bedcover after another of their arguments. It had been a turning point for both of them, in different ways.

"Yeah, right," said Ray in a tired voice, without looking round.

"You can come back to the bedroom now. Ray? Why don't you sleep with ... " Doreen's voice trailed off as she saw her husband cross the landing, go into the spare room and close the door behind him. She knew he was going to change out of his work clothes. She knew he'd be going out again, to the golf club. She ran up the stairs and knocked at his door. "Ray? Ray! Let me in a moment. I want to talk to you."

No sound came from inside the room.

Doreen knocked again, then turned the handle and started to open the door.

"Leave it, Doreen! Just leave it, will you?" Ray stood in the middle of the room in his slacks, pulling a polo-necked sweater over his head. He pushed his fingers through his hair, smoothing it back into place, and slipped on some casual shoes. "I don't want to discuss anything." He looked at his watch. "I'm going to be late."

But Doreen remained in the doorway, hands on her hips, so that her husband couldn't pass. She wasn't feeling well, she had a headache. She'd felt dreadful since she'd got up that morning and not had a drink. She needed one now, and Ray wasn't helping the situation. "What's so urgent at this time of the evening that you can't spend a moment talking to your wife?"

Ray tried to push past her, but she stood her ground. He grasped the tops of her arms firmly and moved her aside and went out of the room. She turned and followed him on to the landing. He went quickly down the stairs. Doreen was right behind him.

"So, who are you in such a hurry to meet tonight?"

No answer. Ray took his coat from the hall cupboard and started to shrug it on.

"Aren't you going to have something to eat before you go? I cooked you dinner. It's in the oven, ready."

Ray would have liked a cup of coffee and a sandwich before going out of the door; he'd had a working lunch with a client and hadn't eaten much during some tough negotiating at the table. But he didn't want to linger in the house with Doreen in such a belligerent mood. He didn't trust himself not to lose his temper. He was tired. He wanted to relax in a pleasant environment with his friends. These days, his home had a more confrontational atmosphere than his office. He needed to get away. Ray chose his words carefully: "Thanks. I'll probably eat it when I get in, later."

"No, you won't."

Did he argue with that, or just get the hell out of there? He was still thinking it through when the phone on the hall table started to ring. He made a movement to answer it, but his wife was standing right beside the table. She picked up the receiver.

"Hullo?" Her tone of voice was more demanding than friendly. "Who? A member of the golf club? What's your name? Mrs Hardwick." Doreen thrust the handset at her husband. "She says it's about a fixture. What kind of fixture, that's the question!"

Ray was sure the caller must have heard those words. He held on to the phone, keeping a hand over the mouthpiece, waiting for Doreen to go into another room. But she stood there, beside him, with her arms folded, looking at him, defiantly.

"Well, go on, then! Speak to your lady friend! Tell her you're on your way, rushing into her arms!" Doreen's eyes flashed at him. Her expression was dark, thunderous. He knew better than to reply. He lifted the phone to his mouth and slid his hand hesitantly off the mouthpiece, ready to put it quickly back again if Doreen began shouting at him.

"Hello, Liz. Thanks for calling. Look, I'm going to the club now. Can I see you up there, and we'll talk about – "

"She can't wait, can she?"

Ray's hand cupped the mouthpiece, quick as a flash. The woman was talking on the other end. He nodded. "Right," he said, and nodded again.

"Go on, run to her! See if I care!" Doreen's face was as flushed with emotion as if she'd been drinking, but there were tears streaming down her face.

"OK, 'bye, Liz." Ray slammed down the phone and turned angrily to his wife. "I suppose you're satisfied, now! God, you're a bitch, Doreen. Bitch! Bitch! Bitch! There's no other word for a woman like you!"

He hurriedly did up the buttons on his coat and started towards the door. She tried to stand in his way but, this time, he pushed her roughly to one side. She fell against the banisters and took a couple of seconds to recover. It gave Ray enough time to open the front door, pass quickly through it and slam the door shut behind him.

Doreen ran at the door and banged both hands against it. She let out a sob, her head fell forward and she began to wail. She remained there, howling and pounding on the door with both fists, again and again.

Stella's head appeared over the landing banisters. She looked down at her mother in the hallway below, sobbing and beating the front door, but she didn't say a word.

Neil blew at the smear on the pane and rubbed it harder. He didn't mind cleaning windows for Mrs Clayforth; it gave him time to think. And it would fill his time this weekend, now that Tanya was ignoring him. He hoped she would come round by next week, that she'd see his point about waiting until he finished university. All he wanted was for her to understand that his studies were important. If he worked hard now, his academic success would give him a springboard to a glittering future. His mother was right: he couldn't live with someone while he was a student; there would be too many distractions. And he didn't think Tanya should waste herself on waitressing in a café for two or three years, just for him. She should stay at home and do a typing course and help her mother. It was the practical thing to do.

Neil loved Tanya, he was sure of that. He loved her so much that he was aching to hold her again, to kiss her and explore her body. It was Sunday morning now, and he hadn't seen her since she'd knocked at his door on Friday evening, full of enthusiasm about following him to university. He was torn: on the one hand, he would have loved to live with Tanya in a cramped flat at any time, or anywhere for that matter. He would have their love-making to look forward to, at the end of every day.

But his father had made sense when he'd sat down with him that night and told him to concentrate on his studies. He'd explained how easy it was to be distracted from a goal and end up with a mediocre degree and a mediocre job. Mr Boyd was ambitious for his son, just as Neil was ambitious for himself. His father had his best interests at heart, he knew that. The studying he did now would affect his job prospects for the rest of his life. It was just that he wanted Tanya every minute of the day. He was miserable without her. He hadn't realised how much she meant to him. He was, he admitted to himself, crazy about her. Would she wait for him? Why did he doubt it?

"'Lo, Neil."

He knew, without looking up, who the voice belonged to: Stella Reynolds was bringing Mrs Clayforth's dog back from its walk.

"'Lo, then" he said, rubbing vigorously at a corner of the window. He wondered if Stella had seen Tanya in the last thirty-six hours. He wondered if she knew they'd had an argument and that Tanya wasn't talking to him at the moment. Neil knew Stella had always had a crush on him. It didn't bother him, one way or the other. Just as it didn't really bother him that Mrs Clayforth pressed her knees against his when they were having coffee. He knew he was a good-looking young man. He accepted it as a bonus in life.

"Is Mrs Clayforth home, d'you know?"

He looked up and gave the girl a half-smile. "Yes, she's inside. Somewhere." He wondered if he should ask Stella if she'd seen Tanya, what she'd said, how she was. He began to think about how he could phrase such a question while Stella went on talking.

"I'll just leave the dog in the kitchen with its water bowl. I don't want to see her, particularly."

"Right." Neil moved his ladder further along the side of the house and started to climb the rungs to the first floor windows. He heard the back door open as Stella deposited the dog inside. He heard her say, "Go on, then, mutt. Get in there." The door slammed and he looked down to see the top of Stella's head as she rolled back down the pathway. Then she stopped and looked up at him and smiled. He decided he preferred not to ask her any questions. He focussed on the window in front of him, hoping she'd go away. If only the girl would lose some weight, he thought. And, then what? Was he starting to fancy Stella Reynolds? Was he that desperate, already? No, not fat Stella! Agreed, he felt sorry for the girl, sometimes. He supposed she'd find a boyfriend, one day. But probably not during the short time he'd be at home. Not before he left for university and the big, wide world beyond.

A deep sigh escaped him as he hooked the bucket at the top of the ladder. He dropped the cloth into the grey water, swirled it about and squeezed it out again. This time next year, he'd be gone from here. He promised himself he would never live in this road again, with its boring people and their unremarkable lives. Even his parents –

Neil froze. There was movement on the other side of the window. He couldn't believe what he was looking at. Mrs Clayforth, clad only in skimpy red and black underwear, was dancing in the middle of the room. He presumed she had some music playing because she was swaying in time to a beat. Her ample hips jerked from side to side, back and forth with a rhythmic thrust. She twirled about, flapping her podgy arms in the air and kicking out with her solid thighs. She wore a blissful expression on her face; her eyes were half closed, her mouth fixed in a semi-grin. It was an astounding sight for the young man to behold. But he continued to stare through the window, fascinated, unable to look away.

Angela executed a heavy pirouette and, holding out her arms, wrists limp, began to side-step across the room. As she jigged along the carpet, she opened her eyes to check where she was going. It was then she caught sight of Neil, clutching the ladder and the cloth, looking at her in wide-eyed disbelief.

Their eyes met. Angela didn't miss a beat. She didn't run to the corner of the room to cover herself up. She didn't even place her hands over her large breasts. Instead, she looked at him with her mouth open, then threw back her head and laughed. Neil watched as she did another twirl in the middle of the room, this time with a small hop in it. Then, to his horror, Mrs Clayforth came over to the window where he stood, still clinging to the ladder. He could see her body in detail now, it's flabbiness, its puckered skin, the parts that wobbled as she moved. She stopped in front of him and gave him a big smile. Suddenly, she curtsied low, holding out the sides of her bikini knickers. She stood up again and let her hands fall to her ample sides and, still smiling, she winked at him.

The moment Stella left Mitzi in the kitchen at Mrs Clayforth's, she went straight to Tanya's house to tell her she'd seen Neil. She liked talking to Tanya about Neil because her friend would tell her things she didn't know about him. She was gradually building up a picture of his likes and dislikes and his plans for the future, all of which she committed to memory. If she couldn't talk to Neil, herself, first hand, she was happy to glean any snippet of information about him from the girl who held the position she coveted: that of Neil's girlfriend. Stella still dreamt of being the object of Neil's affection and had persuaded herself that, one day, she would be. But, for now, she was content to adore the young man from afar, and wait. That Tanya was good-looking and had already captured his heart was a mere detail to Stella. She knew, from observing her parents' marriage at close quarters, that relationships didn't always endure.

"She's upstairs, dear," said Mrs Williams as she opened the door to Stella. "I'm glad you've come round. Tanya's been in a miserable mood all weekend. Try and cheer her up, will you? She hasn't been eating and she won't come out of her bedroom. She hasn't told me what's wrong but," and Mavis, face close to Stella's, finished her sentence in a stage whisper, "I think it's boyfriend trouble." And she nodded, as if to confirm she'd cracked the mystery of her daughter's misery.

"Boyfriend trouble?" Stella asked, wide-eyed and interested, but without waiting for Mavis Williams's reply. She bounded up the stairs and knocked on Tanya's bedroom door and went straight in, closing the door behind her to exclude the mother looking after her in the hall below.

Tanya was lying face down on the bed, her hands around her head and a screwed up handkerchief in one of them. She looked up as Stella closed the door and plonked herself at the end of the bed. The mattress bounced under Stella's weight. Tanya gave a groan when she saw who it was, and let her head drop onto her pillow again.

"Hi, Tanya."

Tanya said nothing, only sniffed.

"What's up then?"

"Go away. Go home."

"Your mum says you're upset about something."

"Go on, Stella. Buzz off, will you? I don't feel like talking today."

Stella sat there, looking round at the posters on the bedroom walls. The Rolling Stones, the Kinks, The Who and The Small Faces gazed back at her with insolent, yet provocative stares. Stella liked Mick Jagger, although he was wearing a lot of mascara and lipstick in this particular picture. She looked at the Kinks, then at the other two posters and made a choice of one band member from each that she would like to have as a boyfriend. Then she remembered Neil. "I saw Neil just now," she said, turning her head to gauge Tanya's reaction.

The head came up and turned in her direction.

"Where?" She sniffed again. "Where did you see him?"

"At Mrs Clayforth's. I took Mitzi out for a walk. He was there, cleaning her windows."

"Oh." Tanya's head returned to her pillow.

"He said 'hello' ".

Tanya swivelled her body round and sat up on the bed. "What, to me?"

"No, to me. He was up a ladder, with a bucket and cloth."

She dabbed at her nose with her sodden handkerchief. "What else did he say?"

Stella frowned, thinking, then shrugged her shoulders. "Nothing, really. He was working. I just went by, underneath his ladder."

"Did he – did he look happy?"

"Happy?" Stella thought again. "I dunno. He was – "

"I know, he was up a ladder."

"Well, it was hard to see, you know? So what's up, then? Your mum said – "

"My mother! My bloody mother! What does she know about anything?"

"She said you'd got boyfriend trouble, whatever that means." Stella was dying to know what the situation was, though she had a pretty good idea. Neil and Tanya had already had one bust-up, and they'd only been going out for a month. She sat, looking at Mick Jagger's pouting lips, and waited.

"It means Neil and I have – have had an argument. We're not talking at the moment, that's all."

"Blimey. Is it serious?"

Tanya took a deep breath, then exhaled. "No, not really. It'll blow over. In fact, I only have to crook my little finger and he'll come running back. I know that."

A slight frown crossed Stella's face. She didn't like the sound of that. She didn't want Neil running after anyone in the long term, except herself. That was how she saw the situation: Tanya leaving home and Neil turning his attention to her, his one true love, although he hadn't yet realised it. She cleared her throat and said, "Come to think of it, he looked pretty cheerful today. He was whistling, I think. Oh yes, I remember now. He said something about – about, what was it? Yes. He said he'd been to a party last night. Said he was tired out. Because of the party." Stella swivelled her eyes in Tanya's direction, to see what effect her words were having.

"He was ... tired?"

"Yup. Tired out." Stella nodded at pouting Mick to confirm it. She heard Tanya start to cry, softly. She leaned over and patted the girl on the shoulder. "Cheer up," she said. "It might not be anything important. Just a one-night stand, or something."

"You – you mean he went to a party with someone else?"

Stella debated how far she could take the story. She'd always had a certain pride in her ability to imagine scenarios. It was how she'd begun to see Neil as the boy she was destined to marry. His openness towards her when they were younger and had all played together was enough for Stella to believe that he cared. Stella's mother, wrapped up in her marital problems and her own low self-esteem, hadn't had the time or inclination to show her daughter any affection. And, with her father absent most of the time, where did a girl go to get the attention she craved? Why, into her imagination, of course. All the love and romance she needed was provided by herself, in her head.

"To be honest," Stella bit her lip, "I don't really know. I mean, he didn't say much about it. Anyway, what did you two quarrel about? If you say it isn't serious."

Tanya wiped her eyes and sighed. "About him going to university in September. I wanted to go with him. You know, get a job and live in a flat with him near the campus." She lowered her head and her voice broke. "But – but he said he didn't – he wanted me to stay here. Stay here and wait for him. Wait for him while he studied at Oxford or Cambridge or wherever he wants to go. He said it was for the best – "

There was a knock and Mrs Williams put her head around the door. She saw the two girls sitting together on the bed; she looked relieved and smiled. "There you are, then! Having a nice chat together. Just like old times, when you sat up here for hours and pressed all those wild flowers. Do you remember?"

The two girls looked at her. Neither of them spoke.

"You had such a lovely time, playing up here in this room when you were younger." She shook her head, wistfully. "Makes me quite nostalgic to see you both here." She turned to Tanya. "So much nicer, dear, to stay home at weekends with your friends and family. You don't want to be gallivanting about, staying up late, going to those parties of Marcia's, do you? I can't tell you how it warms my heart – " An object flew past Mavis Williams's left ear, and hit the wall behind her head.

"Get out, mother! Just leave me alone! Get out, get out, get out!"

The door closed, quickly and quietly. Mrs Williams could be heard going down the stairs. A few seconds later, a door below was slammed shut. Silence for a moment. Then they heard the radio in the kitchen.

"You see! See that?" Tanya had stopped crying. Her face was flushed with rage now and her eyes sparkled with anger. "And Neil wants me to wait for him! To stay here, in this house. With that woman! She's driving me crazy. She won't let me alone for a minute." Tanya turned to Stella, her eyes flashing. "She clings to me. She wants to know where I am all the time, who I'm with. Keeps telling me she wants me at home, with her. She never leaves me alone for a second. Never gives me space. I'm going mad here!" Tanya ruffled her long hair and pulled at it. "And Neil – he expects me to stay in this house and wait for him, for years!"

Stella bit her lip. Here was a problem. Neil was leaving home. For years. How many years, precisely? She would have to know how long she might be engaged to him, before they married. It was important to have these details established, so she could continue day dreaming with her usual pleasure. "My mum doesn't want me to stay at home after I finish school," she said to Tanya. "She says she can't wait for me to leave. She's always saying that."

"Lucky you."

Neither girl spoke for a while. Then Stella asked, "So what are you going to do, Tanya?"

The girl straightened her back and breathed in deeply. "I'll tell you what I'm going to do. I'll tell you exactly what I'm going to do: I'm going to be out of here by the summer, when school finishes. I'm sixteen already; I can leave home. If Neil doesn't want me, then I'll find someone who does. Someone who cares about me enough to take me with him, wherever he's going." She turned to Stella with a triumphant smile. "Hah! Then he'll be sorry! Then he'll wish he'd taken me with him to his rotten university!"

Stella bit her lip and nodded.

"Yes, that's what I'm going to do. Why, I'll probably meet someone at the fête on Saturday week."

"What fête?"

"You know; the Hadham Manor fête. It's next week – "

"Are they having one, this year? I thought, when Sir Charles dropped dead cutting the ribbon last year, that they'd stopped having fêtes. The place is up for sale, that's what my mum said. She said old Lady Trington's gone nutty as a fruitcake. They're putting her in a home and her children are selling up. Everything."

"I don't know about that. I only know they're holding the fête, as usual. And I'm going to make sure I meet someone there – " Tanya cocked her head to one side, as if another thought had come to her. "Or, perhaps I could ask Marcia's brother's friend – what was his name – Roger – to take me. Marcia said that Roger Stowe liked me; he likes me a lot. Well, lets see how much he does." She glanced at Stella, then clapped her hands, laughing. "Let's see what mister high and mighty Neil Boyd thinks about that! Should be an interesting fête, don't you think? I can't wait to see the expression on his face when he sees me with someone else!"

"You're not listening to me, Angela," said Doreen, topping up the gin in both of their glasses.

"Oh, I am," Angela said, smiling with a faraway look. "It's just that I've got a couple of things on my mind – A little more orange in that for me. Now, you were saying: he was on the phone to someone, the other night ... "

"And it wasn't one of his golf club cronies, I can tell you that. He was all lovey-dovey. I know that voice." Doreen took a couple of long sips of her drink. "It's the voice he used on me, years ago."

"Well, if you think there's something in it, have you tried talking to him about it?"

"I've tried everything," snapped Doreen. She regarded the gin and orange in her hand. "I even stopped drinking, since he's always complaining about it." She took another sip. "It didn't make any difference. I think he was using it as an excuse to go out in the evenings."

Angela gave a sympathetic murmur and looked up at the ceiling. Then she looked around the room, but there was nothing in Doreen's sitting room worth an admiring comment. It lacked the tasteful decorations she prided herself on, in her own house. The carpet wasn't deep pile and the sofa was threadbare on the arm rests. There were no pictures on the wall, only a couple of plates, and one of those had been broken and stuck back together. Perhaps Doreen had thrown it at Ray during one of their quarrels, thought Angela. Doreen, she knew, could flare up in an instant. Her friend had a volatile personality. "I wish I could help ... "

"I think – I think it's beyond help." Doreen's voice began to falter, her eyes suffused with tears. "I don't know what else I can do." She pressed her glass against her forehead and held it there. Then she closed her eyes and large tears rolled down both cheeks.

Angela was becoming a little impatient with her friend. Here she was, in the first flush of discovering a new man, urgently needing to share her feelings with someone, and there was Doreen, her usual miserable, maudlin self, spoiling this moment of near-ecstasy. "Maybe, if you ignore it, it'll pass, and he'll come back to you." Angela's voice was a little terse now.

Doreen shook her head, sniffed a couple of times, then drained her drink. "I told you, I've tried everything. There's nothing left I can do."

"Then do nothing, Doreen. Let it take its course. Some things are meant to be." She stared at the shabby wallpaper and the broken plate hanging at an angle. "I know I'm a great believer in destiny." And she began to smile.

Her neighbour looked at her. "What do you mean?"

"I mean," said Angela, turning to her, eyes now sparkling, "there's a new man in my life, and I am over the moon!"

Doreen opened her eyes wide. "Who? Not that boy who saw you dancing in your knickers, the other day?"

Angela put a hand to her mouth and giggled. "Oh, no! That was funny! But he didn't bolt down the ladder when he saw me, so I couldn't have looked that awful to him. No, neither of us said a word about it when I gave him his money. All he said was, 'See you next week, Mrs Clayforth'. Not another word!"

"Who, then?"

"Aha! I'm not in a position to say, at the moment."

"Do I know him?"

Angela considered this. "Mmmm ... Yes. I think you know him quite well."

Doreen forgot her troubles for a moment. "Well, then? When are you going to make this affair public knowledge? I hope I'll be the first to know."

Angela leaned over and patted her on the arm in a friendly, almost conspiratorial manner. "You most certainly will, my dear. And it won't be very long now. In fact, I think you'll find I have a – shall we say – an escort for the fête next week."

"Oh, damn, I forgot about the fête. I always take the children. Not that they can't go on their own, now that they're teenagers. It's just something I've always done. Ray never bothered to come with us. He was always off, playing golf." Doreen thought back to all the times she'd taken her children to events on her own: to sport's days, speech days, music recitals and fêtes. She said, "It's the last one, isn't it, before they sell the manor? The old dear's being packed off to a home, I hear."

"Probably the best place for her, now that Sir Charles has died. Their children have got families of their own and could probably do with the money from the sale. Anyway, Lady Trington is better off in a home." Angela suddenly laughed and slapped her friend on the knee. "It'll come to us all, one day!"

"Thanks."

"Not that I think it's going to happen soon. You know, I feel my life is just beginning, all over again." She looked serious for a moment. "And you know what?"

"What?" said Doreen, reaching across the coffee table for the gin bottle.

"I'm not going to let this chance of happiness slip by," said Angela. "Not for anything in the world. Love is a precious gift. And I'm not going to let anyone take it away from me. Not ever."

CHAPTER 9

"What's wrong, Tanya?" asked John as he opened the front door to her.

"Nothing," the girl said perfunctorily, stepping into the hallway. "Hope I'm not late."

"No, not all," he led the way into the sitting room. "It's good of you to come at short notice. I have to go to my sister-in-law's. I've been sorting through my wife's things and there's some family jewellery that should go to her sister. I shouldn't be long." He indicated upstairs. "The children are playing in their bedrooms, quietly for the moment. I bought them some new board games this week and a couple of jigsaws, just in case it's raining one day when you're looking after them."

"You're good, Mr Taylor; the way you think of everything."

He smiled at her and patted her shoulder. "Well, I wouldn't want to lose such an excellent baby-sitter, would I?" His face came close to hers and he noticed her eyes were misty, as though she were about to cry. "Look," he said, "this is none of my business, but there's clearly something wrong." He led her over to the sofa and Tanya, completely drained of energy, having been awake half the night crying, didn't resist.

John sat her down, placed himself beside her and put his arm along the back of the sofa. "What is it, Tanya? You look unhappy. Is it something you can talk about? Can I help?" He gently tilted her chin, so that she was looking at him. "You're always such a happy, lovely girl. I don't like to see you looking like this." He let his arm fall on her shoulder and he gave her a quick hug. "Come on, tell me all about it. We can't have the twins seeing you crying, can we?"

Tanya found she couldn't hold her emotions in check any longer. She burst into tears. Here was someone showing her sympathy and understanding and who wanted to talk about her problems. Mr Taylor was so different from her mother, or Neil come to that. This man wanted to hear what she had to say, whereas no one else ever listened to her. They only thought of themselves.

"Here, use this." John handed her a newly-pressed handkerchief. He was holding her shoulder again. It felt soft and feminine under his hand. He'd begun to realise, in the last couple of weeks, just how much he missed the touch of a woman. It said a lot for Susan, he reasoned. She had always been wonderful to hold and to kiss: responsive, passionate and loving. It was natural, he thought, to want more of a good experience. He didn't see it as any disrespect to Susan's memory.

Tanya wiped her eyes and her nose, then sniffed a couple of times. "Thank you," she said. "I'm sorry about this, I really am. It's just that – that – "

"I know, I know. There, there." John held her in both arms and rocked her as they sat on the sofa. He felt the girl lean into him, her head nestling under his chin. He breathed in the fresh, sweet smell of her hair and, suddenly, he felt aroused. With each inhalation of the top of her head, he wanted her even more. He closed his eyes and held on to her tight. He rocked her. And Tanya allowed herself to be cradled.

Neither of them spoke for a couple of minutes. They held each other on the sofa, John fighting his impulse to kiss the top of Tanya's head, to smother her in kisses.

Finally, she looked up at him. "You're such a kind man, Mr Taylor – "

"John. Call me John."

"You're so understanding ... John. Not like my mum, or my boyfriend."

With these words, John realised where he was, who he was with, and the danger of his situation. He had been thinking of making love to a schoolgirl, his children's baby-sitter. He had barely been in control of himself, only just in check. What if someone had looked through the window at that moment, or his children had come downstairs? Slowly, without any obvious movement, he held Tanya away from him. He slid his hands from her shoulders and placed them on his knees, then leaned back into the sofa. "Is it boyfriend trouble? Is that the problem?"

She nodded and sniffed deeply, then raised her head. "He's going away, to university. He won't take me with him. He's going to leave me here, all on my own ... "

"You'll never be alone, Tanya. You'll always have friends, wherever you are. You're a popular girl, I'm sure."

"That's what I told myself: let him go. I can find someone else. There are plenty of other fish in the sea."

"Absolutely right. If he doesn't appreciate you, others will."

"So you think I ought to forget him? Let him go, if he wants to?"

John nodded. Then he gave her a broad smile and clapped her on the shoulder. "Come on. Let's get this show on the road. I should have been at June's ten minutes ago. Why don't you take Sally and Ross for a walk in the sunshine. It'll make you feel better and – " he glanced up at the ceiling, "they're suspiciously quiet up there. They could do with using up some energy or they'll never sleep tonight."

And nor will I, thought John, as he pulled Tanya up from the sofa.

He had hardly taken a step out of the front door and on to the path when he saw Mrs Clayforth waving and crossing the road towards him. He thought if he walked fast enough, he might make it to his car in time. But no; his neighbour arrived at the driver's door at the same moment as he did.

"Mrs Clayforth, how are you?" He tried to look as though he was in a hurry. He put his key in the lock, but she placed a hand on his arm to stay him.

"Angela. I said to call me Angela, John." She gave him a wide smile of coral lipstick, then she noticed the carrier bag in his hand. "Are you going out? What a pity. I wanted to talk to you about the fête next Saturday."

"The fête ... " John was thinking fast. He had a feeling the combination of a fête and Angela Clayforth would not be good news for him.

"Yes, it's the last one before they sell the manor house. You know Sir Charles Trington had a heart attack cutting the ribbon at the fête last year. Well, his wife's not all there – in the head, you understand – and they're putting her in one of those nursing homes. It's sad that we're going to lose the village fête, don't you think?" And she looked at him appealingly.

He was being set up for something, he knew. If only he could work out what was coming, he could take avoidance action. He played for time. "Right. Yes, great shame." He opened the car door and slid the carrier bag onto the passenger's seat.

"So, it's a special occasion. Everyone will be there, I'm sure."

"You could be right, Mrs – er, Angela." He couldn't get used to that name.

"So, just briefly – I won't keep you, John, if you're going somewhere – I popped across to ask if you'll be there, too."

John thought hard, computing as many possible outcomes to the situation as he could in that moment. "Well, I don't know ... That is, I hadn't thought about it. I – "

"Next Saturday. In the afternoon. I'll call for you at three. If the weather is like this, we'll have a glorious time – "

"No. Wait. I don't know if I can be there. You see, the children – "

"Oh, yes. Of course! It would be a lovely treat for your children. There's so much going on: the coconut shy and the tombola, guessing how many beans are in the jar, and Mavis Williams and Valerie Boyd always do the cake stall – "

He thought of Tanya, sitting on his sofa where he'd left her, his children playing at her feet. He had it: the best of all possible solutions. "Actually, Tanya's looking after the children. And we'll all be going to the fête together. She's been marvellous with the kids." He glanced back at the house. "She's looking after them right now. They love being with her. She's very good with them. I don't know what I'd do without her, she's been such a help."

A shadow crossed Angela's carefully made-up face, but disappeared in a flash. She smiled brightly again. "Well, we all do what we can to help you, John. You know that."

"I know. And it's appreciated. Now, if you don't mind, I must go to – "

Her manicured hand with its bright red nails darted out and touched his arm. The hand remained there. "You look tired, John. You're still not coping, are you?"

Poor man, thought Angela. He needs a good woman to look after him. And I'm the one to do it. I can hold him in my arms and kiss him goodnight, and then, in the mornings ... She wondered how John would look without his clothes on, lying beside her in bed. She imagined herself in the fuchsia-coloured organdie nightdress she'd bought the previous week, holding his head to her bosom while he slept with a contented expression on his face. She must have been smiling to herself. She heard John's voice saying something about his sister-in-law, how late he was and how she would be worrying about him. She felt his arm leave her hand. Angela blinked and returned to the present. She saw John slide into the driver's seat of his car and raise his hand in a casual wave.

"See you soon, Angela. Thanks for letting me know about the fête. Appreciate it." He turned the key in the ignition and the car coughed into life.

Angela stood on the driveway, waving as John backed onto the road. She was smiling at him, but she was thinking: that's not right. She had come over to him, certain he had not thought about going to the fête next Saturday. She'd expected to have him all to herself. She wanted to parade with him on the manor lawns, arm in arm, perusing the stalls, nodding to the neighbours. She wanted everyone to see she was there with him. She wanted to stake her claim on John Taylor.

The car disappeared around the corner of the Close. The noise of its engine faded and

Angela was left alone, at the roadside. A heavy feeling of acute disappointment came over her. The conversation had not gone according to plan. This wasn't the way it was meant to be. She crossed the road slowly, turning over different thoughts in her head as she walked. By the time she had swung open her gate and reached her back door, Angela knew what she had to do.

She went purposefully into the kitchen, lifted a thick recipe book off the shelf and thumped it on the table. She unhooked her apron from the kitchen door, looped it over her head and quickly tied a bow behind her. She opened the recipe book and ran her finger down the contents page. Her finger stopped about halfway down and she tapped on a chapter heading marked 'Special Occasions'.

Angela stood up and went to a cupboard and took out a frying pan. She began to hum softly to herself as she gathered ingredients from different shelves: herbs, spices, meat from the refrigerator. She smiled as she moved about the kitchen and her humming grew louder. She lifted a heavy casserole dish from a cupboard under the worktop, inspected it and placed it on the counter. Then she stepped back, hands on hips, and addressed the casserole dish. "Tonight, my dear, we shall dine in style, and then, my love, you will be mine."

Doreen looked up from her drink when she heard the back door slam. She listened to the movement in the kitchen, someone opening the fridge door. Thomas was upstairs doing his homework, she knew, and Stella was in her room, devouring yet another paperback and a packet of biscuits. It had to be her husband. But at this hour? She levered herself out of the armchair and stood, swaying slightly, and finished her drink. She went unsteadily towards the kitchen and stopped when she reached the kitchen door. Ray was sitting at the table, eating a sandwich and drinking a glass of milk. He looked up when he saw her standing there, leaning against the door frame.

"You're early," said Doreen, making an effort to get her tongue around the words.

He didn't answer immediately. He took another bite of his sandwich and drank half the tumbler of milk. He gazed ahead of him, avoiding having to look at her flushed features, her dishevelled hair and clothes. "I'm going out again. I want to talk first."

With these words, Doreen's heart soared. Here was her husband, home at a reasonable hour, wanting to talk about their problems. She pushed off from the door jamb and made it to the kitchen table. She fell into the chair opposite

Ray and placed her arms on the table to keep herself upright in her seat. Only then did Doreen realise she needed another drink, something to steady her nerves for the discussion ahead. She hauled herself up and started for the cupboard where she kept the wine and sherry and vermouth. Ray's arm shot out and clamped on hers. He made eye contact with her for the first time that evening, but with a hostile expression on his face.

"Sit down, Doreen. Lay off the sauce for five minutes. I won't keep you from your precious booze for long. I'll only say this once."

Doreen felt herself begin to tremble. Surely, it wasn't the shakes? She needed a drink; her body was crying out for a glass of something alcoholic. She looked at the kitchen cupboard. If she could just pour herself one glass ...

"Here," said Ray, waving the last of his tumbler of milk in front of her face. "Drink this, instead."

She shook her head and batted the glass away with her hand.

He finished the milk. "Yeah, you're probably right. Your body would go into shock if it came into contact with something that was good for you."

"Let me get a drink," she started to get up again.

He pulled her down. "Five minutes, that's all it'll take. Starting now."

"Is that why you came home early? To talk about us?"

Ray wiped the crumbs of his sandwich from his mouth with the back of his hand, took a deep breath and regarded his wife. What a wreck of a woman, he thought. How on earth did we hit rock-bottom, like this?

He spoke as quietly as he could, trying to keep his voice even, trying to keep it from cracking. It was an emotional moment for him: the admittance of the failure of his second marriage. "I'm leaving you, Doreen. There's no good way of saying it. I'm leaving you now, tonight." He looked at her, searching her face for a reaction; the screaming torrent of accusations he expected. But Doreen had closed her eyes. It was as if, by closing them, she could block out his words. She opened them again, but said nothing, only stared at him, mute, dumb.

"I'm going upstairs to pack. Doreen, can you hear me? Are you listening? I said I'm moving out, this evening. I'm not going to tell you where I'm going. If you want to contact me, phone me during the day at the office."

Still, Doreen sat there, staring at him, as if uncomprehending. He scraped his chair back and got up to go. Suddenly, his wife flinched, as though she'd woken up from a bad dream. She lunged at him with both hands, grabbing one of his arms and holding on to him with manic strength. He tried to shake her off, but she held on, making a strange whining sound, her face convulsed.

"Let me go, Doreen. Don't make it any harder for either of us. It's over now. Let go!" He wrenched his arm away, violently, knocking her off balance and sending her sprawling across the floor.

She was moaning now; sobbing, spluttering, her face blotched and red, her eyes and nose streaming. She managed to prop herself up against a cupboard and sit upright on the floor, looking up at him with a frightened, wide-eyed expression. "Don't ... " she moaned. "Don't leave me, Ray. Don't leave us." Her head lolled to one side, then the other. "What about the children? Don't leave us ... " She let her head fall back and she closed her eyes, crying now. "Ray ... " she mewled. "Ray ... " And she stretched out both her arms to him.

He pulled his wife up and put her back in the chair. Her head fell forward and she laid it on the table, sobbing quietly, eyes closed. "I'm going upstairs to pack a case," he said in a determined voice. "Just some clothes. You can have everything else ... " But Doreen wasn't responding. He turned and went out of the kitchen and took the stairs, two at a time.

Ray discovered there wasn't much he wanted to take with him. Just the basics. He wanted to be out of the house as soon as possible. He felt low, a heel, a rat, everything that was despicable. It had taken him a long time, nearly a year, to reach this decision; to jettison all he had worked for a second time round, to start all over, yet again. For a long time, he'd asked himself: What's wrong with me? Why can't I settle with one woman? He had always been a roamer, as far as women were concerned, but he had meant to stay married this time, even if he continued to enjoy other women.

And, when Stella had been born, he'd been over the moon with happiness. They were good times, then. He'd have done anything for his wife and family. It was after Thomas arrived that he started to notice life at home wasn't the same. Doreen seemed unable to cope. He'd told her to go and see the doctor. He supposed, now, he should have given her more help in the evenings and at weekends, but his golf handicap was important to him. All his friends had golf handicaps.

He'd thought about it, long and hard. He hadn't taken the decision lightly to leave his family, no sir. He would provide for Doreen, give her the house and a regular income. And he would come and see the children, and take them out at weekends. Why, he'd seen a notice at the golf club, only a couple of evenings ago: there was going to be a fête up at the old manor, next weekend. He'd take Stella and Thomas along to that. He had felt good when he'd thought of it. It was the moment everything fell into place. All his vague plans for being with Anne suddenly seemed possible if he could take the children for days out, to fêtes and the seaside, to museums in London.

He closed the lid on his second case and flicked the locks. He lifted both cases off the bed and, taking one last look around the room, went out on to the landing. His daughter was standing there in the dark. He wondered if she'd been watching him. He hadn't bothered to close the bedroom door while he'd packed. He put his hand out to touch her cheek, but something stopped him. A kind of revulsion. She was a fat teenager and her expression was sullen most of the time. He had never wanted to be affectionate with Stella; he had never put his arms around her. He couldn't start now, not yet. Maybe, one day.

Ray walked past Stella. She turned and watched him go down the stairs. He set the cases by the front door, without looking back at his daughter. He went into the kitchen. Doreen was still slumped on the kitchen table where he had left her. He placed a hand on his wife's shoulder and shook her gently. She stirred. "Doreen? Doreen, listen to me. I'm going now. Wake up, will you?"

Doreen lifted her head and blinked at him. The light was too strong in her eyes. She could only make out the outline of her husband, a dark shape, surrounded by brightness. Her eyes ached and her throat was parched. She tried to speak, but her words sounded as though they were being drawn across sandpaper. "Ray, don't ... " she croaked.

His hand went lightly to her shoulder again. "It's for the best. It'll be better for all of us. You'll see." He squeezed the top of her arm. "Look after yourself, Doreen." Some hope, he was thinking. She's beyond the point of no return now. She's all washed up, out of it. Her drinking revolts me. I can't stand being in the same room as her. "I'll keep in touch, at work. I won't lose contact with you. I'll take the kids to that fête, next weekend. It'll be better, this way." He paused to let her say something, but she turned her head away from him. Her body seemed lifeless. He was glad he couldn't see her face. "So ... Well ... That's it, then. I'm going now. Say goodbye to the kids for me."

Stella watched her father from the top of the stairs as he opened the front door. She saw him put the two suitcases in the blackness outside, then turn and pull the front door to. She stared at the back of the door where her father had just stood. She thought of Neil, in his house just a few doors up the road and she wondered if she could leave, too. It seemed so easy: just pack a case and step out into the street. Walk away from all the unhappiness, and go and live with Neil.

The Carbonnade à la Flamande was ready by six o'clock. Angela had taken great care in preparing a strong beef stock, then adding brown ale, onions and garlic. She topped the dish with a crust of garlic bread and butter. It smelt delicious when she lifted it carefully from the oven with two thick cloths.

Leaving the casserole on the top to cool, she went to the front window and looked out across the street. He was back: John's car was in the driveway again. Now she would enjoy a long soak in the tub with her favourite bubble bath, then she'd style her hair the way they did it for her at Emile's on Fridays and she'd try out her new perfume. She would decide what to wear later, as the mood took her after she'd relaxed in the bath. She already knew what underwear she would put on. That had been the most important decision.

At seven o'clock, she was ready. Dressed in a dark red clinging dress; very feminine, she thought, and young in style. It wasn't the off-the-shoulder number she'd thought of wearing, originally, but it would slip down a fraction if she moved in the right way. And, after all, she had all evening.

The kids were in bed. He'd bathed them, played rough and tumble with them for half an hour, then read them a couple of stories. Finally, they'd grown quiet and, eventually, they'd fallen asleep. John didn't know where they got their energy from; he was exhausted. He went slowly downstairs, holding the banister for support. He was ready to collapse into an armchair and take forty winks, maybe more. He would make himself a sandwich later. He wasn't hungry right now.

As he went through to the sitting room, the stereogram in the corner caught his attention. It had been his pride and joy when he'd bought it, six months ago. He hadn't thought about using it since Susan had died. He remembered they'd taken the children with them to the big HMV shop in town and spent an afternoon choosing LPs, EPs and singles. They'd been delighted to find so much of their favourite kind of music. John had chosen some jazz records. He loved Dave Brubeck and Jacques Loussier and, also, Segovia. Susie's taste was more commercial. She'd chosen a Matt Monro LP and one by Andy Williams. For the children, they bought Peter and the Wolf, the Sorcerer's Apprentice and Lonnie Donegan singing My Old Man's a Dustman, Cumberland Gap and the Battle of New Orleans.

John smiled as he fingered the records, neatly stacked by the side of the walnut cabinet. It had been a great day out for them all, going up to London like that. They'd come home and played their music until late into the evening. And, when Sally and Ross were tucked up in bed, Susan had come down and put on the Matt Monro LP. They had held hands and danced, leaning into each other as Matt crooned 'My Love And Devotion', 'The Shadow of Your Smile' and 'Softly, as I Leave You'. They had smooched for an hour or so, then they'd gone upstairs to bed. Yes, it had been the perfect day. John flicked the records over, found the Matt Monro LP, took it carefully from its sleeve and put it on the turntable.

After a couple of tracks, he found himself sinking down in the armchair. He didn't mind. He was comfortable. He closed his eyes and thought about Susan. He found himself remembering the first time he'd seen her in the office, reaching into a filing cabinet, wearing a pencil skirt, a pink, V-necked jumper and dainty low-heeled shoes. She'd turned round and looked at him and smiled. And he'd smiled back, thinking how pretty she was. He would have spoken to her but Arthur Hayes had come in and started talking about last night's match on the television.

He'd asked Susan out the next day. He found out she wasn't engaged to anyone and that she lived at home with her parents. He was in a hurry to get to know her before any other bloke in the office did. He wanted to marry her, have kids with her. John smiled as he thought about it. What a lucky devil he'd been. There was Ian Stone and – what was his name? – Vic, yes, that was it, Vic Caulfield; they'd married the two other secretaries there. The three of them had got hitched around the same time. Well, Vic was on his third wife now; kids everywhere, costing him a fortune, and Ian, poor fella, he'd lost Iris to cancer. Then John remembered, he'd lost his wife, too.

But no one could take away his memories. He'd always have those pictures of Susie in his mind. Matt was singing 'You've Made Me So Very Happy' and John felt his emotions rising. He kept his eyes closed. He didn't want to cry. He wanted his happiness back. He wanted to resume his perfect life. He thought of Tanya: sixteen years old and crying her heart out over some boy. She hadn't lived the half of it, yet. Tanya would get over her first love, in time, and she'd marry someone else, who'd make her cry, too, probably. He'd never made Susan cry. At least, he didn't think so. He knew he'd made her happy; she'd told him so, just before she died.

The double chime of the doorbell cut across his reverie. John immediately had a sinking feeling. He knew who it was. He pulled himself up, out of the chair, and turned down the volume on the stereogram. He took a deep breath as he walked out of the sitting room and into the hall, towards the front door. He was becoming a little weary of Mrs Clayforth, in spite of her good neighbourliness, her kindnesses in thinking of him and the children with her home cooking. He hoped she wouldn't keep him long, tonight. He wouldn't invite her in. He would make it clear that he wanted to be alone this evening. If necessary, he would make it very clear.

CHAPTER 10

There wasn't a cloud in the sky on the morning of the garden fête at Hadham Manor. The whole of the village seemed to be milling about on the immaculate terraces, banging in tent pegs for the marquees, helping with the stalls, organising competitions and games, selling glasses of lemonade and squares of cake to families and friends as they arrived.

Mavis Williams and Valerie Boyd stationed themselves behind the cake stall. Both women had been making Dundees, Madeiras and other delights for over a week, carefully storing the fruits of their labours in airtight tins and baking batches of sponges and pastries until late the previous evening. Their stall had been placed on the second terrace, not far from the table where people paid their entrance fee, bought raffle tickets and wrote their names and addresses on chits for the balloons that would be released at the end of the fête.

"There now," said Mavis, moving a Victoria sponge a fraction so that it wasn't touching the cherry cake next to it. "I think we've arranged everything nicely."

"I hope the iced fancies don't dry up in the sun. I wish we'd asked for a canopy. We could do with some shade, don't you think?" Valerie looked up at the blue expanse of sky, shading her eyes from the glaring sun.

"Oh, I expect everything will go fairly quickly. Besides, they forecast rain for later, so it might cloud over soon." Mavis placed a square tin lid, full of small change, at the back of the stall next to a pile of cut up sheets of greaseproof paper. She stood back and surveyed the stall, one last time, to satisfy herself that everything was in order.

"Good heavens, Mavis," Valerie Boyd murmured in a low voice. "Don't stare, but look who's here; over at the entrance table. Unbelievable."

Mrs Williams moved her head, in a carefully casual manner, in the direction of the entrance to the fête. Ray Reynolds was paying for a wad of raffle tickets and distributing them to his children, Stella and Thomas, who received them silently, without smiling. He then offered some to his wife, who had been standing sullenly in the background. She shook her head and looked away. They didn't seem to be a happy family.

"Well, I never," said Mavis, moving the coppers around in the small change tin so that she looked occupied as the Reynolds family went slowly by. "Not that my daughter tells me very much these days, but she did say Ray had left Doreen. Maybe they've made it up; trying to get back together again. I must say, they don't look very happy about it." She glanced at the family as they moved towards the tombola. "I suppose they've got to make a start somewhere."

Valerie served two customers while Mavis scanned the terraced lawns for her daughter. Tanya had told her Mr Taylor wanted her to go with him to the fête, to help him with his children. Mavis was pleased that Tanya had stopped moping around the house, brooding over her quarrel with Neil Boyd. Valerie Boyd was a good neighbour and her eldest son was a nice boy, she thought. But Tanya was far too young to get involved with the opposite sex. At least, she didn't want her daughter ending up pregnant, as she had done with Jim. It was what Mavis feared most of all: losing Tanya to a young man, or the girl having a child of her own. She wanted to keep her daughter close to her for the rest of her life, if possible. They'd been so happy together when Tanya was a little girl ... But she mustn't think of that now, there were customers to be served. The garden was filling up. Heavens, what a turnout. Oh, there's that awful Mrs Clayforth.

"That must be your daughter, Mavis," Valerie pointed to the other side of the terrace. "By the Hoop-La, with Mr Taylor and his children. How's the baby-sitting job working out, by the way? Tanya hasn't been over to see Neil for a couple of weeks now. I must say, it's not a bad thing. Gives Neil a chance to concentrate on his studies – Oh, hello Irene! Isn't Jack with you? Yes, that one's a Dundee cake, a shilling a slice."

Mavis saw Tanya standing, holding little Ross Taylor's hand, laughing as John Taylor paid for a handful of hoop-la rings. The girl patted John on the back to wish him luck and took hold of Sally with her free hand. Together, the three of them watched as he tried to ring the prizes at the back of the stall. Ross was jumping up and down and pointing to a train on the highest shelf while Sally looked longingly at a doll with a gingham bow in its hair. Tanya crouched down to the children's level to watch John throw again. One of the rings fell over a small teddy bear and Tanya and the twins clapped and whooped for joy. John Taylor looked round, beaming, and he clapped his hands with them. Thought Mavis: they could be any happy family, out for the afternoon.

Someone else was watching John Taylor, from the other side of the lawn. Angela Clayforth had placed herself by the soft drinks stand and was sipping from a beaker of lemonade. Her face was like thunder, in spite of the sunshine. She had half-decided not to come. She had been hysterical last night. She had shouted, she had cried, she had screamed at him. What had started out as a very pleasant evening in the company of a single man had, somehow, turned into a nightmare of the worst kind.

It had begun well enough: Angela had rung the door at seven o'clock, holding the Carbonnade casserole in both hands, waiting for John to answer the door. But he didn't answer. She rang again, and waited. Finally, she put the casserole on the step and rang and rang, perhaps a little too insistently. She thought she saw a shadow through the frosted glass, on the other side of the door. Was he standing there? Was he deliberately making her wait on the step? When he opened the door, she gave him her biggest and best smile. "John! I've made you a wonderful casserole for tonight. Carbonnade à la Flamande, you'll love it!"

John stood there and blinked at Angela. He looked down at the lidded pot on his step; he hesitated. He seemed about to say something.

"Well, aren't you going to invite me in?" Angela bent and picked up the casserole and handed it to him. He fell back a step, holding the dish, still looking as though he wanted to speak, but couldn't. Angela thought how grateful he was probably feeling, how alone he must have been, another evening by himself. She stepped into the space he had created when he'd fallen back and she was soon in the hallway, hanging up the silk scarf she'd draped across her shoulders as a last-minute touch before leaving her house.

She had wriggled into the dark red number she'd decided to wear, but it had seemed a little tight, tighter than when she'd tried it on in the shop. Well, that couldn't be helped. Wear it, she would. It was low cut, which she liked. She had a good bosom, she knew. None of that flat-chested rubbish that you saw in the magazines, these days. Angela wanted John Taylor to know she was all woman. He was clearly the type of man who needed a lot of encouragement.

John had always seemed to draw back, gently, politely, whenever Angela tried to get close to him. This had happened in his kitchen, when she'd brought over the Osso Buco and accompanying rice dish, just over a week ago. He had been standing in a corner, leaning against the worktop, nodding and smiling nervously, as he always did, when Angela suddenly had a desire to be near him, in the same corner of the kitchen. She had inched closer to him. He had been unable to move, but he'd turned his head away from her and made some inconsequential remark about the tea caddy on the counter. It had been his mother's, apparently. That didn't interest Angela. But she'd backed off, for the moment.

And now, she went through to the kitchen again. John followed her, carrying the casserole. He placed it on the worktop. "Look, Angela. I don't know how to say this ... "

She put a finger to her lips. "Sshh," she whispered, conspiratorially. "Don't say anything. I'll just pop this in the oven, and we can go into the other room and have a drink while it's warming. I've put some vegetables in it." She lifted the casserole and placed it on the middle shelf of the oven and turned on the gas. "There, that's done," she turned and beamed at him.

"The thing is – "

"I know. You're a little lost for words, right now. That's the kind of person you are, John: too reticent to say what you feel. I understand. You're not a forward type of man – "

"Look, Angela. I appreciate all the cooking you've done in the last month or so, but – "

"Tell me about it while we're relaxing in the other room," said Angela, breezing into the sitting room. "I'd love a drink, John. What do you have?" She glanced at the long-playing records on the sofa, with the cover of Matt Monro's 'Moment to Moment' propped up where John could look at it from his chair.

He gave up what he was trying to say, for the moment. He came and stood at the door while she moved his LPs and place herself on the sofa. "Would you like a vermouth, Angela? Red or white? Something with it, or plain?"

"Oh, a little water or lemonade will be fine," she fluttered her eyelashes, smiling up at him.

John disappeared back into the kitchen, while Angela perused his record covers. She wasn't sure about the jazz; it seemed a little avant-garde to her. She had no idea who Segovia was; he looked foreign, so it wasn't surprising she hadn't heard of him. She didn't think Lonnie Donegan was quite the thing for a sophisticated evening, tête à tête, but Andy Williams and Matt Monro met with her approval.

She sighed contentedly and looked around the room. Here she was, spending her first evening alone with a man in – how long? – too many years. She remembered sitting on the sofa at Frank's mother's and holding hands with – No, no; she didn't want to think about Frank right now. Angela gazed around the walls, at the pictures, the book case, the dresser full of jugs and plates too rustic for her taste. She would soon change all that. Where would they live? In her house, or his? Angela's mind raced on, planning her future happiness, making minor adjustments, here and there, to accommodate some of his furniture and his children, although she didn't intend to have much to do with them.

What am I going to say to her? wondered John as he set out the tumblers on the worktop and splashed vermouth into each of them. How am I going to say it? He opened the children's bottle of lemonade and topped up the two glasses. I've got to make it clear. I've got to be firm. She has to understand that I want – no – need to be alone at the moment, with Ross and Sally, and, of course, Tanya. Yes, that's it: I can say it's just for the moment. Surely the woman can take a hint? She's lonely, that's her problem. Been on her own, over there, far too long. When did her old man die? Must have been about a year ago, I suppose. I didn't really pay any attention to it, only what Susie said. I remember now: Susan said she should invite Mrs Clayforth over sometime. She might have mentioned the woman was lonely, I have no idea.

John carried the drinks through to the sitting room and presented one of the tumblers to Angela. She took it with a gracious smile and patted the space on the sofa, beside her. John glanced at his armchair in the corner, hesitated, and perched next to Angela, sitting uncomfortably close to the edge of the seat.

"Cheers."

"Cheers, John." Angela gave an almost imperceptible shrug of her shoulders, hoping the top of her dress would reveal a little more of herself to her neighbour. John stared straight ahead, sipping mechanically at his vermouth. He had to do it tonight: he had to tell her, even though it would be awkward for both of them. He couldn't have this woman barging into his home every time she needed company.

Angela turned to face him, swivelling her hips and inching ever so slightly in his direction. "Shall we have some music, John?" She gave him a glossy-lipstick smile. John looked away. He fixed on the shelves of the bookcase. He tried to arrange the words in his head, to make a sentence: Why don't you get the bloody hell out of here, Mrs Clayforth, and stop pestering me?

"I'm very fond of Matt Monro, you know … "

He blinked and shook his head slightly. "Umm, what?"

Angela leaned across him, gently pressing her shoulder against his chest as she lifted up the LP the other side of him and waved it in the air.

"How about listening to this one?"

"Well, uh, no, not now, really"

Angela forced a tinkling laugh. "Oh, alright. Then how about this?" Again, she leaned into him as she reached over to pick up another LP. "Andy Williams. I adore Andy Williams. The song about watching the girls go by is so ... oh, I don't know ... so happy, don't you think?"

John finished his drink. He wanted another, badly. He took the record from Angela and put it on the lid of the stereogram. "Another drink, Angela? A top up?"

"Oooh, I don't know. What are you trying to do to me, John Taylor? Are you trying to get me tipsy?" She wagged a bright red-varnished nail at him. "Just a little one, then. The night is young, as they say ... "

Oh, Christ! John snatched up the glasses and bolted from the room. In the kitchen he leaned against the worktop, took several deep breaths then shook his head. Right, this has got to be it. Here. Now. Say it.

He poured more drinks and took them through. Angela was standing by the radiogram. She had the Andy Williams record out of its cover. She turned and smiled at him. "Do you dance, John?" She opened her arms wide, holding the long-playing record in one hand and its cover in the other, and swayed her hips at him. John placed the drinks on the low table. He sat down. He wasn't smiling.

"Sit down for a minute, Angela. There's something I'd like to discuss with you."

Angela's whole body seemed to lift an inch into the air. Her eyes widened and her waxy lips formed a large 'O'. She glided to the sofa and sat close to him, shoulders turned towards him, her head angled in a coquettish way. She looked at him expectantly, her face flushed with eagerness. "Yes, John? Tell me what it is you want to say."

"The thing is, Angela – " God, he wished she'd stop batting those false eyelashes at him; they reminded him of fat spiders trampolining on their webs. "I don't know how to tell you this … You've been so kind – "

Her hand, heavy bracelets jangling at the wrist, clamped on his knee. "Oh, think nothing of it! A little labour of – affection!" And she began to giggle in a girlish way.

"It's just that – well, I'd rather you didn't cook for me any more, Angela. No offence. Your cooking is – very nice, indeed. But I'd prefer it if you didn't keep calling on me, like this."

His neighbour's face froze in a wide-eyed expression: non-comprehending, non-believing, bewildered. "I don't know what you mean, John. You think I'm going to too much trouble, don't you?" She shook her head while attempting to smile. "But it's no trouble, believe me. I enjoy cooking for you. Really, I do – "

"No, that's not the problem, Angela." Her hand had loosened its grip on his knee and he took the opportunity to shift further along the sofa. "It's just that – and please don't be offended by what I have to say – "

"There's someone else, isn't there?" She regarded him with a sorrowful expression. "Is that what you're trying to tell me, John? You've met someone else! Is that what you wanted to say?"

It was John's turned to be bewildered. What was the woman talking about? He'd met someone who could cook for him, or what? It was clear that Mrs Clayforth's idea of neighbourliness ran to more than a casserole and a fireside chat. He seized on her words, her assumption; it was his way out. "Yes," he said. "That's right. I've met someone. I wanted to tell you." He looked up and saw she had tears in her eyes. The fat spiders were wet, bedraggled. Black rivulets had started to run from the corners of her eyes, down her rouged cheeks. "Here, let me get you a handkerchief – "

"No!" she hissed at him. Suddenly, there was a glint in Angela Clayforth's black-ringed eyes, a steeliness to her voice. She was struggling to maintain her composure while her world collapsed around her. She had planned so much: the candlelit dinners for two, the dinner parties for six or eight, the holidays abroad; the decorations for their home, the long nights spent in passionate love-making and the languorous mornings after. All her hopes were falling away with each sentence John Taylor uttered.

How could she face the world? How could she face Doreen Reynolds? And the embarrassment of it all: she'd told Doreen she would be bringing her new man to the fête on Saturday. No one should be treated in this way. No one. He had led her up the garden path, taken advantage of her generous nature. He had allowed her to build up her hopes, only to pull the rug from under her when it suited him. He had no more use for her now, she was surplus to requirements. She was sure he was laughing at her; feeling smug with himself, superior.

Angela rose and smoothed the skirt of her dress down over her knees. She pulled herself up to her full height and looked down at John, where he sat, looking uncomfortable. "I am not staying in this house a moment longer. You are a devious brute of a man, John Taylor. May you rot in hell for your sins!"

She strode towards the door. He got up and went after her, into the hallway. "No, wait, Angela. Don't take it that way. I didn't mean – What I meant was – I just don't want you to cook for me – for us – any more. It'd be better – better for you. Don't you see?"

Angela yanked her silk scarf off the peg and fixed him with a haughty look. "Don't think I will forget this, the way you've treated me, Mr Taylor. Don't think you can live in a small road like this and take advantage of your neighbours and expect to carry on, as usual. I can tell you, you can't. People will soon begin to talk." She waved the garish-coloured scarf at him and he flinched and stepped backwards. "Please open the door and I'll bid you goodnight."

"Angela, don't be like this. Can't we talk about this in a reasonable – "

His neighbour opened the front door, herself, and stepped out, into the fading light of early evening. "Bon appetit and goodnight, is all I've got to say." And with those words, Angela swept down the pathway. She marched across the road, head held high, looking neither left or right at any of her neighbours' homes. John stood and watched her stride down the side of her house and disappear through the back door. He let out long, deep exhalation of relief, shook his head slightly, and turned and closed his front door.

Doreen wasn't in the mood to notice Angela parading up and down the terraced lawns at the fête, or the new floral print dress her friend had on, or her wide-brimmed hat with cabbage roses fixed to one side. She trailed behind her husband and children around the various stalls and sideshows, taking little interest in the proceedings, her thoughts on what she could do to get Ray back and wondering who the woman was he had left her for.

Give him his due: he had kept up all his financial commitments to her and the children, so far, though he had only been gone for a week. Time would tell if he would be consistent in this, especially if the new love of his life started to resent such a large portion of his income going to support another woman. She wondered, not for the first time, when Ray would ask her for a divorce. It was the next step, the logical one, when a couple had parted.

Doreen noted that neither of her children had said anything about their father not living with them any more. They had not tried to sit down and talk things through with her; not a word of comfort or commiseration. Her daughter had maintained the sullen aloofness she had adopted two or three years earlier. Perhaps, thought Doreen, she had lashed out at Stella once too often in the past. The girl seemed to avoid her whenever she could, these days. They were not close, mother and daughter, and probably never would be.

Thomas had also withdrawn into his own world. He had his school friends, his school work, which he seemed to enjoy and have no difficulty with, and he had his sports interests. He seemed to spend more and more time, these days, playing rugby and cricket. And Ray had said something this afternoon about teaching him to play golf. Everyone in the family was coping with the new arrangement, except for Doreen. She was as distraught as she had been the evening Ray had walked out on her. She hadn't even seen Angela to talk things over. Not that she wanted to see anyone. She had tried to stop drinking again, one more time, and had failed. Now, she just wanted to lay down and die.

But she was here, putting on a brave face at the village fête, for the sake of appearances. Why was she bothering, she wondered? Who was she trying to kid? Somewhere, deep in her drink-addled brain, she'd thought the afternoon might bring her and Ray closer, might heal the rift a little, might start to build bridges. But he had virtually ignored her from the moment he'd called for them all at the house. He had kept up a patter in the car to Thomas about the British Open Golf Championship, which he was hoping to go and see later in the year with a couple of friends from the club. Doreen wondered if the new woman in her husband's life was a golf-player, too. Doreen had tried to learn, once, but had much preferred what the members called the nineteenth hole: the clubhouse bar. In fact, she'd enjoyed the bar far too much. After the time she staggered into the bar stools and sent both the stools and herself sprawling onto the floor, Ray had never taken her to the club again.

Ray was helping Thomas with the Lucky Dip. Stella was looking bored, not noticing anything very much. Doreen looked around at the crowds milling on the lawns. She asked herself if Ray's new woman was here, watching them trailing from stall to stall, so obviously miserable together. Doreen imagined some smart, attractive woman coming up to them and introducing herself, as pre-arranged with Ray. It would be the ultimate insult, the final degradation. Doreen cast about the terraces, full of smiling families with excited children, some of whom she knew. It was then she saw Angela, examining some trinkets at the handmade jewellery stand. Her friend was looking intensely at one particular necklace, holding it up to the light and turning it over in her hands. But the strand of beads didn't seem to be bringing her much pleasure. Doreen noted Angela was looking as miserable as she, herself, was feeling.

John Taylor was concerned about Mrs Clayforth but, after the way she had behaved towards him the previous evening, he thought it best to give his neighbour a wide berth, at least for the duration of the fête. He was happy to be out for the afternoon with his children, and Tanya was an added bonus. The girl was looking very pretty in a simple, sleeveless, pale pink cotton dress, her long blonde hair flowing over her slim shoulders and down her straight back. John had wanted to touch Tanya, to put his arm around her shoulder, to hold her hand and squeeze it. He reckoned this impulse stemmed from years of habit: holding hands with his wife whenever they'd taken the kids out for the day. It was natural to want to be close to someone. He was beginning to miss that intimacy, now that he was starting to come to terms with the loss of Susan.

For weeks, he had been numb. He'd had no desires or inclinations, as far as the opposite sex was concerned. He'd simply thought about Susan and the good times they'd had. He'd wallowed in self-pity, cried himself to sleep, seeing nothing but an emotional void stretching before him for the rest of his life. He couldn't imagine his future; he hadn't wanted to contemplate life without Susie. It had taken nearly two months for him to notice the world around him again, to rediscover the delights of seeing his children play and hearing them learn new words. Now he wanted to share that joy with someone. He needed to talk to another person about what he saw and thought, on a daily basis. He knew he was lonely. What he didn't need was the obvious come-on that Angela Clayforth had offered him the previous evening. He wanted a soft, gentle, unthreatening woman, as Susan had been.

Tanya held on to Ross's hand as he pulled her towards the Coconut Shy. He jumped up and down, excitedly. "Want one! Want one!" He jabbed his small finger at the coconuts positioned in metal rings on long poles of varying heights.

John came up behind them and placed a hand on Tanya's shoulder as he looked down at his son. "Say, please!" he regarded the boy with a semi-stern expression.

"Please! Please!" The boy bounced around them like a Mexican jumping bean.

Tanya laughed and flicked some strands of hair back over her shoulders. They fell across

John's hand and the lower part of his arm. They felt soft and warm in the sunlight. He wanted to keep his arm there, to prolong the closeness to her, but he knew he should move away. Reluctantly, he slipped his hand from the girl's shoulder and busied himself looking around for his daughter. Sally was a few feet away, with her back to them, clutching a stick of candy floss and watching a clown on stilts as he loped through the crowds, bending down to talk to children who squealed in delight.

"Coconut! Please!" Ross tugged at his father's hand, pulling him in the direction of the coconut shy and the crowd that had gathered around it.

"OK, young man. Let's see what we can do. Tanya, can you hold on to Sally for a minute. She's got candy floss all over her face, already."

John paid for six balls and stood in line, ready to take a crack at the dozen or so coconuts on the stand. When it came to his turn, Tanya stood with the twins on one side of the stall. She crouched down beside them and held a hand of each child. The children were wide-eyed and silent, their attention wholly focussed on their father as he pitched the hard balls at the exotic fruit held in the metal rings. John aimed the first ball at a coconut in the middle; he missed and the ball went sailing into the heavy tarpaulin at the back. He lobbed the next ball at the nearest coconut, in the front line. Incredibly, he missed that too.

A low moan came from the twins. "Oh, Daddy!" That was Ross's voice. John knew he had to win a prize for his son. The boy expected it; he believed his father could do anything.

The third ball dislodged a coconut on the left, but it remained in place, at an angle. "Bad luck, sir!" called out the stallholder. The fourth ball pounded the tenting at the back of the stand, just as his first ball had done. Two shots left. John carefully took aim. If he could hit the coconut he had already caused to tilt in its ring, it should, with luck, fall to the ground. The fifth ball narrowly missed its target, dropping heavily to the ground and rolling a little way before stopping dead. Last ball: John screwed up his eyes and concentrated all his attention on the coconut still sitting at a precarious angle. He drew back his arm and hurled the ball with all his might, and watched it make contact with the fruit, dead centre. The coconut seemed almost to jump in surprise, out of its ring, and land at the foot of the metal pole on which it had been sitting for half the afternoon.

A loud cheer went up from the small crowd which had gathered around the stall. John turned and, with his arms flung wide, went towards his children. "Daddy! You won!" Ross ran and threw himself at his father. John gathered him up and hugged him. Then he deposited the boy back on the ground and put his arms around his daughter, not minding the candy floss kisses. He turned to Tanya, who was clapping her hands and laughing and congratulating him. He put his arms around her and held her tight and rocked her back and forth. She seemed to yield to his embrace and he turned his head and planted a kiss on her cheek. It was over in a few seconds and they fell back, both of them laughing. John glanced around, covertly checking the reaction of the people standing there. That was when he noticed Angela Clayforth, glowering at him from the jewellery stand across the way.

CHAPTER 11

Neil had promised to man the Lucky Dip for a couple of hours while his father went across to help his mother taking money at the cake stall. Neil was happy to stand there, supervising the children plunging their small hands into the barrel, pulling out a package and feverishly unwrapping it. He enjoyed seeing their faces light up and hearing their whoops of pleasure as they tore off the last of the wrapping paper and found a toy car or tiny doll or a set of paints or coloured pencils. But the families who gathered around the Lucky Dip were only partially holding his attention. Whenever he could, at every interval between customers, he would slide his eyes in the direction of the Taylor family and Tanya as they made their way around the different stalls.

He'd been thinking about Tanya for most of his waking hours in the last couple of weeks. Try as he may, he couldn't get her out of his mind. His studies no longer interested him. He lusted after his ex-girlfriend, he admitted it to himself. He wanted her. He needed her. The very thought of her was sending him into spasms of longing, worse than any hunger he had known. His eyes devoured her as she crossed the lawns, holding hands with Mr Taylor's children and hugging them at intervals. When Mr Taylor had won that coconut, a couple of minutes earlier, and had thrown his arms around Tanya and kissed her, Neil had felt something like a knife stabbing him in the heart, as well as in the throat.

" 'Lo, Neil." A toneless voice cut across his thoughts.

" 'Lo, Stella."

She came and stood beside him, her head drooping slightly, as if she wasn't sure he would want her there. "How's it going, then?" she ventured.

"Alright." Neil continued to watch Tanya, though appearing to be glancing about the lawns in general. He hadn't even looked at Stella. He knew she would stand there, regardless of his off-handedness. He knew she liked him a lot. She often lingered around him, he'd noticed that, but her presence never bothered him, one way or the other. He was totally indifferent to the girl: he could take or leave her company. His preoccupation would always be with Tanya. She was the centre of his world, and he'd begun to realise that in the last couple of weeks.

They stood in silence for a minute or so. Then Stella said: "Did you know about my mum and my dad?"

"No. What?" He shaded his eyes and saw Mr Taylor buying ice creams. As the man distributed the cornets, piled high with whipped ice cream and chocolate flakes, Tanya said something and smiled at him, shyly. Neil guessed she'd made some joke about her figure; he wished he knew for sure. He wanted to know everything she was saying and thinking. Mr Taylor laughed at Tanya and shook his head, and his hand patted her hip for a moment, almost imperceptibly.

"They've split up. My dad's left us. He's found another woman. My mum's crying all over the place and it's driving me mad, she's so miserable all the time."

"I'm sorry to hear that," Neil made an effort to say. Tanya was enjoying her ice cream, running her pink tongue sensuously around the edges of the cornet.

"Yes. And now Mrs Clayforth's just gone over and butted in, talking nineteen to the dozen, like she does. I can't stand it, once she starts. I had to get away from them. My mum's getting fed up with her, too, I reckon."

"Right."

"She's chatting up my dad right now, making gooey eyes at him; stupid cow. He's just laughing at her, of course. She'll go for anything in trousers, that old bat."

"Right."

Tanya was moving off with the Taylor family, disappearing round the corner of a tall laurel hedge. Neil strained to catch his very last glimpse of her as she vanished from view. He sighed to himself and looked down at the Lucky Dip barrel, poked at the wood shavings on the top and bit his lip.

"She'll be after Mr Taylor, next. All that cooking she does for him. Trots across there with those casserole dishes, practically every night. I've seen her."

Neil took a deep breath and looked up from the barrel. "Probably do them both good. Give them some company in the evenings."

Just then, a father with three children, aged about ten, seven and four, bought three Lucky Dips and Neil busied himself watching them plunge their hands into the barrel and explore the wood shavings for one of the small gifts he'd spent the morning helping his father to wrap.

When they'd gone, Stella said: "Fancy going to see a film with me next Saturday, Neil? They've got 'The Ipcress File' on at the Astoria."

It was a film he would have liked to have seen, to have taken Tanya to. He would have sat in the back row with her and held her hand and kissed her, and she probably would have let him fondle her breasts. "No, I can't," he said. "I've got work to do. Got exams coming up, soon. And I've got to mow Mrs Clayforth's lawn for her, tomorrow morning."

"Well, maybe after your exams, then?"

"Right. After the exams," he said automatically, hardly hearing his own reply. Tanya was back, standing just across the lawn from them, looking over some paintings by a local artist and pointing out the different scenes to Sally Taylor, who was nodding her head.

Stella hugged herself and smiled. After his exams, he'd said. He said he'd go to the pictures with her. They'd sit there in the dark and, maybe, they'd hold hands. She looked up at Neil, ready to give him a grateful smile, but she saw his eyes narrow and focus on the stall across the way. She followed his gaze to John Taylor and his two small children, standing there with Tanya Williams. Stella couldn't help letting her smile broaden into a wide grin. Tanya would rue the day, she thought, that she ever let Neil go. The girl had told her she'd find someone else. Well, that couldn't be better news. With Tanya out of the way, the field would be clear for Stella to get to know Neil, to make him her boyfriend. She would be more patient with him than Tanya had been. She wouldn't stand in the way of his studies, either at home or university. And he would see that she was always there for him, and he would appreciate that, and come to love her for it. And they would get married and she would be so happy. They would be together, side by side, just as she was standing beside him now.

"You know what I'd really like?"

"What's that?" Ray asked, inclining his head towards Angela, an amused expression on his face.

"I'd love to look over the manor house," she said. "I mean, see all those beautiful rooms. It must be quite impressive inside."

They were walking, arm in arm, ahead of Doreen, who'd hardly said a word since her neighbour had joined them. Angela had suddenly darted over to them, just as John Taylor and his children and Tanya Williams had arrived at the Coconut Shy, next to the jewellery stall where she was standing. She'd immediately started talking to Doreen about the necklace she'd been looking at, and saying how well it would go with the dress she'd bought last week. Doreen was feeling so miserable, standing with

Ray, and yet not with him, she'd hardly responded to her friend, even though they hadn't seen each other for over a week.

"Then, let's go!" Ray squeezed Angela's hand where it lay on his arm. "Anything to please a lady. We'll ask for a guided tour. We'll say we're prospective buyers – "

"Don't be silly!" Angela tapped his arm, playfully. "They've already sold the place to a developer. They're going to pull it down and build new homes. I hope they'll be decent ones."

Ray had been relieved when Angela had joined them. He was already tired of the hurt silence Doreen had maintained all afternoon and by his children's lack of response to his attempts at conversation. Thomas had run off, as soon as he'd seen a boy who was in his class at school, and Stella had maintained her usual detached stare into the middle distance, avoiding eye contact with either of her parents. He had made an effort to visit his family this afternoon, when he would have much rather stayed at home with Anne or gone with her to the club for a round of golf.

Ray had vowed he would support and visit his children and keep an eye on his wife's drinking problem. He didn't think he was responsible for Doreen's alcoholism but he didn't want to be the cause of her deteriorating beyond the point of no return. He'd always hoped she'd get better. But it clearly wasn't going to be while he was around. He accepted he'd made a mistake, leaving his first wife for Doreen but, having done that, and having had children with her, he wasn't going to leave her without some sort of support.

And Anne had been so good about that. They had known each other for five years now, and she'd never complained when he'd had to go home or spend time with his family over Christmas and for birthdays. It was Ray who'd become less enthusiastic about being with his wife and children, not Anne. Especially since Doreen's drinking problem had not improved. It had become a vicious circle: Doreen drank, so Ray was inclined to stay away; Ray stayed away, so Doreen drank. One of them had to get off the merry-go-round, and it didn't look as though it would be his wife.

Ray was so happy with Anne. Her house was a haven of calm, a nest of love and affection. But, just one hour back in Hadham with his wife and kids, and Ray was feeling depressed already. Angela Clayforth's talkativeness was the perfect antidote for the afternoon. He'd never taken much notice of Angela and Frank Clayforth, or Angela on her own when he'd come home lately and found her in his sitting room, deep in conversation with Doreen. But he was grateful for her company to see him through these next few hours of familial duty. Then he'd make his escape back to Anne and they'd go out for a good meal, and this whole unsavoury afternoon would be virtually forgotten.

"Let's walk around the house and see if we can look through the windows," he suggested to Angela, hoping Doreen would stay where she was and give him a break from her reproachful and morose gaze. "They can only tell us to go away. Come on, my dear. I must say, you're looking delightful in that dress."

Angela giggled, a little too loudly. One or two people looked round at the pair of them, still arm in arm. Who cares, thought Ray; I'll be out of this place soon. But Angela cared a great deal who had heard her. She particularly wanted John Taylor to hear. She desperately wanted him to see she could have a good time without him, that he hadn't devastated her with his words the previous evening. She hadn't realised, until last night, how much her daydreaming about John Taylor had taken over her life. She'd been so sure he would fall in love with her and rescue her from the loneliness of widowhood.

Angela needed to feel loved, and she needed a man to love. She had wanted John to love her but, apparently, he had someone else in mind. Angela wondered, for a moment if the new person in his life could possibly be the Williams girl. They had looked happy enough together this afternoon, particularly when he'd won at the Coconut Shy. Tanya Williams was wayward enough to try to entice him, thought Angela, and she had youth on her side. Angela was older than John, but she felt she had other qualities: maturity, an adult approach to life, and experience, both in the kitchen and in the bedroom. Why couldn't John see that she, Angela, was the perfect replacement for his late wife? Well, perhaps he would see it, in time. And she could wait; she had time. She had too much time, in fact. She was lonely, and she didn't think she could bear it much longer.

Tanya was watching Neil through lowered lashes. She had been glancing at him, surreptitiously, from the moment they'd arrived at the fête. She'd smiled and laughed with John Taylor and his children and she'd been enjoying herself, a little. But all the time she was conscious of Neil, stationed by the Lucky Dip on the lower terrace.

She had imagined she would be over Neil Boyd, by now. After all, she'd only intended to use him to help her leave home, to get away from her suffocating mother. True, she'd enjoyed making love with him. And it had been wonderful, the way he'd responded to her; how he'd worshipped her body, and his obvious delight in giving her physical pleasure. What more could a girl want? This was where her plan had misfired: she had only meant to have fun with Neil on a temporary basis. But, somehow, he had got under her skin, into her system. He had penetrated her heart, her soul. Tanya ached for Neil. She knew now that she cared deeply for him, that she loved him, that she would never be happy until she was back in a relationship with him. She'd lain awake for nights, wondering what he was doing, worrying that he would find someone else. If he would just give her sign, a word, just an indication that he still liked her, she would run straight back into his arms and cover him with kisses and never leave him again.

"Would you like a cup of tea, or a lemonade, Tanya?" John Taylor put his arm around her as he spoke. He was always doing that, thought Tanya, with some irritation. Always touching her. It was friendly but, for some reason, she didn't feel like being friendly today. Still, she had to keep up appearances. At any moment, Neil might look up and see her. She didn't want to appear to be miserable. Her pride wouldn't allow her to give herself away. Also, she felt a little angry, frustrated: she was supposed to be going out with Marcia Ackroyd's brother's friend, by now. Marcia had practically guaranteed it; said she had it all set up. But Roger Stowe had been away on an engineering course, almost since the day she had split up with Neil. Tanya wondered if it was simply boredom that had turned her longing to be with Neil, once more, into an obsession.

"A lemonade would be fine. What about you, Sally? Ross, would you like an orange drink? Don't pull the chair away from Sally like that. Ross, behave yourself. Come back here!"

"You'd better go and get him," John said to her. There was that hand again, touching her. Tanya didn't like it, at all.

"He's hiding behind the hedge. I can see him!" shouted Sally, pointing in the direction of the bushes they'd walked by, a moment ago.

Tanya got up and took the path back to the lower terrace. There was Ross, crouching behind some low branches, imagining, like an ostrich with its head in the sand, that he couldn't be seen. "Come along, little man." Tanya held her hand out to him. As she spoke, she glanced across the lawn to the Lucky Dip. Neil was standing there, talking to Stella Reynolds. She was smiling shyly up at him, regarding him with doe eyes. But Neil wasn't looking at Stella as they spoke. He was staring down into the Lucky

Dip barrel and knocking the toe of his shoe against its base in a bored or, maybe, nervous fashion; Tanya couldn't tell.

"No! I want play hide-and-seek! I want you to play with me!" Ross's demand cut across her thoughts.

"Come and have a lemonade first. Then we'll see, after that." Tanya yanked at the boy's hand and pulled him back onto the path. Stella Reynolds, she thought as she led Ross back to the tea tent where John Taylor and Sally were sitting. I hope she doesn't think she stands a chance with him. On the other hand, how much did she trust Neil not to grab the first girl who came along, just to spite her? Yes, but not Stella Reynolds, surely? Well, all things were possible.

John Taylor rose and pulled a chair out for Tanya. He seated his son next to him, placed a lemonade in front of the boy and smiled across at her. "It's been a wonderful afternoon, Tanya. I want you to know that. This is the happiest I've been for a long time. Really. And I know the kids are having a good time, too."

Tanya gave John a perfunctory smile.

"We must do this again: take the children out somewhere, maybe to the coast. You'd like that wouldn't you, Ross, Sally?"

"Yes!" chorused the twins.

John reached across and touched her arm. Tanya almost flinched, but managed to stop herself. And all the time she was thinking: if Neil goes out with Stella, I don't know what I'll do. How could he contemplate going anywhere near that big lump? But I bet she'll run after him now, and she'll probably wear him down, and that'll be that; I'll have lost him. There was a rumble of thunder in the distance. Tanya looked up and saw the sky to the West was full of black clouds. The wind had suddenly come up and she pulled at the low neckline of her dress in an attempt to keep her shoulders warm.

"Don't worry about your dress. You're looking good the way you are," said John, folding his arms and giving her an admiring look.

What am I going to do? thought Tanya, biting her lip. She was suddenly conscious of what she'd thrown away, all for the sake of winning a point in a stupid argument with Neil. God, I want him back. I don't want John Taylor and I don't want Roger Stowe. And I don't want Stella Reynolds butting in and taking what's mine.

Who does she think she is, parading arm in arm with my husband for all the world to see? Doreen muttered to herself as she made her way along the terrace path to the tea tent. She couldn't believe how insensitive her friend had been towards her. She fell heavily onto a folding chair at one of the tables and looked around, but Ray and Angela had disappeared from sight. They were probably around the other side of the house, by now. Angela had said she wanted to look at the manor house, close up, and Ray had seemed to latch on to the idea, immediately. He had almost dragged Angela across the lawn, leaving Doreen standing on her own, watching them depart. And her friend had been very willing, almost too willing, to go with him. The two had come together the moment Angela had arrived.

Doreen glanced at the other tables in front of the tent. Her eyes rested on John Taylor and his children, having tea with Mavis Williams's girl. They all looked happy enough, enjoying their glasses of lemonade. Doreen sighed. Was she the only one in the world who was miserable? Even her daughter seemed to have found someone to talk to. The girl had been standing by the Lucky Dip with Valerie Boyd's eldest son for nearly an hour now. Was he her boyfriend? She doubted it. She knew her daughter wasn't the most attractive girl around, and she'd thought Tanya Williams had something going with young Neil.

But perhaps that was over. The girl didn't seem to be very interested in Neil today. She had spent all her time with John Taylor's two children, who seemed to adore her. Doreen was sure that if Tanya had been a few years older, she would have suited John Taylor, admirably. They seemed to be getting along well, sitting there, smiling and laughing together. Doreen saw John reach out and squeeze Tanya's arm, and the girl had given him a big smile in return. Now, that would give Mavis a turn, thought Doreen; if her precious daughter were to take up with their neighbour. Doreen had always believed Mavis was too possessive about Tanya. She clung to her daughter, fretting each time the girl was out of her sight. It wasn't healthy, smothering the child, like that. It was natural for the girl to want to be with her friends, and enjoy the company of the opposite sex. Mavis was going to drive her daughter away, one day. Doreen was sure of it. And then the woman's whole world would collapse. She would have brought about the very thing she feared most, simply by putting her own needs above those of her child. Doreen shook her head. She'd have been delighted if Stella had found someone to be with, instead of slouching around at home with that miserable expression on her face all the time.

Brrr! She was starting to feel chilly, sitting alone at the table. Where were Ray and Angela? Surely, they should have walked around the old house by now? The wind was getting up; the sun had disappeared behind a range of dark clouds. Angela would get cold in that flimsy dress she was wearing, exposing half her bosom like that. Her friend had always been proud of her bosom. Personally, Doreen thought there was a little too much of it to be elegant or feminine. She'd asked Ray once what he'd thought about it. He hadn't seemed to know what she was talking about. "Men like woman with a bit of flesh on them," he'd finally mumbled from behind the paper.

"Yes, but Angela's a bit top heavy, don't you think?" Doreen had insisted.

"If you say so. I hadn't really noticed." The newspaper had rustled a fraction and that had been the end of the conversation.

But Ray must have noticed that bosom, Doreen thought. He had been humouring her, that was all. He hadn't wanted to talk to her, as usual. Angela's bust wasn't something one could avoid noticing. The woman wore those awful plunging necklines, nearly all the time. So ridiculous at her age, mutton dressed up as lamb. She'd even worn a low-cut dress, in black, to Frank's funeral, Doreen remembered. Yes, she'd forgotten about that. It had made one or two of the male mourners smile, though not their wives. That was the trouble with Angela, she said to herself: the woman was too forward, brazen almost. Why, she'd practically flung herself at Ray, this afternoon.

A rumble of thunder meant that rain was on its way. Doreen saw John Taylor get up from his table and shepherd Tanya and his children away, presumably to his car. She wondered what Mr Taylor had thought of Angela's plunging necklines when she'd arrived on his doorstep, night after night, with those casseroles she'd concocted. Funny, Doreen had imagined Angela would have been with John Taylor at the fête today. After all, she'd said she'd be here with the new love of her life, and sounded quite excited about it. Well, she was wasting her time with Ray; he'd already moved out and was living with someone else. But Doreen hadn't seen Angela for a few days, so hadn't had a chance to tell her Ray had left. She'd been hoping she could find out who the woman was, and be able to discuss the situation fully with her neighbour. Normally, she saw Angela on Friday evenings but, last night, she had been alone with a bottle of fortified wine.

She would give Ray and Angela five minutes more, then she would go home and leave her friend to call round later. Then she would tell her about Ray. Although, perhaps Angela already knew he'd left her. Maybe that was why she'd come on so strong with her husband this afternoon. Perhaps she thought Ray was available. Come to think of it, Angela had always flirted with Ray when he'd come home in the evenings and found them talking over a few drinks in the sitting room. Ray had always had time to swap a line or two of banter with Angela. Maybe he was ogling her bosom at the same time. It wouldn't have surprised Doreen.

Suddenly, she sat up straight. Rigid. A terrible, nightmarish thought flashed through her mind, like a hot knife searing her brain. What if Ray had left home with Angela? No, that wasn't possible! It was entirely possible. Why not? Angela hadn't been around for a few days. And neither had Ray. They were certainly together this afternoon and delighting in each other's company. So, that was it: Ray had left her for Angela, the neighbour she had always trusted. Her friend had been making up to her husband whenever she'd had the opportunity to do so. Yes, it all made sense now: Angela staying away last night, not wanting to confront her. Why, her friend had been laughing at her, all along. And Ray, as well. He'd known his wife was going to be in for a shock, one day soon.

Doreen slumped back in the wooden chair. She no longer felt the chill in the air. She had even broken out in a sweat. God, she needed a drink. She must get home. She couldn't sit here, waiting for them both to saunter round the laurel bushes and say they had something to tell her; that now was the moment for her to know they were in love. Of course! How could she have been so blind as not to notice. Ray hadn't had to look far for his next dalliance. He had always been a Don Juan; that was how Doreen had taken him away from his first wife. And Angela had been there for the taking. Perfectly convenient for the both of them. Oh, you fool! You stupid woman! You were so busy feeling sorry for yourself, you hadn't noticed what the problem really was. It was right there, under you nose. Did Stella know? And Thomas? What about everyone else in the Close? Valerie Boyd? Mavis Williams? Oh, God; please not Mavis Williams.

Doreen looked around her at the deserted tea tables, the wind whipping the edges of the checked tablecloths. The two women behind the counter were watching her, she felt sure. She stood up and looked at her watch. Angela and Ray had been gone for nearly an hour. It certainly didn't take all that time to walk around the manor house, no matter how many windows they peered through, no matter how interested in the internal decor Angela professed to be.

She would go home. She would lock herself away. She felt so ashamed of herself. Everybody must have heard about Ray and Angela. She was the last one to know. The wind was getting up now. The sky had become dark, full of ink-black, louring clouds. The tea ladies were closing up the tent and people were scurrying in different directions across the lawns, heads down, clutching the fronts of their jackets. Doreen hurried back to the lower terrace to see if Ray and Angela had gone over to talk to Stella or had found Thomas and his school friend.

But, no. The gardens were deserted. Everyone seemed to have packed up their stalls, knowing a serious thunderstorm was on its way. Doreen turned in every direction, hoping to see her husband sheltering under an awning, waiting for her so that he could walk her home. A large spot of rain landed on her arm. Then another, and another, coming fast now, pelting her like tiny balls of ice. Doreen backed away from the terrace, holding her hand above her head in a futile attempt to ward off the weather. She walked unsteadily in her high heels along a side path that led to the car park, heavy droplets streaming down her cheeks, which could have been rain or tears.

CHAPTER 12

When Neil arrived to clip Mrs Clayforth's back hedge the following morning, the house was unusually quiet, almost as if no one was there. Normally, the woman had the radio blaring in the kitchen; not forgetting what he'd seen up the ladder when he'd been cleaning her bedroom window. He rang the side bell for the third time, and was just thinking about going round to the front, when the back door opened and Mrs Clayforth's drawn, red-eyed face appeared in the crack of the door.

"Oh – Of course ... " She gave a slight sniff and dabbed her nose with her hand. "Come in, Neil. I forgot today's Sunday. Have a cup of coffee with me." Her voice wavered. "I need someone to talk to."

Neil was used to having a coffee with Mrs Clayforth before he started work. She liked to talk, and he always listened and ate her biscuits. But, today, she didn't sound particularly animated and she didn't look very happy. She was still in her long padded dressing gown. She didn't look as though she'd slept well, if at all.

But it wasn't his place to comment. Neil went through to the kitchen and sat down, hands clasped under the table, and waited for his coffee. Mrs Clayforth kept her back to him while she busied herself with the kettle. Occasionally, he heard her snuffle but she didn't turn round and talk to him, as she usually did.

"Here you are, young man," she passed him a mug and sat down opposite him. "Excuse me not being dressed, but I've had a bad night, and I'm so ... " her voice trailed off. She dropped her head into her hands and let out a small sob.

Neil had no idea what to say. He took a swig of his coffee and lifted a couple of chocolate biscuits from the plate in front of him. He heard Angela take a deep breath, then sigh.

She lifted her head and tried to smile at him. "At least you're here. Not everyone's deserted me. You're the one person I can rely on. I know I can talk to you." Her eyes began to water again and she dabbed at her nose with a sodden handkerchief. "More biscuits?" She held the plate towards him.

"No, thanks. I'd better start work in a minute. I'll just finish this." He gulped down the last of his coffee and rose, scraping back the chair.

Angela's hand shot out and caught hold of his own. "No, don't go. Stay here for moment.

The hedge can wait. I'll pay you anyway, never mind that."

Neil slowly sat down again, not sure how to reply. He sat there and waited. Clearly, the woman was upset. He didn't think it had anything to do with him. Still, if she said she was going to pay him for sitting and listening to her troubles, who was he to argue? But he wasn't sure his mother would approve of him lounging about in Mrs Clayforth's kitchen.

In fact, his mother had become less sympathetic towards the woman, lately, than she had been. She had even suggested to Neil that he give up doing jobs for their neighbour at weekends, now that his exams were nearly upon him. And he'd overheard her talking to his father while they were watching a television programme, the other night. She'd been telling him she thought Mrs Clayforth was bothering Mr Taylor too much. Almost chasing him, she said; taking over those meals, practically every evening. He heard his father murmur in the right places in the conversation, without expressing any opinion himself.

Perhaps his mother had already spoken to Mrs Clayforth about him stopping work and concentrating on his studies. He knew that if he did give up jobbing for the woman, he would only spend more time thinking about Tanya. He had woken up that morning, driven practically mad by his desire for her. It was all he could think about as he'd got ready to come across to Mrs Clayforth's. So, he was happy to listen to the woman spout on about her own problems. He'd even try to listen to her and sympathise. He felt a bit sorry for Angela Clayforth. She wasn't a bad old stick, for an older woman.

"I saw you doing the Lucky Dip, yesterday," she was saying to him. "I hope you made some money for the Trust."

"Yes. My father's writing a cheque to The Wildlife Trust today. My mum made a fair amount from her cake stall with Mrs Williams, too, and the money's all going to be sent together, in one donation."

"It was nice to see so many people there," continued Angela. She was looking less upset now, her face had brightened. Neil thought she didn't look too bad in the morning light without makeup. He smiled at her, hoping to cheer her up a little. He supposed he felt sorry for her. She had always been friendly towards him. He didn't like to see her looking sad.

He said, "I saw you with Stella Reynolds' dad, walking around the manor house. Stella came over and talked to me for a while." He didn't think he should mention Mr Taylor, if his mother was right about Mrs Clayforth chasing the guy. Besides, it might mean mentioning Tanya, who'd been with helping out with his children. Neil didn't want to go there. His feelings were too raw.

"Yes. We were interested in seeing the inside of the old house before they knocked it down."

"Is that what they're going to do with it?"

"They've sold it to a developer, so I've heard."

They sat in silence for a minute, having run out of things to say about the manor house. Then Angela cleared her throat and said, "It's a pity it rained when it did. I wanted to come over and talk to you. But we bumped into your father, getting fresh change for your mother's stall and we chatted with him for about half an hour. When we came back, everyone had gone. The lawns were deserted and it was pouring with rain. Ray – Mr Reynolds drove me home to save me getting wet. It was kind of him. Did you know he's left his wife?"

Neil nodded. He wasn't sure he should be discussing such things with another adult, just yet. He was seventeen years of age, but he wasn't sure how grown up that made him in the eyes of others. Finishing school, going to college, these were milestones on the way to adulthood. And he had made love to a woman, already. That

Tanya was a woman, he had no doubt. His mind clicked back: he was lying beside her in their camp in Hadham woods. Now he was pressing against her, mounting her – Mrs Clayforth was talking to him, saying something about Mrs Reynolds.

"Of course, it's miserable, being left on your own. A woman can get so lonely, you know. I've been on my own for over a year now and, Neil, I can tell you, it's no fun." She looked at him, mournfully, and shook her head. "No fun, at all." Her hand closed over one of his. He had forgotten to keep them under the table, as he usually did. She squeezed his fingers. He didn't like to draw his hand away.

"Yes," was all he could think of to say. He wondered when her knees would begin to press against his, as happened every Sunday morning over coffee. But it didn't happen. She simply held his hand in hers.

"Of course, you're young. Look at you. You have your youth and your whole life before you ... "

"You're not so old, Mrs Clayforth – "

She beamed at him. "Call me Angela," she said, her voice suddenly sounding more positive. "You don't think so?"

"No, you're – well, you're a nice lady."

She put her head to one side and smiled brightly at him, the sunlight streaming into the kitchen and lighting up her face.

"You really think that?" She was still holding his hand.

"I've always thought that." He was pleased to have cheered her up so quickly.

"Really?"

"Yes, of course. I always thought you were a – a nice looking woman." He nodded to confirm his words.

Her other hand reached across the table and clasped his. "You're so sweet to say that, Neil. I never knew. All this time ... " She was looking at him, her eyes sparkling now.

They sat in silence again. Neil felt obliged to say something else. He was pleased he could make her happy. A job well done, he reckoned. "And you looked pretty good when you were dancing the other day. I mean, when I was cleaning the window, and all that." He wasn't sure he should have mentioned the incident, but he'd run out of topics to talk about.

Angela withdrew her hands, slowly. She was looking at him in a strange way, he thought. She got up and came around the table and stood beside him. To his surprise, she began unbuttoning her dressing gown. She let the garment fall to the floor. He felt her take hold of his head in her hands and, next thing, she was pressing his face into her big pillowy breasts. He realised, straight away, that she didn't have any underwear on, but he didn't pull his head away. He did nothing to discourage her. Instead, he lifted his hands and placed them on her hips. He felt her body give a small shudder of delight. And he was aware of his own sensation of pleasure, too.

He pushed back his chair and stood, looking at Angela, waiting for her next move, willing to be led. She put her face close to his and pressed herself against him. Then she kissed him, full on the lips. He responded, leaning into her. His breathing changed. She ran her hands over him and kissed him again, this time in a long, passionate embrace. When Neil felt Angela moving against him, it excited him even more. He pushed his tongue into her mouth and they remained locked together, in the middle of the kitchen, exploring each other for a full ten minutes.

Gently, Angela broke away from him and, with a knowing smile, took hold of his hands and pulled him towards the door. She led him out into the hall and up the stairs to her bedroom, pausing at the door to undo the ribbons on her negligée. Neil cupped her breasts with his hands and lifted them and kissed them.

Locked in an urgent passion, they manoeuvred their way towards Angela's giant-sized bed. Neil felt his shirt opening as Angela's hands moved quickly down the front of him. He loosened his belt, then his trousers. He slid Angela's negligée off her shoulders.

She stood there, naked, in front of him; her arms outstretched, inviting him into her bed. Her body was not unattractive. It was well-proportioned, she had curves in all the right places. Perhaps her breasts were a fraction low and her bottom was fully-rounded, rather than pert, but Neil wanted Angela very much at that moment. He was out of his clothes in a couple of seconds and they were writhing on the bed together two seconds after that.

"Slowly," Angela moaned in a low voice. "There's no hurry. We have the whole morning."

Neil tried his best to curb the urgency he felt. He half-succeeded. He buried his head in her breasts, then between her legs, until she began to move in a rhythmical fashion. Then he was inside her and she was clinging to him, pulling him deeper into her body. When he heard her cry out: a long, gasping, animal sound, he abandoned all restraint and shouted out loud with her. As their cries subsided and their movements lessened, they clung to each other, still gasping for breath, still kissing. Then their moans of ecstasy eased into sighs of pleasure, followed by slow, deep breaths of satiated desire.

After a while, Neil disengaged himself from Angela's voluptuous body. He rolled over and sank his head into the mountain of perfumed pillows at the head of the bed. He lay there, looking at the ceiling, marvelling at the morning's events. He felt a contentment he hadn't experienced in a long time. He stretched out a hand and laid it on Angela's soft stomach. She shuffled her body closer to his and her hand rested on his chest. They lay there for a long time, not moving, not talking. Neither of them had anything to say.

Finally, Angela murmured. "You're an excellent lover, Mr Boyd."

Neil turned his head and smiled at her. "You're excellent, yourself, Mrs Clayforth. The best."

"You mean that?"

"Of course."

Angela propped herself up on an elbow and looked at him. She laid a finger on his shoulder and said in a playful voice: "Better than that girl you've been seeing – what's her name – Tanya Williams?"

Her words were a bolt from the blue. He hadn't expected her to mention to Tanya. After all, he had just made love to this woman. Though he supposed everyone in the Close knew about him and Tanya. It was the last thing he wanted to discuss right now, especially as his relationship with Tanya had come to an end.

He leaned across and kissed her. "You're the best."

She gave a girlish laugh and snuggled down, pulling him with her. They wrestled under the sheets for a moment, then Angela said: "You're not seeing her any more, are you?"

He lifted his head and looked at her. "Who?" He knew very well who she was talking about, but he really wanted to avoid the subject.

"You know," Angela gave an impatient snort. "Anyway, she's taken up with John Taylor, opposite. Didn't you know? Did you see them at the fête, yesterday? Love's young dream ... "

Neil moved away from her and lay on his back, studying the ceiling. He couldn't believe what she was saying to him. His emotions were in turmoil. He was having to view the situation from another angle, for the first time. He had spent the previous afternoon watching Tanya and the Taylor family, but he'd never imagined the kind of thing Angela was telling him.

Yes, he'd seen John Taylor pat Tanya on the back a couple of times and, of course, when he'd won that coconut, they'd all shouted and hugged each other. But never, in his wildest dreams, had he imagined Tanya was having an affair with their neighbour. It didn't seem to fit: Mr Taylor was kind of old – well, not young; not their age, at any rate. When had this begun? Was it when Neil was still going out with her?

He closed his eyes and tried to think of any signs he had missed, any clue to Tanya's fondness for the man whose children she baby-sitted. Nothing there. Tanya had always been enthusiastic in their love-making. She'd been upset when he'd said he needed to spend more time studying. She'd been distraught when he'd told her not to follow him to university. And now, she'd switched her affections to John Taylor, just like that. He had nothing against Mr Taylor, but he couldn't believe Tanya could transfer her feelings to another man in such a short period of time.

"You're not still seeing her, are you?" Angela's voice interrupted his thoughts and brought him back to reality; to the cream and lavender decor of the bedroom, the wide, softly-sprung bed, the warm body laying beside him. "Are you?"

"No." What business was it of hers, anyway, who he saw? Angela wasn't his age, she wasn't his type. She was just there, and so was he, and something had happened, and it had been a good roll in the hay, that was all.

"Good. Then I've got you all to myself," she purred, running her painted fingernails up and down his chest.

He lay there quietly, letting her caress him, trying not to think of anything in particular. He would sort out his feelings about Tanya and Mr Taylor later. Too much was happening to him, right now. Angela pressed herself against him. He responded. They began to move together, to explore each other, all over again. Then Angela rolled her curvaceous body on top of him and smothered him with her generous bosom. He could see nothing, he could hear practically nothing, and he thought of nothing except making love to the woman, one more time.

Stella had never been so happy. Neil had spoken to her, and only her, for practically the whole afternoon. At least, it had seemed like the whole of the fête. And she had helped him bring the Lucky Dip into one of the marquees when it had begun to rain.

Tanya hadn't reappeared with Mr Taylor and his children after they'd gone over to the tea tent. Stella supposed they had gone straight home. She had stood with Neil, by the entrance to the marquee, waiting for the cloudburst to end. She hoped he'd suggest walking home with her, and then they could really talk to each other, without all these people milling around. But he had said something about finding his father to sort out the Lucky Dip takings. He'd pushed off from the post he'd been leaning against and left her staring at the rain, pounding the lawns and paths, while he disappeared into the dark interior of the tent, looking for his parents.

Not since they were children, playing in Hadham Woods together, had she spent so much time alone in Neil's company. She was glad Tanya and Neil had broken up. She realised now, it was what she'd always hoped for. Stella lay back on her bed and let her imagination wander wherever it chose to go. She could picture herself with Neil in the woods, just walking together and talking, holding hands. Then they would sit for a while on the soft grass, still deep in conversation. They would lie back with their heads close together on the cool earth and, then, they would kiss. He'd hold her in his arms and she would bury her face in his broad chest and listen to his heartbeat. It would be pounding because he'd be excited at being near her.

And he'd want her, and she would want him. They'd lie there, holding each other and kissing with their tongues, like they did in the novels Stella got from the library. Then Neil would start to unbutton her blouse. Stella replayed this scene, several times. She would have on the new bra she'd bought in Marks and Spencer's in Croydon, the previous Thursday.

Then it would all become a romantic haze of indefinite detail. There would be an orchestra, somewhere in the trees, and the music would build to a crescendo as they kissed more passionately and rolled out of focus in the picture. They would be out of shot for a long while. Maybe a few waves crashing on a beach somewhere, but she'd think of something better, more original than that, next time. And, finally, Neil would stand up and gather her in his arms again for a last, passionate kiss before they had to go home for tea. He would tell her that he didn't want to leave her, that he couldn't bear being parted from her. He would make her promise to be his, forever. He would put his hand under her chin and tilt her head up, and ask: 'Stella, will you – will you marry me? Would you wait for me while I finish college?' And she would smile up at him, shyly, and timidly nod her head. Then he would let out a deep sigh of happiness and cover her face in kisses. And they would walk, hand in hand, out of the forest. Maybe lots of violins at this point. And he would kiss her goodnight, one last time –

There was a thud on her bedroom door. "Stella? Stella! What are you doing in there? It's time you took Mrs Clayforth's dog for a walk. Come on, you lazy, good-for-nothing girl. Get yourself up and dressed. Just because it's Sunday!" God, thought Doreen, plodding back down the stairs, what have I done to deserve such a girl? She's fat, she's lazy; she's not even intelligent. All she does is slouch around the house, all day, with a miserable expression. No wonder I always need a drink!

Doreen went into the kitchen and opened a wall cupboard. She selected a bottle of white wine. It was, after all, Sunday morning. Something light. It would simply give her a boost, help her through the morning without pulling the rug from under her. These days, Doreen found it didn't take much to get her drunk to the point of being incapable. She had to think about what she drank if she wanted to see out the day.

And today, she wanted to have her wits about her. Doreen had some thinking to do. What she'd witnessed yesterday afternoon, at the fête, had kept her awake all night. And she still needed to think, a lot more. One thing was sure, she wasn't going to give Angela the satisfaction of seeing she was upset about what she'd seen. Even if she'd cried buckets over Ray in front of Angela in the past, she wouldn't let the woman see she still cared about her husband. God, they must have been laughing at her for weeks, maybe months. For how long? Had Ray simply left their house and walked a few doors down the road, let himself into Angela's and got into her bed?

Well, Doreen would show them both. She could wait. She'd have the last laugh. Who was it who said, 'Revenge is a dish best served cold'? She would go round to Angela's, later on, with a bottle. She could imagine her so-called friend greeting her with a big smile on her face. She'd be looking very pleased with herself, imagining Doreen didn't understand the situation. She'd welcome her into her home. And Doreen would notice a small suitcase in the hall. But she wouldn't ask Angela about it. She wouldn't have to; she would know.

The best course of action was to take none at all, for the moment. Doreen popped the cork on the wine and filled a tumbler, almost to the top. Give them enough rope and they'll hang themselves, was another cliché that swirled in her brain as she drank deep and refilled her glass. Then she took the bottle and the tumbler over to the table, sat down heavily and put her chin in her hands.

Now, how would she work it? How could she break up this little love-nest, permanently? Doreen gulped down more wine and, suddenly, she found she couldn't see the situation as clearly as before. She'd woken up with a headache, but she nearly always had a headache and a raging thirst in the mornings. She resolved to sit down and plan how she would clip Angela Clayforth's wings, once and for all. Angela was a loose cannon, these days, who would take any husband who appeared to be half-available. Other women would thank Doreen for putting Angela Clayforth out of circulation, she was sure.

"But why don't you want to go?"

"I've told you. Don't you listen to anything I say?" Tanya, seated at her dressing table and brushing her hair with long strokes, turned to where her mother was standing at the bedroom door.

"But Mr Taylor's such a nice man, and those children would be a lot for him to manage on his own. It'll be fun to have a day at the coast with them all. You were enjoying yourself at the fête, I saw you. And when Mr Taylor won that coconut, you were as thrilled as he was – "

Tanya slammed down the hairbrush and turned to face Mavis again. "I think I'm spending too much time at Mr Taylor's, these days. I was only supposed to look after the twins until he got home from work. That was the idea. Remember?"

"But you can't let him down like this, Tanya. You've already said you'll go with them. And think of the children. They'll be so disappointed if you don't. You have to think of other people, sometimes. You can't always do what you want – "

Tanya swung back to the dressing table mirror and glared at her mother in the glass. "Oh, stop telling me what to do, woman! I'm sixteen years of age and I've nearly finished school. Stop interfering in my life, will you? Let me make my own decisions."

Mavis bit her bottom lip and held the edge of the door, looking at her daughter, reproachfully. She said in a small voice: "You wouldn't be able to behave like this if your father was alive. He'd have given you the discipline you need. God knows, I can't do anything with you ..." Her voice trailed off and she turned and left the room, closing the door quietly behind her, as if all the fight had gone from her.

Her daughter remained sitting rigid at her dressing table, staring into the mirror. She heard her mother go slowly down the stairs and into the kitchen. She heard the clatter of pots on the stove.

"I'm not putting up with this any longer than I have to," Tanya muttered to herself. She picked up the hairbrush again and started pulling it violently through her hair. After a couple of minutes of this, she suddenly stopped, put down the brush and regarded herself in the mirror. Her mouth began to tremble and her eyes filled with water. "There's nothing for me here," she breathed. "I'm sick to death of it all." She lowered her head and let her long hair slip forward and cover her face.

She knew the truth of it now: she missed Neil. She missed making love with him, she missed the way he held her. She longed to touch his firm, muscular body again. She had half a mind to go and knock at his door, right now, and tell him she would wait for him to finish university, if only they could get back together. A small part of Neil would be better than no Neil, at all. It wasn't just because he was her ticket out of here; there was much more to it than that, she realised now. Tanya took a deep breath, sat up straight and wiped her eyes. There was nothing for it: she would get dressed and go and see him. She couldn't carry on like this. She couldn't stand another moment without him.

Angela stood naked on the deep pile carpet, eyeing her body in the long wardrobe mirror. She turned sideways and ran her hands down her breasts, across her stomach and over her plump bottom. Not bad, she thought to herself. You're not in bad shape, at all, Angela.

She turned to face the mirror, full on, and put her hands on her hips as she swivelled her shoulders, first one way, then the other. It's no surprise that he wanted you, she smiled at the mirror. He's probably wanted you for weeks, months probably. After all, a woman with your experience knows just how to please. It must have made a change for him, after fumbling with that schoolgirl in the dark. Now he's tasted honey, there'll be no going back. She hugged herself and twirled about on the carpet. I've got a young man, now, to make love to me whenever I want. Well done, Angela; not many women can say that for themselves.

She looked at the rumpled bed sheets where they had lain, not an hour ago. There was an indentation in the large frilly pillow where he had laid his head and gazed at her. The outline of his body could still be discerned on one side of the soft mattress. She climbed back on the bed and lay where he had lain, squirming in the sheets with delight as she remembered how their passion had climaxed, not once but twice, on this very counterpane. She lay there, imagining the future: Sunday mornings wholly taken up with lovemaking and, maybe, some evenings, too. It was so wonderful to contemplate, the two of them –

The back door bell rang twice, three times, insistently. The dog began to bark in the kitchen. Drat that girl! It was Doreen's chubby daughter, no doubt, come to take the dog for a walk. Angela got up quickly and slipped on an old candlewick dressing gown that she used for cleaning the bathroom. As she went down the stairs, tying the belt in a double knot in front of her, she thought of Doreen sitting alone in her house. Her friend had looked so miserable at the fête, yesterday afternoon, that Angela had been too irritated to make small talk with her. At least Ray had made the effort to be sociable. He'd been quite friendly, in fact. And it had been just what she'd needed, with John Taylor standing there, showing off his young floozie to the world.

"Quiet, Mitzi!" Angela took the dog's lead from a peg by the back door, arranged her mouth in a smile and opened the door to Stella.

"'Lo, Mrs Clayforth."

"Hello, Stella." She handed the lead to the girl. "Here you are. Take her for a long run, will you? She needs the exercise." And so do you, my tubby friend, thought Angela, still annoyed at having her daydreams interrupted. Then she had an idea. "Look, next weekend, don't bother to ring the bell. I'll be having a lie-in, I expect. Just take Mitzi out, as usual. I'll leave the back door open for you."

"Right you are, Mrs Clayforth," Stella replied, bending to attach the lead to the dachshund's collar. Then she clicked her tongue a couple of times and said "Come on, dog! Time for a run in the woods."

Angela watched the girl and the dog, waddling in unison down the path to the gate. She gave a sigh of irritation. She couldn't have this sort of disturbance when she had her young man upstairs in her bed.

Now then, where was she? Ah, yes. She'd have a long, luxurious bubble bath and lie there, remembering her beautiful morning. Then she'd play some music; waltz around to Dean Martin's 'Amore' and think about what to wear. And, during the week, she'd buy some new clothes, and a couple more negligées, saucy ones. Angela went back upstairs and ran the bath, humming 'Amore' as she emptied half a bottle of pink bubble bath under the gushing taps.

CHAPTER 13

John Taylor's conscience was starting to trouble him a little. He hadn't said a word to Angela Clayforth at the fête and he was beginning to feel it might have been rude of him. After all, the poor woman had practically offered herself to him, a few nights ago, and he hadn't handled the situation in the most diplomatic of ways. Not that he blamed himself, entirely. Angela hadn't given him much of a chance to say what he'd wanted to say. That was the trouble with Mrs Clayforth: she had her own slant on the world and she couldn't see the situation from another's point of view.

But he'd been surprised at how quickly she'd turned on him, in the space of just a few minutes. She'd transformed herself from a pussycat into a hissing mountain cat and, for a moment there, he had been a little afraid of her. It seemed to him she was possessed by some kind of powerful, tamped emotion that bubbled just below the surface, ready to erupt. And, like a volcano, when Angela blew, she would engulf everything in her path. John reckoned he should take the lid off the situation before the woman got out of hand. He had a vision of Mrs Clayforth telling the neighbours that he had led her on. And it would be her that they'd believe, not him. He was sure of that.

John closed the front door quietly and stood for a moment, looking across the road to number twelve. He couldn't see Angela peering from behind her net curtains, as he had done on many occasions. He took a deep breath and started down the path, rehearsing as he went what he'd say to her. He'd even let her cook for him again, if that was what she wanted to do. Anything for a peaceful existence.

He knocked at the front door and waited. There was no reply. He wondered if Angela was home. He rang the bell, in case she hadn't heard the knocker. He stepped back and glanced at each window to see if there was any sign of movement. Finally, he decided to ring the bell again, one last time. As he waited on the step, he turned and looked at his own house, then he glanced, first in one direction, then the other, at the other houses in the Close. They all stared back at him. This is like living in a goldfish bowl, he thought to himself. Everyone knows everyone else's business. You can't breathe in this place, you can't move a muscle, without the rest of the road knowing exactly what you're doing. It was the first time the idea of moving house entered John's mind, but he hardly had time to register the thought when the front door opened.

Angela Clayforth stood there, barefoot, in a dark blue silk housecoat with a towel wrapped around her head. She had opened the door with a ready smile on her face, but when she saw who it was, she glared at him. "Yes?"

"Ah – Angela," John began. "I'm sorry to disturb you. I'll come back later, if it's not a convenient moment." He started to back down the step, but Angela held the door open, still without a smile on her face.

"You'd better come in. I was in the bath. I'll catch a death of cold, standing here, like this." She stood back and allowed John to step inside. It was the first time he'd ever been in the Clayforths' house. Susie had never got around to calling on Mrs Clayforth and he'd only ever nodded to Frank Clayforth across the low hedges that bordered their front gardens. A strong, sweet odour of bath salts, or something similar, assailed his nostrils. Angela was pink and glowing from her recent ablutions. John thought she actually looked more attractive without the usual thick layer of makeup on her face, but he dared not pay her a compliment; it might start her up again, misinterpreting his attempts at friendship and neighbourliness.

"Well?" She folded her hands across her bosom and tapped a bare foot on the lavender-blue carpet. "If you've come to apologise for the other night, don't bother. I've completely forgotten all about it."

"I'm glad about that, Angela. Really, I am. I probably said the wrong things, in the wrong way. I wanted to say sorry, yesterday, when I saw you at the fête, but – "

"But you were with your young bit of stuff," she spat out the words and looked him up and down with a haughty expression on her face.

"What?" John started guiltily. Had his feelings for Tanya been that obvious? Had others noticed, too? Had Tanya noticed? "No, you've got it all wrong. Tanya helps me with the children, that's all. Her mother volunteered her, when I first lost Susan. You remember? You were all so kind to me. You're all wonderful neighbours. That was what I came to say, really." He hung his head, staring at her painted toenails; blood-red.

Angela felt triumphant. She allowed herself to smile at John Taylor. He was missing her, already. No doubt about that. This was his way of making up to her: slowly, with little compliments, as though nothing had changed between them. The question was: should she make him beg for forgiveness? No, she was too generous a woman for that. Her love-making with Neil had purged her of all ill-feeling towards John Taylor. The man didn't know what he wanted, that was all. She gave him one of her sweetest smiles. "I'm sure we can be good friends again, John. I'd like that."

"I'd like that, too." He was relieved. She'd smiled at him. That was all he wanted. It was what he'd come for: absolution. No more anxiety about what she might say to the neighbours. He could rest easy; Angela Clayforth was no longer on the rampage. He grinned at her, relaxing now. He wanted to pat her on the shoulder, shake hands on it. But what was she doing – ?

Slowly, smiling back at him, Angela began to undo the belt of her housecoat. The belt fell to the floor and the housecoat slipped from her shoulders. She stood there, naked, before him. Then she lifted her arms and took a step towards him. "Lets make up, properly, John." She took another step. He recoiled, horrified.

He looked around the hall, everywhere but at Angela. He did all he could to avoid gazing at her nude body. He hadn't been prepared for this. He was embarrassed, frightened by her strong sexuality, her passion. It was the last thing he'd expected when he'd rung her bell. But here he was, in her house, trapped in a corner of her hallway, and she was advancing on him with her arms outstretched, ready to encircle him in a tentacled grip. That was how he saw the situation.

Too late. She had her arms around him now. Her hot, damp body, still perspiring from her bath, was pressing against him. He had nowhere to go, he was unable to move. He stood there, while his neighbour plucked at the folds of his shirt, trying to undo the buttons. "Angela ... "

"Sshh. Don't say a word. Come with me." Her hand slipped down his side and into his hand. She pulled him towards the bottom of the staircase.

He resisted. She pulled harder. The towel around her head came loose and fell to the ground; her damp, tousled hair giving her the appearance of a scarecrow. He wrenched his hand from hers with a violent twist. "No! This – this isn't right! Please put your clothes on. Please!" He made a dash for the front door and fumbled with the lock, his hands shaking, his eyes almost closed as he tried to avoid seeing any more of Angela.

She stood dead still in surprise at the foot of the stairs. She couldn't understand what was happening. She could see John Taylor with his back to her, pulling at the front door. In a second, he would have it open and there might be people outside, passing by. She sprinted over to her housecoat and shrugged it on and tied the belt as fast as she could. Then she ran over to John and clung to his back. "What are you doing? Where are you going? Come back! Don't go!"

Roughly, he threw her off him. She tottered backwards into a glass-fronted cabinet on the far side. But she pushed off, angry now, understanding he'd rejected her. "You can't go, just like that! John! You can't make advances, then play games with me!"

But John had wrenched open the door and was halfway down the path. Angela stopped at the door and clutched the frame, her face scarlet with anger, her hair wild, sticking out at all angles. She looked like Medusa with her head covered in writhing snakes, ready to strike at anything within reach. She screamed at John. "You Don Juan! You – you Casanova! You bastard! You can't do this to me!" But John was already crossing the road, reaching for the catch on his gate.

Suddenly, Angela noticed her. Standing on the pavement, outside John Taylor's house, her mouth open, staring first at John as he ran across the road, then at Angela. Tanya had never seen such an extraordinary sight. She tried to work out what was happening. Clearly, Mrs Clayforth was upset. Equally clear was Mr

Taylor's hurry to get away from her. And why was she calling him a Casanova, a Don Juan? Had he been trying to take advantage of Mrs Clayforth? Tanya hesitated. Should she turn back? Should she go home? She'd only come to tell Mr Taylor that she couldn't go to the coast with him, that she was busy with end of term exams for the next couple of weeks.

John hadn't seen Tanya. He hadn't dared look round or back as he'd half-run up the path to his door. His hand was still shaking as he tried to put the key in the lock. Finally, he managed it and fell inside and slammed the door. He stood there, on the other side, leaning heavily against the door and gasping for breath, his eyes wide in disbelief at what had happened. Never – never, in a thousand years – would he have imagined something like that happening to him. He had thought all women were soft and gentle, like Susie. But this woman's aggressiveness had scared him rigid. And now, the whole Close knew about it: they had heard her shouting at him. They would think he'd tried to seduce her and she'd sent him packing. What was he going to do? What about the children? Would they take them away from him? Would he be arrested for attempted rape? My God, the possibilities were infinite.

The doorbell made him jump. His heart boomeranged around his chest. She had come after him. She was going to make a scene on his doorstep. There was no escaping her now. Slowly and carefully, trying not to make a sound, he pushed off from the door and started treading gingerly towards the back of the house. He had only taken a few steps when the doorbell sounded again. This time, whoever was doing the ringing was holding their finger on the bell. He turned and faced the door, willing the noise to stop; but it didn't. He couldn't bear the sound. His nerves were shot through. He had been through so much trauma in the last two months that his threshold of pain was at an all-time low. He went to the door and flung it open, his muscles tense with anticipation, ready to face a further attack. It took him several seconds to realise it was Tanya, not Mrs Clayforth, standing there. He could only stare at her, wide-eyed with surprise.

"Hello, Mr Taylor." She was looking at him warily, not sure if she should give her usual friendly smile after what she had seen in the street.

John didn't, couldn't respond. He was still struggling to dispel the image of a naked Angela Clayforth from his mind, although it was the blazing anger on her face which had shaken him the most.

"I'm sorry to bother you ... " She waited for him to say something, even if it was just a greeting, but he continued to stare at her, his mouth slightly open. She pushed on: "I just dropped by to say that – about going to the coast next Sunday – I'm – "

"Oh, yes. Come in Tanya. Sorry, I wasn't thinking. My mind was somewhere else. Come in, won't you?" He held the door wide, keeping himself well behind it so that he couldn't be seen from the street, especially by the person who lived opposite.

"I can't – I won't come in. I'm sort of busy at the moment." She peered into the hallway where John lingered, almost hidden by the door. "My mum wants me to do something for her, so I've got to be getting back. I just called to say I can't make next week. You know, going to the coast for the day. I mean, I thought I could. I really did. But I can't now. So ... " her voice trailed off.

John Taylor was looking at her as if she were talking a foreign language, as if she were saying something beyond his realm of understanding.

"I can't go with you next weekend," Tanya repeated in a more definite tone. "That's all I came to say. In fact, I don't know about the baby-sitting, any more."

John understood now. He understood everything. He realised what had happened to him in the last half an hour. Not only had Angela Clayforth tried to ruin his reputation in the Close but, by screaming at him in the street, she had destroyed the one relationship, apart from his precious children, that he'd clung to for his sanity. The woman was destructive: she was like a large tank, an automaton mowing down everything in its path, flattening any opposition. Seeing her like that, he was suddenly less afraid of Angela. Instead, he was angry as hell with her.

While he was turning these thoughts over in his mind, his anger rising by the second, Tanya turned to go, having said all she felt it was necessary to say.

"Just a minute, Tanya." He came out from the shadow of the door and stood full-square on the step, hands on hips, for all the world to see. "There's no need to run off. Come in and have a coffee and we can work this out."

She shook her head as she retreated down the path, giving him an apologetic smile as she opened the gate.

"Tanya! Wait a minute! Don't go! If it's what you saw just now, forget it. Mrs Clayforth's not –" He was lost for words, how to explain.

" – not anything," he finished, lamely. But the girl was already out of earshot, hurrying along the pavement in the direction of her house.

John slammed his front door so hard that the force sent the barometer on the wall beside it crashing to the floor. It was the final straw: Susan had bought him that barometer for their first wedding anniversary. It had a million memories attached to it; it was like a holy relic for John. He crouched down and examined the instrument and found the glass front was broken. It was Victorian; he didn't know if it could be repaired. He ran his finger over the face, then gently picked up the apparatus and placed it on the sideboard. Then he noticed he'd cut his hand on the cracked glass and it was bleeding in heavy droplets on the carpet.

Instinctively, John clamped his other hand over the wound. He studied the dark red splatterings around his feet. He knew the time had come for him to get a hold on his life, to abandon this terrible passivity that had gripped him and allowed people to use him for their own purposes. He would stand his ground with that bullying woman across the street, for a start. He would do more than that. He would tell her what he thought of her, and he would let others know, as well. Women like that were a menace to the community. Yes, that was the word: a menace.

They should be put away, locked up, put down, taken out. They were a threat to ordinary folk who were simply trying to get on with their lives.

Tanya didn't go straight home after she left John Taylor's. A sense of relief, as if a great weight had been lifted off her shoulders, overwhelmed her and put a spring in her step. She went past her own house and stopped at the gate of number twenty-one. She hesitated only for a moment, then pushed open the gate and went quickly up the path. As she reached the step she took a deep breath, then lifted the polished knocker and banged it hard against the wood.

Mrs Boyd opened the door. She was wearing an apron with a bib, her sleeves were rolled up and her hands dusted with flour. She regarded Tanya with surprise for a moment then, with a visible effort, changed her expression and smiled at the girl. "Hello, young lady. We haven't seen you for while. Come in. I'm just doing some baking. I'll call him – Neil!" And she shut the door behind Tanya.

There was no response from upstairs. "Neil!" called Valerie Boyd, again. She shook her head in exasperation. "I know he's up there."

"I'll go up and see him, if you like, Mrs Boyd," offered Tanya.

"Well, OK. I must get back to my cooking. Tell him dinner won't be long, so don't you keep him talking. He's got exams next week. This is an important time – "

"Yes, Mrs Boyd. I'll tell him."

Tanya took the stairs two at a time, her long legs hardly touching the steps. She got to Neil's door, with its familiar stickers of football teams, cricket tours and rugby finals stuck all over it at a variety of angles. She knocked once, then immediately opened the door. There was Neil, lying on the bed, staring up at the ceiling, with a book open on his chest. He turned his head as the door opened. When he saw who it was, he immediately swivelled round and sprang to his feet, the book falling to the floor with a thud.

Neither of the young persons spoke. Neil wondered if he was dreaming and Tanya was terrified he would tell her to go away. They stood there, drinking in the sight of each other. Then Neil stepped forward and put his arms around Tanya and held her tight. She flung her arms around him and pressed her face against his. They clung together, deliriously happy, then Neil drew back and began to kiss her passionately. She returned his kisses with the same fervour. He drew her to the bed. "Your mum ... " she started to say, but he was kissing her again and his hands were undoing her blouse. There was an urgency to their love-making and they didn't take long. Afterwards, they lay on Neil's bed, their bodies entwined, their heads close together. And they vowed to each other they would never, ever, be parted again.

Stella was disappointed not to have seen Neil cleaning Mrs Clayforth's windows or mowing her lawn that morning. She deposited a tired, well-exercised Mitzi back at the house while managing to avoid an encounter Mrs Clayforth, herself. She left the animal in the kitchen with its water bowl and dog basket, closed the back door quietly, and, reluctantly, went home. Her mother had been in a particularly bad mood since the fête, the previous day, and Stella, whose instinct for self-preservation made her aware of such things, had sensed the black cloud hanging over her home the moment she'd come in the back door.

But the atmosphere in the house couldn't cancel out the exhilaration she felt at having spent an hour or so with Neil at the Lucky Dip. From now on, she planned to see him whenever she could. They would have more conversations, intimate ones, and they'd soon form a close relationship. This was how Stella saw the situation: progress, all the way. From the first tentative phrases they had exchanged yesterday would blossom a love so strong that they were bound to get married and live happily ever after. Stella had a purpose in life now, a direction, a goal. It made living at home with her mother and her problems much easier to bear.

That evening, when Angela's door bell rang, her thoughts flew immediately to Neil Boyd. He had to see her again; he couldn't stay away from her. He needed to feel her body close to him once more in the bed. As Angela hurried to the door, it crossed her mind it could equally be John Taylor, having thought about what she'd offered him earlier and regretting his shyness. That young Williams' girl was no substitute for a real woman, experienced in love-making. Neil had discovered that. John Taylor would realise it, too.

"Oh," was all Angela could think of to say when she opened the door and saw Doreen Reynolds standing under the porch light. She tried to hide her disappointment. Her neighbour held a bottle of wine in her hands and, like Angela, seemed to be having trouble forming a smile on her face.

"You were expecting someone else?" said Doreen, with an almost accusatory look. "Have I intruded on something? Is he hiding behind the sofa, afraid to show his face?"

At this, Angela threw back her head and laughed. "Not quite. I thought you were him, to tell you the truth. Never mind. Come in. We hardly had a moment to talk, yesterday. And so much has happened since then."

Doreen stepped into the hall, wearing a grim expression on her face. It had taken a lot of courage for her to knock on Angela's door and demand an explanation for her behaviour at the fête. She wanted the woman's affair with her husband to be out in the open, once and for all. And, when Angela broke down and admitted it and begged for forgiveness, Doreen planned to hit her over the head with the bottle she'd brought; and hit her again, and again, until Angela was senseless. Then she would go into the kitchen and get a knife from the drawer and finish the woman off. It didn't matter that the police would come and take her away, or that she would spend the rest of her life in prison. She had nothing to live for now, anyway. At least she would have the satisfaction of knowing that Ray and Angela hadn't found happiness at her expense.

"Come through," said Angela, leading the way into the sitting room. "I've got something to tell you. Something wonderful has happened to me. I can't keep it to myself much longer."

Hearing these words, Doreen could hardly contain the bitterness and anger she felt towards her neighbour. The woman had professed to be her friend, had listened to her problems over the years, had offered advice and, then, she'd taken her husband from her. Doreen sat back in one of Angela's plush armchairs, waiting her opportunity to carry out her plan. She was determined now. No going back. Her life was over; why shouldn't Angela's life be over, too?

"Let me open this, first," said Angela, carrying Doreen's bottle through to the kitchen. Doreen looked around the room that had become so familiar to her over the years. How many evenings had she sat in this chair and drunk wine and laughed with her friend, sharing their grievances over their respective marriages? And, when Frank had died, she had envied Angela her new-found freedom. She had no idea her friend's need for male company would destroy her own fragile marriage. Well, it was done now; water under the bridge. She'd been betrayed by the one person in the Close she thought she could trust. Why, she had even got her daughter to walk Angela's yappy dog for her.

She had been blind, so naïve, so utterly stupid in trusting this woman.

"There now," said Angela, returning with the opened wine and a couple of glasses which she set on the low table between them. That's right, thought Doreen, put the bottle where I can reach it. I'll have a glass or two first, to give me Dutch courage, then I'll get up and grab the bottle and brain her with it. The bottle will be easier to lift when it's not so full, and it would be a shame to spill the wine on the floor and waste it. So, carry on talking Angela. Tell me how you've sat here in the evenings, making love to my husband. I promise I won't say a word. You'll get the surprise of your life; the final surprise.

"Well, cheers. Here's to 'L'amour'!" Angela passed a full tumbler of wine to Doreen and splashed a much smaller amount in her own glass. She'd had such an emotional day, particularly the unexpected passion of her encounter with Neil, that she didn't want to dull her senses, just yet. She wanted to relive the experience, to give her friend a moment by moment account of the young man's agility and ability to please. She thought it would cheer Doreen up; maybe inspire the woman to find a lover of her own. Why, she'd even push poor John Taylor in Doreen's direction. Yes, that would be a good turn. Doreen needed something to shake her out of her torpor. Ray had clearly left the nest, not just physically but emotionally. He had been marvellous company for her yesterday afternoon; he was obviously in love with someone, and it wasn't Doreen.

"You've knocked that back quickly," observed Angela, pushing the bottle in Doreen's direction. "Here, help yourself." Poor woman, she thought. She's dying inside.

"Don't mind if I do. Down the hasshh!" Doreen's tongue was already getting in the way of her words. Another full tumbler. One more would do; she didn't even have to finish it. Just lighten the load in the bottle, then – oh, hell – How did that happen? She felt the coldness of the wine as it soaked the front of her skirt. Somehow, she had missed her mouth completely with her glass. She had been thinking so hard about how she would lift the bottle and bring it down on Angela's head that she'd lost her spatial bearings. Well, never mind. Doesn't mean a change of plan.

"Here, wait a minute. I'll get a cloth from the kitchen. It's all down your skirt." Angela got up, turned her back on her friend to leave the room, and let her smile transform into a grim expression. She was concerned about her chair cover and her deep-pile carpet. Red wine stains weren't the easiest of marks to shift. She'd had enough of Doreen for one evening, already. She would persuade the woman to go home, as soon as she could. She didn't need Doreen's problems, tonight.

She took a clean cloth from the cupboard and moistened it under the tap. When she came back into the sitting room, Doreen immediately got up and, swaying on her feet, took hold of the wine bottle on the coffee table by its neck. "No, don't!" said Angela, alarmed. "You'll spill some more, Doreen. Put it down! Put it back on the table –"

Doreen took a couple of unsteady steps towards her neighbour, without seeming to notice the coffee table that stood between them. Angela watched, helplessly, as her friend fell across the tiled top, still clutching the bottle of wine, and lay stupefied, belly-down, while the last of the red wine trickled from the downward-angled bottle onto her precious cream carpet.

CHAPTER 14

Tanya lay in bed, gazing up at the ceiling with a dreamy smile on her face. She'd thought of nothing but Neil since they'd made up, the weekend before. Her life was complete now. She knew what she wanted, and she had nearly lost it a while back. Now, nothing would get in the way of her happiness; she would make quite sure of that.

They had seriously discussed their future together in the last few days, especially when, after school, they'd lain on the floor of the camp in Hadham Woods, after making love. Neil was still ambitious and wanted to go to university and become a top lawyer. Tanya found she was ambitious for him, too; reasoning that a happy, fulfilled man made a good partner. They made plans to share a flat near the university. Tanya would do a secretarial course in the nearest town and Neil would study hard for his degree. And they would be together, from now on. That, for Tanya, was the most important thing in the world.

The front door banged shut and Tanya heard her mother run up the stairs with quick, nimble steps. Tanya barely had time to turn her head on the pillow when her door flew open and her mother was standing in the middle of the room. Mavis looked flushed, she sounded breathless, and there was a light in her eyes that held more of a steely glint than a warm sparkle.

"I've just been speaking to Valerie Boyd." Her mother ran her hands down her floral apron. She had been wearing floral aprons over the same style of skirts and blouses, ever since Tanya could remember. The only change the girl had noticed over the years was the grey that had replaced her mother's sandy-coloured hair. Tanya wished she wouldn't wear it swept severely back in a French pleat, like that. She had begged her many times to have a younger, softer hairstyle. And now, looking at Mavis, arms akimbo in a confrontational posture, Tanya knew there was trouble brewing, and she knew, if her mother had been talking to Mrs Boyd, it had to do with her going out with Neil. She propped herself up on her elbows, waiting for the torrent of words that could only lead to the usual row.

"She tells me you're seeing her son again. Seeing him after school, preventing him from doing his studies." Mavis stared at Tanya, willing her daughter to provide an explanation, an excuse, a promise that she wouldn't see Neil again.

Tanya looked straight back at her mother. She pursed her lips and said nothing. There was nothing to say, nothing to waste her energy explaining. She was the happiest person alive and even her mother wasn't going to spoil how she was feeling today.

"You told me you weren't going to see that boy, any more. Is this why you told Mr Taylor you couldn't go with him to the coast tomorrow? Hmm? Is that the reason? Well, say something, girl! Don't just lie there with a sulk on your face. You've got a tongue in your head, haven't you?"

"Mum, there's nothing to say." Tanya sat up, swivelled her long legs out from under the eiderdown and slipped her feet into her fluffy blue slippers. "Yes, I'm seeing Neil again. No, it's not going to affect his studies. He's as keen as ever to get his exams and go to university." She stood up and put on her thin cotton dressing gown, tying the sash around her slim waist in a double knot. She felt more confident about holding her own in an argument with her mother if she was more or less dressed instead of recumbent in the bed. She went to her dressing table and picked up her hairbrush, gave her hair a few strokes and turned to her mother.

"But I think you should know that I'm going with him when he goes away in October. We're going to share a flat together, in the town."

"What?" Mavis looked aghast, ashen. Her thin hands flew to her breast where she held them as if she was experiencing some kind of heart palpitation. "You can't leave home, Tanya! You're too young. You're only sixteen – "

"Mum, we've been through all this. We just go round in circles, time and time again." She returned to brushing her hair, then she turned to her mother again. "And I'm not too young to leave home. The truth of the matter is that you don't want me to leave. You want to keep me here, at home, all to yourself. You don't want to lose me because you've got no one else. That's why you don't want me to see Neil, or any other boy, for that matter. You're terrified that, one day, I'll settle down with someone else, and you'll be left on your own, permanently."

Mavis recoiled at her daughter's words. Her eyes widened in protestation. "Don't be so ridiculous," she said, shaking her head in vigorous denial. "I would never think like that. I only want you to be happy, Tanya. You know that."

"You want to be happy," said Tanya, pointing the hairbrush at her mother. "You're not interested in my happiness. You're just thinking of yourself."

"Don't talk rubbish – "

"Is this how you carried on with Dad? Well, is it? Pretending to make sacrifices and suffer for him; making him feel guilty about any small pleasure in his life? And, all the while, leading the life you wanted and keeping the reins on him. Until he couldn't stand it any longer and he – "

"Don't you bring that up again! Haven't I suffered enough? Haven't I done everything I could to bring you up in a nice home? Haven't I lived completely for you? To make sure you have the best in life?"

Tanya threw the hairbrush on the bed and folded her arms in front of her. The light in her eye matched that in her mother's now. The two women squared up to each other in the centre of the room. "Why do you always resort to this – this emotional blackmail, mother? Why do you always have to bring it down to your lifetime of sacrifices for others? Can't you accept that other people see the world differently? That they want different things?" She prodded her bosom with her index finger to make a further point. "I want you to be happy, Mum. As happy as I am. I don't want to see you making yourself miserable on my account. If I'm making you go without things or stopping you doing what you want to do, then tell me what it is you want from me, and I'll try to make you happy. But you must do the same for me – "

Mavis started crying. Her shoulders heaved and large tears began to roll down her face from red-rimmed eyes. "Don't go, Tanya," she sobbed. "Don't leave me all alone."

Tanya took a deep breath and blew out her cheeks. "Oh, for God's sake, Mum. You always do this: you always start crying when you can't get your own way."

Mavis sobbed even louder. She bowed her head and put her hands up to her eyes, forming bony fists in the sockets. "I can't bear it. I can't take any more ... I'm so miserable!"

Tanya shook her head and went over to her mother. She put a hand on her shoulder. Mavis began to cry even louder. "Stop it, Mum. That's enough. Pack it in, will you? We don't have to talk about this now."

Her mother whimpered and kept her knuckles in her eyes. "I can't bear it," she whined. "I couldn't stand it if you were to leave me on my own ... "

Tanya kept her hand on Mavis's shoulder and gave her a despairing look. "Don't worry about it, Mum. Not now. Nothing's going to change yet. I'm still here; look."

Mavis slowly lowered her hands, lifted her head and regarded her daughter, sorrowfully. She sniffed. "I don't know what I'd do if I lost you, Tanya." She shook her head, piteously. "I couldn't bear to live if I didn't have you near. You're my life, you know. I only live for you."

Her daughter pulled a wry expression. "I know that, Mum," she said in a placating tone, as though trying to calm a child. "Don't think I don't know that. Here, let me get you a tissue. Your nose is running. We don't want that, do we?"

Valerie Boyd put the teapot on the breakfast table, looked at her eldest son and frowned. "You're late down this morning, Neil. Aren't you supposed to be at Mrs Clayforth's by half-ten?"

Neil kept his head down and carried on buttering his toast, taking his time and scraping the butter carefully into each corner, right to the edge of the crust.

"Answer your mother, will you?" his father's voice came from behind his Sunday paper.

"I don't think so," Neil mumbled, reaching for the pot of marmalade.

"Why ever not?" His mother sat down at the table, alert now to her son's reluctance to discuss the matter but determined to know what the problem was.

"She probably doesn't need me today. I mean, I'm pretty up to date with the jobs over there."

"This doesn't have anything to do with your seeing Tanya again, does it?"

Neil chewed thoughtfully at his toast and marmalade. His father's face looked out from the newspaper and gave him a stern look. Neil said, quickly, "Of course it doesn't. Why should it?"

Valerie sighed. "I knew this would happen. I knew, the moment I saw that girl on the doorstep, she'd be disrupting your life again. You can't let Mrs Clayforth down. It's not right. She's expecting you. She's our neighbour."

Neil took another slice of toast from the rack and busied himself with the butter dish again.

The newspaper was lowered and his father said, "You finish that piece of toast, young man, then you go round to Mrs Clayforth and apologise for being late. You can't let people down when you feel like it. You'll be getting a reputation for being unreliable. And you don't want that. Not if you aim to make a success of your life." The newspaper rose again. His father had spoken. There was nothing more to be said on the subject.

Slowly, reluctantly and confused about the situation he now found himself in, Neil trailed along the pavement to Mrs Clayforth's, praying the woman would have given up waiting for him and gone out for the day. Or she had fallen down and broken her ankle, or her arm, or incapacitated herself in some other way. He imagined a range of scenarios in which he would offer his condolences as she lay in her enormous bed, swathed in bandages after falling down the stairs.

He passed Tanya's house and looked up at the first floor windows. He knew which was her bedroom and he was relieved to see the curtains were still drawn. Something like fear gripped him: the fear of losing Tanya once more. He knew he couldn't bear it. What if Tanya found out he had slept with Mrs Clayforth? That must never happen. And yet, here he was, going over to the woman's house again; making himself available to someone he didn't particularly like. You must need your head examined, he said to himself as he lifted the latch on the elaborate wrought-iron gate at number twelve.

But what could he do about it? How could he explain to his parents that Angela Clayforth had other ideas for him on a Sunday morning, these days? It would probably kill them, he thought; his respectable, suburban parents. They'd never speak to him again. But they'd speak to Mrs Clayforth about it, he was sure. They'd tell her just what they thought of her, seducing their innocent son. And Angela would go ballistic and then the whole of the Close would hear about it, including Tanya. The family would have to move away, and his father would never speak to him again.

No; it didn't bear thinking about, the fall-out from coming clean about the situation. Better to keep a lid on it and hope for the best. Anyway, he'd be at college soon, and Tanya would be with him, full-time. The heaviness he'd felt as he'd walked down Angela's path began to lessen as he thought of his girlfriend and their life to come. He knocked at the back door, still praying for a miracle that would prevent Mrs Clayforth from opening it. His hopes were demolished when the door opened, almost immediately. There stood Angela, in a pink version of the lavender negligée she had been wearing the previous Sunday; all frills and bows and a deeply-cut neckline. The garment had been left open from head to toe, revealing her ample breasts, her soft belly and substantial thighs.

"You're late, my sweet! No matter!" trilled Angela in a voice that betrayed her relief he had finally come. She took hold of his hand and pulled him inside. As he stood there, in the middle of the kitchen, his arms limp at his sides, she held his face and gave him a long lingering kiss, her negligée slipping from her shoulders, her body pressed against his.

Neil had no idea how he ought to react. He was supposed to be playing it cool, trying to put her off. But he had no plan; no idea what to say to the woman to make her leave him alone. He knew he had to extricate himself from the situation, gently but firmly. He had to talk to her, persuade her that last week had been a one-off, just a bit of fun, nothing more than that. He felt her pulling at his belt, then his shirt buttons, her hands sliding down to his thighs and front.

"Listen, can we stop this for a moment?" he managed to say between the bombardment of kisses. "We need to talk. Please." He took hold of the tops of her arms and held her away from him. But she was still smiling crazily at him, her hands clawing the air to get at him. "Let's sit down for a minute." He guided her towards a chair and sat her down. And before she could reach out to him again, he scooted round the kitchen table and sat down on the other side.

"Look, Angela," he began, doing up his shirt buttons as he spoke. "There's something I need to say. It's about last Sunday – "

"Ah! You don't have to worry, sweetheart. I won't tell a soul about it. It's our secret." She tapped the side of her nose and winked at him. "Why on earth should I want anyone to know about our little bit of pleasure? That's our business, isn't it? Just we two – "

"No, that's not what I mean. It's just that – well, I didn't – I wasn't – prepared for last Sunday. It just kind of happened and I – "

"You don't need to worry about that! I won't get pregnant. I've had an operation. So, you see, darling, there's nothing to worry about, at all – "

Neil shook his head in exasperation. "No, that wasn't what I meant. I didn't mean about taking precautions. I'm talking about us; what we did. The thing is – "

Angela leapt up from the chair and tripped swiftly round the table. She came up behind him and clasped his shoulders, bending over him, overwhelming him with her powerful perfume. "You were superb last Sunday," she purred in his ear. "The very best. You know just how to turn a woman on." Her hands moved to his front again, and undid the buttons on his shirt. "Let's not stay downstairs too long.

Someone may come to the door. We can do our talking upstairs, in bed."

Neil had a horrible vision of his mother knocking at the door, or worse, his father checking up on him, making sure he'd gone across to Mrs Clayforth's and was hard at work, mowing her lawn or cleaning the windows. He allowed himself to be led from his chair, out of the kitchen and into the hallway. He hesitated for a moment in the hall, but honestly couldn't see what else he could do. Angela led him up the staircase, just as she had the previous Sunday morning, stopping on the landing beside a large floral arrangement of ferns and gladioli to kiss him again. "Afterwards," she murmured in his ear as she nibbled the lobe, "we can relax in the bath together and I'll wash your back, then I'll put oil on you and give you a massage, and you can do the same to me."

Neil wasn't thinking any more. He'd given up on thoughts for the day. He followed Angela into the bedroom and took off his shirt and trousers. As he lay on the bed, he refused to think of anything at all. He closed his eyes and gave himself up to a creeping pleasure and its attendant sensations. He had no idea of time, or even place, or, in the end, who he was with.

Stella pulled at the lead, urging Mitzi to trot faster along the pavement. But the dog insisted on checking every lamp post and low wall and wooden fence in the Close. Stella was in a hurry: she knew Neil would be working at Mrs Clayforth's until noon and she wanted to ask him if he would take her to the pictures next Saturday.

She looked expectantly around the front garden as she came up the path and was disappointed not to see Neil trimming the hedge or washing Mrs Clayforth's car. Perhaps he was round the back, although she couldn't hear the lawn mower. Maybe he was doing a job for the woman inside the house.

Stella remembered Mrs Clayforth had said not to disturb her on Sunday mornings. She could open the back door without knocking and go right in and leave Mitzi with her water bowl. Stella was happy to do this; she didn't like making conversation with Mrs Clayforth very much. The woman seemed to talk down to her, if she spoke to her at all. And Stella could never think of anything to say in return. It may have been that, being a friend of her mother's, Stella saw Angela Clayforth in the same category of persons: someone who was hostile to her, someone to be avoided.

She opened the back door and let Mitzi scoot in, ahead of her. The dog pattered over to her bowl and lapped noisily at the water while Stella unhooked the lead from her collar and hung it on the peg by the door. She stood and listened for a moment, hoping to hear Neil whistling while he did some task in the house. But all she could hear was Mitzi drinking enthusiastically from her bowl.

"You need some more water, dog," said Stella, seeing the nearly empty bowl. "Here, let me fill this. You were thirsty, weren't you?" She held the bowl under the tap, rinsed it out and refilled it with water and put it down beside Mitzi's basket. But the dachshund was no longer interested in liquid refreshment. She climbed into her basket, circled round in it a couple of times, then collapsed on the cushions with a sigh and closed her eyes.

It was while Stella was bending over the basket, giving Mitzi a pat goodbye, that she heard someone come down the stairs. She stood up and looked towards the door. Neil came into the kitchen, his shirt open and hanging out of his trousers, his head lowered as he concentrated on doing up his belt buckle. Stella stared at him, trying to work out the reason for his state of undress. Two seconds later, she knew. Mrs Clayforth glided into the room behind Neil, wearing a filmy negligée that was almost transparent. The garment was open and Stella could see quite plainly the woman was wearing nothing underneath it. Angela almost collided into the back of Neil as he looked up and saw Stella standing by the dog basket.

"Ah ... " was the only sound Neil was able to utter. He stood there, rooted to the spot, dumb-struck, his hands still grasping the buckle of his belt. Angela was right behind him, holding him by the shoulders. He could feel the frills and ribbons of her negligée brushing him on the back. He realised immediately how it must look. He didn't have a clue what he could say to Stella. She was staring at him, wide-eyed, her mouth opening and closing like a fish.

It was Angela who, to his relief, said something to break the silence. "Stella, you've brought Mitzi back." She quickly wrapped the negligée around her and secured it with a pink-ribboned belt. Then she went over to the dachshund, who had opened its eyes to take in the new arrivals and was thrashing its tail against the side of the wicker basket. "Has she had a good walkies?" Mrs Clayforth simpered as she leant over the dog. "She looks tired out. Well done, Stella. I'll pay you next week. I'm rather busy, right now."

Angela didn't sound at all embarrassed by the situation and Neil suspected she was actually finding it amusing. Her last sentence had made him wince. He'd felt it was unnecessary. And Stella hadn't moved or said anything, at all. He desperately wished the fat girl would leave. He didn't like the way she was staring at him, with a mixture of deep shock and despair. He wanted to turn and rush out of the kitchen and hide in the hallway until she'd gone.

Now Angela was pushing Stella towards the back door, opening it and shoving the girl outside. As she closed the door, she turned to Neil and started to laugh: a loud guffawing sound. Then she began to undo the ribboned belt of her negligée as she slowly came towards him. Neil held up his hands to ward her off and took a couple of steps backwards. He was in a state of panic. He wanted to get away from her, to run out of the house and never come back.

"It's alright, my darling! The girl's gone now. She won't say a thing to anyone. Nobody talks to her."

Angela went to embrace him but he backed away again, then found he was blocked by the door to the hallway. He quickly side-stepped the woman and, tucking in his shirt, he made for the back door.

"Don't go yet ... " she said, giving him an appealing look. "Surely, you can stay for a while longer?"

He shook his head. He checked his shirt buttons, his belt buckle and his trouser flies. Without another word, he opened the back door, fell out and half-ran down the path. Angela rushed to the window in the hall and watched him open the front gate. Even then, she could admire Neil's young, muscular body. It gave her a small thrill to think she had enjoyed him in her bed for most of the morning. She smiled to herself behind the net curtain and gave a happy shrug of her shoulders. It wasn't just the physical side of the relationship that gave her so much pleasure. She adored Neil: his soft, intelligent voice, his easy manner, the way his eyes creased at the corners when he smiled at her ...

She dropped the curtain and turned and went dreamily back into the kitchen. She filled the kettle and got down a coffee cup. Was it love she felt for Neil, she asked herself? She certainly had much stronger feelings for this young man than she'd ever had for Frank. Frank: portly, boring Frank. His presence in the house seemed light years ago. Now, when Angela moved through the rooms, it was Neil she could see and hear, not Frank. She could smell him on her sheets, on her negligée, on her skin. Yes, she told herself, she could easily be in love. At least, she felt a strong, almost uncontrollable passion for the teenager every time she saw him. And she thought about him constantly. She lived for his Sunday visits now; she didn't think she could survive without them. Neil had brought a light and a warmth into her life that she hadn't felt in years, if ever. She needed him; and she knew it wasn't just a physical desire that gripped her but an emotional one, as well. She needed Neil to touch her, to make love to her, to lie with her and talk to her, which he sometimes did between her kisses.

The coffee cleared her thoughts. Angela put her longing for Neil to one side, in a compartment in her head all on its own. As long as she had those sweet hours of lovemaking to look forward to, nothing could mar her days, not even Doreen Reynolds getting drunk and spilling red wine on her chair covers and cream carpet.

She shook her head and tied her negligée belt more securely. She would have a bath and put on some old clothes, then she would have another go at trying to remove those wine stains. She had thought Doreen might call and apologise for the damage she had caused. But, probably, the woman was still comatose from the night before. Angela had practically had to carry her home, she was so drunk. No wonder her house was in such a mess and her daughter looked so slovenly. How had Ray stood it, all those years? Angela thought Doreen had got everything she deserved. And, she thought, I have what I deserve: a wonderful young man all to myself. He's mine, and no one else's; and that's the way it's going to stay.

Neil went straight from Angela's to Tanya's house. He needed to see his girlfriend, to hold her, to be reassured by her. He needed to tell her that he loved her and he wanted to hear her say she loved him. He was racked with guilt about Angela Clayforth and, more than that, for being caught in her kitchen by Stella Reynolds.

What if the girl told Tanya what she'd seen? Would she do that? He thought she might. He would have to talk with Stella, and quite soon, not leave the situation to fester. Fortunately, the girl was gooey-eyed about him, that much he knew. He was sure he could smooth the incident over. He would even lie to the girl and say he had taken off his shirt to fix one of Mrs Clayforth's pipes. And Stella wouldn't argue with him; she always hung on his every word. He could hear her flat, monotone voice now: "Lo, Neil. How are you?' He shook his head. Hallelujah, what a turn-off that female was.

Stella ran home without looking back at Mrs Clayforth's house. Large, hot tears rolled down her cheeks and her nose was running, but she hardly noticed. She couldn't get out of her head the image of Neil, half-dressed, and Mrs Clayforth, completely undressed and looking proud of it. And he'd looked so guilty when he'd glanced up and seen her standing there. And Mrs Clayforth had thought the whole thing very funny, that was obvious.

Stella couldn't believe it: Neil had actually given up Tanya for Angela Clayforth. She would never have thought of them together in a million years. What could he possibly see in her? She was her mother's friend; she was old, she wore horribly bright lipstick and had yellow hair. And her big bosom! Stella had caught sight of those pendulous breasts through her negligée and thought they were the most unattractive appendages she had ever seen. And to think, Neil had – had touched those; probably kissed them. No! It didn't bear thinking about.

She ran upstairs and slammed the bedroom door behind her, but the images multiplied. She saw Neil in bed with Mrs Clayforth: he was on top of her, his long, thick hair practically touching her face as he moved in time with her. And she was wailing with pleasure in that high-pitched voice she used when she was excited about something, or angry with her dog, or hooting with laughter with her mother. Did her mother know Mrs Clayforth was sleeping with Neil? Did Tanya know? Did Mrs Boyd know? What about Mr Taylor? She'd thought Mrs Clayforth was sweet on him.

Stella threw herself on the bed and buried her face in her hands. It wouldn't do; it wouldn't do, at all. All her hopes, all the love and affection she possessed had been channelled in Neil's direction for years and years. And she had been prepared to wait. She would have waited almost forever for Neil. She knew he was the one she was meant to be with. Tanya, she reckoned, was too flirtatious to wait for him while he finished his studies. But Mrs Clayforth: here was a whole new situation she never dreamt she'd have to deal with.

Mrs Clayforth. Mrs Clayforth. Stella repeated the name, hissing it under her breath, over and over. How was she going to deal with Mrs Clayforth? How was she going to get that awful woman away from Neil? Then a thought prompted Stella to stop crying. She blinked her eyes and sniffed, long and hard, a couple of times. She rolled on her back and lay there, staring at a spider's web suspended from her ceiling light, imagining accidents that could befall Mrs Clayforth, so that Neil would be hers again.

CHAPTER 15

The sooner I get this over with, the better, thought Neil as he walked determinedly down the Close to the Reynolds' house. It had been over five hours since Stella had seen him in the kitchen at Angela's and he knew time was running out if he wanted to talk things through with her. If he didn't speak with her – well, he was taking a big gamble: the girl was bound to let something slip to Tanya; he knew how girls talked when they got together. He didn't think Stella knew he was going out with Tanya again, that they'd made up and were going strong. But if Tanya mentioned it, Stella was bound to tell her what she'd seen in Angela's kitchen. No; he couldn't take a chance on that. His whole happiness was at stake.

The Reynolds' house was at the other end of the road, near the beginning of the Close where it joined Hadham Lane. Neil paused at the entrance, not wanting to go up the path, not wanting to knock at the door. He took a deep breath and put his hand on the wooden gate. It had been painted green, long ago, but the weather had penetrated the paint and the wood was swollen and rotten. It hung on one hinge and gave a high-pitched squeak as he opened it. The front lawn, he noticed, needed cutting, badly, and there was an air of shabbiness about the house, too. Everything at the Reynolds' place needed a coat of paint or repairing.

As he stood on the front step, he thought about the unpleasant task ahead. He eyed the blue gloss curling off the windowsills and the drainpipe coming away from the wall, and a sinking feeling gripped him. Just do it, he said to himself; just talk it through with her and then you can go home. He gave a firm nod to himself and rang the bell and waited. A light went on in the hallway and he knew there was no turning back.

Doreen Reynolds peered out, into the dusk, taking a moment to focus on him. She didn't have a drink in her hand but he could smell the alcohol only a few seconds after she'd opened the door. He wasn't sure if she was sober enough to recognise him. In which case, he'd have some awkward explaining to do. But a lopsided smile spread across her flushed face. "Neil Boyd! Well, what a surprise. I don't have any jobs for you to do here, I'm afraid." She swayed as she gestured behind her, into the hall. "Ackshully, we don't have any money to pay you, that's the truth – "

"No, that's not why I called, Mrs Reynolds." He didn't want to hear her hard luck story. He knew Mr Reynolds had left her, and he could understand why. "I just wanted to talk to – Is Stella in? Could I have a word with her?"

Doreen stepped back unsteadily, holding on to the front door. "Come in, dear boy." She looked at him with a soppy, conspiratorial expression. "Is there something I should know? Is this the start of a new romance?" Her bloodshot eyes swivelled round in mock secrecy.

"I just want a word with her, if that's possible," said Neil, already wishing he was somewhere else and getting ready to depart. It crossed his mind that Stella might be out and he'd wasted his time coming round, in any case.

But Doreen said: "She's upstairs. Come in." She hung on to the door as he stepped into the hallway, and the alcohol fumes were immediately stronger. Doreen swung the door shut behind him and tottered over to the bottom of the stairs. She clasped the newel post and shouted, "Stella!"

No reply.

"Stella! Your boyfriend's here to see you!" Doreen looked back at him and gave a chuckle and attempted to wink. "That'll get her down here – "

A door opened and light flooded the landing upstairs. They heard it slam and the landing dimmed again. Footsteps clumped along the floor above, then Stella appeared at the top of the stairs. She looked down and froze when she saw Neil standing with her mother, who was clutching the banister rail, clearly the worse for wear.

She stared at him with the same expression she'd worn in Angela Clayforth's kitchen, hours earlier, and Neil pleaded silently: Don't say anything, Stella. Don't mention this morning. He said: "Hi, there. Can I have a word with you, for a moment?"

Doreen put a hand on his shoulder. It felt heavy, as though she were using him for support. "Why don't we all go into the sitting room and have a nice drink?" She looked from Neil to her daughter, and back again.

"No, mother," Stella spoke from the top of the stairs. Her voice sounded strained, choked with emotion. As she trod heavily down the stairs Neil could see her eyes were red-rimmed. Had she been drinking, too? he wondered. Pray God, she wasn't in the same condition as her mother.

They stood there in the hall, the three of them, looking at each other. No one spoke. Neil was trying to work out how he could talk to

Stella alone, how he could get rid of the inebriated mother. He supposed Stella knew why he was there. The question was: did she want her mother to know, which would be the same as telling the whole world.

"Mum, go back and watch your TV programme. We want to talk on our own, don't we Neil?"

He nodded his head, glad that she had called him by his name.

"I see," said her mother, giving them a knowing look. She pushed off from Neil's shoulder and went, diagonally, across the hallway. She found the sitting room door at the second attempt, grasped the handle and disappeared through the door.

Stella looked at Neil, then shook her head. "She's not well," she said, by way of explanation

"Not well," repeated Neil. It was of no interest to him; he only wanted to say his piece and be out of there.

"So, what did you want to talk to me about?" Her voice sounded less tense, more relaxed now that her mother had gone.

Neil was about to say something about that morning, but suddenly felt exposed, standing there in the hallway. "Is there somewhere we can talk?"

"There's my bedroom," said Stella, perhaps a little too readily.

Neil had had enough of bedrooms for one day. "The kitchen. Can we sit in there and talk?"

"Oh, yes. Of course."

"Can we be overheard in the other room?"

Stella shook her head. "No. Probably not. And my mother ... well, she's not – "

"Not well," he nodded his head.

They settled themselves at the kitchen table. The room was shabby and dark. Neil noticed the walls and the paintwork were spotted with grease and the surfaces needed a good wipe with a cloth. There were crumbs on the table and Neil wondered how long they had been there. But Stella didn't seem to notice them. She put her elbows on the table and clasped her hands together and looked at him, expectantly.

"The thing is," Neil began, thinking fast how he could phrase what he'd come to say, "I think I owe you an explanation." He waited.

Stella said nothing, only gazed at him.

"I mean, about this morning. At Mrs Clayforth's. It wasn't what you think."

She stared at him, her head slightly on one side.

"I wanted you to know that. You might have got it wrong."

Stella unclasped her hands and laid them flat on the table. Then she picked up a toast crumb and studied it, rolling it between her thumb and index finger.

"It was just a joke thing, you know?" This is sounding ridiculous, he thought to himself. But what else can I say?

She looked at him with a half-smile of disbelief. In that moment, Neil knew he would have to be honest with her. Here goes, he thought; I'm completely at her mercy now.

"She's lonely, that's all: that Mrs Clayforth. She's all alone. I feel sorry for her."

Stella gave a slight snort and dropped the breadcrumb.

"I mean, it was nothing serious. Just a laugh. You won't tell anyone about it, will you?"

She looked at him hard, unsmiling. "Is she your new girlfriend?" she asked, watching him carefully.

"No! No way! Are you kidding? Old Angela?" He tried to sound amused by her suggestion but his voice was pitched too high and sounded strained.

"Then ... " Stella's heavy face folded in a frown. "You're not going to see her ... ?"

"Oh, come on. I told you: a joke, a one-off." Neil thought it was none of Stella's business who he saw, who he jumped into bed with. But the girl seemed to be looking for some kind of reassurance that he was basically chaste. And he was happy to give her that impression, whatever she wanted.

But Stella didn't seem satisfied. Apparently, she wanted more. "I thought we were friends ... " she traced a greasy patch on the table top with her finger. "I mean, after the fête last weekend."

Oh, God! Is this what it's all about? thought Neil. She's been reading things into whatever I said to her, the other Saturday. He tried to remember some of their conversation, any part of it. But he couldn't recall having said that much to her. He'd been watching Tanya most of the time. That, he did remember. "We're friends, Stella. We'll always be friends, I hope."

She nodded, her big brown eyes seeming almost dog-like in their adoration of him. Neil began to understand, then, what it was that Stella wanted to hear. She wanted him to talk about them, Neil and Stella, not Mrs Clayforth, or anyone else. She would forget the incident with Angela if she had something else to focus on. She was waiting for him to hint at a relationship she'd already decided they had. He could say anything and she would believe it because it fitted in with her hopes and dreams. She had her emotional check-list and she was prompting him, so that she could tick the boxes. All he had to do was answer correctly and she was putty in his hands.

"You know I think a lot of you," he said, testing the phrase for effect.

The response was immediate. Stella smiled at him and her hand slid across the table towards him. "I – I think a lot about you, too. I always have."

I know that, he nearly said. "So we have our secrets, Stella. Just the two of us."

She nodded and beamed at him. "Us against the world!"

"Right. Us." He thought it appropriate to touch her hand, in a grateful sort of way. But, as he put out his hand, she took hold of it and held on to it. And she didn't let go.

"Us." She gave his hand a squeeze, then put her other hand over the top of it. There was no way he could withdraw his hand now, encased as it was in both of hers. They sat and looked at each other for a long minute; Stella smiling, Neil trying to do the same. He'd got the assurance he needed; the girl wasn't going to blab. Now he had to get himself out of there. But he had to keep Stella sweet.

He cleared his throat. "Well, old friend, it's time for me to go."

She looked crestfallen. She still had hold of his hand.

He brought his other hand up, from under the table, and patted her hands in an affectionate way. Then he rose, pushing out the chair with the backs of his knees. Stella rose with him, at last relinquishing his hand. But she moved around the table and stood close to him; too close, he thought, with her chin upturned. Oh, Christ, he thought. She wants me to kiss her.

While he was wondering how he could step backwards and to one side without giving offence, she suddenly stood on tip-toe and kissed him, full on the lips. He pulled his head back, so that the kiss was brief, almost just a brushing of the lips. Then, worried he'd been too obvious in recoiling from her, planted a peck on her cheek, in return.

But she turned her head, just as he was placing his lips against her cheek, and she kissed him on his mouth again, forcefully, this time. Neil dared not move his head, dared not move a muscle. There was nothing he could do but kiss her back with a certain amount of meaningful pressure. He timed the act: five seconds and he could release himself. She clung to him but he gently held her away from him.

"I really have to go. My studies ... " he said, as if that explained it all. To his relief, she nodded and looked down, shyly, at the kitchen floor. He could see he'd done enough to placate her. She would never tell on him now.

"When will I see you again?" she whispered, kissing him quickly and lightly on the cheek as she opened the front door.

"Oh, soon. I mean, all the time. I'll see you around." He gave her a small wave on the path. "And thanks for keeping our little secret."

She grinned at him, her chubby face creased with pleasure, and blew him a kiss. He was obliged to smile and vaguely repeat her gesture back to her. Then he turned and went quickly down the path, out of the gate and, very fast, back to his own house.

Stella closed the front door quietly, to avoid alerting her mother to Neil's departure. She didn't want any questions from the woman tonight; she needed to be alone with her thoughts. She touched her cheek, then her lips, and her face took on a kind of glow. She leant back against the front door and gazed at nothing in particular. Then a slight frown crossed her features and she pushed off from the door. She went slowly over to the stairs and up to her bedroom.

Laying on the bed and staring up, as she did nearly every evening, at the ceiling with its uninhabited spider's web, Stella reviewed her evening with Neil: what he'd said, how he'd said it; the kisses, the smiles, the half-promises, the heat of his hand in hers. I know he's using me, she said to herself. But I don't care. It's not important. If that's the only way I can have him to myself, I'll do anything he wants. And he's promised me he won't go near that awful woman again, and I believe him. Why else would he want to convince me it was nothing to him except a mad fling?

What counts, Stella lectured herself, isn't winning small battles, but the victory, overall. Why make a big fuss about something that's happened and can't be changed? Why not look to the future, instead of dwelling on the past? The thing is, she ticked off the points on her fingers, he's finished with Tanya now, and he's not going near Mrs Clayforth again; he promised. That leaves what? That leaves me and him; Neil and myself. She touched her cheek again, where he had kissed her, and slid her fingertips round to her mouth and smiled. There would be many more evenings like this, she told herself. Tonight was only the beginning.

Then Stella remembered she was going to ask Neil to take her to the cinema next Saturday. It had gone completely out of her mind when she'd been with him in the kitchen. No matter;

she would see him all the time, now. He had said that, and she believed it to be true. She let out a contented sigh and settled further into her eiderdown and started making plans.

She would go on a diet, of course. Although Neil seemed to like her just the way she was. She would buy some new underwear; the stuff she wore to school had turned grey from throwing it in the washing machine with Thomas's football kit and the coloured blouses her mother wore. And what could she do with her hair? She thought of having blonde highlights, the same colour as Tanya's hair was naturally. She twisted a limp strand between her fingers and held it out to examine it.

But, no matter how hard Stella tried, her mind kept returning to the same image: there she was, in the kitchen with Neil, and he was kissing her, not once but several times, and on the lips. She found it hard to believe this had really happened to her, here, downstairs, tonight. But it had. So she abandoned all other thoughts except those of Neil and herself, standing by the kitchen table, their hands touching, their mouths pressed to each other's in the dim kitchen light. It was the only picture she wanted to hold in her head now. And she wanted to experience that moment again, and again. Stella decided she would do anything to have Neil to herself. She would keep quiet about Mrs Clayforth, pretend it hadn't happened. He would have her complete loyalty, forever, if he would continue to love her like tonight. That was all he had to do: just keep loving her.

"Another two weeks, and I'm finished with these exams," said Neil as they stood at the bus stop, holding hands, after school.

"Then we'll have the whole summer before you start college," Tanya smiled at him. "I can't wait. We'll be together every single day."

He squeezed her hand and they kissed, then the bus came along. Neil should, he knew, have been blissfully happy. But, all the time, he was looking down the street to see if Stella Reynolds was walking their way. It would be a lot easier for him once his exams had finished. He could devote a few hours to Stella to keep her happy and still spend most of his time with Tanya.

He wondered how he'd got into this situation in the first place. He put it down to trying to please others which, he reckoned, was his nature and his upbringing. His parents had always stressed the importance of getting on with people. You never knew when you'd need a friend or a neighbour, or a business contact. So he thought he was doing the right thing, trying to placate both Angela and Stella. But that didn't stop him wanting Tanya; she was his raison d'être, his whole reason for existing.

By the time they got off the bus at Hadham, Neil's mood had become lighter. Stella hadn't been on either deck of the bus – he'd checked – and there wouldn't be another one along for an hour. So he could take his time, walking slowly with Tanya along Hadham Lane, and they could even slip into the woods for a while. It would probably be the last time, before his exams, that they could be completely alone. He would make this afternoon special: he would make love to Tanya like he never had before. She had said she'd wait for him; she wouldn't make demands on his time during the next fortnight. She said she understood he was doing his exams for both of them, their future. And now, he would show her how much he appreciated her consideration. This next hour or two would be precious for both of them and would sustain him throughout the long fortnight of exams.

Stella hadn't seen Tanya to talk to, all day. She'd thought they were friends again, but Tanya had spent every break with Marcia Ackroyd and her gang of three. Every time Stella had looked up, she'd seen the four of them, whispering and giggling, in one corner or another. Even in the few minutes between classes, when they'd moved along the corridors from lesson to lesson, carrying their bags and books, Tanya had been too busy talking to Marcia and Jennifer and Gillian, to fall in step with Stella and ask her how she was.

This had been frustrating for Stella. She had so much to tell Tanya. She was bursting to let her friend know she was seeing Neil Boyd. She wouldn't tell the girl everything, of course. She had promised not to talk about Mrs Clayforth to anyone, and it wasn't in her interest to do so. But she was dying to tell someone about her boyfriend, for that was what Neil had become in the last twenty-four hours. It had taken only one night of lying awake, turning over the evening's events in her head, and she had been able to embellish every look and every word he had directed at her. By Monday morning, Stella was seriously in love and wanted to tell the whole world.

But there was no one to tell. She had very few friends at school with whom she could talk intimately. There had really only been Tanya since they'd started at Broadfield Lodge, after they'd both failed their eleven-plus exams. It was a second-rate private school with top-rate fees, which was enough for their parents to believe they were doing the best for their daughters. Doreen Reynolds thought it gave Stella the chance to make the right sort of friends. It would give her an entrée to a certain social milieu and stand her in good stead for the rest of her life.

But Stella, with her combination of weight problems and a slow wit, and her love of being on her own with her nose stuck in a book, had not made any friends. She was probably the most unpopular girl in the class. It was only because she had known Tanya at primary school that she was able to talk to the girl, on occasions. But Tanya soon made new friends who weren't interested in Stella tagging along. Stella had no experience of boys to contribute to the girls' conversations, and she certainly couldn't wear the latest fashions, being overweight, lank-haired and, for a period, incredibly spotty.

Stella got off the bus, feeling low after another day alone at school but looking forward to going over to Neil's house and spending an hour or so with him. It didn't matter, any more, that she was snubbed at school. She could leave at the end of the year, like Tanya, if she wanted. She could leave home, too, and never have to put up with her mother's bad temper again. Then it began to dawn on Stella that she could do what Tanya had planned to do: she could follow Neil to university and get a job and share a flat with him.

The more she thought about this, the more the idea grew, until it became a certainty; something to plan for, something to talk about with Neil when she saw him that evening. The thought spawned a whole new daydream that kept her mind occupied nearly all the way along Hadham Lane. She began to think about the decor for their flat, the linen, the curtains, the ornaments. She was halfway through planning the kind of meals she would cook for Neil when she realised she was walking past the woods of the old manor. She began another daydream: she was in the woods with Neil, in the old camp where they had played as children. It didn't matter that she'd come across Neil there with Tanya, a while ago. That was all in the past. Tanya was history. Now she, Stella, was Neil's girlfriend, and the hideaway in the woods was Stella's special place now, as much as it had been Tanya's.

She left the lane and shouldered her way through the bushes that formed the boundary to Hadham Woods. Slowly, dreamily, happily, she made her way along the winding paths that led to the old camp. She just wanted to see the place again, as it was now, ready to be occupied by Neil and herself in the long afternoons of the coming summer. The ground was soft under her feet after the heavy rain which had fallen the previous night. The world smelt fresh and clean, and her old loneliness had been washed away with the bad weather.

Stella glanced up and blinked at the sunlight glittering in the highest branches of the trees. She felt a new contentment, a tranquillity, an inner peace that she hadn't experienced during the years of domestic chaos and problems at school. At last, Stella had someone who cared for her, a boyfriend she could care for, in return. She belonged to Neil Boyd now; a person to call her own. And she would make sure she stayed with him for the rest of time. No Angela Clayforth, or anyone else, was going to spoil this precious love for her. She would see to that.

She was almost at the camp when she heard the cry. Her heart boomeranged in her ribcage, then sank like a stone. She knew that sound, she knew what it meant. Tanya was making love in the camp, and there could only be one person she was with. Or could there? Stella said a quick prayer, although she wasn't at all religious. Could Tanya be with one of Marcia Ackroyd's friends? That Roger Stowe she'd been keen on when she'd first split up with Neil?

Slowly, carefully, silently, Stella moved from tree to tree, drawing nearer to the camp. But she knew, even though she couldn't admit it to herself, that it was Neil in the camp with Tanya. She paused behind a large oak and asked herself if she wanted to see this, if she really wanted to smash her dreams, forever; to have nothing left to hope for. But she couldn't pull herself away. She had to know for sure. She inched her way forward, biting her lips so hard that they almost bled. And then she saw them through the bracken, quite clearly, lying on the floor of the old camp. Their naked bodies moving as one, melded in a joyous union.

Stella backed away; her face distorted, twisted, dark, murderous. She turned and careered through the woods, crashing through the undergrowth, not minding the brambles and branches that tried to bar her way. Wide-eyed with shock, she couldn't even cry. She could make no sound, except the heavy snorting of a bovine creature. She stumbled out into the lane and lumbered, panting, up the road towards home. Her one thought was to hide herself away in her bedroom, then stuff her eiderdown in her mouth to stifle her screams.

She could feel herself shaking, trembling, as she turned the corner into Manor Close. Then she saw the worst possible sight she could have imagined at that moment. Angela Clayforth and Mavis Williams were standing by the gate, talking to her mother. Mrs Clayforth was doing all the talking. Tanya's mother had her arms folded and was pursing her lips, as if she were only just able to tolerate what Angela was saying. Her own mother was holding on to the gate, probably out of necessity, and she was a major obstacle in Stella's route to her bedroom.

"Ah, it's your daughter, Doreen. Stella, you look as though you've been through a hedge, backwards! Look at your uniform – "

"I'll deal with my own daughter, if you don't mind, Angela," said Doreen in a low voice that was distinctly less than friendly.

Mavis said, "Where's Tanya, Stella? Didn't she come home on the bus with you? Her tea's ready and she's got homework to do – "

Stella's words burst from her in a volcanic explosion. All the pain and anger tamped inside her suddenly erupted in a deadly, vicious flow. "She's in Hadham Woods, having sexual intercourse with Neil Boyd. I just saw them! You can go and see for yourself, if you don't mind viewing them without their clothes on!"

The three women looked at her in shocked disbelief. Stella barged through them and pushed the gate open, sending her mother reeling backwards. Mrs Clayforth was the first to recover. "Stella, what are you talking about? What do you mean?"

Stella stopped on the garden path and turned to face them. The image of Mrs Clayforth in an open negligée and Neil fumbling with the belt of his trousers had not left her. The scenario had burned itself permanently into her brain. "Surprised, are you? That nice young man who visits you on Sundays – "

"Shut up, girl!" shouted Angela. "You don't know what you're talking about!"

Stella didn't have a chance to respond. Mrs Clayforth immediately wheeled round and took off down the Close towards Hadham Lane. The women looked after her as she broke into a run and turned into the lane in the direction of the woods. Doreen started to say something to Stella as she followed her into the house. But her daughter, unable to trust herself in the company of her mother at that moment, dived through the back door and up the stairs and slammed the bedroom door behind her.

Only Mavis Williams remained at the garden gate. She put one hand up to her face; the other, clutching the gate post, held her steady. She stared, wide-eyed, at the hibiscus, withered and dying, in the middle of the Reynolds' lawn, and shook her head distractedly, muttering, "Tanya! My Tanya!" over and again.

CHAPTER 16

Angela half-ran the length of Hadham Lane, her face pink with exertion, her bosoms heaving. She zig-zagged along the road, waving her arms wildly in the air, rehearsing the accusations she would deliver when she found Neil and the Williams girl. Only when she reached the broken wall bordering the woods did she stop and pause for breath, but her mind was already racing ahead as she drew in great gulps of air.

She could see them now, cowering under the hail of her invective. She would tell the girl how free this young man was with his favours, how happy he was to make love to a woman with experience. And she would make it plain she wasn't going to give up her Sunday mornings for anyone; that she could get Neil into her bed anytime she liked. And the girl would start crying because she didn't understand, because she'd thought Neil was hers alone, that he loved her faithfully. And Neil would be standing there, not knowing what to say, having been caught in a compromising situation.

He would expect to lose both women, Angela was sure. But that would be where her maturity would win the day. She'd let him know he was still welcome in her bed, that she understood a man's needs and temptations. And he'd admire her for her worldly attitude and, in spite of their age difference, his admiration would grow into love. And they would become more than lovers and, maybe, one day, they'd get married and he would never stray from her arms again.

Angela jumped over a pile of stones that lay heaped in a gap in the crumbling wall. Without pausing to get her bearings, she plunged straight into the wood, heading for its dark interior. She was still talking to herself as she crashed though the undergrowth, the thick brambles and low branches tearing at her too-tight clothes, veering on to each narrow path that presented itself, pushing back low boughs which hung in front of her face.

She was determined not to cry. She would not let Neil see how upset she was over this infidelity. But, in her heart, she was howling with pain. He had entered a place in her soul that she'd never dreamt existed. Not only had he lifted her to great heights with his lovemaking, but he had now brought her lower than she'd ever thought possible. She had never known such extremes of emotion with Frank; she had hardly known emotion, at all, with him.

It was all that girl's fault; Mavis Williams's daughter. She'd been the one John Taylor had gone weak at the knees over. The girl was the cause of all Angela's problems. She had spoiled each love affair Angela had tried to nurture. Tanya Williams would have to go, that much was certain. Angela vowed she would drive the girl out of the Close, out of the village, out of the county. She would not have Neil snatched from under her nose, as well as John Taylor. Why, the girl might set her sights on Ray Reynolds next! No man was safe, and there wasn't a woman in the Close who could enjoy peace of mind as long as a female on heat like that was around. Angela began to imagine a number of scenarios, accidents that might befall Tanya Williams in Hadham Woods.

"What's that noise?" said Tanya, suddenly sitting up.

"I don't know," Neil answered, but he'd heard it, too. Someone was making their way through the woods, and in their direction. "Quick! Get dressed!" he scrambled up and handed Tanya her blouse.

They just had time to do up their shirts, but not to put on their school blazers, when Neil caught a glimpse of someone moving between the trees. It must be Stella Reynolds, he thought.

He would have some explaining to do, but he thought he could handle the situation if he kept his wits about him.

Suddenly, she was there, standing before them in the clearing. Angela Clayforth confronted them, hands on hips, glowering, her expression pure rage.

"So! You thought you could get away with it? You thought you could sneak down here, whenever you liked, and have your bit of fun!"

Neil knew Angela's words were directed at him, not Tanya. He prayed she would say her piece and leave. The woman was in a highly emotional state, that much was obvious. Her normally perfect hairstyle was in disarray and there were a couple of broken twigs sticking out of it. Her face was fuchsia-pink and her eyes flashed moist and bright. Her mouth was curled in a cruel, sneering fashion, made more menacing by her dark red lipstick.

"Well? Answer me! What do you think you're doing here? After all the things you said, only yester – "

"Please, Mrs Clayforth," said Tanya, stepping forward to talk to the woman. "I don't think you should be here. This has nothing to do with you."

"It has everything to do with me!" Angela aimed an accusatory red fingernail at Neil as he lingered behind Tanya. "You ask him! Go on! Let him tell you the truth!"

"Angela, leave it ... " said Neil, shaking his head with a pleading look.

"Well, if he won't tell you, I will!" Angela's eyes glinted with fury. "That young man of yours, or the young man you think is yours – "

"Stop it!" shouted Tanya, putting her hands over her ears. "I don't want to hear! Whatever bad things you're trying to say about us – it doesn't matter! You have no right to be here! This is a private place!"

"And nor do you have any right, you brazen girl! Do you think you're the only one – "

"Angela! That's enough!" Neil stepped in front of Tanya and waved the woman back with an angry, dismissive gesture. His blood was up now, and he wanted Angela to be gone. He would speak to her later, if it were absolutely necessary, but seeing her here, in their special place, made her an intruder, an aggressor; a thoroughly unpleasant sight.

But it was Tanya who made the first move. Full of indignation at the way their lovemaking had been interrupted and encouraged by Neil's obvious hostility to their neighbour, she stood beside her lover and waved a fist at Angela. "Go home, Mrs Clayforth!

You're too old to understand what's going on here."

The reference to her age sent Angela's mind into a spin. How dare she? How dare the girl talk to her like that! When she saw Tanya's balled hand shooting out towards her, her reaction was swift, automatic, and violent. Her own tamped fist shot out and caught Tanya on the chin, knocking the girl backwards in several tottering steps until she fell against a tree. Neil heard the crack as Tanya's head came into contact with the thick trunk of the oak. He turned and, frozen with horror, saw Tanya's eyes swivel then roll inwards in a cross-eyed fashion. As the girl began to slide down the tree, he saw a thin trickle of blood leak from the corner of her mouth.

Neil watched helplessly as Tanya crumpled and fell onto the soft earth at the foot of the tree. Angela stood equally transfixed, not believing what was happening.

"Tanya!" To Neil, his voice sounded far away and, as he tried to reach out to her, he seemed to be stepping towards her in slow motion. He fell to his knees beside the girl and lifted up her head. Her face was pale, her body limp. Frantically, he took hold of her wrist and searched for a pulse.

"She hit her head on the tree, that's all! I hardly touched her – "

Neil could hear Angela's quavering voice protesting behind him. He laid Tanya back on the ground and tried to find the pulse at her neck. He felt for a heart beat, he shook her gently. "Tanya!" he sobbed, knowing the worst, already. "Tanya!" Then he tilted back her head, opened her mouth and began mouth to mouth resuscitation. Regularly and rhythmically, he breathed air into her lungs and pressed down on her rib cage.

"I didn't do anything!" Angela was saying. "The girl threatened me. I acted in self-defence; you saw!"

Neil refused to give up on Tanya. For ten minutes, fifteen minutes, twenty, he breathed air inside her and squeezed it out again, but the girl didn't respond. Once more, he felt for a pulse. He couldn't get one. Tanya was starting to feel cooler, colder. He felt the rigidity of death creeping through her body. Finally, he sat back on his knees and stared at his girlfriend's lifeless form. Tears rolled down his face. His mouth, thick and numb from the effort of trying to revive her, trembled as he wept.

He tried to think what to do next. Phone for an ambulance, he decided; he must get to a phone. There would be one up at the manor house. He got up shakily, waiting for the circulation to return to his legs. Then he became aware of Angela, still standing at the edge of the glade, not far from the oak tree. The woman seemed calm now. She hadn't uttered a word since he'd begun trying to breathe life into Tanya. He turned and looked at her. But her face showed no emotion. "We must get to a phone ..." he said.

"We must bury her, that's what we have to do."

"What?"

"I said bury her, here."

"Are you crazy? You can't leave her like this. We've got to get her to hospital. There still might be a chance."

"She's dead. I can see that. She needs burying. We need shovels."

Neil blinked at Angela. "I don't believe I'm hearing this – "

"We must do it, now. We have no choice. Go and get two shovels from my garden shed and bring them back here, as fast as you can." She folded her arms with an air of finality, like someone issuing orders to a subordinate.

"Angela, are you mad? We have to phone for an ambulance. The police – and Mrs Williams – "

Angela slid her manicured hands down to her hips. "And just what are you going to tell them?"

"The truth, of course! Tanya fell and hit the tree – "

"And is anyone going to believe you?"

"Of course they will! There's no reason not to. Look, we're wasting time – "

"No, we're not." She flashed a fiery look at him. "You listen to me!" She went over to him, her eyes narrowed to slits, her mouth set in two thin lines, rigid and unyielding. "What are the police going to think when they find a dead girl here? That you banged her head against a tree? That you killed her?"

"Don't be ridiculous! We'll tell them what happened. We'll tell them exactly how it – "

"We?"

Neil looked at her, as if he were having trouble understanding what she'd said.

"If you want 'we', Neil, darling" said Angela, allowing him a hint of a smile, "you'll do this my way, with as little fuss as possible. And I think you'll find it's in your own interest, long-term, as well as mine."

Neil jerked his head up a fraction. "I don't know what you mean by that."

"I mean there's no point getting involved in something we can't do anything about. Now, go and get those shovels. We have to work fast and be out of here."

All at once, Neil felt his knees weaken. He swayed for a moment, then took a deep breath. "You can't make someone disappear, just like that. What are you going to tell Tanya's mother when she doesn't come home?"

"Me?" said Angela. "Me?" She put a hand to her bosom and regarded him with mock surprise. "This is nothing to do with me. I haven't seen the girl. I met you in the lane, that's all."

"You're crazy! You're – you're an evil woman, that's what! They'll know Tanya was with me – "

"Not if you don't tell them." Angela smiled in a superior, knowing way. "You can say you saw her, briefly, and that she said she didn't want to see you again. Use your imagination. You'll think of something, I'm sure. Now, hurry. And trust me."

Neil hesitated. He was torn between wanting to do the right thing for Tanya and his instinct for survival; to avoid taking the blame for what had happened. If he were honest and went to the police and told them the truth, would they believe him? Was Angela right? Would the result of any enquiry into the accident be that he, himself, was blamed? There was no reason for Angela to have been in the vicinity, unless he was prepared to tell the world he'd been having an affair with her. And was he prepared to do that? No, he was not. His mother would never recover from the revelation.

Tanya: his dear, sweet love was dead, and there was nothing he could do to bring her back. He wished with all his heart that he could do something, but how could he help her now? He looked at her, lying so peacefully under the tree. She seemed to be sleeping, that was all. She hadn't suffered. The blow to the head had been instant. And he'd done everything he could to revive her. Now he had to think about himself, his future. An incident like this could ruin his career before it had begun. All he could do was try to keep himself out of the situation. Tanya would have understood. He would give her a loving burial under the trees where they had found so much happiness together. And he would visit her often. He would never forget her.

Neil crashed through the undergrowth towards the lane, still debating with himself on the best course of action. He was already doing as Angela said: he was about to cover up the scene of the accident. But was it for the best? What would be the consequences in the long term? There was so much to think about and he wanted more time to weigh up the options. He felt he was being swept along in a tide of circumstances that was out of his control. He stopped on the pathway and leant against a tree. He wiped the sweat from his forehead with the back of his hand. But, still, he couldn't think clearly. No obvious solution to his problem came to mind. He shook his head and let out an exasperated sob. Then he pushed off from the tree and continued running along the path towards Hadham Lane.

Angela paced the perimeter of the clearing, crossing and uncrossing her arms, walking first in one direction and then in the other, her eye falling at intervals on Tanya's inert body. She hadn't meant for the girl to die. That hadn't been the reason why she'd confronted the lovers in the wood. All she'd wanted to do was create a scene, to expose Neil as the two-timing young man he was, and get him back, all to herself.

If only the girl hadn't shouted at her, if only she hadn't made that reference to her age. It was something Angela had never quite been able to forget when she'd lain in bed with Neil. His body had been so smooth, so taut, so muscular, and there was this girl, in the bloom of youth, pointing out a defect Angela could do nothing about. It had sent her wild. It had been the reason she'd struck out. All the frustration she'd felt about losing the plump, firm body of her youth had been focussed in that one swing at Tanya, in that one fateful second. The girl could have said something else, anything at all, but she'd been wrong to accuse Angela of being too old to understand about love-making.

And now, she was dead. Perhaps it wasn't such a bad thing, thought Angela, as she kicked a clod of earth that had been loosened when Tanya had staggered backwards. The girl had been promiscuous, Angela reasoned. She had already spent the weekend with John Taylor and, now, she wanted Neil, as well. It had been hard enough for Angela to stomach seeing John with the young girl, and their looking so happy together. But she had got over that and focussed her feelings on Neil Boyd, instead. And she would have been content – very content – for everything to have run on in that way. If she couldn't have John, well, Neil was a younger, more exciting liaison for a woman of a certain age. And that, if Angela was honest with herself, was the heart of the problem. Tanya had been young and pretty, and Angela was jealous of her. The girl had been a threat to Angela's own happiness. It wasn't a bad thing that she'd been removed from the playing field.

Neil reached the corner of the Close and glanced down the road. There was no one about, as far as he could see. His best bet, he decided, was to sprint as fast as he could to Angela's and hope that no one came out of their house or drove by in their car at that moment. There was nothing else he could do. He took a deep breath, and ran for it. He was through the gate and up the path and around to the garden shed in seconds. He wrenched open the shed door and fell inside. He didn't think he'd been seen.

Panting for breath, he hung over the handles of the lawn mower for a couple of minutes. His legs felt weak again. What am I doing here? he asked himself, shaking his head in disbelief, droplets of perspiration spraying the dusty boards. He had no idea how he'd got into this situation. And, suddenly, he didn't care. All he knew was he had to get out of the shed and back to the woods, as soon as possible.

He glanced at the garden tools, stacked carefully in order of size and frequency of use by himself when he'd first started working for Angela. He selected two shovels. Again, he couldn't believe he was doing this. He thought of Tanya, lying there in the woods, and his hand began to shake as he lifted the second spade from its wall hook. What else can I do? he asked himself. Do I go to the police, and bring the whole world crashing down about everyone's ears? He snatched up the two spades and held them to his chest. He took a deep breath once more, opened the shed door and began to run.

As he sprinted along the side of the house, Mitzi began to bark vociferously. She'd been incarcerated in the kitchen for several hours and needed to go out. Neil cringed at the incessant yapping, ducked his head and ran for all he was worth along the Close. He dared not look up at his neighbours' windows to see who was observing him. His sole aim was to get back to Hadham Woods as soon as he could, and bury Tanya and come away. He never wanted to go near that place again, ever, in his life. He wanted the whole episode behind him; he wanted to return to a normal existence. He wanted to finish his exams and go to university, and never come back to this part of the world.

But, if Neil had glanced up at the Reynolds' house, he would have seen Stella's head, haloed by the light of her desk lamp, craning towards her bedroom window with a puzzled, frowning expression. He would have seen her get up from her desk and press her forehead against the window pane. He would have seen her staring down at him, following him with her eyes as he ran along the Close, clutching the two shovels to his chest. When he reached the end of the road and turned into Hadham Lane and disappeared from view, Stella also disappeared from the window.

He's not coming back, thought Angela. Of all the low-down tricks, he's left me here with the girl's body. What if he's gone to the police? Would he do that? He might, but he'd have some explaining to do. How could he have known about the body if he hadn't been at the scene of the crime, himself? The crime? What crime? There's been no crime here; only a simple accident. The girl became aggressive towards me; I had to defend myself, that's all. Yes, that's it! I struck out in self-defence. Anyone would have done the same. It was her or me. I had no choice.

Angela listened carefully. The woods were silent. Even the birds seemed to have stopped singing; the sun had gone behind a cloud. She rubbed the tops of her arms as she paced to and fro in the clearing. She looked at the girl, lying pale and still on the ground. Even in death, thought Angela, she looks beautiful. Damn her. She could understand why Neil had found the girl impossibly attractive. It wasn't fair, she thought; I deserve to be loved, too. And I will be loved; I've got him now. We're bound together in this. He needs me, just as I need him. He can't go to the police. If he does, I'll make sure he takes the blame, as well. I'll fix it so that his precious career goes to the wall. And I'll be able to tell his mother a thing or two, and the neighbours – She heard a twig snap, the rustle of branches. She saw someone making their way through the trees, towards the clearing.

"You're back! What took you so long?" Angela almost barked at Neil with relief, seeing him with the shovels.

"I was as quick as I could be," he said defensively. "Here," he held out one of the spades to her and she took it.

"Did anyone see you?"

"I don't know. I certainly didn't hang around to find out."

He went over to Tanya and stood, looking at her. Then he knelt down beside her and leant over and kissed her on the lips.

"Come on! We don't have much time. Where shall we start digging?" Angela glanced about the clearing for a dark, soft-looking spot on the woodland floor. "Here?"

Neil gave Tanya a last lingering look, then he sighed and stood up and looked across to where Angela was standing, shovel poised to strike the leafy soil. He nodded, and watched her spear the ground with the spade. The earth yielded. He went over and began striking the same patch of ground. The two of them dug away without a word, each wrapped in their own thoughts.

Why? Why am I helping her? Why don't I call the police? Neil turned these questions over in his mind as he hacked at the earth, not looking at the woman beside him. When he'd arrived back at the clearing and seen Angela's almost hostile expression towards him, he knew he'd have to sever whatever ties she thought she had with him. Once he had lain Tanya to rest, he would never see or speak to the woman again. Why on earth had he got involved with her in the first place? He couldn't believe his stupidity.

But it had seemed harmless enough: a roll in the sheets with Mrs Clayforth; a bit of a laugh on a Sunday morning. He had no idea how possessive the woman would become. He'd never dreamt it would come to this. Now, he had lost Tanya, the only girl he'd really cared about, and Mrs Clayforth was treating him as though she owned him.

Angela stood up straight to get her breath. She surveyed the hole that was growing under their spadework. She wiped her forehead with the back of her hand, checked her nails for dirt and looked at Neil. "At this rate, we're going to be a couple of hours, at least."

He didn't reply, or even look up. He continued to hack at the earth with his shovel, lifting large clods of soil and throwing them to one side. He knew that if he spoke, he would tell her what he really thought of her, and that might bring him further trouble. Instead, he concentrated on channelling all his anger and emotion into the task of burying Tanya.

He had managed his life badly so far, he knew. He had only meant to enjoy himself. But, what had been an hour or so of fun at the weekend had turned out to have disastrous consequences, and not just for him. He knew his own selfishness had brought about Tanya's death. And now he had to think and act carefully if he was going to extricate himself from the situation. He would play it by ear, proceed cautiously and see how things panned out. If an opportunity arose, he would be ready and he'd take it. He was not about to spend the rest of his life under the thumb of Mrs Clayforth.

Angela paused and leaned on the handle of her shovel, her breath laboured, her face flushed. She looked across at Neil, watching him carefully. "You know, I thought for a moment that you weren't coming back."

Neil kept digging, head down. "Why's that?" he said, eventually.

"I thought you might have gone to the police." She studied every muscle on his face, searching for a clue to what he might be thinking.

"Why would I do that?" She was testing him, he knew.

"You might think that you could. But you can't. We're in this together, for the long haul."

"I'll be going to university soon. I've got my exams at the moment, then I'll get a holiday job. I'll probably go down to the West Country and get a job in a pub, or go up north for a couple of months. I'll be leaving home for good in a few weeks time. We don't need to see each other after this, ever again."

Angela's body straightened and stiffened. She held on to the handle of her shovel with both hands and spoke in a low, constrained voice. "You can't leave me now. Not after this. I won't let you go, Neil. I want us to be together, always."

He stopped digging, stood up and regarded at her. It was the first time he'd really looked at her since Tanya had collapsed under the tree. What he saw made him feel alarmed and exasperated. This older woman, nearly the same age as his mother, trying to cling to him, to manipulate him, trying to take over his life. He was revolted by the thought of it, the idea of spending the rest of his days with this big, vulgar woman with her imperious voice. For that was what she sounded like to him: a bossy matron who was desperate for company and trying to hold on to the only man she could. But she couldn't have him. He would separate himself from her by any means he could. He would kill her if he had to – Did he mean that? Yes, he meant it. He would do whatever it took to get this dreadful woman out of his life.

"I want you to come to me next Sunday morning, as usual," Angela was saying as she worked the shovel into the ground again. "It'll be good for us both. We were good together. There's no reason why we can't continue to make love."

Neil's mind was working fast. He dug to a rhythm, raising the shovel just a little higher, each time. One swing to the back of the woman's head, would be all it would take. He waited until she had bent over her work again. Now she had her back to him. Shovel in the ground, swing the earth to one side, shovel in the ground, swing the earth and –

Something moved in the trees. He saw a flash of bright red clothing dart across to his right. He lowered the shovel and peered into the woodland but, whatever it was, it had gone. He listened, but all he could hear was birdsong.

Someone was watching them, he was sure of it. He fought the urge to fling down his shovel and run, helter-skelter, through the woods and out of this never-ending nightmare. He told himself it was too late; he would achieve nothing by running away. There was nothing he could do, for the moment, but continue to dig. He prayed that whoever was there hadn't seen Tanya's body, that they hadn't wondered why Neil and Angela were digging a large hole in the forest floor. A forlorn hope. His problems were increasing by the minute. He felt a surge of panic. His life was spinning out of control.

CHAPTER 17

"That's enough for me," Angela stood up, stretched her back and leaned on her shovel. "It must be deep enough now."

Neil would have liked the hole to have been longer, wider, much deeper, for Tanya's sake as well as for his own peace of mind, but the flash of movement in the woods had brought a new urgency to the work. All he wanted to do now was bury Tanya in the shallow grave and get out of Hadham Woods as soon as possible. He'd sort out the problem of Angela Clayforth another day. One problem at a time. She was becoming the least of his worries. Who the hell had seen them digging the hole in the woods?

"Anyway," continued Angela while he worked on the last corner of the trench, "you wouldn't have been able to telephone from the manor house. It's empty now. The family moved out last week, after the fête. They'll be building houses here soon, I expect. Expensive ones, like ours." She swept a bangled arm around her, taking in the clearing. "All this will be built over. It'll be someone's driveway, here. And we'll go on living in Manor Close, just the way we did before. And the girl's disappearance will be completely forgotten."

Neil stood up abruptly. He didn't want to hear any more of Angela's ideas for his future. "Let's bury her and get out of here," he said, going over to where Tanya lay. Gently, he slipped his hands under the girl's arms and waited for Angela to take hold of the ankles. Together, they carried Tanya over to the trench and laid her down in the dark, rich soil. Neil arranged her long hair on her shoulders and crossed her hands on her breast. Then he paused for a minute and said a silent prayer over the body while Angela stood there, examining her chipped nail varnish.

Then they piled the earth on top of Tanya; Angela seeing to the end where the feet lay and Neil shovelling earth onto the rest of the body. He left her head until last. He dreaded obliterating his girlfriend completely and began to put the earth back more slowly.

"Look, I've done enough," said Angela, with more than a trace impatience in her voice. "I'll leave you to finish this. I'm going back now. We shouldn't go home together, in any case."

"OK."

"I'll see you on Sunday morning." She waited for his reply.

He continued to shovel earth over Tanya, slowly, almost sprinkling it with his spade.

"My place. Usual time."

He didn't respond.

"Don't forget, Neil, we're in this together."

He gently shook more soil, this time under Tanya's chin.

"We need each other, Neil. You and I." It was almost a question.

He looked up and gave her an ugly look. She had never seen his face look so dark and twisted with hate. Angela turned and hurried away from him, taking the path back to Hadham Lane and her immaculate home, and normality.

Neil watched her go for a moment, then turned back to Tanya. He knelt down by her face with its peaceful, sleeping expression. "I promise you, Tanya, I will never forget you. You'll be the love of my life, always. I'll get rid of that woman, you'll see. I'll do it for you. You know she was nothing to me."

He bowed his head and said another prayer. He wasn't particularly religious but prayers, to him, added a solemnity to the burial. Then he took hold of his shovel and moved the rest of the earth at double speed, not looking at the beautiful face the soil was obliterating. When he'd finished, he broke off some small branches and laid them on the earth. He found some ox-eye daisies growing at the edge of the clearing; he picked them and laid them at the head of the grave.

A last look around, and Neil gathered up the two shovels. The grass around Tanya's grave was trampled and churned, but it would soon settle and grow again; nature renewing itself. He knew Tanya had loved nature and wild flowers. She was at rest in a spot she had been fond of, and that gave him a sort of comfort.

He turned to go. His knees nearly gave way when he saw her standing there. Not five feet from him, Stella Reynolds stood beside the thick trunk of a beech tree, regarding him with a slight smile on her face, her head to one side.

"'Lo, Neil."

"Why, Stella!" He tried to sound light, pleased to see her, but he knew the horrified look on his face gave him away. "How long have you been standing there?" He needed to know.

She shrugged her shoulders. "A while," she said.

He wanted to ask her how much she knew, exactly what she'd seen. He almost felt like giving up, there and then, and going straight to the police. "Did you see who else was here?"

She nodded. Infuriatingly, she was giving nothing away.

"Who, then?"

"You were here with Mrs Clayforth. You told me you'd never see her again."

Her words were a chink of light in the blackness of his situation: she was concerned about his relationship with Angela, not what had happened to Tanya. He clutched at this straw of hope. "I didn't ask her to come here. She followed me, that's all."

Stella nodded. "I told her you were here with Tanya. I was walking here and I saw you with her, in the camp." She gazed at the mound of earth with the branches and flowers arranged on top of it. Then she looked at him, waiting for him to speak.

She knows, he thought to himself. She saw me with Tanya and that upset her, so she tried to stir things with Angela. She must have followed the woman back to the wood and seen her hit out at Tanya. So, she saw the girl crack her head against the tree, saw me trying to revive her. Then she saw us bury the body. She knows it all. Yet, she hasn't said anything about going to the police. Neil computed all this at lightning speed while he stood there, holding the shovels.

But why hasn't she mentioned going to the police? he asked himself. Then he provided his own answer: because that's not what's concerning her. She's jealous of Angela, that's all. She doesn't care about the rest. That means it's me she wants, not an enquiry into the death of Tanya. He felt a surge of hope. If I'm nice to her, he wondered, will she forget everything she saw? He had to gamble on that being the case.

He dropped the shovels and walked up to Stella. He took hold of her and he kissed her. She didn't back away from him. He felt her respond. He kissed her again. She put her arms around him and clung to him, kissing him with the same passionate force as Angela Clayforth always did.

He relaxed. Relief flooded through his body. He was happy, even excited, to discover he had control over this awkward girl. He pressed against her. It was like a new adventure, a new conquest. He almost wanted to make love to her, there and then. He knew he could have her, and that she wanted him. Then he became conscious of the mound of earth behind him. He thought of Tanya, still warm in her grave, and he was disgusted with himself.

"We have to be getting back," he said, holding Stella away from him. Then he looked at her, sharply. "You wouldn't do anything to hurt me, would you, Stella? You know, I'm very fond of you."

She shook her head, earnestly. "I could never do anything to harm my future husband."

"Your what?"

"We will get married, one day, won't we, Neil?"

He suppressed the urge to laugh out loud. "Hmm. Yes, one day." Why not humour the girl? He needed her, for the moment.

Her face lit up. Her eyes shone with a child-like happiness. She stood on tip-toe and kissed him again. She wanted to hug him, cling to him, never let him go. All that she had been through, all the tears and jealousy over the months and years, had been worth it. She had known her patience would finally win through. Neil was hers now, and forever. He had just asked her to marry him. He had forgiven her for telling Mrs Clayforth about Tanya and him, and thereby causing Tanya's death.

It stood to reason, if Stella had kept quiet about seeing Neil and Tanya in the woods, Mrs Clayforth would never have known where to find the couple. The woman would never have gone there to confront them, and Tanya would still be alive. The guilt Stella had been feeling over the incident was starting to evaporate already. Neil hadn't accused her of anything at all. In fact, he seemed to want her to be there for him, to support him through his ordeal. He'd clearly had no feelings for Tanya, and Stella reckoned she'd been stupid to overreact as she had. And he'd simply been having a 'laugh' with the older woman, as he'd called his affair with Mrs Clayforth; Stella understood this now. Neil was obviously a man with strong needs and, as his wife, she might have to look the other way, occasionally.

She watched him throw Angela's shovels into the bushes then, together, they trailed back along the lane to Manor Close. Both were silent, each lost in their own thoughts: Neil trying to work out what he would say if questioned about seeing Tanya; Stella planning a white wedding at St Joseph's and a honeymoon in the West Country.

When they got to Stella's gate, Neil didn't kiss her again. Instead, he said, "Remember, Stella, you've seen nothing. Leave me to explain about Tanya going missing." As a gesture, he brushed her hand with his, and it was enough for the girl. She nodded, mutely. She was relieved of any responsibility over her friend's death and she had Neil to herself for the rest of her life. Stella couldn't believe her luck. When she opened the back door, her mother was waiting for her in the kitchen. Doreen struck her daughter hard across the face.

"How dare you!" shouted her mother as Stella toppled backwards into the kitchen table. "How dare you show me up in front of my friends and neighbours!"

Stella held the side of her face. Her cheek was beginning to burn and redden. She could smell drink on her mother's breath. Nothing unusual there. What she couldn't understand was why her mother was being so emotional. Two drinks, and she was normally semi-comatose. There must be other forces at work, decided Stella. Who, or what, had awoken the sleeping monster?

She was so busy watching out for the next blow that it was a minute or two before she noticed the gash on her mother's forehead. Her mother had fallen and hurt herself before: she had often misjudged a door or the staircase. But this wound was a new addition, right in the centre of her brow. Stella tried not to stare, but her mother noticed her looking at the mark and her hand flew to her temple.

"Yes, you can gawk, my girl! You did this to me!"

"I did? No! I couldn't possibly have – "

"You pushed me over in the garden, in front of Mrs Williams and Mrs Clayforth. You just barged past me when you came home from school. You're a clumsy oaf of a girl! God knows, I deserve better than you!"

And I deserve better than you, thought Stella, but experience had taught her not to voice an opinion. So, her mother had fallen over again; probably in the house after Stella had followed Neil to Hadham Woods. Doreen often used Stella as an excuse, somehow, when she collided with a wall or a cupboard. None of this had mattered to Stella for a long time now, as long as she could avoid her mother's blows. She could never remember a time when her mother hadn't hit her, often on the slightest pretext. For years, she'd believed she deserved the abuse, she'd thought she was a bad child who drove her mother mad. But, as her mother's drinking problem grew worse, and Stella looked around at the marriages of her classmates' parents, she began to see that Doreen was the source of her own unhappiness. Worse than that, she had made life at home almost intolerable for Stella and her brother, and was the reason her father had left them.

"That cut's fresh," said Stella, standing back, well out of range of her mother's hand. "You did that no more than half an hour ago. What's upset you, this time? Has Dad phoned? Has he been round to collect some clothes?"

At these words, Doreen's anger seemed to ebb from her. Her head drooped and her shoulders hunched forward. She collapsed onto a kitchen chair and laid her head on the table and sobbed into her hands without restraint. Stella didn't go over to the table to comfort her. Her mother's mood could change in a flash, without warning. She remained in the corner of the kitchen, watching Doreen's shoulders heaving, and thanking heaven she would soon be able to leave home, never to return.

Finally, her mother lifted her head. She looked a wreck: her face was red and blotchy and her mascara had run, leaving black smudges around her eyes. Her forehead was beginning to swell around the gash and the skin was dark with bruising, her hair was lank and tangled and the roots needed retouching. She blinked at Stella and shook her head slowly. "Your father," she mewed, before giving a long sniff and wiping her nose with the back of her hand, "isn't coming back – "

"I know that."

"And I suppose you know who he's gone to, don't you?"

"Some woman from the golf club, I expect."

Doreen shook her head. She looked pathetic, thought Stella. She needed to pull herself together. No one was going to sort out her problems for her; she had to do it for herself. Stella knew she was going to hear the same old complaints about the many evenings her father had spent away from home, at his golf club with his friends. Her mother could never understand why he preferred the clubhouse to his home life, or why he had finally been attracted to another woman.

But Doreen had a new twist to the saga, tonight: "Your father is having an affair with Angela Clayforth. You saw them at the fête the other week, I'm sure."

"You're joking!"

Her mother looked indignant. "I am certainly not joking. Your father told me he's met someone else and Mrs Clayforth has said the same thing."

Stella wanted to laugh out loud. If only her mother knew about their neighbour and Neil Boyd. Though that was all over; Neil belonged to Stella now. But if Neil was right and his Sunday morning with Angela Clayforth had been only 'a laugh', then it was possible that Mrs Clayforth had made a beeline for her father, and got him. After all, the man was lonely and needed company. Why shouldn't he fall for his neighbour and spend his evenings with her, pretending he was at his golf club?

"How do you know they're together? Dad's not living in her house. We'd have known about it; we'd have seen him going in and out of there."

Doreen sniffed and wiped her nose again. "I think he's waiting for her to join him, somewhere else. I think she sees him at his new flat, somewhere in town."

Stella still didn't want to believe it: her father with that odious creature, the woman who had made love to her future husband. Angela Clayforth was pushing into every corner of her life, taking from her the men she loved best in the world. "Well, go and talk to her," Stella said to her mother. "And tell her to leave Dad alone."

Doreen straightened in her chair and laid her hands flat on the table. "I intend to. I'm going to have it out with her, once and for all."

Stella saw an advantage in this: her mother having a major spat with Mrs Clayforth would keep the pair of them occupied for a while. It would give Stella time to figure out how to eliminate the woman from their lives. She already hated Angela Clayforth for going with Neil, and now she loathed their neighbour for being with her father. With the Clayforth woman gone, her father might return to them and her mother would stop drinking. Stella pushed off from the worktop and went slowly out of the kitchen, leaving her mother slumped over the table, quietly sobbing to herself again.

The decision was made: John Taylor was moving out of Manor Close. He would see Tanya one more time before he went and, maybe, she would come with him and the children to Ireland where he'd got an interview for a job in County Cork. It was a small hope, but he couldn't go without asking her. There was a chance that she'd say yes. He knew she wanted to leave home. Well, she could come with him and start a new life, away from the prying eyes of neighbours like Angela Clayforth. If it hadn't been for that woman, turning up at his house at all hours, Tanya might have seen him in a different light. And now the neighbours thought he had come on strong with Angela, only to ditch her the moment it suited him.

He opened his front door, cautiously. It was ridiculous, he told himself, the way he had to sneak in and out of his own home, these days. But if Angela Clayforth saw him, she would probably create a scene in the middle of the street for all the world to hear. She was an actress of the first order, no doubt about that, and a strong character who was used to getting her own way in life. It was not that John was a coward, but he was not a man who enjoyed confrontations, of any sort. Yet, he was beginning to experience hostile feelings towards his neighbour: she had ruined his chance of finding happiness again, after the loss of the woman he'd loved. He felt that if he saw Mrs Clayforth, one more time, he wouldn't be as polite to her as he had been in the past. And, if she provoked him again, he might even strike her. She was starting to have that effect on him.

No sign of Angela in the garden opposite. He slipped out of the door, closed it carefully and quietly, went quickly down the path, out of the gate and turned left towards the Williams's house. Tanya's gate squeaked loudly as he lifted the latch and pushed it open. He would offer to oil it for them. It must be hard to take care of everything, two women on their own.

He knocked and waited. Knocked again; waited. The third time, he banged the knocker much harder than he'd meant to, then quickly looked in the direction of Angela Clayforth's house. The last thing he wanted was for her to see him calling on Tanya. But there was no sign of movement anywhere in the Close. He wondered if the girl and her mother were out. The house appeared to be empty; there was no sound, no twitch of the curtain. He knocked one more time, telling himself he would go home if no one came to the door within a couple of minutes.

But the door did open. Mavis Williams's haunted face peered out from the dark interior. She looked at him without expression.

John Taylor was taken aback for a moment. The woman looked unwell: her eyes were red-rimmed and there were dark, puffy rings around them. Perhaps she'd been quarrelling with her daughter again. Tanya had told John she was fed up with the constant rows she'd been having with her mother. "Mrs Williams, it's John Taylor." He wasn't sure she recognised him. "I'd like to have a word with Tanya, if I may."

Mavis regarded him blankly. When she spoke, her voice sounded faint and scratchy, like an old 78 rpm record. "Tanya ... yes ... " And she continued to stare at John.

"Tanya: is she there? Can I speak to her for a moment? It's important. I'm going away soon."

"Gone away ... yes. Gone. That's what they said ... "

"Mrs Williams, are you alright? Can I come in for a minute? You don't seem to be well."

"She's gone. They told me. Gone somewhere ... "

John gently took hold of Mrs Williams's hand and steered her inside and closed the front door behind them. He led her into the kitchen. He had never been in the Williams's house before and was surprised at how untidy it was, a film of dust on the surfaces. Mavis wore the same air of neglect: a dark stain on the front her skirt, the cuffs of her blouse grubby and a button missing, her hair loosely pinned but slipping over her thin neck. He sat her down at the table. She stared at him, passively. There was food on the table: old, stale and brittle. Several cups of half-drunk tea had coatings of rancid milk across their surfaces.

He took one of her papery hands in his and held it. He was beginning to realise what had happened. Tanya had already left home and her mother was devastated, unable to carry on without her beloved daughter. John knew Mavis adored Tanya, that her daughter was her whole life, and that Tanya had been struggling to leave the nest for some time now. If only he had called a few days earlier, he could have persuaded the girl to come with him and the children. And he would have made sure she kept in touch with her mother. The woman wouldn't have been left, abandoned, in this way.

"Where is she, Mrs Williams? Where has Tanya gone? Where can I get in touch with her?"

Mavis made a whimpering sound and shook her head. She seemed to have no tears left for crying.

"Is she in London?" He waited, but she didn't respond. "Do you have a phone number for her? An address? "Is she with anyone? Does she have a job?"

Mavis gave a dry rattle at the back of her throat. "She's gone. Left me for good. That young man: Neil; she told him she was leaving. Then she went. She didn't say goodbye. She just went."

"Has she gone with him? Have they gone somewhere together?"

Mavis slowly shook her head. "She's gone on her own. She wanted to leave me. Imagine that ... "

John could imagine it, alright. This was no place for someone as happy and vivacious as Tanya. The house was like a morgue: dark, gloomy, foul-smelling. Even her mother's breath smelt stale as she leant across the table towards him. He should have come to see the girl earlier. He could be with her, right now, if only he'd known how stifled she'd been in this place. But he hadn't dared make a move with that bitch Clayforth watching him from her window, opposite. He felt the anger Angela always invoked in him start to rise again. He had missed an opportunity to be with Tanya, only by a few days. There was nothing left but to leave, too. He had no reason to stay, anymore.

"Look, Mrs Williams, I'm moving. I'm taking the children to Ireland. I'll send you my address." He studied her face to see if she was listening to him. It was hard to know. The woman looked half-demented. "If Tanya contacts you, will you give her my new address? Can I phone you in a few weeks time and let you know where I am?"

This woman's neglecting herself, thought John. She should see a doctor. If she goes on like this, much longer, she'll be in a hospital. I bet she hasn't eaten for days. He noticed her eyes were almost glazed, as if she'd retreated to a world where reality couldn't intrude and hurt her. He wondered if he should speak to one of her neighbours and suggest they get a doctor in. He would have done just that: spoken to someone about Mavis, but he wasn't sure what his standing was in the road, after Angela Clayforth had said she would tell everyone how he'd treated her.

No, he decided. It was none of his business. He just wanted to get out of there and leave the past behind. He got up from the table. Mavis Williams remained seated, as if unaware of his presence. He put his hand on her shoulder, but she stared straight ahead. "I'm going now. Look after yourself, won't you?"

The woman regarded the kitchen sink in front of her, glassy-eyed.

He walked over to the door, then looked back once more at Mavis. There was a carving knife on the table. John would recall, in later years, wondering if he should put it away in a drawer, out of her reach. She wasn't in a fit state to have big knives lying around. She could do herself a mischief with a blade like that.

Then he was out of the door and into the street and heading for home as fast as he could. All he could think was that he had lost the chance to be with Tanya in Ireland. He flicked his eyes in the direction of Mrs Clayforth's house as he turned into the gate. That woman: if he ever saw her again, he'd be tempted to do her harm.

It was the morning Neil had dreaded all week. But it had to be taken care of. He had to get Angela Clayforth out of his life, for good; then he could deal with Stella Reynolds. He had nearly finished his exams and all he wanted now was to leave home and start his life again, in another part of the country. Tanya would always have a special place in his heart. He would remember her, all his life, with affection and love.

The hardest thing he'd had to do, ever, was to speak to Tanya's mother; to tell her Tanya wasn't coming home any more. He'd made up some story about the girl telling him she was going away, that she didn't want to see her mother again. It had torn him apart to see how Mrs Williams had taken the news, how she'd swayed on her feet and clutched the table to steady herself. He'd helped her to the sofa and got her a glass of water. He'd always known Mavis Williams had lived for her daughter, that Tanya was her whole life.

From that moment, the woman seemed to retreat into a kind of shell, a strange world of her own. She rambled on to Neil, saying she already knew that Tanya had gone; that his visit was no surprise to her and she'd been expecting it. At first, he'd imagined the woman was distraught with grief. But, then, a more sinister idea crept forward from the back of his mind. He had not forgotten the flash of red clothing he'd seen moving between the trees while he and Angela had buried Tanya. It had been nagging at him all week: Stella was wearing a blue dress with yellow and white flowers when she'd appeared in the woodland clearing just after Angela had gone. He'd tried hard to remember if he'd ever seen Mrs Williams wearing a red cardigan or a blouse of the same colour. Or, perhaps, his mother, or Doreen Reynolds. Or John Taylor in a red weekend shirt, or one of his children.

It was one of the loose ends he had to tie up before he went to college. He needed to tidy up his life so he wouldn't have to give the incident any more thought. It was his future that counted. The past was done, finished with, and it couldn't be changed. He'd made a few mistakes, granted; but he wasn't going to let that ruin his life. He was a young man with ambition. He was handsome, intelligent and capable. He had everything to look forward to; he'd had it planned for years.

Only Tanya had thrown him off course when he'd realised how much he loved her. But now Tanya was gone, and nothing else mattered and no one else was going to stand in his way. He dreamed of a brilliant career with a beautiful, rich and well-connected woman by his side. He would have a partnership in a top law firm in the City, a large house in the Home Counties and a small chateau in France. He would play golf, of course, as one did to make business contacts. His children would go to the best schools and his sons would follow him into the law. He would probably have a mistress and he would keep her in a flat in Mayfair, near Shepherd's Market. One of the boys at Neil's school had a father who kept a woman there, so he knew it was the right place for extra-marital pleasure.

He would work hard and he would play hard and, who knows, one day he might be Lord Mayor of London. He would not let Angela Clayforth stand in the way of all that. He was destined for higher things, and he would make that plain to her today. It would be unpleasant, but it couldn't be avoided.

Neil's jaw was already set as he approached number twelve, Manor Close. He gave the gate a violent shove, sending the wrought iron clanging against the low brick wall that bordered the property. He strode up the path and round to the side of the house and snatched at the handle of the back door. He was in no mood for compromise: he'd reached his limit. Angela Clayforth had caused him more trouble than he'd ever imagined at this stage of his life. It was not the right way to start his career, and it was not the way he meant to go on.

CHAPTER 18

She was waiting for him in the kitchen. She had on a black negligée this time, with red silk ribbons threaded through the edges. Her hair was brushed out, looking softer, instead of stiff with hair spray as usual. Her face wore a hungry expression. She went towards him as soon as he stepped inside and closed the door.

"I knew you'd come!" Angela flung her arms around him, letting the negligée fall open. Neil stepped to one side and held her at arms' length without looking at her naked body. He wasn't smiling, she noticed. His eyes were cold and grey in the morning light. She did up the ribbons on her negligée but there wasn't enough material to cover her bosom. She was pleased about that: he would soon be in the mood for her, even if he seemed distant at the moment.

"I'm not staying, Angela. I've come to tell you it's all over between us – "

"You can't leave me now!" cried Angela, holding out her arms to him; but, again, he moved away from her. "Too much has happened. We have secrets together. You don't want the whole world to know about us, do you?"

"Nobody will know anything unless you tell them, Angela. And I don't think you want the police involved. Just think what your neighbours would say."

"They're your neighbours, too! What would your mother say if she heard about us?"

Neil looked at her with a steely expression. "You've already threatened me with that one. Go ahead, if you want, and tell the world. I don't think you want to ruin my life. You've nothing to gain from that."

"Oh, yes I have!" Angela was not about to show any weakness in front of this young man. She'd always had a streak of bravado in her. She racked her brains to think of something, anything, she could threaten him with; something that would keep him close to her. She knew she needed him.

"If you think you can tell people I killed Tanya, there's something you should know. Somebody saw us in the woods; someone saw you hit Tanya – "

"I don't believe you! You're making this up!"

Neil shook his head and, for the first time, he smiled. But it wasn't a friendly look; it was full of disdain for her. "After we buried the body, after you went, there was someone else standing there, watching me."

"Don't lie to me!" Angela tore at her negligée distractedly.

He gave a short laugh. "There's no reason to lie to you. I spoke to the person. And that person told me what they'd seen. It'd be two against one, if you tried to go to the police, Angela. Give it up. Stop trying to threaten me."

"I'm not trying to threaten you," she simpered, trying another tack and looking at him with cow eyes. "I want you, Neil."

But he held steady, sensing victory. He could look confident, even if he didn't feel it. He was still worried Angela would go to the police, or worse, tell the whole world about their Sunday mornings together. He would die of shame. His career and his life would be over.

"So, how about it?" said Angela in a wheedling voice, toying with her negligée ribbons and smiling at him coyly. "Come upstairs and play for an hour – "

Dammit, she wasn't listening to him. Was he never going to be free of her? "You're a lonely old woman, Angela. Find yourself a man your own age. Get married again. Stop chasing people half your age – "

"How dare you! I am not old and I am certainly not lonely! You haven't lived yet, that's your trouble! You're not the Casanova you think you are!"

Neil blew out his cheeks. "OK, fine. I'm not good enough for you. That's not a problem. I'm going now – " and he turned towards the door.

"Wait!" Angela launched herself at him. She clung to his back, her arms locked around his waist. "Don't go. You don't have to – "

He threw her off, roughly, and she fell to the floor. Then he began to panic, suddenly feeling trapped. He wanted to run away from this woman and all that she stood for: the forbidden sex, Tanya's death, the destruction of his future career. He could see Angela wasn't going to let him go quietly; she wasn't going to let him go, at all. She would cling to him, drag him down, he would never be free of her.

Just then, the back door opened. Mitzi bounded into the kitchen, followed by Stella Reynolds. Neil froze in horror. It was his worst nightmare: Stella thinking he was being unfaithful to her. He looked back at Angela, still lying on the floor where he had thrown her down. He looked at Stella. Her fleshy face, her eyes bulging, her mouth opening and closing, gulping for air. He couldn't bear to be in the same room as these women for another second. He pushed past Stella and ran out of the back door, down the path and out on to the street, heading for home.

Angela lifted her head and looked at Stella Reynolds, standing there with Mitzi's lead in her hand. The girl dropped the lead to the floor and took a step back, still staring at her mother's friend, crumpled on the tiles.

"Stella, I know what you're thinking ... " began Angela.

But the girl already had one hand on the back door handle.

"It's not what you think. Let me explain – "

But Stella was not in the mood for explanations. She could see, quite clearly, the way things were. Mrs Clayforth had not only taken away her father but was determined to have Neil for herself, as well. Stella hadn't the words; she couldn't articulate the hate she felt for this woman. She had kept anger and resentment suppressed at home for so many years, she couldn't just call it up now, on tap. She had no idea how to tell this woman what she felt, what she would like to do to her.

"Stella, wait –" called Angela, holding up an arm to the girl as she disappeared out of the door. Mitzi pattered over to her mistress and began to lick her hand, her arm, her leg. Angela didn't push the dog away. No one else was going to show her any affection. Even Doreen's fat daughter was refusing to talk to her now.

She shook her head. She couldn't understand it: the harder she loved, the less she got in return. The more passion she felt for a man, the more he backed away. Angela had tried to control her feelings for Neil, for John Taylor, and even for Frank when she was younger. But she was an open, emotional, feeling woman. When she wanted a man, she wanted the whole of him; there could be no half-measures.

Even Doreen, the neighbour she'd thought was a friend, had stopped talking to her lately. Not that it was a great loss: Doreen had practically ruined her sitting room carpet with that red wine. No wonder her husband had left her. Angela wondered where Ray had gone. He'd been so sweet to her at the fête, she could have fallen for him, if she'd known he was free. Had he been trying to get friendly with her? Angela shook her head. She didn't know. How could she know anything about men, anymore? Women were supposed to be the fickle ones but, in her experience, it was men who blew hot and cold –

The door bell rang. Angela got up and went to the front window. She saw John Taylor placing a casserole dish on the step. It was the one she'd taken across to him the evening he'd told her he'd met someone else. A yearning, something like hope, surged inside Angela. The young person John had met, the girl he'd wanted to be with, no longer existed. He was free now, more available than Neil Boyd had ever been.

She pulled aside the net curtain and tapped on the window pane. John Taylor started and looked round, just as he was about to step back on the path. She motioned for him to come around to the side entrance and bring the casserole with him. He hesitated. She nodded her head, vigorously, and waved him round to the back door. Reluctantly, he picked up the dish and, looking uncomfortable, walked round to the side of the house.

Angela opened the door wide. "John!" One bulbous breast freed itself from the black negligée.

John Taylor recoiled, a hand flying up to shield his view of Angela, the casserole dish falling from the other and smashing on the side path. "God!" he exclaimed, turning away with a mixture of disgust and horror on his face.

Angela was suddenly aware of her breast and coaxed it back into the negligée. "Oh, John, I was just going to take a shower. But won't you come in for a coffee ... " She was talking to an empty space. The man was no longer there. She peered out of the back door, only to see the back of John Taylor as he strode quickly down the path and out of the front gate.

Angela ducked inside the door again, then caught sight of the broken pieces of crockery scattered around the step. She shook her head, regretfully. She had bought the dish as part of her trousseau, all those years ago, when she'd got engaged to Frank. And now it was broken, like all her dreams of happiness and love; shattered by yet another man who thought only of himself.

She closed the door and leant her back against it. Tears welled up in her eyes. She had started the day so happily, looking forward to holding Neil in her arms. But she had gone from elation to despondency in a matter of only a few hours. Why was it that life buoyed her up, then hurled her down like this, she wondered? Why couldn't she lead a calm and contented life with a good man by her side? It was all she had ever wanted: a shared affection and comfortable intimacy with someone who accepted her as she was. Angela understood she had a strong personality, but there were advantages in that, she knew. Men loved to receive attention from a woman, and she gave it to them by the bucket load.

Distraught, Angela threw herself into a chair at the kitchen table. Was this to be her life from now on? she asked herself, miserably. Was she never to find happiness? Was there no one who'd give her the love she craved and allow her to return it, one hundred per cent? Her problem wasn't loneliness, as Neil had said it was; she had plenty of neighbours and she could join a club, if she wanted to. It was an intimate, loving relationship that was missing. Surely, that wasn't too much to ask: someone to have and to hold, as they say; someone to share her life? Angela ached to be passionate about someone. Anyone. She simply needed a man.

John Taylor had brought the casserole dish across because he'd wanted to see her again, she was sure. He had wanted to make up with her. Was it her fault that, in her haste to talk to him, she'd spilled out of her negligée? She had only bought the garment a couple of days ago and it was the first time she'd worn it. She had pounced on it in the shop because it had the kind of revealing neckline she knew suited her. But low-cut garments have their disadvantages. Surely, he understood that? He was a shy man, John Taylor. She could help him overcome that.

Angela levered herself out of the chair and drifted from the kitchen. She would have a long soak in the bath, then put on the matching sweater and slacks she'd bought last season but had never worn. She would do her face and, looking cheerful, go across to John Taylor and apologise for popping out of her negligée, like that. He would understand and they'd have coffee together and, soon – What was that, in the hallway?

Lying on the front door mat was a buff-coloured foolscap envelope. Angela picked it up and turned it over. It had her name on it, written by hand, but she didn't recognise the writing. She turned it over. It was sealed. She slid a finger under the flap and tore along the top. There was a single sheet of note paper inside, folded into three. She opened up the letter and sat down at the bottom of the stairs to read it. There were only a few lines, written with a blue ball-point pen, in the same handwriting as the envelope:

I know you killed Tanya Williams.
Meet me at Hadham Manor House
on the first floor at nine o'clock tonight
or I will go to the police

It wasn't signed. Angela turned the letter over. There was nothing written on the other side. She turned it back and read the lines again. Her heart began to pound. She was glad she was sitting down; her legs might have given way.

She tried not to panic. She needed to think. Who knew about Tanya? Who had written this? And why? Did they want to blackmail her? It seemed the most likely explanation. But there could be another motive: the writer wanted to help her in some way, to get her out of this awkward situation. And that person knew she wouldn't come to the manor house unless the alternative was too terrible to contemplate, hence the threat of going to the police. Angela liked that explanation better.

But why the old manor house? Why not simply ring her door bell tonight and speak to her in the comfort of her own home? Because whoever it was didn't want to be seen anywhere near her house. Who was this person? Was it Neil Boyd? Was he trying to get his own back on her? Or did he simply want her to set him free from the terrible secret they shared? He had said as much, this morning. He'd said he didn't want to see her any more, but she'd reminded him they were tied to each other for the rest of their lives. He had gone away and thought about this and had decided they needed to talk. He didn't want to risk coming to the house again. He wanted to meet her on neutral territory, far from the prying eyes of their neighbours.

But, wait a minute! Neil had told her he'd seen someone in the woods when they were burying Tanya. He hadn't told her who that person was, but he had spoken to him. Hadn't he said it was a man? Angela looked closely at the handwriting on the letter. Yes, it could be a man's hand. An older man, not a young man like Neil. Who could this older man be? No one from the manor. The Trington family had put Lady Trington in a nursing home, just after the fête, and the staff had left around the same time, including the gardeners who'd maintained the woodland; Angela had read all that in the local paper. So, who had seen them there? Should she contact Neil and show him the letter? She could knock at his door as soon as she'd had her bath. She had planned to see John Taylor – Angela sat up, rigid, on the stairs.

The letter had not been on the mat, first thing this morning. But she'd found it there after John Taylor had called. He'd come to the front door, first of all, and put the casserole dish on the step. It was only because Angela had seen him from the window and waved him round to the side that he'd spoken to her, at all. He'd probably posted the note through the letterbox when he'd put the dish on the front step. He had meant for her to connect the letter to the dish, to understand he wanted to meet her and talk. Angela knew, then, she had been right: John Taylor wanted to recommence their relationship. But he wanted to meet her somewhere away from the gaze of their neighbours. How romantic of him to think of the manor house! She had always wanted to take a look inside the old place.

Angela glanced up at the hall clock. She had plenty of time before she saw him; it was only mid-morning now. She would relax in a bubble bath and think about what she would say to John. She would, of course, admonish him for being shy with her and making it so difficult for them to begin their relationship. So, it had been John Taylor in the woods that day! He had followed the Williams girl, no doubt, and he'd been upset by what he had seen: the accident when Tanya had hit her head. But Tanya had been unfaithful to him; he must have seen that, too.

Poor John Taylor: he had probably been in such emotional turmoil after that, he hadn't known what to say or do. He wouldn't know how to speak to Neil after that day; the boy had taken his girlfriend away from him. So, it was natural that he'd want to talk it through with Angela. He knew her well enough; he knew she was someone who cared about him. They would sort out any misunderstandings they'd had in the past. She would let Neil Boyd go; John Taylor was the one for her.

It was about a quarter to nine that evening when Angela left the house. She'd spent most of the afternoon rehearsing what she would say to John. She knew now she had no need to worry. She scolded herself for having felt afraid when she'd first read his letter. Like a lot of men, he was shy and unable to say what he really felt. Perhaps he didn't really know, himself. She must be gentle with him; she had nearly frightened him away, more than once, she knew that now. But this time tomorrow, thought Angela, as she squirted generous amounts of Chanel No. 5 on her pulse points, we'll have spent a night in romance and passion in the old manor house. She wondered if the Trington family had left a four poster bed or a chaise longue or two on the premises. That would make the perfect setting for a tryst, almost like a film set. Angela let her imagination roam Hadham Manor the whole afternoon. By a quarter to nine, she was nervous with anticipation, primping her hair in the mirror several times before she left.

The manor house was only a ten-minute walk along the road. Angela had no wish to go through the woods and pass by the grave of Tanya Williams, even though the summer twilight would light her way along the woodland paths. She wanted to forget the past, especially the recent past, and live in the present and look forward to the future. There was a spring in her step when she left the house. She glanced up at John Taylor's house as she turned out of the gate. She wondered if he'd already left to go to the manor. If she walked fast, she might catch him up along the way.

But Angela saw no one on the road. The narrow lane to the big house was deserted. Not even a car passed her. She stood at the entrance of the driveway to the house, remembering her promenade, arm in arm, with Ray Reynolds, only a couple of weeks earlier. Yes, she thought, it could so easily have been Ray she'd fallen for; he had always been friendly towards her. She wondered, for a moment, if Ray had written her the letter. It would be appropriate that they should meet here again, after the fête.

But, no. She dismissed the idea from her mind. She was committed to John Taylor now. She had made a decision. Don't be greedy, Angela, she said to herself. And she started up the driveway with a contented expression on her face, her stiletto heels tapping on the cobbled stones leading up to the studded oak entrance door.

She was relieved to see the front door was open a fraction. He was here, already. That was as it should be. Angela paused on the worn steps to savour the moment. She felt a deep satisfaction, as well as eager anticipation. She turned and gazed across the lawns and the flower beds, to the ancient trees on the perimeter, swaying in the evening breeze. The house had been deserted for a fortnight and, already, the grass badly needed cutting. But the borders were a picture: a riot of blooms of different shades, colours and hues. It was the height of the rose season and their heady perfumes hung in the evening air. Bouquets of Rosa Mundi, Celsiana and Rosa Centifolia intoxicated Angela, and they heightened her desire for John Taylor.

She took a deep breath and exhaled slowly. At last, she felt at peace with the world. All her troubles were over. She was going to her destiny. She had waited a long time for this and, now, her time had come. She turned her back on the summer evening and pushed with both hands on the heavy door. It creaked open a fraction, enough for Angela to slip inside and into the gloom of the hall with its dark oak panelling. Immediately, the musty smell of a deserted house assailed her nostrils. She gave an involuntary shiver and rubbed the tops of her arms and wished she'd brought a cardigan with her.

The letter had asked her to go up to the first floor but, as her eyes got used to the dimness, she could see snatches of interiors through open doors leading off the entrance hall and she wanted to explore. John would wait. Angela had often dreamed of visiting Hadham Manor, and had even entertained the idea of joining the Women's Institute and making jam and cakes when she heard that Lady Trington was a member. But, as her marriage to Frank had deteriorated, Angela had felt less inclined to socialise in Hadham village. She remained curious, however, about the interior of the manor house, and had an overwhelming desire to explore it now, before the light faded, which wouldn't be for another half an hour.

Angela made straight for the rear of the house on the ground floor, where she guessed the main sitting room would open on to the terraces. She was not disappointed. The long room, with its linenfold panelling and ornate plaster ceiling bearing family crests and entwined fruits and flowers, was a breathtaking sight, running the length of the building, from east to west. She entered the room timidly, at first, then, feeling bolder, walked to the middle of the floor and gazed at the walls and above her. She tried to imagine the room full of richly upholstered furniture, brocade curtains and enormous oil paintings of ancestors of the Trington family. There was already a film of dust over the intricate parquet flooring; an aluminium camping chair had been left in the cavernous hearth of the fireplace. Empty cardboard boxes and balls of scrunched-up newspaper were strewn about the room. Already, there were cobwebs on the long French windows, illuminated by the blood-red sunset which lit up the walls and plasterwork.

A noise, coming from the floor above. Of course; he didn't know she was here. He was getting impatient. She should go to him. They could explore the rest of the house together. But, perhaps, he had something else in mind ... He had waited so long for her, and she for him. Angela went quickly back to the entrance hall and started up the grand staircase. Halfway up, she heard a floorboard creak on the first floor, but she couldn't work out from which direction the sound had come. When she reached the top of the staircase, she paused with one hand on the gallery rail. Then she called out, "Hello?" and listened.

Silence.

"John?"

No reply.

"It's me, Angela."

Nothing.

"Is anyone there?"

But someone was there; she sensed it. And she thought she knew where he was. Angela made her way along the main gallery. The sun had nearly set and it was almost dark in the long corridor. She turned in to the first door she came to. The room gave on to the front of the house. It was marginally lighter because of a long casement window. Someone had left it open. Angela was glad of the fresh air. She was beginning to feel oppressed by the damp and the closeness in this uninhabited house. And she was starting to get irritated with John for playing hide and seek with her, in this way.

"John, if you don't come out now, I'm going home. I've had enough of your stupid games." Angela stood still and put her head to one side, listening as acutely as she could.

There it was again: the sound of a floorboard creaking. But the noise had come from another room, further along the gallery. She turned on her heels and went quickly, and as noisily as she could, to the far end of the corridor. She strode through the door of the last room off the gallery and peered into the gloom. There was no one there; not in front of her. Then she heard a slight rustle behind her, somewhere near the door. She turned. A shadow moved towards her. She gave a small jump and raised her arms, automatically. "Oh, you frightened me – "

Something plunged into her breast. She felt a searing pain. She knew, immediately, that she'd been stabbed. She looked down at the large knife protruding from the front of her, then up to see her attacker. In another moment, the knife was pulled from her and thrust into her again. Angela staggered. She tried desperately to see who was in the room with her. She fell backwards, towards the window and the last vestiges of evening light. The other person followed her. A hand went out to the knife, and Angela screamed with pain as the weapon was pulled from her again. Her knees gave way. She fell heavily to the floor, clutching her breast with one hand and holding on to her stomach with the other. As she lay on the dusty boards, she saw the feet of her assailant out of the corner of her eye. A woman. And she recognised those feet. She knew who was trying to murder her now.

"Don't," cried Angela, feebly. She raised a hand, covered in warm blood, and tried to grab at an ankle, but the woman kicked her arm away.

She saw the woman bend over her and raise the knife again. It looked like a carving knife and, in that moment, Angela knew she was going to die. She felt the knife: the hot, excruciating pain. She looked up, beseechingly, at the woman. She felt the air leave her lungs. It was as though she were drowning. She was starting to lose consciousness. Her vision was clouding over. With one, last swooning effort Angela breathed, "You ... " then her head fell to one side, motionless.

The woman stood over her, looking down at the bleeding body, not moving for a long time. She didn't withdraw the knife again. She slowly turned and left the room; her footsteps echoing along the gallery, down the stairs and out, into the night.

CHAPTER 19

Stella attached the lead to Mitzi's collar and pulled the dog towards the back door. The dachshund had been over the moon to see her, jumping up, barking and wagging her tail until Stella had been obliged to shout at her and push her away. She assumed Mrs Clayforth was still in bed, after her exertions with Neil in the kitchen the day before. "She's lucky I turned up to walk her mangy dog," Stella muttered under her breath. "She could work off her energy walking the animal, herself, instead of chasing after other people's fiancées."

Stella had been shaken by the way Neil had pushed past her in Angela's kitchen, the previous morning. But, she reasoned later, if she stood by him when he was so obviously under stress with his exams, he'd appreciate her and, in time, fall in love with her, as he had with Tanya. It was this belief that sustained Stella: a rosy picture of the two of them, walking, hand in hand, into the sunset, and Neil turning to her and saying how much he admired her and had grown to love her.

Mitzi relieved herself on the garden path as soon as they got outside, and Stella wondered how long the dog had been cooped up in the house. Mrs Clayforth was a disgrace; Stella had half a mind to report the woman for cruelty to animals. They made their way, as usual, along Hadham Lane and into the woods at the back of the manor house. Stella avoided going anywhere near where Tanya lay. She wasn't yet used to the idea of the girl's death, even though it had been a kind of accident. The sooner she and Neil left Manor Close and went to live near his university, the better she would like it. She wanted to get as far away as possible from Angela Clayforth.

Mitzi started barking again; running a short distance along the path then scampering back to Stella and yapping, insistently. Stella decided she'd had enough of the neurotic dog for one morning and turned to go back down the path, the way they'd come. "Come on, mutt! This way!" she called. But the dachshund was still playing up, refusing to follow her. "Suit yourself!" Stella shouted and started to head for home. After a few minutes, she reckoned she ought to go back and put the dog on its lead and drag it home with her.

She could hear the animal barking, barking, barking. It was a yelping, high-pitched

417

noise that went right through Stella, and she was starting to get a headache. This would definitely be the last time she'd walk this dog, she promised herself. She put on a spurt, almost running along the path, trying to catch up with Mitzi, whose tiny legs were scrabbling on the twigs and leaves, carrying her towards the wide lawns and terraces of the manor house.

"No, not there! Mitzi! Come back, you stupid dog!" But, each time Stella nearly caught up with the animal, it darted off again, towards the house.

She saw the dachshund disappear around the side of the building and sprinted after her, coming out on the driveway at the front of the house. She stood there, partly to get her breath but, also, to locate Mitzi. She listened. Everywhere seemed silent and still; eerily quiet. Then the high-pitched barking began again. It sounded as though it was coming from inside the house. Stella wheeled round. The front door was ajar. The stupid dog had got itself trapped somewhere in one of the rooms, and now she would have to go and rescue it.

Stella sighed. She would be late for school, at this rate. Not that she cared much about class work, but she had wanted to see Neil at the bus stop. She went up the wide, stone steps and, gingerly, pushed on the thick oak door. It gave a fraction, complaining with a long drawn out creaking sound. But there was enough space for Stella to edge through, and she quickly went inside. She blinked in the dusty half-light of the entrance hall and wrinkled up her nose at the damp, musty odour of the place. Mitzi yelped again. Stella's heart sank. The dachshund had got itself trapped upstairs, probably under a floorboard.

Exasperated, and using swear words she'd heard her mother use, she plodded up the oak staircase and stood at the top and listened. There it was again: that same persistent yapping. It was coming from the far end of a long gallery. Stella frowned, clicked her tongue impatiently, and started down the corridor. When she reached the last doorway, she could hear the dog's claws scraping the bare boards as it scuffled about, probably in an excited circle. "OK, you stupid dog. That's enough for – "

Stella stopped in her tracks and opened her eyes wide. She wasn't sure what she was looking at. She had a horrible suspicion it was human, and it was lying in a heap on the floor. The dog was running round the body, jumping up at it, pawing it, licking the bloody hands and the face. A wave of nausea swept over Stella and her legs began to tremble. She held on to the door jamb with one hand and clapped the other over her mouth. The corpse was covered in dark, congealed blood. It had poured from the torso onto the floor and seeped through the gaps in the boards. The white face was unmarked, but the expression on it was horrific: the glassy eyes were fixed, staring at the ceiling. The mouth was open, as if the body was about to utter some indignant sound. Stella stared and held the door, and continued to stare. She couldn't move; her feet were welded to the floor. She had no idea how the dead person had got here, but she knew, for sure, it was Angela Clayforth.

Detective Inspector Bill Collins leaned back in his chair and blew out his cheeks. In all his thirty years in the police force, he'd never dealt with a murder as bizarre as this. A respectable widow found dead in a deserted manor house; slashed repeatedly with a kitchen carving knife and no obvious suspect. It was going to be a long, drawn out enquiry, involving most of the neighbourhood, as well as the folks who had lived at the manor until recently. He had six months in which to handle the case before he retired and devoted himself to his garden and his roses. He shook his head. He wasn't sure there would be time enough for him to close the case. Jack Baker might have to take over.

The inspector took a deep breath and opened the green foolscap file in front of him. First up: the young girl who'd found the body. Must have been quite a shock for her, he imagined. He read the name at the top of the page: Miss Stella Reynolds, aged sixteen years; lives a few doors down from the deceased. He picked up the phone. "Show her in, Keith." He put down the phone and waited for the door to open. A tubby teenager with a blotchy face, probably from crying and shock, stood in the doorway. "Come in, sit down," he said, indicating the chair the other side of his desk.

"Now then, Stella. I can call you Stella, can't I?"

She nodded. Her eyes were bloodshot and glistening.

Poor kid, thought Bill. She's had the shock of her life.

Hell; I hope they don't think it was me, Stella's mind was racing.

"Right, young lady. I'm going to ask you a few questions. Nothing to worry about. Don't be nervous." She looks scared as hell, he thought, watching her closely. Maybe she knows something but doesn't want to talk about it, for some reason. Better go softly on this one, until we get some more leads.

What if they start digging in the woods? Stella's mind galloped. She was sure Mrs Clayforth's murder was connected in some way with the death of Tanya Williams. She thought of Neil, but she wasn't convinced he'd been that upset by Tanya's death. It hadn't stopped him making love to Stella in the woods, that same afternoon. And he seemed to be having some sort of relationship with Angela Clayforth; at least, that was the impression she'd got when she'd surprised them in Angela's kitchen –

"Have you any idea, at all?" the detective was asking her.

"What? I'm sorry?"

"That's alright. Take your time, Stella. I said, do you know of anyone who didn't like Mrs Clayforth? A neighbour, perhaps, who'd quarrelled with her? Someone who might have wished her harm?"

Without knowing why, a picture of her mother popped into Stella's head. She could see Doreen swaying against the worktop, rifling the cutlery drawer, searching for a sharp knife with which to cut a lemon for her gin. If Mrs Clayforth had been having an affair with her father, her mother had every reason to hate the woman. Suddenly, Stella wanted to go home; she needed to ask her mother a few questions.

Had Doreen slipped out of the house and gone to the manor during the previous evening? Would Stella have known about it, if she had? No, she would not have known, for Stella had been engrossed in a book: 'How to Get Your Man and Keep Him' by the well-known agony aunt, Laetitia Wensberry. But it was not something Stella was going to admit, especially to a policeman old enough to be her grandfather.

"No," she said, looking down at her hands, her feet, around the room; anywhere but at Inspector Collins.

"And did you see or hear anyone while you were in the manor house? Any footsteps? Was there anyone in the grounds? Did the dog appear to see or hear anything unusual? Take your time, Stella; think hard. Who would have wanted to kill Mrs Clayforth?"

Stella examined her hands again. She decided her nails needed cutting. She had a lot to do today: cut nails, speak to mother, discuss Mrs Clayforth's death with Neil. Finally, she shook her head and exhaled slowly. She felt exhausted now. She wanted to go home and lie on her bed and think things through, quietly, without interruption.

"OK, young lady. I won't keep you any longer," Bill Collins said in an avuncular tone, trying to sound kindly. "Now, I want you to think about what I've said and, if you remember anything at all, no matter how small or unimportant the detail may seem, I want you to get in touch with us. The sergeant on the desk will give you a phone number."

"Right." Stella scraped the chair back and stood up and turned to leave.

Just then, there was a knock and the sergeant put his head around the door. "The young lad's here, sir. Shall I show him in?"

Stella peered through the gap in the door and saw Neil sitting on the wooden bench that ran the length of one side of the waiting room. He looked up and saw her, too. He shot her an intense look: urgent and pleading. She stared back at him, wide-eyed, not knowing what to think. Did the police suspect Neil had something to do with Mrs Clayforth? Were they going to arrest him? Would they lock him up; take him away from her for years?

She was shown out of the office. In the waiting room, she said "Lo, Neil."

"Hello, Stella. How are you feeling?" His hand squeezed her arm, with affection and concern, she thought.

And it was enough: all Stella's vague suspicions about Neil's involvement in Mrs Clayforth's death evaporated. She looked up at him and mustered a smile. "I'll wait for you, " she breathed. "I'll be here when you come out."

His hand slipped down her arm and briefly touched her own hand. He looked relieved and her heart leapt for joy. He wanted her to be there for him. She had a place in his life. She stood and watched as the sergeant ushered him into Inspector Collins's room, then she went over to the long bench and sat down to wait. The seat was still warm where Neil had been sitting, and that made Stella feel even warmer inside.

"Sit down," said the detective, showing Neil the chair in front of him. "Neil Boyd, isn't it?" Inspector Collins consulted his file.

"Yes." Neil tried to sound confident, but it was the last thing he was feeling. The cards were stacked against him; he knew that. Did they know about him and Angela?

"Now then, it says here you did odd jobs for Mrs Clayforth at weekends. Went to her house regularly, on a Sunday morning." The older man looked up, waiting for Neil to reply. "Is that right?"

"Yes, that's right." What else could he say?

"And you were at her house yesterday morning, as usual?"

"Yes." No denying that.

"And did Mrs Clayforth seem upset or agitated, in any way, to you?"

Neil shook his head. "No, sir."

That was nice: Bill liked the 'sir'. Not many young people respected their elders, these days. Long-haired louts, most of them. Pop music and hashish. This boy had the right attitude. Hardworking, too, probably, if he had a weekend job.

Bill leaned forward and looked at him hard. "And would you say Mrs Clayforth was a popular woman in Manor Close? Well-liked? Got on with the neighbours, did she?"

It was time to be economical with the truth. Neil shrugged and looked at a loss for something to say. "I only cleaned her windows and polished her car, did her lawn and things like that. My mother asked me to help out when Mr Clayforth died, last year. I didn't always see her. She was in the house most of the time. I only went in for coffee, mid-morning."

"So you don't know if she'd had a disagreement with anyone in the Close? A neighbour, perhaps? Did you hear her arguing with anyone? Not just recently, but at any time in, say, the last year?"

Neil shook his head again and looked apologetic. "I wish I could help, sir. It's awful, what's happened. My mother can't believe it, and nor can my Dad. We all saw Mrs Clayforth at the fête, the other week, up at the manor. She looked happy enough, then. It's a real shock, you know. Unbelievable, really. Everyone knew Mrs Clayforth. She was – well – in the centre of things. Always there." He shook his head once more, for good measure, and looked at the policeman with a steady gaze.

Bill Collins's stomach began to rumble. It was lunch time and, with his digestive problems, he had to eat regularly; the doctor had told him that. He brought his hands down on the desk, then closed the file in front of him. "OK, young man. Here's what I want you to do: if you see or hear anything that might help us with our enquiries, I want you to get in touch with us, pronto. Do you understand?"

"Yes, sir. Of course, sir."

"Good, then." Bill stood up and held out his hand.

Neil got up from his chair and shook the policeman's hand, firmly. A sense of relief washed over him and he felt his jaw muscles begin to relax. He knew they could ask him back, at any time, and they probably would. But he'd got through today, and that was enough for now. "Thank you, sir," he said, smiling, as he turned and left the interview room.

Outside, Stella rose as he came through the door. "Neil, I – "

"Sshh!" he hissed quietly. "Come with me," and he held out his hand.

Stella took hold of it gratefully and, together, they left Hadham police station. They walked quickly down the road without talking, without looking back. It was only when they turned into Hadham Lane that Neil let go of her hand and dropped his pace. He stood in the middle of the lane and took a deep breath, then blew out his cheeks. He put his hands on his head. "Hallelujah!" he said. Then he laughed. Turning to her, he smiled and took her hand again. "Let's walk a while. Let's go into the woods."

"But, we can't – "

He put his finger to his lips. "We can. We can do anything we want. Let's go."

"But the police; they're up at the manor house – "

"That's alright. We're not going near the house. I want to talk to you, Stella. I want to know what they asked you."

They entered the woods by the broken wall, as they had done so many times in the past. Stella was in seventh heaven, basking in the glory of Neil's attention. As they wound their way through the trees, he asked her what she'd seen at the manor house when she'd found Angela, what the police had asked her, what she thought about the murder; that is, who she thought had done it. Stella stopped walking and looked up at Neil. "All I know is: you didn't do it, Neil. And that's all I care about. I'm not going to let Mrs Clayforth's death stand in the way of our happiness. I want to get married, Neil. I want us to be together, from now on."

Neil led Stella along the pathway, deep into the woods. When they got to the clearing, they paused for a moment by Tanya's grave, still holding hands. Neither of them felt the need to express what they were thinking. Both seemed to feel there was nothing more to say. They climbed inside the bracken walls of the camp where they had played when they were children, and where Neil had loved Tanya with all his soul. He kissed Stella, a little reluctantly at first, she felt. But she returned his kisses with the fiery passion that burned within her.

They lay down on the soft earth and held each other. Neil undid Stella's blouse and skirt and removed her underwear. He made love to her in an expert, slightly perfunctory manner. It was Stella who cried out with joy, with unbridled exultation. It set the pattern for their love life together. It was how it would be: the one who performed the act of love, and the one who loved with a burning desire. It was not an imbalance Stella noticed on that day. It was the happiest day of her life.

Jack Baker tapped on Bill Collins's door and opened it, a sheaf of papers and a coffee cup in one hand.

"Got a lead on that bloke who lived opposite Angela Clayforth, Bill."

"Oh, yes?" Collins looked up from his paperwork. He needed a break in this case.

"Apparently," said Jack, seating himself in the chair Neil had recently occupied and depositing his coffee and papers on Bill's desk, "this John Taylor's done a runner to Ireland. The Garda have tracked him down to Cork. He's working there. Living with some widow called ... " Jack squinted at the top sheet of his papers, "Eileen Dwyer."

"Good on you, Jack. Let's get the bastard back here. Stupid idiot, skipping off like that, just after committing a crime."

"We don't know that it was him."

"We don't know it wasn't," responded Bill. "A bit of tough questioning, that'll soon sort him out."

The phone rang and Collins snatched it up. He listened, nodded and said, 'Right. Thanks,' then dropped the receiver back on its cradle. He looked across at Jack Baker and a broad grin spread across his ruddy face. "Got him," he said. "They're bringing him in for questioning now. Looks like we'll have this one in the bag by the end of the week."

"If you say so," said Baker, rising from his chair. "I'm going to interview some of Mrs Clayforth's neighbours. They must know a couple of things that'll give us a lead. The woman wasn't a recluse, we know that already – "

"And we know something was going on between her and this John Taylor," Bill told him. "A Mrs Sheila Hodge volunteered a bit of gossip to the sergeant this morning while I was interviewing that chubby teenager."

"Should be interesting to hear what he's got to say," Jack opened the door to leave. As he did so, the desk sergeant brought in a haggard-looking John Taylor. He looked as though he'd been travelling all night from Ireland.

"Sit down, Mr Taylor," Bill motioned towards the chair Jack Baker had just vacated. "We're hoping you can help us with our enquiries. We're dealing with a particularly vicious murder, here, and I gather you knew the victim well."

John started in his chair, as if protesting. "I didn't know her well," he said. "She was a neighbour, that was all. She tried to help out when my wife died, earlier on this year. She did some cooking for me and the children. But, in the end, I told her we were fine. We were managing alright and I didn't need her coming round – "

"I gather you gave her the message, loud and clear," Inspector Collins appeared to consult his notes. "One of your neighbours says you threw a casserole dish at Mrs Clayforth; left it in pieces on the side path – "

"That's a lie! I took the dish back to her when I was packing to move to Ireland. I dropped it on the path, that was all. I'd been going to leave it by the front door, so as not to disturb her. But she saw me coming down the path and opened the door to me. She – she ... "

"Yes? Go on, Mr Taylor."

John was feeling desperate, already. And he'd only been in the room with the inspector for a few minutes. He realised that every sentence he uttered was digging him further, deeper into a mire of suspicion. He knew things were looking bad for him. He thought he'd escaped the clutches of Angela Clayforth but here she was, reaching out to him from beyond the grave. "She wasn't dressed. I'd come at an awkward moment. As soon as I saw she was in her – her – some kind of wrap, I – well, dropped the dish with surprise, I think."

"You're not very clear on this, are you?" The policeman looked at John, closely.

"I am," Taylor insisted. "I'm very clear on everything. I don't know why you've dragged me back here, all the way from Cork. I've got nothing to say, nothing that will help you. I wasn't involved with the woman, if that's what you mean – "

"Your suggestion, not mine, Mr Taylor." Collins gave him a knowing smile.

The room began to revolve. John felt his face flush with emotion; beads of sweat began to trickle from his forehead. "Look, Inspector," he wiped a hand across his brow, "I swear to you, I've never been involved with Angela – Mrs Clayforth. She wanted – Well, she liked me – a lot – but I told her – I had to tell her – "

"You spurned her advances, you mean?" The inspector raised his eyebrows; the half-smile remained.

"Yes, that's it," said John with some relief that the policeman understood him. "She kept coming round to my house, making suggestions about – about the two of us. In the end, I had to tell her I'd met someone else, just to make her understand I wasn't interested in her."

"And had you met someone else?"

"No! Well, not really. I just wanted to move out of the road, and go somewhere, far away. And when this job came up in Cork, I grabbed at – "

"And how did Mrs Clayforth feel about you leaving her?" Collins leaned forward. The smile had lessened now.

"I don't know. That is, it wasn't any of her business."

"But she didn't want you to go?"

"I didn't tell her I was moving."

"You saw no reason to tell her?"

"That's right – "

"Because you'd already planned to kill her, then leave for Ireland – "

"No! You've got this all wrong! Please, Inspector. You, and now the press; they're out there, asking me questions, implying that I killed Angela Clayforth, when I didn't!"

"That's for us to establish, Mr Taylor. There's another matter I'd like to discuss with you. Perhaps you can shed some light on the disappearance of a young girl we know used to baby-sit for you, until recently. We're told – "

"By that gossip Sheila Hodge, no doubt," John spat out the words and folded his arms across his chest, defiantly.

"You were often seen with the girl, Tanya Williams. You seemed close to her at the village fête, recently. And now, she's gone missing. Her mother's out of her mind with worry, too distracted, even, to report her daughter's disappearance. But your neighbour seems to think you might have taken the girl to Ireland with you – "

"No! I never did! I've met someone else over there. A Mrs Dwyer, Eileen Dwyer. She'll tell you I came to Cork on my own with my children – "

"And you don't know where this young girl has gone?"

"Of course not!" John couldn't believe the turn of conversation. Was he being accused of not one, but two murders now, on the hearsay of a gossipy neighbour? "She looked after my children for me, for a while, that was all."

"And she refused to go with you to Ireland – "

"I never asked her to come with me!"

"You mean you quarrelled with her before you left?"

"For God's sake! You've got no evidence for any of this. You're just repeating what that bitch Hodge said. She's been talking to the newspapers all morning, too; enjoying the attention, by the looks of things. I saw her outside the building when you brought me in for questioning. You're hounding me, inspector. I'm an innocent man. I want to see a lawyer!"

Jack Baker knocked at the door of number seventeen, Manor Close, stood back and looked up at the house for signs of life. He'd already spoken to Valerie Boyd, the mother of the young man who'd come to the station, voluntarily, for questioning, and she'd told him that Mrs Williams had fallen into some kind of state of decline since her daughter had gone missing. Jack leaned on the bell and banged with the knocker again. He didn't want to have to break the door down but he'd got a young officer in the car who'd help him do just that, if necessary. Then the door opened a fraction and a lost-looking face peered out at him, questioningly.

"Mrs Mavis Williams?" said Jack in a clear, strong voice, in case the woman had lost her hearing as well as her mind.

The woman nodded slightly.

"Police, madam." He waved his walleted badge at her. "I'd like to ask you some questions. May I come in?"

She nodded her head a little and opened the door, wider. Jack stepped inside. The smell in the hallway nearly felled him: rotting food, probably.

"Shall we go through to your sitting room, madam?" he asked. He wasn't sure he wanted to see what was decaying in the kitchen.

Mavis shuffled through the door to the front room and Jack followed, noting in the gloom the layer of dust that coated the furniture and the window sills and the floor. The woman clearly wasn't coping, not looking after herself. He glanced at the low table in front of the sofa. It was piled high with various objects that could have belonged to a teenage girl: makeup, records, books, articles of clothing. Mrs Williams perched on the edge of the sofa. Jack sat opposite her in a large armchair. The woman picked up a blouse and held it to her face. She wore a faraway expression, as if she didn't see him there.

"My Tanya ... " she said in a small voice. "She's gone. She didn't take her clothes ... " Mavis put the blouse to her nose and inhaled, slowly, then breathed out. "I've still got her things. I'll look after them for her."

"Yes, Mrs Williams; you do that." This woman needs looking after, herself, thought Jack. She needs care; needs to go into a home. "I won't keep you long," he said in a slow, deliberate voice, hoping he was getting through to her. "I need to ask you what you know about your neighbour, Mrs Angela Clayforth. You know she was murdered, up at the manor house, last night? Did you know Mrs Clayforth well? What can you tell me about her?"

Mavis picked up a lipstick and took the top off it. She daubed some on her lips. It was a pale pink and did nothing for the woman's sickly pallor. It was like sitting opposite a ghost, reckoned Jack.

"She's gone away, now."

"Who's gone away, Mrs Williams? Mrs Clayforth? Your daughter, Tanya?"

Mavis slowly nodded her head. "Yes," she said, staring at the objects on the table. "All finished now. Gone away. I have to look after her things. She'll miss them. I know she will."

This is going nowhere, said Jack to himself. I'm wasting my time with this half-baked woman. He stood up to go. "Mrs Williams?"

She stared ahead of her.

"Mrs Williams, we're going to arrange some help for you. We'll get a doctor to look at you. You're ill. You need looking after."

Mavis raised her gaunt, pale face and looked vaguely at the policeman. "She's not coming back. I'm looking after her things for her. This one," she held up a 45 rpm record to the inspector. "She'll miss this. Used to play it all the time."

"How'd it go, sir?" said the police constable when Jack got back to the car.

"Useless. Bloody useless. The woman's out of her mind. Get someone round to look at her, will you? She needs putting in a home. And that house needs fumigating. Miss Haversham's got nothing on what's inside that place. I'm going down to number eight," he looked along the Close. "A Mrs Doreen Reynolds. Mother of the girl who found the body. I'll see you down there. Wait outside in the car for me. Radio for a doctor for that woman, first, will you?"

The Reynolds' garden was almost as overgrown as the one at number seventeen. He wondered if he'd find another half-lunatic inside. Might be something in the water, he said to himself as he knocked at the door. To his relief, a smart, neat woman opened the door, almost immediately. "Mrs Doreen Reynolds?" He flashed his badge again.

"Yes. Do come in, won't you?" she smiled at him. Jack felt relieved. If only they were all as compos mentis as this, his job would be a lot easier.

The house didn't smell and the rooms were tidy and clean. Mrs Reynolds showed him through to the lounge. "Would you like a cup of tea or coffee, Inspector? Please sit down."

"Nothing for me, thank you," he sank into the armchair. "I won't keep you long, Mrs

Reynolds. Nasty business, this. You're daughter must have had quite a shock."

"Oh, yes. She did," Doreen nodded in agreement.

"We've spoken to her, as you know. What we'd like to ask you is how well you knew the deceased, and if you can tell us anything that might help us find the person who did this."

Doreen sat up straight on the edge of the sofa, eager to be of some use. "I'd be happy to tell you anything I know, Inspector. But I didn't know Mrs Clayforth very well. She was a neighbour, but we hardly ever spoke. I'm so busy with my family ... " Doreen gestured, as if despairing of her lack of time. "My husband's away. I have it all to do," she smiled. "Are you sure you wouldn't like a cup of tea? It's no trouble."

Jack shook his head. "No, thanks, Mrs Reynolds. Can I ask: did Mrs Clayforth have a man friend, do you know?"

The woman appeared to ponder his words, frowning a little. "No ... " she said slowly, giving it a little more thought. "I don't think so ... "

"You're sure? She didn't quarrel with anyone who lives in the street?"

Doreen concentrated on the question, shrugged, shook her head and looked apologetic. "Not that I know of, Inspector. But, you know, I hardly have time to look up from the housework, let alone listen to neighbourhood chatter."

Jack smiled. "I understand, Mrs Reynolds." He stood up and closed his notebook. "I'd ask you to let us know if you think of anything, any small detail, that you feel could help us with this case."

"Of course, Inspector," said Doreen rising, too, and smiling at him. "Let me see you to the door. I do hope you catch this awful person. One doesn't feel safe ... "

"Don't worry, madam. We'll have this case solved before long." I wish, thought Jack as the woman opened the front door for him. When she closed it behind him, she took a long, deep breath. Then she looked up and saw her daughter standing there.

"Well?" Doreen demanded. "What are you looking at?"

"You. You're different," said Stella, coming slowly down the stairs.

"What on earth do you mean?" Doreen turned away and went hurriedly through to the kitchen and moved some cups around on the worktop.

"You haven't been drinking." Stella followed her into the room.

"So? What's wrong with that? Why shouldn't I have a cup of coffee, if I want one? I don't have to drink alcohol, all of the time."

"Why have you stopped drinking?" persisted Stella.

At this, Doreen's patience snapped. She wheeled round and faced the girl, brandishing a cup at her. "Because I can do what I like, my girl! It's none of your business whether I drink or not! I don't feel like drinking at the moment, that's all. I want to get on with my life. And you get on with yours, and stop pestering me, you horrible child."

The funeral of Angela Clayforth took place one week to the day after her body had been found by Stella Reynolds. It was a sad affair, thought Inspector Jack Baker as he stood beside his colleague, Bill Collins, and watched the coffin being lowered into the earth. They were the only ones in Hadham Churchyard besides the vicar and the chauffeur and coffin bearers from the funeral home. The dozen or so journalists who'd followed the cortège from the undertakers had been locked out of the cemetery and were observing them through the gates.

Jack wasn't happy: the case hadn't been solved. They'd had to let John Taylor go back to Ireland; lack of evidence. All they had to go on was a letter they'd found in Angela Clayforth's kitchen, accusing her of killing Tanya Williams and arranging to meet her at the manor house the night she was killed. Jack sighed. Bill was retiring soon; he'd be handling this case on his own. All he could do was stop the housing development up at the manor while he searched the place for clues. And go through all the files again. Maybe talk to the local gossip, once more. What was her name? That Mrs Hodge.

CHAPTER 20

Stella should have known on her wedding night that something was wrong. He hadn't noticed her sheer nightdress, or that she'd lost weight for him. Not that Neil had delayed the wedding, at all. In fact, he'd been keen to tie the knot as soon as possible, and they'd married just two weeks after he'd started university. It was romantic, she thought, being so young and poor and living in a damp, cramped flat near the college campus. But Neil hadn't been happy. He hated the flat, despised her attempts to cook, and spent more and more time in the university library, late at night.

But she didn't mind. She was Mrs Neil Boyd; living away from home and her mother. She'd got a job, waiting at tables in a local café, and gone to evening classes to learn shorthand and typing. By the time Neil had got his degree and started his articles in London, she was able to support them both, with a certain amount of economising. She knew Neil appreciated it. He would be earning much more money, one day, and he would look after her then, as she was looking after him now.

They settled in a flat in a Bloomsbury square, near Lincoln's Inn, and Neil's star rose through the contacts he made and through Stella's renowned dinner parties. They were happy enough: life was much easier now. Stella longed for a baby, but Neil said it was too soon. Too much of a disruption, he said.

"But you're hardly ever here," Stella protested. "You're out, nearly every evening – "

"It's business. I have to wine and dine my clients; you know that. You want me to be successful, don't you, woman?"

"Of course. But, darling," Stella went over to where Neil was making himself a coffee before going out again for an evening at one of the best restaurants in St James's. "I spend so much time on my own; I always did – "

Neil wheeled round, jabbing the coffee spoon at her, accusingly. "You knew I would have to work hard. I'm doing this for both of us, goddam it!"

"I know ... "

"No, you don't know! You know nothing at all, you selfish bitch! I'm sick of you! I've had it up to here!" He slammed down the coffee mug and the liquid spilled over the worktop.

"I'll get it," said Stella, going to the sink to get a cloth. As she dabbed at the worktop, she heard the front door bang. She stopped and listened. Silence. He was gone. Another evening on her own.

She sighed, threw the cloth in the sink and left it there. She went through to the lounge, stood front of the drinks cabinet and ran her fingers along the top of it. She opened the cabinet doors, took out a bottle of vermouth and a large glass and took them over to the low table. A tear rolled down her cheek as she sat on the sofa and unscrewed the top of the vermouth. The neck of the bottle clunked against the edge of the glass as she filled it to the rim. Stella drank deeply, then filled the glass again. She sank back into the sofa and let the tears fall freely. A few minutes later, she leaned forward and filled the glass again.

"Pooh, you stink!" Doreen wrinkled her nose as her daughter drew up a chair in the residents' sitting room of Hillview Home for the Elderly.

"Glad to see me, as usual, mother," said Stella, sitting down beside her.

"You want to stop that drinking, my girl. Doesn't solve marriage problems. From one who knows. Don't hang on to him. Kick the bastard out. Start again, before you're over the hill." She screwed up her eyes at her daughter. "You haven't got long. You look bloody awful, you do."

"And how are you, mother?" Stella replied in a deliberate tone.

Doreen sniffed and raised her eyebrows, dismissively. "Same as ever. They've got me all padded up now, since the last accident. Can't get to the loo, these days; scared I'll fall over if go fast. They'll think I'm on the gin ... " She looked closely at Stella again. "Lay off the sauce, girl. Those buggers aren't worth it. Didn't bring your father back, and it won't stop your one straying, either. Think I don't know?"

"Is that why you stopped drinking? You worked that one out?"

Doreen stared at the aspidistra in a brass pot by the window. "Something like that."

"But you thought Dad was having an affair with Angela Clayforth. The moment somebody murdered her, you didn't touch a drop, ever again."

Her mother continued to stare at the potted plant. "Gave me a lot to think about, Angela's death. I was mistaken, I admit that. But you can't undo what's done." She shrugged. "Waste of time, worrying about your father, like that. It was all a wasted effort."

"His wife's got some wasting disease now. She can't play golf with him, any more. He's nursing her at home, but he says she's got to go into a hospice, soon."

Doreen shifted in her high-backed chair. "Can't say I sympathise. Not my problem. Got enough to think about, watching Mavis Williams going round the twist. She's started going for walks in the night. They've had to tie her down. Took a wrong turn and fell down the stairs, the other night. I didn't even know she was gone. They're moving her out of our room next week; putting her in a nursing home. Then, maybe, I'll get some sleep."

"But you'll have to share the room with someone else, if she goes. It's a double room; it's got two beds in it."

Doreen shook her head. "I'm moving to a smaller room at the back. Got a view of the garden, it has. Nice and quiet. I was going to ask you to sort my stuff and move it for me. I don't trust those girls: Sharon, or that Gina. A lot of Mavis's stuff has gone missing since she's been here, and I don't think she lost all of it by herself."

"You're too suspicious, Mum. That's your trouble. You want to trust people more – "

Just then, Mavis Williams shuffled into the room, leaning on a walking frame, her eyes wide with a vacant stare as she looked this way and that, not seeing.

"Over here, Mavis," Doreen lifted a hand and beckoned her. But either Mavis didn't see her room mate or she didn't hear her, or both.

She looks pathetic, thought Stella. The old woman's hair was matted and there was food down the front of her cardigan. Her thick stockings were wrinkled and bunched around the ankles of her stick-thin legs. Her face was gaunt, sunken. An old plastic bag, full of holes, dangled from one of her thin wrists. It was full of bits and pieces: an old 45 rpm record stuck out of the top of it, and an op-art blouse that Stella recognised from a long time ago.

Suddenly, Mavis fixed on them, sitting there by the window. She nodded at them, her face becoming animated. "I'm going out for tea. I'm going to see Tanya, up at the manor," she informed them in a reed-like, warbling voice. "I've got her things. She's missed her records and her make-up, silly girl. She shouldn't have left them behind."

Stella went rigid. What was the woman saying? Did she know where her daughter was buried? Had she seen them, that day? No, it wasn't possible! These were just the ramblings of an old woman with senile dementia. Mavis had never recovered from losing Tanya, she knew. But, then, nor had Neil, Stella reckoned. It had to be the reason for the way he treated her; always out with other women. Stella hadn't been his first love, she knew that was true. And Angela Clayforth, she remembered, had been his second.

"Mrs Boyd? Mrs Neil Boyd?" the man asked when she picked up the phone.

"Yes?"

"Right. I'm sorry to be phoning at this time of the evening. I know it's late. But I also know your husband isn't there."

Stella took another sip from her wine glass and didn't reply. She waited for the voice to continue.

"He's out with my wife. They're having an affair." The voice paused.

Stella gulped at her Beaujolais.

"They've been seeing each other for over a year, but I've – I've only just found out. My name is Lewis, by the way; Richard Lewis. My wife is a lawyer, a partner in your husband's firm. I found a letter from him ... a love letter to her. I confronted her last night – " His voice seemed to crack, but he regained control of it after a moment. "She – she didn't deny it. Says it's serious. Hello? Mrs Boyd? Are you there?"

"Yes. I'm here."

"The thing is, Mrs Boyd, what are we going to do?"

But Stella couldn't think. The room was going round. She swayed and fell backwards into the telephone chair, still holding her glass and the phone.

"I want my wife back, Mrs Boyd. I must tell you that. I don't want to lose what we — we've had. Can we help each other on this? Can we — Oh, I don't know what. I'm out of my mind with worry. I just want her back. Can you help me?" Lewis tried to choke back a sob, but failed. Stella heard him dissolve, crying uncontrollably.

Slowly, without getting up, she reached over and put the phone back on the hook. She sat there, holding her glass with both hands and staring at the mirror on the opposite wall. She must have gazed at her reflection for half an hour or more; she wasn't sure. She let her mind go blank. She was tired of thinking. Who could she talk to? Who could she phone? Her brother? He had no time for her since he'd married his rich, older wife. He didn't even visit his mother. There was Naomi at the office. Stella could talk to Naomi ... No, she couldn't. Neil had fancied Naomi once, when she'd brought her friend home for supper. Had they had an affair, back then? It was possible. Naomi was always asking after Neil. Always interested in him.

At one in the morning, the key turned in the lock. Neil stepped quietly into the flat and carefully closed the front door behind him. He turned and took a step into the hall, then saw Stella sitting on the chair, looking at him, cradling an empty glass.

"For God's sake!" he hissed at her. "Go to bed, you drunken bitch."

She looked at him. "Have fun with Mrs Lewis tonight, did you? Her husband phoned. Says it's official: you're an item."

Neil scowled and waved an arm at her, dismissively. "I don't want to talk about it. Go to bed. I'm sleeping on the couch."

Stella rose and placed the wine glass on the hall table, next to the telephone. "As far as I'm concerned, you can move out as soon as you like. Just pack your things and go. I've had enough, Neil."

"Suits me fine. I don't know how I've put up with you, all these years." He stood in the doorway and looked at her, an expression of disgust on his face. "Just like your mother: drinking like a fish all the time. Have you any idea what I've had to put up with?"

Now, at last, Stella felt the anger she'd suppressed throughout the marriage sweep over her. She heard herself shout at him, "Have you any idea what I've put up with?" She pointed at the empty glass on the table. "That has been my prop during your affairs, your infidelities. That has anaesthetised my pain. You were unfaithful to me, right from the beginning; right from the time I found you with Angela Clayforth – "

Her husband seemed to stiffen at the mention of that name. This didn't escape Stella's notice. She couldn't help a triumphant smile. "And that was it, wasn't it? You thought I didn't know? You didn't think I understood why you'd married me?"

"Shut up, woman," said Neil, irritably, starting to go into the sitting room.

"Aha! But I did know! I knew all the time. You married me so that I'd keep quiet about you and Mrs Clayforth –"

"Shut up! Bitch!"

"You didn't want the police to know you were having an affair with her, did you? And why was that, Neil?" Stella stood with her arms akimbo; a superior, taunting smile on her face.

In one stride, he was over to her. His hand swung across her face, sending her flying against the wall. She held her mouth and felt warm blood trickling over her hand as she slid down the wall. She lay in a crumpled heap, head pulled into her shoulders, waiting for the next blow. She had spoken the unspeakable. Pandora's box was open.

The divorce was surprisingly quick. Only a matter of months. Neil didn't contest the adultery charge; he let her keep the flat. She wondered if he was afraid of her; afraid that she would go to the police, all these years on. But she wasn't interested in Mrs Clayforth's murder. Stella had met someone else. The chance of a new life. The chance to be loved. The chance to be happy, this time.

Tony Martin was younger than she was. Had a barrow in the North End Road market. She'd got talking to him when she'd bought some grapefruits for her new diet. By the time her divorce was through, they'd moved into a flat at World's End. Six months after that, they were married. Six months later, Stella was living there on her own.

When Tony had gone down for receiving stolen goods, Stella had vowed she would wait for him. Then a girl had turned up on her doorstep, two weeks after Tony had been moved to Wandsworth. The girl was pregnant. Expecting Tony's child, any day now.

He signed the papers, one visiting session, and she took them back to her lawyer. Stella never saw Tony again. She often wondered if he'd married the girl when he'd got out of prison. She calculated that the child was almost a teenager now.

Her mother's last heart attack came just a few months before they found Tanya Williams in Hadham Woods. The woman had had a long life, in the end: ninety-two years when she died. Stella spent the best part of a day clearing out the room at Hillview. She had no idea her mother had kept her old school essay book or so many photographs and letters.

The worst part of the afternoon was sorting through Doreen's clothes. The ones she had worn towards the end of her life had an unsavoury odour and were caked with dried baby food. Stella filled nearly a dozen sacks. There was very little she wanted to keep. She pushed the photos and the letters she'd found at the bottom of the wardrobe into a couple of carrier bags. She would sort through them when she got back to the flat. The home said they needed the room for a new guest who was coming at six o'clock that evening.

Stella wasn't sure how she felt about her mother's death. She supposed she should be upset, or sad, at least. But, although their relationship had been, on the whole, a stable one since Doreen had stopped drinking, all those years ago, she could never forget the traumatic years when she'd lived in her parents' home. It had been a battlefield and Stella had been seriously wounded. She had healed, but she carried the scars. She had a feeling her mother understood that.

In later years, they had avoided discussing the past, except in a perfunctory way when a reference to something or someone was unavoidable. She sifted through the photos her mother had kept: the smiles on the faces of her family in their ridiculous clothes and hairstyles, hiding the real pain. Stella sighed and threw the pictures back into the carrier bags. She turned to the letters. They were more interesting; there were several from her father.

Ray Reynolds had died of cancer the previous year. He had been a widower for five years before that, but he'd never visited Doreen in the home, or even asked about her. They were ships that had passed in the night, leaving a couple of bewildered offspring in their wake. There were several of her father's letters that had been written to her mother before they'd married and were full of tender phrases. Stella had no idea he had been such a romantic. But the stunted phrases in the scribbled notes accompanying his cheques to support the family, later on, showed clearly that, whatever

Ray and Doreen had once had going for them, it had disappeared forever and was never coming back.

That evening, sorting through more papers, Stella came across the letter she had never thought she would read. It had been folded into three and placed in a plain envelope; it hadn't been sealed. There was no address on the envelope; it could have been intended for anyone, everyone, to read. It was dated two days after the murder of Angela Clayforth. It was a confession. She read the letter through, her heart beating like a ship's engine. She read it again, then again. She looked up, her eyes casting wildly about the room as she wondered where she could hide the piece of paper.

She got up and went over to her writing bureau, opened the top flap and pulled out a small drawer inside. She lifted a wad of bills, placed the letter at the bottom of the drawer and placed the correspondence on top of it. She closed the desk lid and went through to the kitchen and made herself a cup of strong coffee. As she leaned against the worktop, sipping her hot drink, Stella reflected on what she'd suspected for years. It seemed odd that, finally, she knew for certain who had murdered Angela Clayforth. The question was: who should she tell?

"Alright. You can go now, Mrs Martin," said Detective Barry Carver, waving a chubby finger at her. "But we'll want to see you again, along with the others – "

"Others? What others?" As if Stella needed to ask.

Carver consulted his file, as if he needed to. They both knew who they were talking about. "Your ex-husband, for a start. And a Mr John Taylor. You three are the only people left who knew Mrs Clayforth well."

"But I didn't know her well," said Stella, for what seemed like the thousandth time.

Detective Binns chimed in, "You discovered the body. She was a close friend of your mother's. You walked the woman's dog, every day. We say: you knew her well enough."

"By the way, do you keep in touch with your ex-husband, Mrs Martin?"

Stella shook her head. "Of course not. Why would I want to?"

"Neil Boyd, I'm talking about; the lawyer. Not your second husband. He's inside again: armed robbery. They never learn. Do better to play the fucking lottery."

"I don't see either of them, and I've no intention of doing so."

Barry Carver leaned over his file and fixed her with his steel-grey eyes. "If you hear from them, either John Taylor or Neil Boyd, I want to know about it. Understand?"

"Can't you speak to them, yourself?"

"We've already spoken to Mr Taylor, and we'll be talking to Boyd, shortly. Keep away from them, Mrs Martin. Don't let me think the three of you are hiding something from the police. You don't want to go the same way as Tony Martin, do you? Twenty years behind bars? Bloody waste of a life."

"You don't need to lecture me."

"Glad to hear it. Go home, Mrs Martin. Leave us to solve this murder. The case remains open until we find out who did it."

Stella rose and scraped back her chair. It had been a long night and it had got them nowhere, just as she'd expected. But it had helped her make up her mind about one thing: she would destroy the letter she'd slipped into her back pocket before they'd brought her in for questioning. There seemed no reason to rake up tragedies from the past. What good would it do anyone now? It wouldn't bring back Tanya, or help Angela Clayforth. Lives had been played out: winners and losers.

Funny thing, mused Stella as she left the police station, turning up her jacket collar against the chill of the early morning frost glittering on the pavements, how feeling passionate about someone can tip you off course, bugger up your life, send you in one direction instead of another. What had old Angela's crime been? Wanting Neil? Wanting someone to call her own?

And there he was: standing on the other side of the road. Older, less hair now, rounder in the face; but it was Neil, waiting for her to finish talking to the police. He must be worried sick, thought Stella. After all, it was why we married: so I wouldn't tell them what I'd seen. But they'd found Tanya's body, anyway.

"'Lo, Neil."

"Hello, Stella." He nodded at her, keeping his hands in his coat pockets.

"Can't think why you want to see me, after all this time."

He smiled, trying not to look sheepish. "Can we have a coffee, somewhere? I'd like to talk."

"We're not supposed to confer. You know that? Police rules."

"Just a chat, for old time's sake." He withdrew a hand from a pocket and slipped his arm through one of hers.

Stella shook her head, giving him an ironic smile. "I'd feel honoured, if I didn't know better,"

They found a warm, steam-filled café, a couple of streets away, and sat down at a table at the back of the premises, well away from the window.

"You're married again?" Stella asked him, after the waitress had taken their order for two large coffees.

He nodded.

The Lewis woman? The one I named in the divorce papers?

He shook his head. "There were other women around at the time. Plenty of others. I met someone a couple of years after that. Two kids now. Want to see their picture?" He brought out his wallet and opened it up, displaying a family photo: four people smiling in the seaside sunshine at the camera.

Stella was about to make a polite, neutral comment about the family group when the waitress brought over their coffees. Instead, she fumbled under her jacket and pulled a piece of paper from the back pocket of her jeans. She placed it on the table, between them. "This is what you're after," she said. "This is what you want to know about."

He looked at her, questioningly. "What is it?"

She met his gaze, still with that half-smile.

He reached out to pick up the folded letter, but Stella was too quick for him. Her arm shot out and she snatched back the paper. "I'll read it to you," she said, opening it up. "I found it in my mother's things when she died. It's about Angela Clayforth. It's written by the person who killed her – "

"Stella, it wasn't me – " began Neil.

"I know that."

"I often thought, all those years ago, that it might be you." he said, watching her closely.

"What? You're joking, of course! I thought it was you: getting your own back on Angela for Tanya."

"Bloody hell ..." Neil murmured under his breath. Then he looked away, shaking his head.

"Anyway, it doesn't matter now." Stella shrugged and took a sip of her coffee. "Turns out we were both wrong. But what happened destroyed any chance of happiness we might have had. I wish I'd come across this, years ago – "

"Read it to me," Neil said, impatiently, turning to face her again.

"OK. Here we go: ' To whom it may concern,' it says." Stella glanced at him across the table, enjoying the moment, his hanging on her every word. "Then it goes: ' This is my confession to the murder of that woman, Mrs Angela Clayforth, who I killed in the house at Hadham Manor, yesterday evening, the 7th of July. I did it because – ' "

"That's no good," interrupted Neil. "It doesn't give the year. You couldn't use this in court. They'd run motorways though it – "

"It's not going to be used in court," said Stella. "I'm going to read it to you, that's all. Now, do you want me to go on? Do you want to hear it, or not?"

"Yes," he hissed, under his breath. Why had this woman always irritated him so much? He was tempted to slap her smug, jowly face, as he had done in the past. Fortunately, for her, they were in a public place. She was getting off lightly.

" '7th of July,' " Stella repeated. " 'I did it because she was an evil woman. She brought so much unhappiness into the world. I saw her kill my daughter, Tanya – ' "

Neil started in his chair, almost leapt out of it. Stella stopped reading and looked up. "Go on," he told her in a low voice. He hadn't bargained for this revelation when he'd decided to see her again. It was better than he could ever have hoped for.

" ' When Doreen's fat daughter – ' Er ... " Stella paused and cleared her throat, then started again. " – ' said my daughter was with that Neil Boyd in the woods, I ran down there to tell her to come home. But I was too late. Angela Clayforth was already there, shouting at my Tanya. She hit my daughter in the face and my girl fell against a tree. I saw it all. That woman killed my child; the only person I had in the world. She killed me, too; robbed me of my happiness. Now, I'm dead inside. I've no feeling left. Everything's gone numb. The light has gone from my life. That light was Tanya. Angela Clayforth had to pay for what she did.

' So I wrote the woman a letter, saying I'd seen her kill Tanya. I told her to meet me at the manor house, that evening. And she came; curious to know who had written to her, I suppose. And I stabbed her with a kitchen knife. It was easy. I was so full of hate. Then I stabbed her again, and again. I don't know how many times: until I knew she was dead, that's all. I don't feel any better for having killed her. It hasn't brought my darling girl back to me. But why should that woman live if my daughter can't? There's no justice in this world, but it was as close as I could get to it.

' I'm ready to die, myself, now. They can come and get me; I don't care. It's a rotten world. Everybody's rotten. May they all rot in hell. I saw them bury my girl: that Neil Boyd and Angela Clayforth. I don't want to disturb Tanya now. Why should I? She's lying there, with the flowers and trees that she loved so much. She always loved nature when she was a child.

' May she rest in peace, my Tanya. I won't find peace until I'm with her. I'm waiting to die. There's nothing left for me on this earth. I'm glad Angela Clayforth is dead and I would do it again, if it would bring my Tanya back. Signed: Mavis Vera Williams. 8th July, 1965.' There's your date," said Stella.

"How do you know this is genuine? Anyone could have written it. You could have done this, yourself."

Stella looked up from the letter. "Mavis shared a room with my mother at the old people's home. She must have given it to Mum to look after. I don't suppose she really knew what she was doing. She had senile dementia – "

"Your mother could have written that," insisted Neil. "She could have killed Angela and written the letter to shift the blame on to Mavis, who was already out of her mind over her daughter."

Stella bridled. "My mother didn't kill Angela Clayforth. She was at home that evening, drunk as a skunk; I remember. She hadn't the co-ordination to get out of the front door, let alone execute a murder."

Neil pondered this. It seemed to fit. Doreen Reynolds had been a lush at that time, even if she did pull herself together, later. "Well, this lets John Taylor off the hook, good and proper. You'd better let him know. What are you going to do with the letter?"

Stella shrugged. "Burn it. It's no use to anyone now. The police have no evidence against Mr Taylor, and they never will have. It's only the press who want to make a meal of him, and that'll die down, soon enough."

"Give the letter to me. I'll destroy it." Neil held out his hand to her.

She pulled back and stuck out her chin, defiantly. "No. You've caused enough problems in my life, already."

"Would you have told me about this if I hadn't been there, outside the police station?"

Stella considered this, then shook her head. "I've had this piece of paper for over six months now and, in all that time, I never thought of contacting you. But, when they found Tanya, I knew you'd contact me. I didn't think you could keep away. And I was right on that, wasn't I?"

He nodded. They looked at each other. It seemed they had nothing more to say. Stella stood up. Neil rose and pulled out his wallet, paid the bill and left a tip. Together, they went out of the café door into the street. The sun was trying to break through the grey clouds. Perhaps it would be a nice day, later on.

They stood and faced each other. Neil proffered his hand. Stella didn't raise hers to take it. She simply looked at him, sadly, as if for the last time. The moment he understood the rebuff, he turned on his heel and walked quickly away. She watched him go for a moment, then set off in the other direction.

She stopped by the first waste bin she saw, attached to a lamp post at the next crossroads. As Stella waited for the lights to change, she tore Mavis's letter into squares, then into smaller squares, finally dropping the pieces of paper into the litter bin.

The lights changed and Stella crossed the road with half a dozen other people. She was hardly aware of them. She was lost in thought, reflecting on Angela Clayforth and how one woman's needs had affected the lives of so many, even from beyond the grave. But, by the time she reached the kerb, Stella had moved on, in her mind as well as on the street. She began to plan what she was going to do tomorrow and, for that matter, with the rest of her life.

About the Author

Lindsay Greatwood was born in London, gained an Honours degree in English from the University of Sussex and taught English as a foreign language. She has ghost-written autobiographies for several personalities and published *Fame and Fortune in Switzerland*, *The Alpine Set in Switzerland*, *The Glitterati in Switzerland* and *The Fall of Ozog*. She lived in Switzerland for many years and now lives in France with her Swiss francophone husband.

By the same Author

Fame and Fortune in Switzerland

A number of well-known personalities were attracted to the shores of Lake Geneva in the second half of the twentieth century. Many of them knew each other well and their lives were intertwined. One or two fell deeply in love; others came to blows. Each faced more than one personal crisis, at least as dramatic as the situations they portrayed on screen or in print.

Ian Fleming: his time in Geneva coloured the world of James Bond - **Richard Burton:** the locals called his home a 'bicoque' – a shack - **Alistair MacLean:** a writer who came to blows with Burton - **Peter Ustinov:** took a long personal journey to a wine-growing region - **Audrey Hepburn:** fled from kidnappers to her 'place of peace' - **Yul Brynner:** lived in splendour on Lake Geneva - **William Holden:** fell in love with Audrey Hepburn - **Coco Chanel:** lived in exile after the war with her German lover - **Capucine:** jumped from the eighth floor of her apartment building.

ISBN: 978-2-8399-0509-1

The Alpine Set in Switzerland

Darling, we're known as The Alpine Set! wrote the actress Benita Hume to a Hollywood friend in the late Sixties. She had just moved to the picturesque tax haven of Lausanne on Lake Geneva with her husband, matinée idol George Sanders. George had many reasons for wanting to enjoy the clean air and mountain views of Switzerland: he could keep most of the money he earned from various and unusual sources and enjoy the highest standard of living; he was only an hour by air from the major European movie capitals and he would avoid being hounded by Hollywood gossip columnists who wanted to know more about his past and present. Most of all, he could continue to build a financial scam that stretched from Italy to Los Angeles and would take in the British government and a good number of famous Swiss residents.

Frank Zappa: his concert inspired Deep Purple's *Smoke on the Water* - **Georges Simenon:** compared begging letters with Charlie Chaplin - **Charlie Chaplin:** his body was dug up and held to ransom - **Graham Greene:** lost a fortune in a tax scam - **George Sanders:** his 'rip-snorter' cost the British government millions of pounds - **James Mason:** lay in a Swiss bank vault for years - **Vladimir Nabokov:** was rescued from a Swiss mountain - **Freddie Mercury:** swung from a chandelier in his Montreux hotel.

ISBN: 978-2-8399-0660-9

The Glitterati in Switzerland

There were many entertainers who made their homes on the shores of Lake Geneva; the list is impressively long and star-studded: David Bowie, Freddie Mercury, Keith Richards, Christopher Lee, Van Johnson, Noël Coward, David Niven, Peter Sellers, Elizabeth Taylor, Roger Moore, Richard Burton, Alistair MacLean, Peter Ustinov, Audrey Hepburn, Yul Brynner, William Holden, Capucine, Coco Chanel, Georges Simenon, Charlie Chaplin, Graham Greene, George Sanders, James Mason, Vladimir Nabokov and many others; all international artists whose work continues to dazzle. They were rightly called the Glitterati: their lives were glamorous, dramatic and headline-grabbing. But, if they believed they could escape professional pressures and lead quiet, orderly existences in Switzerland, they soon found out they would have to think again.

David Bowie: his open marriage led to a Swiss divorce - **Keith Richards**: entered a Swiss clinic to come off heroin - **Christopher Lee**: saw the mountains reach the foot of his bed - **Van Johnson**: his violent behaviour caused his wife to leave - **Noël Coward**: 'Boxers' with Niv began with Bloody Marys *à la gare* - **David Niven**: his wife refused to be buried with him - **Princess Diana**: loved to ski but was homesick for England - **Peter Sellers**: his chalet was a fortress of technology and garden gnomes - **Elizabeth Taylor**: loved and lived with several husbands in Gstaad - **Roger Moore**: fell out with David Niven's widow on the eve of the funeral.

ISBN: 978-2-940509-02-7

Célébrités et Fortunes en Suisse

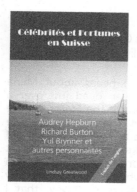

Dans la seconde moitié du vingtième siècle un grand nombre de célébrités étaient attirées par les rives du Lac de Genève. Plusieurs d'entre elles se connaissaient bien et leurs vies s'interconnectaient. Quelques-unes tombèrent follement amoureuses ; d'autres en vinrent aux mains. Chacune dut faire face à plus d'une crise, au moins aussi dramatiques que celles qu'elles jouaient à l'écran ou dans leurs écrits.

Ian Fleming : son séjour à Genève a teinté le monde de James Bond - **Richard Burton :** les gens appelaient sa maison une « bicoque » - **Alistair MacLean :** un écrivain qui s'est battu avec Burton - **Peter Ustinov :** rejoignit une région viticole après avoir essayé d'autres endroits - **Audrey Hepburn :** retrouva son « havre de paix » pour fuir des kidnappeurs - **Yul Brynner :** vécut dans le luxe autour du Lac de Genève - **William Holden :** tomba amoureux d'Audrey Hepburn - **Coco Chanel :** vécut en exil après la guerre avec son amoureux allemand - **Capucine :** se jeta du huitième étage de son appartement.

ISBN: 978-2-940509-08-9

The Fall of Ozog

A Swiss-Lavaux Thriller

The great Rock of Ozog, high above Lake Geneva, is cracking up –
and so are the lives of those who live in its shadow

The first time I heard about Maria Ceccini she'd been dead just over a month. I'd been in the States for the summer when she'd taken a dive under the paddle-wheel of an old steamer on Lake Geneva, and it wasn't until a week or so after I got back to Switzerland, when Gruber dropped by my picture gallery in Vevey, that I realised I had an investigation on my hands that would tip my personal life into the final stages of chaos.

I have never, in all my forty-two mostly law-abiding years, wanted to be a policeman. Buying and selling modern art has been my game ever since my second marriage went into terminal decline. But about eight years back, Gruber's pals at the European Intelligence Agency in The Hague decided Europol needed to expand its network of undercover agents and they reckoned I fitted the bill; which is pretty amazing since I'm American, born and bred. But then, I'd married a Swiss lady around that time and settled near Lausanne, papers and all; though my wife and I had different addresses and a third divorce was in the air when I first heard of Maria Ceccini.

Set in the scenic vineyards of the Lavaux region on the Swiss Riviera, The Fall of Ozog traces the destruction of a family of winegrowers and those whose lives are crushed in the fall -

ISBN: 978-2-940509-07-2

The Secret Passion of Angela Clayforth

An English Murder Mystery

There is, in fact, rather a history to the house which could be useful for – ah – publicity. A talking point, perhaps. Apart from the ghost, someone was found here once ...

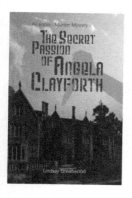

She could still see the old manor house as it was on that summer's evening: abandoned, ready to be bulldozed by the developers; beautiful in an empty, haunted way. Inside, field mice scuttled behind the wainscoting of echoing rooms, rats nested in fireplaces and bats hung upside down from the ancient rafters. Some of these creatures, thought Stella, must have seen Mrs Clayforth lying in one of the upstairs rooms, cold and white, eyes staring at the ornate ceiling. They might even have seen the knife enter the woman's body, over and over, in that furious attack.

But it would be years, whole decades, before Stella would find out what really happened on that July night, back in 1965; though she'd long had her suspicions. And, even when the evidence finally stared her in the face, she had good reasons, she told herself, for not going to the police.

Set in the Home Counties of southern England, the demolition of an old manor house signals the destruction of the suburban community surrounding it. As tensions rise, a grisly murder is committed and a young girl goes missing. Will local residents ever find peace again?

ISBN: 978-2-940509-09-6

Lightning Source UK Ltd.
Milton Keynes UK
UKOW01f1107240517
301907UK00001B/34/P